A twisting, action-packed plot explores themes of loyalty, nipulation, moral ambiguity and violence with an under-
g search for redemption and love. A must for fans…

    Sally Morris, *Daily Mail*

s is both accessible and sophisticated, handling big sub-
terrorism, feminism, genocide, love – in prose that is
and heart-stopping. A fat book likely to be devoured
e sitting.

    Nicolette Jones, *Sunday Times*

sterly exercise in the art of storytelling, the product of
werful imagination and engaged with themes to which a
ung readership should easily relate.

    Robert Dunbar, *Irish Times*

Original and suspenseful.

    Amanda Craig, *The Times*

s is an incredibly accomplished effort, striking the
ect balance between stylistic originality, gripping story-
ing and powerful ethical deliberation.

    Tom Donegan, *INIS*

As gripping as *The Knife of Never Letting Go*, this is a tough but compelling story which takes readers into shocking and moving territory.

Julia Eccleshare, *Lovereading4kids*

The Ask and the Answer ... delivers a gripping, fast-paced maze-like page turner full of surprising twists and turns.

The Ultimate Book Guide

The breakneck pace belies what is a wonderfully-realized and tremendously subtle dystopian novel about power and control and love and loyalty. I loved it.

Jill Murphy, *The Bookbag*

A harrowing read but I could not put it down.

Fiona Noble, *Bookseller*

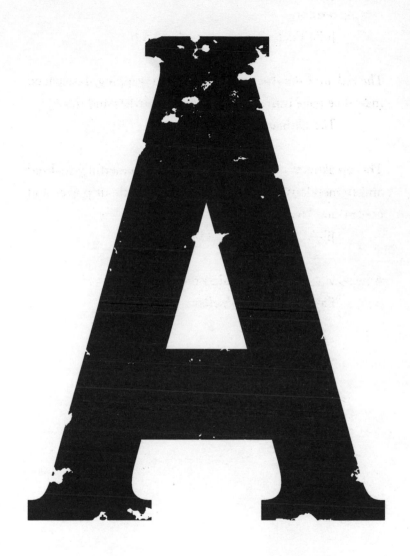

PATRICK NESS

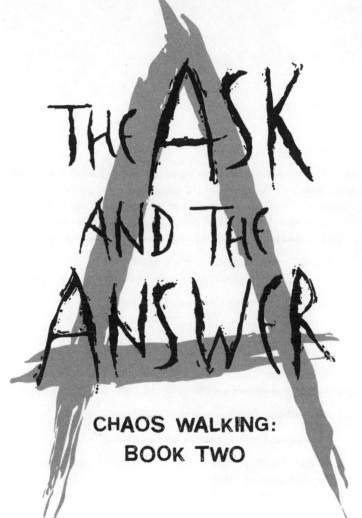

THE ASK
AND THE
ANSWER

CHAOS WALKING:
BOOK TWO

WALKER
BOOKS

First published 2009 by Walker Books Ltd
87 Vauxhall Walk, London SE11 5HJ

This edition published 2009

4 6 8 10 9 7 5 3

Text © 2009 Patrick Ness

This book has been typeset in Fairfield and Tiepolo

Printed and bound in Great Britain by Clays Ltd, St Ives plc

British Library Cataloguing in Publication Data:
a catalogue record for this book is available from the British Library

ISBN 978-1-4063-2247-7

www.walker.co.uk

For Patrick Gale

Battle not with monsters
lest you become a monster
and if you gaze into the abyss
the abyss gazes into you.

Friedrich Nietzsche

THE END

"YOUR NOISE REVEALS YOU, TODD HEWITT."

A voice–

In the darkness–

I blink open my eyes. Everything is shadows and blur and it feels like the world's spinning and my blood is too hot and my brain is clogged and I can't think and it's dark–

I blink again.

Wait–

No, *wait*–

Just now, just *now* we were in the square–

Just now she was in my arms–

She was *dying* in my arms–

"Where is she?" I spit into the dark, tasting blood, my voice croaking, my Noise rising like a sudden hurricane, high and red and furious. "*WHERE IS SHE?*"

"I will be the one doing the asking here, Todd."

That voice.

His voice.

Somewhere in the dark.

Somewhere behind me, somewhere unseen.

Mayor Prentiss.

I blink again and the murk starts to turn into a vast room, the only light coming from a single window, a wide circle up high and far away, its glass not clear but coloured into shapes of New World and its two circling moons, the light from it slanting down onto me and nothing else.

"*What have you done with her?*" I say, loud, blinking against fresh blood trickling into my eyes. I try to reach up to clear it away but I find my hands are tied behind my back and panic rises in me and I struggle against the binds and my breathing speeds up and I shout again, "*WHERE IS SHE?*"

A fist comes from nowhere and punches me in the stomach.

I lean forward into the shock of it and realize I'm tied to a wooden chair, my feet bound to its legs, my shirt gone somewhere up on a dusty hillside and as I'm throwing up my empty stomach I notice there's carpet beneath me, repeating the same pattern of New World and its moons, over and over and over, stretching out for ever.

And I'm remembering we were in the square, in the square where I'd run, holding her, carrying her, telling her to stay alive, stay alive till we got safe, till we got to Haven so I could save her—

But there *weren't* no safety, no safety at all, there was just *him* and his men and they took her from me, they *took* her from my arms—

"You notice that he does not ask, *Where am I?*" says the Mayor's voice, moving out there, somewhere. "His first words are, *Where is she?*, and his Noise says the same. Interesting."

My head's throbbing along with my stomach and I'm waking up some more and I'm remembering I *fought* them, I fought them when they took her till the butt of a gun smashed against my temple and knocked me into blackness—

I swallow away the tightness in my throat, swallow away the panic and the fear—

Cuz this is the end, ain't it?

The end of it all.

The Mayor has me.

The Mayor has her.

"If you hurt her—" I say, the punch still aching in my belly. Mr Collins stands in front of me, half in shadow, Mr Collins who farmed corn and cauliflower and who tended the Mayor's horses and who stands over me now with a pistol in a holster, a rifle slung round his back and a fist rearing up to punch me again.

"She seemed quite hurt enough already, Todd," the Mayor says, stopping Mr Collins. "The poor thing."

My fists clench in their bindings. My Noise feels lumpy and half-battered but it still rises with the memory of Davy Prentiss's gun pointed at us, of her falling into my arms, of her bleeding and gasping—

And then I make it go even redder with the feel of my own fist landing on Davy Prentiss's face, of Davy Prentiss falling from his horse, his foot caught in the stirrup, dragged away like so much trash.

"Well," the Mayor says, "that explains the mysterious whereabouts of my *son*."

And if I didn't know better, I'd say he sounded almost *amused*.

But I notice the only way I can tell this is from the sound of his voice, a voice sharper and smarter than any old Prentisstown voice he might once have had, and that the nothing I heard coming from him when I ran into Haven is still a big nothing in whatever room this is and it's matched by a big nothing from Mr Collins.

They ain't got Noise.

Neither of 'em.

The only Noise here is mine, bellering like an injured calf.

I twist my neck to find the Mayor but it hurts too much to turn very far and all I can tell is that I'm sitting in the single beam of dusty, coloured sunlight in the middle of a room so big I can barely make out the walls in the far distance.

And then I do see a little table in the darkness, set back just far enough so I can't make out what's on it.

Just the shine of metal, glinting and promising things I don't wanna think about.

"He still thinks of me as Mayor," his voice says, sounding light and amused again.

"It's President Prentiss now, boy," grunts Mr Collins. "You'd do well to remember that."

"What have you done with her?" I say, trying to turn again, this way and that, wincing at the pain in my neck. "If you *touch* her, I'll–"

"You arrive in my town this very morning," interrupts the Mayor, "with nothing in your possession, not even the shirt on your back, just a girl in your arms who has suffered a terrible accident–"

My Noise surges. "It was no *accident*–"

"A very bad accident indeed," continues the Mayor, his voice giving the first hint of the impayshunce I heard when we met in the square. "So very bad that she is near death and here is the boy who we have spent so much of our time and energy trying to find, the boy who has caused us so much trouble, offering himself up to us *willingly*, offering to do anything we wish if we just *save the girl* and yet when we try to do just that–"

"Is she all right? Is she safe?"

The Mayor stops and Mr Collins steps forward and backhands me across the face. There's a long moment as the sting spreads across my cheek and I sit there, panting.

Then the Mayor steps into the circle of light, right in front of me.

He's still in his good clothes, crisp and clean as ever, as if there ain't a man underneath there at all, just a walking talking block of ice. Even Mr Collins has sweat marks and dirt and the smell you'd expect but not the Mayor, no.

The Mayor makes you look like yer nothing but a mess that needs cleaning up.

He faces me, leans down so he's looking into my eyes.

And then he gives me an asking, like he's only curious.

"What is her name, Todd?"

I blink, surprised. "What?"

"What is her name?" he repeats.

Surely he must know her name. Surely it must be in my Noise–

"You know her name," I say.

"I want you to tell me."

I look from him to Mr Collins, standing there with his arms crossed, his silence doing nothing to hide a look on his face that would happily pound me into the ground.

"One more time, Todd," says the Mayor lightly, "and I would very much like for you to answer. What is her name? This girl from across the worlds."

"If you know she's from across the worlds," I say, "then you must know her name."

And then the Mayor smiles, actually *smiles*.

And I feel more afraid than ever.

"That's not how this works, Todd. How this works is that I ask and you answer. Now. What is her name?"

"Where is she?"

"What's her name?"

"Tell me where she is and I'll tell you her name."

He sighs, as if I've let him down. He nods once to Mr Collins, who steps forward and punches me again in the stomach.

"This is a simple transaction, Todd," the Mayor says, as I gag onto the carpet. "All you have to do is tell me what I want to know and this ends. The choice is yours. Genuinely, I have no wish to harm you further."

I'm breathing heavy, bent forward, the ache in my gut making it difficult to get enough air in me. I can feel my weight pulling at the bonds on my wrists and I can feel the blood on my face, sticky and drying, and I look out bleary-eyed from my little prison of light in the middle of this room, this room with no exits–

This room where I'm gonna die–

This room–

This room where she ain't.

And something in me chooses.

If this is it, then something in me decides.

Decides not to say.

"You know her name," I say. "Kill me if you want but you know her name already."

And the Mayor just watches me.

The longest minute of my life passes with him watching me, reading me, seeing that I mean it.

And then he steps to the little wooden table.

I look to see but his back's hiding what he's doing. I hear him fiddling with things on top of it, a *thunk* of metal scraping against wood.

"*I'll do anything you want,*" he says and I reckernize he's aping my own words back at me. "*Just save her and I'll do anything you want.*"

"I ain't afraid of you," I say, tho my Noise says otherwise, thinking of all the things that could be on that table. "I ain't afraid to die."

And I wonder if I mean it.

He turns to me, keeping his hands behind his back so I can't see what he's picked up. "Because you're a man, Todd? Because a man isn't afraid to die?"

"Yeah," I say. "Cuz I'm a man."

"If I'm correct, your birthday is not for another fourteen days."

"That's just a number." I'm breathing heavy, my stomach flip-flopping from talking like this. "It don't mean *nothing*. If I was on Old World, I'd be—"

"You ain't on Old World, *boy*," Mr Collins says.

"I don't believe that's what he means, Mr Collins," the Mayor says, still looking at me. "Is it, Todd?"

I look back and forth twixt the two of 'em. "I've killed," I say. "I've killed."

"Yes, I believe you've killed," says the Mayor. "I can see the shame of it all over you. But the asking is who? *Who* did you kill?" He steps into the darkness outside the circle of light, whatever he picked up from the table still hidden as he walks behind me. "Or should I say *what*?"

"I killed Aaron," I say, trying to follow him, failing.

"Did you, now?" His lack of Noise is an awful thing, especially when you can't see him. It's not like the silence of a girl, a girl's silence is still active, still a living thing that makes a shape in all the Noise that clatters round it.

(I think of her, I think of her silence, the ache of it)

(I don't think of her name)

But with the Mayor, however he's done it, however he's made it so he and Mr Collins don't got Noise, it's like it's nothing, like a dead thing, no more shape nor Noise nor life in the world than a stone or a wall, a fortress you ain't never gonna conquer. I'm guessing he's reading my Noise but how can you tell with a man who's made himself of stone?

I show him what he wants anyway. I put the church under the waterfall at the front of my Noise. I put up all the truthful fight with Aaron, all the struggle and the blood, I put me fighting him and beating him and knocking him to the ground, I put me taking out my knife.

I put me stabbing Aaron in the neck.

"There's truth there," says the Mayor. "But is it the whole truth?"

"It is," I say, raising my Noise loud and high to block out anything else he might hear. "It's the truth."

His voice is still amused. "I think you're lying to me, Todd."

"I ain't!" I practically shout. "I done what Aaron wanted! I murdered him! I became a man by yer own laws and you can have me in yer army and I'll do whatever you want, just tell me what you've done with her!"

I see Mr Collins notice a sign from behind me and he steps forward again, fist back and–

(I can't help it)

I jerk away from him so hard I drag the chair a few inches to the side–

(shut up)

And the punch never falls.

"Good," says the Mayor, sounding quietly pleased. "Good." He begins to move again in the darkness. "Let me explain a few things to you, Todd," he says. "You are in the main office of what was formerly the Cathedral of Haven and what yesterday became the Presidential Palace. I have brought you into my home in the hope of helping you. Helping you see that you are mistaken in this hopeless fight you put up against me, against us."

His voice moves behind Mr Collins–

His voice–

For a second it feels like he's not talking out loud–

Like he's talking right in my head—

Then it passes.

"My soldiers should arrive here tomorrow afternoon," he says, still moving. "You, Todd Hewitt, will first tell me what I ask of you and then you will be true to your word and you will assist me in our creation of a new society."

He steps into the light again, stopping in front of me, his hands still behind his back, whatever he picked up still hidden.

"But the process I want to begin here, Todd," he says, "is the one where you learn that I am not your enemy."

I'm so surprised I stop being afraid for a second.

Not my enemy?

I open my eyes wide.

Not my enemy?

"No, Todd," he says. "Not your enemy."

"Yer a murderer," I say, without thinking.

"I am a general," he says. "Nothing more, nothing less."

I stare at him. "You killed people on yer march here. You killed the people of Farbranch."

"Regrettable things happen in wartime, but that war is now over."

"I saw you shoot them," I say, hating how the words of a man without Noise sound so solid, so much like unmoveable stone.

"Me personally, Todd?"

I swallow away a sour taste. "No, but it was a war *you started!*"

"It was necessary," he says. "To save a sick and dying planet."

My breathing is getting faster, my mind getting cloudier, my head heavier than ever. But my Noise is redder, too. "You murdered Cillian."

"Deeply regrettable," he says. "He would have made a fine soldier."

"You killed my mother," I say, my voice catching (shut up), my Noise filling with rage and grief, my eyes screwing up with tears (shut up, shut up, shut up). "You killed all the women of Prentisstown."

"Do you believe everything you hear, Todd?"

There's a silence, a real one, as even my own Noise takes this in. "I have no desire to kill women," he adds. "I never did."

My mouth drops open. "Yes, you *did*–"

"Now is not the time for a history lesson."

"Yer a *liar*!"

"And you presume to know everything, do you?" His voice goes cold and he steps away from me and Mr Collins strikes me so hard on the side of the head I nearly fall over onto the floor.

"Yer a LIAR AND A MURDERER!" I shout, my ears still ringing from the punch.

Mr Collins hits me again the other way, hard as a block of wood.

"I am *not* your enemy, Todd," the Mayor says again. "Please stop making me do this to you."

My head is hurting so bad I don't say nothing. I *can't* say nothing. I can't say the word he wants. I can't say nothing else without getting beaten senseless.

This is the end. It's gotta be the end. They won't let me live. They won't let *her* live.

It's gotta be the end.

"I hope it *is* the end," the Mayor says, his voice actually making the sounds of truth. "I hope you'll tell me what I want to know so we can stop all this."

And then he says—

Then he says—

He says, "Please."

I look up, blinking thru the swelling coming up round my eyes.

His face has a look of concern on it, a look of almost *pleading*.

What the hell? What the ruddy hell?

And I hear the buzz of it inside my head again—

Different than just hearing someone's Noise—

PLEASE like it's said in my own voice—

PLEASE like it's coming from me—

Pressing on me—

On my insides—

Making me feel like I wanna say it—

PLEASE—

"The things you think you know, Todd," the Mayor says, his voice still twining around inside my own head. "Those things aren't true."

And then I remember—

I remember Ben—

I remember Ben saying the same thing to me—

Ben who I lost—

And my Noise hardens, right there.

Cutting him off.

The Mayor's face loses the look of pleading.

"All right," he says, frowning a little. "But remember that it is your choice." He stands up straight. "What is her name?"

"You know her name."

Mr Collins strikes me across the head, careening me sideways.

"What is her name?"

"You already know it—"

Boom, another blow, this time the other way.

"What is her name?"

"No."

Boom.

"Tell me her name."

"No!"

BOOM!

"What is her *name*, Todd?"

"EFF YOU!"

Except I don't say "eff" and Mr Collins hits me so hard my head whips back and the chair over-balances and I do topple sideways to the floor, taking the chair with me. I slam into the carpet, hands tied so I can't catch myself, my eyes filling up with little New Worlds till there ain't nothing else to see.

I breathe into the carpet.

The toes of the Mayor's boots approach my face.

"I am not your enemy, Todd Hewitt," he says one more time. "Just tell me her name and this will all stop."

I take in a breath and have to cough it away.

I take in another and say what I have to say.

"Yer a murderer."

Another silence.

"So be it," says the Mayor.

His feet move away and I feel Mr Collins pull my chair up from the floor, taking me up with it, my body groaning against its own weight, till I'm sat up again in the circle of coloured light. My eyes are so swollen now I can't hardly see Mr Collins at all even tho he's right in front of me.

I hear the Mayor at the small table again. I hear him moving things round on the top. I hear again the scrape of metal.

I hear him step up beside me.

And after all that promising, here it really, finally is.

My end.

I'm sorry, I think. *I'm so, so sorry.*

The Mayor puts a hand on my shoulder and I flinch away from it but he keeps it there, pressing down steadily. I can't see what he's holding, but he's bringing something towards me, towards my face, something hard and metal and filled with pain and ready to make me suffer and end my life and there's a hole inside me that I need to crawl into, away from all this, down deep and black, and I know this is the end, the end of all things, I can never escape from here and he'll kill me and kill her and there's no chance, no life, no hope, nothing.

I'm sorry.

And the Mayor lays a bandage across my face.

I gasp from the coolness of it and jerk away from his hands but he keeps pressing it gently into the lump on my forehead and onto the wounds on my face and chin, his body so close I can smell it, the cleanliness of it, the woody odour of his soap, the breath from his nose brushing over my cheek, his fingers touching my cuts almost tenderly, dressing the swelling round my eyes, the splits on my lip, and I can feel the bandages get to work almost instantly, feel the swelling going right down, the painkillers flooding into my system, and I think for a second how *good* the bandages are in Haven, how much like *her* bandages, and the relief comes so quick, so unexpected that my throat clenches and I have to swallow it away.

"I am not the man you think I am, Todd," the Mayor says quietly, almost right into my ear, putting another bandage on my neck. "I did not do the things you think I did. I asked my son to bring you back. I did not ask him to shoot anyone. I did not ask Aaron to kill you."

"Yer a liar," I say but my voice is weak and I'm shaking from the effort of keeping the weep out of it (shut up).

The Mayor puts more bandages across the bruises on my chest and stomach, so gentle I can barely stand it, so gentle it's almost like he cares how it feels.

"I *do* care, Todd," he says. "There will be time for you to learn the truth of that."

He moves behind me and puts another bandage around the bindings on my wrists, taking my hands and rubbing feeling back into them with his thumbs.

"There will be time," he says, "for you to come to trust me. For you, perhaps, to come to even *like* me. To even think of me, one day, as a kind of father to you, Todd."

It feels like my Noise is melting away with all the drugs, with all the pain disappearing, with me disappearing along with it, like he's killing me after all, but with the cure instead of the punishment.

I can't keep the weep from my throat, my eyes, my voice. "Please," I say. "Please."

But I don't know what I mean.

"The war is over, Todd," the Mayor says again. "We are making a new world. This planet finally and truly living up to its name. Believe me when I say, once you see it, you'll *want* to be part of it."

I breathe into the darkness.

"You could be a leader of men, Todd. You have proven yourself very special."

I keep breathing, trying to hold on to it but feeling myself slip away.

"How can I know?" I finally say, my voice a croak, a slur, a thing not quite real. "How can I know she's even still alive?"

"You can't," says the Mayor. "You only have my word."

And waits again.

"And if I do it," I say. "If I do what you say, you'll save her?"

"We will do whatever's necessary," he says.

Without pain, it feels almost like I don't have a body at all, almost like I'm a ghost, sitting in a chair, blinded and eternal.

Like I'm dead already.

Cuz how do you know yer alive if you don't hurt?

"We are the choices we make, Todd," the Mayor says. "Nothing more, nothing less. I'd like you to choose to tell me. I would like that very much indeed."

Under the bandages is just further darkness.

Just me, alone in the black.

Alone with his voice.

I don't know what to do.

I don't know anything.

(what do I do?)

But if there's a chance, if there's even a *chance*–

"Is it really such a sacrifice, Todd?" the Mayor says, listening to me think. "Here, at the end of the past? At the beginning of the future?"

No. No, I can't. He's a liar and a murderer, no matter what he says–

"I'm waiting, Todd."

But she might be alive, he might keep her alive–

"We are nearing your last opportunity, Todd."

I raise my head. The movement opens the bandages some and I squint up into the light, up towards the Mayor's face.

It's blank as ever.

It's the empty, lifeless wall.

I might as well be talking into a bottomless pit.

I might as well *be* the bottomless pit.

I look away. I look down.

"Viola," I say into the carpet. "Her name's Viola."

The Mayor lets out a long, pleased-sounding breath. "Good, Todd," he says. "I thank you."

He turns to Mr Collins.

"Lock him up."

PART I

TODD IN THE TOWER

1

THE OLD MAYOR

[TODD]

MR COLLINS PUSHES ME up a narrow, windowless staircase, up and up and up, turning on sharp landings but always straight up. Just when I think my legs can't take no more, we reach a door. He opens it and shoves me hard and I go tumbling into the room and down onto a wooden floor, my arms so stiff I can't even catch myself and I groan and roll to one side.

And look down over a thirty-metre drop.

Mr Collins laughs as I scrabble back away from it. I'm on a ledge not more than five boards wide that runs round the walls of a square room. In the middle is just an enormous hole with some ropes dangling down thru the centre. I follow 'em up thru a tall shaft to the biggest set of bells I ever saw, two of 'em hanging from a single wooden beam, huge things, big as a room you could live in, archways cut into the sides of the tower so the bell-ringing can be heard.

I jump when Mr Collins slams the door, locking it with a *ker-thunk* sound that don't brook no thoughts of escape.

I get myself up and lean against the wall till I can breathe again.

I close my eyes.

I am Todd Hewitt, I think. *I am the son of Cillian Boyd and Ben Moore. My birthday is in fourteen days but I am a man.*

I am Todd Hewitt and I am a man.

(a man who told the Mayor her name)

"I'm sorry," I whisper. "I'm so sorry."

After a while, I open my eyes and look up and around. There are small rectangular openings at eye level all around this floor of the tower, three on each wall, fading light shining in thru the dust.

I go to the nearest opening. I'm in the bell tower of the cathedral, obviously, way up high, looking out the front, down onto the square where I first entered the town, only this morning but it already feels like a lifetime ago. Dusk is falling, so I musta been out cold for a bit before the Mayor woke me, time where he coulda done anything to her, time where he coulda–

(shut up, just shut up)

I look out over the square. It's still empty, still the quiet of a silent town, a town with no Noise, a town waiting for an army to come and conquer it.

A town that didn't even try to fight.

The Mayor just turned up and they handed it right over

to him. *Sometimes the rumour of an army is just as effective as the army itself,* he told me and wasn't he right?

All that time, running here as fast as we could, not thinking bout what Haven'd be like once we got here, not saying it out loud but hoping it'd be safe, hoping it'd be paradise.

I'm telling you there's hope, Ben said.

But he was wrong. It wasn't Haven at all.

It was New Prentisstown.

I frown, feeling my chest tighten and I look out west across the square, across the treetops that spread out into the farther silent houses and streets and on up to the waterfall, smashing down from the rim of the valley in the near distance, the zigzag road zipping up the hill beside it, the road where I fought Davy Prentiss Jr, the road where Viola—

I turn back into the room.

My eyes are adjusting to the fading light but there don't seem to be nothing here anyway but boards and a faint stink. The bell ropes dangle about two metres from any side. I look up to see where they're tied fast to the bells to make 'em chime. I squint down into the hole but it's too dark to see clearly what might be at the bottom. Probably just hard brick.

Two metres ain't that much at all, tho. You could jump it easy and grab onto a rope to climb yer way down.

But then—

"It's quite ingenious, really," says a voice from the far corner.

I jerk back, fists up, my Noise spiking. A man is standing up from where he was sitting, another Noiseless man.

Except—

"If you try to escape by climbing down the ropes left so temptingly available," he continues, "every person in town is going to know about it."

"Who are you?" I say, my stomach high and light but my fists clenching.

"Yes," he says. "I could tell you weren't from Haven." He steps away from the corner, letting light catch his face. I see a blackened eye and a cut lip that looks like it's only just scabbed over. No bandages spared for him, obviously. "Funny how quickly one forgets the *loudness* of it," he says, almost to himself.

He's a small man, shorter than me, wider, too, older than Ben tho not by much, but I can also see he's soft all over, soft even in his face. A softness I could beat if I had to.

"Yes," he says, "I imagine you could."

"Who are you?" I say again.

"Who am I?" repeats the man softly, then raises his voice like he's playing at something. "I am Con Ledger, my boy. Mayor of Haven." He smiles in a dazed way. "But not Mayor of New Prentisstown." He shakes his head a little as he looks at me. "We even gave the refugees the cure when they started pouring in."

And then I see that his smile ain't a smile, it's a *wince*.

"Good God, boy," he says. "How Noisy you are."

"I ain't a boy," I say, my fists still up.

"I completely fail to see how that's any sort of point."

I got ten million things I wanna say but my curiosity wins out first. "So there *is* a cure then? For the Noise?"

"Oh, yes," he says, his face twitching a bit at me, like he's tasting something bad. "Native plant with a natural neurochemical mixed with a few things we could synthesize and there you go. Quiet falls at last on New World."

"Not *all* of New World."

"No, well," he says, turning to look out the rectangle with his hands clasped behind his back. "It's very hard to make, isn't it? A long and slow process. We only got it right late last year and that was after twenty years of trying. We made enough for ourselves and were just on the point of starting to export it when…"

He trails off, looking firmly out onto the town below.

"When you surrendered," I say, my Noise rumbling, low and red. "Like cowards."

He turns back to me, the wincing smile gone, *way* gone. "And why should the opinion of a boy matter to me?"

"I *ain't* a boy," I say again and are my fists still clenched? Yes, they are.

"Clearly you are," he says, "for a *man* would know the necessary choices that have to be made when one is facing one's oblivion."

I narrow my eyes. "You ain't got nothing you can teach me bout oblivion."

He blinks a little, seeing the truth of it in my Noise as if it were bright flashes trying to blind him, and then his stance slumps. "Forgive me," he says. "This isn't me." He puts a hand up to his face and rubs it, smarting at the bruise around his eye. "Yesterday, I was the benevolent Mayor of a beautiful town." He seems to laugh at some private joke. "But that was yesterday."

"How many people in Haven?" I say, not quite ready to let it go.

He looks over at me. "Boy—"

"My name is Todd Hewitt," I say. "You can call me Mr Hewitt."

"He promised us a new beginning—"

"Even *I* know he's a liar. *How many people?*"

He sighs. "Including refugees, three thousand, three hundred."

"The army ain't a third that size," I say. "You coulda fought."

"Women and children," he says. "Farmers."

"Women and children fought in other towns. Women and children *died.*"

He steps forward, his face getting stormy. "Yes, and now the women and children of this city will *not* die! Because *I* reached a peace!"

"A peace that blacked yer eye," I say. "A peace that split yer lip."

He looks at me for another second and then gives a sad snort. "The words of a sage," he says, "in the voice of a hick."

And he turns back to look out the opening.

Which is when I notice the low buzz.

Asking marks fill my Noise but before I can open my mouth, the Mayor, the *old* Mayor, says, "Yes, that's me you hear."

"You?" I say. "What about the cure?"

"Would you give your conquered enemy his favourite medicine?"

I lick my upper lip. "It comes back? The Noise?"

"Oh, yes." He turns to me again. "If you don't take your daily dose, it most definitely comes back." He returns to his corner and slowly sits himself down. "You'll notice there are no toilets," he says. "I apologize in advance for the unpleasantness."

I watch him sit, my Noise still rattling red and sore and full of askings.

"It *was* you, if I'm not mistaken?" he says. "This morning? The one who the town was cleared for, the one the new President greeted himself on horseback?"

I don't answer him. But my Noise does.

"So, who are you then, Todd Hewitt?" he says. "What makes you so special?"

Now *that*, I think, is a very good asking.

Night falls quick and full, Mayor Ledger saying less and less and fidgeting more and more till he finally can't stand it and starts to pace. All the while, his buzz gets louder till even if we wanted to talk, we'd have to shout to do it.

I stand at the front of the tower and watch the stars come out, night covering the valley below.

And I'm thinking and I'm trying not to think cuz when I do, my stomach turns and I feel sick, or my throat clenches and I feel sick, or my eyes wet and I feel sick.

Cuz she's out there somewhere.

(*please* be out there somewhere)

(*please* be okay)

(*please*)

"Do you always have to be so bloody *loud*?" Mayor Ledger snaps. I turn to him, ready to snap back, and he holds up his hands in apology. "I'm sorry. I'm not like this."

He starts fidgeting his fingers again. "It's difficult having one's cure taken away so abruptly."

I look back out over New Prentisstown as lights start coming on in people's houses. I ain't hardly seen no one out there the whole day, everyone staying indoors, probably under the Mayor's orders.

"They all going thru this out there, then?" I say.

"Oh, everyone will have their little stockpile at home," Mayor Ledger says. "They'll have to have it pried out of their hands, I imagine."

"I don't reckon that'll be a problem when the army gets here," I say.

The moons rise, crawling up the sky as if there was nothing to hurry about. They shine bright enough to light up New Prentisstown and I see how the river cuts thru town but that there ain't nothing much north of it except fields, empty in the moonlight, then a sharp rise of rocky cliffs that make up the north wall of the valley. To the north, you can also see a thin road coming outta the hills before cutting its way back into town, the other road that Viola and I didn't take after Farbranch, the other road the Mayor *did* take and got here first.

To the east, the river and the main road just carry on, going god knows where, round corners and farther hills, the town petering out as it goes. There's another road, not much paved, that heads south from the square and past more buildings and houses and into a wood and up a hill with a notch on the top.

And that's all there is of New Prentisstown.

Home to three thousand, three hundred people, all

hiding in their houses, so quiet they might be dead.

Not one of them lifting a hand to save theirselves from what's coming, hoping if they're meek enough, if they're *weak* enough, then the monster won't eat 'em.

This is where we spent all our time running to.

I see movement down on the square, a shadow flitting, but it's only a dog. **Home, home, home,** I can just about hear him think. **Home, home, home.**

Dogs don't got the problems of people.

Dogs can be happy any old time.

I take a minute to breathe away the tightness that comes over my chest, the water in my eyes.

Take a minute to stop thinking bout my own dog.

When I can look out again, I see someone not a dog at all.

He's got his head slumped forward and he's walking his horse slow across the town square, the hoofs clopping against the brick and, as he approaches, even tho Mayor Ledger's **buzz** has started to become such a nuisance I don't know how I'm ever gonna sleep, I can still hear it out there.

Noise.

Across the quiet of a waiting city, I can hear the man's Noise.

And he can hear mine.

Todd Hewitt? he thinks.

And I can hear the smile growing on his face, too.

Found something, Todd, he says, across the square, up the tower, seeking me out in the moonlight. **Found something of yers.**

I don't say nothing. I don't *think* nothing.

I just watch as he reaches behind him and holds something up towards me.

Even this far away, even by the light of the moons, I know what it is.

My ma's book.

Davy Prentiss has my ma's book.

2

THE FOOT UPON
THE NECK

[TODD]

EARLY NEXT MORNING, a platform with a microphone on it gets built noisily and quickly near the base of the bell tower and, as the morning turns to afternoon, the men of New Prentisstown gather in front of it.

"Why?" I say, looking out over 'em.

"Why do you think?" Mayor Ledger says, sitting in a darkened corner, rubbing his temples, his Noise *buzz* sawing away, hot and metallic. "To meet the new man in charge."

The men don't say much, their faces pale and grim, tho who can know what they're thinking when you can't hear their Noise? But they look cleaner than the men in my town used to, shorter hair, shaved faces, better clothes. A good number of 'em are rounded and soft like Mayor Ledger.

Haven musta been a comfortable place, a place where men weren't fighting every day just to survive.

Maybe too much comfort was the problem.

Mayor Ledger snorts to himself but don't say nothing.

Mayor Prentiss's men are on horseback at strategic spots across the square, ten or twelve of 'em, rifles ready, to make sure everyone behaves tho the threat of an army coming seems to have done most of the work. I see Mr Tate and Mr Morgan and Mr O'Hare, men I grew up with, men I used to see every day being farmers, men who were just men till suddenly they became something else.

I don't see Davy Prentiss nowhere and my Noise starts rumbling again at the thought of him.

He musta come back down the hillside from wherever his horse dragged him and found the rucksack. All it had in it any more was a bunch of ruined clothes and the book.

My ma's book.

My ma's words to me.

Written when I was born. Written till just before she died.

Before she was murdered.

My wondrous son who I swear will see this world come good.

Words read to me by Viola cuz I couldn't–

And now *Davy bloody Prentiss*–

"Can you please," Mayor Ledger says thru gritted teeth, "at least *try*–" He stops himself and looks at me apologetically. "I'm sorry," he says, for the millionth time since Mr Collins woke us up with breakfast.

Before I can say anything back I feel the hardest, sudden tug on my heart, so surprising I nearly gasp.

I look out again.

The women of New Prentisstown are coming.

They start to appear farther away, in groups down side streets away from the main body of men, kept there by the Mayor's men patrolling on horseback.

I feel their silence in a way I can't feel the men's. It's like a loss, like great groupings of sorrow against the sound of the world and I have to wipe my eyes again but I press myself closer to the opening, trying to see 'em, trying to see every single one of 'em.

Trying to see if she's there.

But she ain't.

She ain't.

They look like the men, most of 'em wearing trousers and shirts of different cuts, some of 'em wearing long skirts, but most looking clean and comfortable and well-fed. Their hair has more variety, pulled back or up or over or short or long and not nearly as many of 'em are blonde as they are in the Noise of the menfolk where I come from.

And I see that more of their arms are crossed, more of their faces looking doubtful.

More anger there than on the faces of the men.

"Did anyone fight you?" I ask Mayor Ledger while I keep on looking. "Did anyone not wanna give up?"

"This is a democracy, Todd," he sighs. "Do you know what that is?"

"No idea," I say, still looking, still not finding.

"It means the minority is listened to," he says, "but the majority rules."

I look at him. "All these people wanted to surrender?"

"The President made a *proposal*," he says, touching his

35

split lip, "to the elected Council, promising that the city would be unharmed if we agreed to this."

"And you believed him?"

His eyes flash at me. "You are either forgetting or do not know that we already fought a great war, a war to end *all* wars, at just about the time you would have been born. If any repeat of that can be avoided–"

"Then yer willing to hand yerselves over to a murderer."

He sighs again. "The majority of the Council, led by myself, decided this was the best way to save the most lives." He rests his head against the brick. "Not everything is black and white, Todd. In fact, almost nothing is."

"But what if–"

Ker-thunk. The lock on the door slides back and Mr Collins enters, pistol pointed.

He looks straight at Mayor Ledger. "Get up," he says.

I look back and forth twixt 'em both. "What's going on?" I say.

Mayor Ledger stands from his corner. "It seems the piper must be paid, Todd," he says, his voice trying to sound light but I hear his buzz rev up with fear. "This was a beautiful town," he says to me. "And I was a better man. Remember that, please."

"What are you talking about?" I say.

Mr Collins takes him by the arm and shoves him out the door.

"Hey!" I shout, coming after them. "Where are you taking him?"

Mr Collins raises a fist to punch me–

And I flinch away.

(shut *up*)

He laughs and locks the door behind him.

Ker-thunk.

And I'm left alone in the tower.

And as Mayor Ledger's *buzz* disappears down the stairs, that's when I hear it.

March march march, way in the distance.

I go to an opening.

They're here.

The conquering army, marching into Haven.

They flow down the zigzag road like a black river, dusty and dirty and coming like a dam's burst. They march four or five across and the first of them disappear into the far trees at the base of the hill as the last finally crest the top. The crowd watches them, the men turning back from the platform, the women looking out from the side streets.

The *march march march* grows louder, echoing down the city streets. Like a clock ticking its way down.

The crowd waits. I wait with them.

And then, thru the trees, at the turning of the road—

Here they are.

The army.

Mr Hammar at their front.

Mr Hammar who lived in the petrol stayshun back home, Mr Hammar who thought vile, violent things no boy should ever hear, Mr Hammar who shot the people of Farbranch in the back as they fled.

Mr Hammar leads the army.

I can hear him now, calling out marching words to keep everyone in time together. *The foot*, he's yelling to the rhythm of the march.

The foot.

The foot.

The foot upon the neck.

They march into the square and turn down its side, cutting twixt the men and the women like an unstoppable force. Mr Hammar's close enough so I can see the smile, a smile I know full well, a smile that clubs, a smile that beats, a smile that dominates.

And as he gets closer, I grow more sure.

It's a smile without Noise.

Someone, one of those men on horseback maybe, has gone out to meet the army on the road. Someone carrying the cure with him. The army ain't making a sound except with its feet and with its chant.

The foot, the foot, the foot upon the neck.

They march round the side of the square to the platform. Mr Hammar stops at a corner, letting the men start to make up formayshuns behind the platform, lining up with their backs to me, facing the crowd now turned to watch them.

I start to reckernize the soldiers as they line up. Mr Wallace. Mr Smith the younger. Mr Phelps the store-keeper. Men from Prentisstown and many, many more men besides.

The army that grew as it came.

I see Ivan, the man from the barn at Farbranch, the man who secretly told me there were men in sympathy. He stands at the head of one of the formayshuns and everything that proves him right is standing behind him, arms at attenshun, rifles at the ready.

The last soldier marches into place with a final chant.

The foot upon the NECK!

And then there ain't nothing but silence, blowing over New Prentisstown like a wind.

Till I hear the doors of the cathedral open down below me.

And Mayor Prentiss steps out to address his new city.

"Right now," he says into the microphone, having saluted Mr Hammar and climbed his way up the platform steps, "you are afraid."

The men of the town look back up at him, saying nothing, making no sound of Noise nor buzzing.

The women stay in the side streets, also silent.

The army stands at attenshun, ready for anything.

I realize I'm holding my breath.

"Right now," he continues, "you think you are conquered. You think there is no hope. You think I come up here to read out your doom."

His back is to me but from speakers hidden in the four corners, his voice booms clear over the square, over the city, probably over the whole valley and beyond. Cuz who else is there to hear him talk? Who else is there on all of New World that ain't either gathered here or under the ground?

Mayor Prentiss is talking to the whole planet.

"And you're right," he says and I tell you I'm certain I

hear the smile. "You *are* conquered. You *are* defeated. And I read to you your doom."

He lets this sink in for a moment. My Noise rumbles and I see a few of the men look up to the top of the tower. I try to keep it quiet but who are these people? Who are these clean and comfortable and not-at-all-hungry people who just handed theirselves over?

"But it is not I who conquered you," the Mayor says. "It is not I who has beaten you or defeated you or enslaved you."

He pauses, looking out over the crowd. He's dressed all in white, white hat, white boots, and with the white cloths covering the platform and the afternoon sun shining on down, he's practically blinding.

"You are enslaved by your idleness," says the Mayor. "You are defeated by your complacency. You are *doomed*" – and here his voice rises suddenly, hitting *doomed* so hard half the crowd jumps – "by your good intentions!"

He's working himself up now, heavy breaths into the microphone.

"You have allowed yourselves to become so *weak*, so *feeble* in the face of the challenges of this world that in a single generation you have become a people who would surrender to *RUMOUR!*"

He starts to pace the stage, microphone in hand. Every frightened face in the crowd, every face in the army, turns to watch him move back and forth, back and forth.

I'm watching, too.

"You let an army *walk* into your town and instead of making them *take* it, you *offer it willingly!*"

He's still pacing, his voice still rising.

"And so you know what I did. I *took*. I took *you*. I took your freedom. I took your town. I took your future."

He laughs, like he can't believe his luck.

"I expected a war," he says.

Some of the crowd look at their feet, away from each other's eyes.

I wonder if they're ashamed.

I hope so.

"But instead of a war," the Mayor says, "I got a conversation. A conversation that began, *Please don't hurt us* and ended with *Please take anything you want.*"

He stops in the middle of the platform.

"I expected a WAR!" he shouts again, thrusting his fist at them.

And they flinch.

If a crowd can flinch, they flinch.

More than a thousand men flinch under the fist of just one.

I don't see what the women do.

"And because you did not give me a war," the Mayor says, his voice light, "you will face the consequences."

I hear the doors to the cathedral open again and Mr Collins comes out pushing Mayor Ledger forward thru the ranks of the army, hands tied behind his back.

Mayor Prentiss watches him come, arms crossed. Murmurs finally start in the crowd of men, louder in the crowds of women, and the men on horseback do some waving of their rifles to stop it. The Mayor don't even look back at the sound, like it's beneath his notice. He just watches Mr Collins push Mayor Ledger up the stairs at the back of the platform.

Mayor Ledger stops at the top of the steps, looking out over the crowd. They stare back at him, some of them squinting at the shrillness of his Noise *buzz*, a *buzz* I realize is now starting to shout some real words, words of fear, *pictures* of fear, pictures of Mr Collins giving him the bruised eye and the split lip, pictures of him agreeing to surrender and being locked in the tower.

"Kneel," Mayor Prentiss says and tho he says it quietly, tho he says it away from the microphone, somehow I hear it clear as a bell chime in the middle of my head, and from the intake of breath in the crowd, I wonder if that's how they heard it, too.

And before it looks like he even knows what he's doing, Mayor Ledger is kneeling on the platform, looking surprised that he's down there.

The whole town watches him do it.

Mayor Prentiss waits a moment.

And then he steps over to him.

And takes out a knife.

It's a big, no-kidding, death of a thing, shining in the sun.

The Mayor holds it up high over his head.

He turns slowly, so everyone can see what's about to happen.

So that everyone can see the knife.

My gut falls and for a second I think–

But it ain't mine—

It ain't—

And then someone calls, "Murderer!" from across the square.

A single voice, carrying above the silence.

It came from the women.

My heart jumps for a second—

But of course it can't be her—

But at least there's someone. At least there's *someone.*

Mayor Prentiss walks calmly to the microphone. "Your victorious enemy addresses you," he says, almost politely, as if the person who shouted was simply not understanding. "Your leaders are to be executed as the inevitable result of your defeat."

He turns to look at Mayor Ledger, kneeling there on the platform. His face is trying to look calm but everyone can hear how badly he don't wanna die, how childlike his wishes are sounding, how loud his newly uncured Noise is spilling out all over the place.

"And now you will learn," Mayor Prentiss says, turning back to the crowd, "what kind of man your new President is. And what he will demand from you."

Silence, still silence, save for Mayor Ledger's mewling.

Mayor Prentiss walks over to him, knife glinting. Another murmur starts spreading thru the crowd as they finally get what they're about to see. Mayor Prentiss steps behind Mayor Ledger and holds up the knife again. He stands there, watching the crowd watch him, watching their faces as they look and listen to their former Mayor try and fail to contain his Noise.

"BEHOLD!" Mayor Prentiss shouts. "YOUR FUTURE!"

He turns the knife to a stabbing angle, as if to say again, *behold*—

The murmuring of the crowd rises—

Mayor Prentiss raises his arm—

A voice, a female one, maybe the same one, cries out, "No!"

And then suddenly I realize I know exactly what's gonna happen.

In the chair, in the room with the circle of coloured glass, he brought me to defeat, he brought me to the edge of death, he made me *know* that it would come—

And then he put a bandage on me.

And *that's* when I did what he wanted.

The knife swishes thru the air and slices thru the binds on Mayor Ledger's hands.

There's a town-sized gasp, a *planet*-sized one.

Mayor Prentiss waits for a moment, then says once more, "Behold your future," quietly, not even into the microphone.

But there it is again, right inside yer mind.

He puts the knife away in a belt behind his back and returns to the microphone.

And starts to put bandages on the crowd.

"I am not the man you think I am," he says. "I am not a tyrant come to slaughter his enemies. I am not a madman come to destroy even that which would save himself. I am *not–*" he looks over at Mayor Ledger "–your executioner."

The crowds, men and women, are so quiet now the square might as well be empty.

"The war is *over*," the Mayor continues. "And a new peace will take its place."

He points to the sky. People look up, like he might be conjuring something up there to fall on them.

"You may have heard a rumour," he says. "That there are new settlers coming."

My stomach twists again.

"I tell you as your President," he says. "The rumour is true."

How does he know? How does he ruddy *know*?

The crowd starts to murmur at this news, men and women. The Mayor lets them, happily talking over them.

"We will be ready to greet them!" he says. "We will be a proud society ready to welcome them into a new Eden!" His voice is rising again. "We will show them that they have left Old World and entered PARADISE!"

Lots more murmuring now, talking everywhere.

"I am going to take your cure away from you," the Mayor says.

And boy, does the murmuring *stop*.

The Mayor lets it, lets the silence build up, and then he says, "For now."

The men look at one another and back to the Mayor.

"We are entering a new era," Mayor Prentiss says. "You will earn my trust by joining me in creating a new society. As that new society is built and as we meet our first challenges and celebrate our first successes, you will earn the right to be called men again. You will earn the right to have your cure returned to you and that will be the moment all men truly will be brothers."

He's not looking at the women. Neither are the men in the crowd. Women got no use for the reward of a cure, do they?

"It will be difficult," he continues. "I don't pretend otherwise. But it *will* be rewarding." He gestures towards the army. "My deputies have already begun to organize you. You will continue to follow their instructions but I assure you they will never be too onerous and you will soon see that I am not your conqueror. I am not your doom. I am not," he pauses again, "your enemy."

He turns his head across the crowd of men one last time.

"I am your saviour," he says.

And even without hearing their Noise, I watch the crowd wonder if there's a chance he's telling the truth, if maybe things'll be okay after all, if maybe, despite what they feared, they've been let off the hook.

You ain't, I think. *Not by a long shot.*

Even before the crowds have started to properly leave after the Mayor's finished, there's a *ker-thunk* at my door.

"Good evening, Todd," the Mayor says, stepping into the bell-ringing jail and looking around him, wrinkling his nose a little at the smell. "Did you like my speech?"

"How do you know there are settlers coming?" I say. "Have you been talking to her? Is she all right?"

He don't answer this but he don't hit me for it neither. He just smiles and says, "All in good time, Todd."

We hear Noise coming up the stairs outside the door. **Alive, I'm alive** it says **alive alive alive** and into the room comes Mayor Ledger, pushed by Mr Collins.

He pulls up his step when he sees Mayor Prentiss standing there.

"New bedding will arrive tomorrow," Mayor Prentiss says, still looking at me. "As will toilet privileges."

Mayor Ledger's moving his jaw but it takes a few tries before any words come out. "Mr President–"

Mayor Prentiss ignores him. "Your first job will also begin tomorrow, Todd."

"*Job?*" I say.

"Everyone has to work, Todd," he says. "Work is the path to freedom. I will be working. So will Mr Ledger."

"I will?" Mayor Ledger says.

"But we're in jail," I say.

He smiles again and there's more amusement in it and I wonder how I'm about to be stung.

"Get some sleep," he says, stepping to the door and looking me in the eye. "My son will collect you first thing in the morning."

3

THE NEW LIFE

[TODD]

BUT IT TURNS OUT IT ain't Davy that worries
me when I get dragged into the cold of the next morning in
front of the cathedral. It ain't even Davy I look at.

It's the horse.

Boy colt, it says, shifting from hoof to hoof, looking
down at me, eyes wide in that horse craziness, like I need a
good stomping.

"I don't know nothing bout horses," I say.

"She's from my private herd," Mayor Prentiss says atop
his own horse, Morpeth. "Her name is Angharrad and she
will treat you well, Todd."

Morpeth is looking at my horse and all he's thinking is
Submit, submit, submit, making my horse even
more nervous and that's a ton of nervous animal I'm sposed
to ride.

"Whatsa matter?" Davy Prentiss sneers from the saddle
of a third horse. "You scared?"

"Whatsa matter?" I say. "Daddy not give you the cure yet?"

His Noise immediately rises. "You little piece of–"

"My, my," says the Mayor. "Not ten words in and the fight's already begun."

"He started it," Davy says.

"And he would finish it, too, I wager," says the Mayor, looking at me, reading the red, jittery state of my Noise, filled with urgent red askings about Viola, with more askings I wanna take outta Davy Prentiss's hide. "Come, Todd," the Mayor says, reining his horse. "Ready to be a leader of men?"

"It's a simple division," he says as we trot thru the early morning, way faster than I'd like. "The men will move to the west end of the valley in front of the cathedral and the women to the east behind it."

We're riding east down the main street of New Prentisstown, the one that starts at the zigzag road by the falls, carries thru to the town square and around the cathedral and now out the back into the farther valley. Small squads of soldiers march up and down side roads and the men of New Prentisstown come past us the other way on foot, carrying rucksacks and other luggage.

"I don't see no women," Davy says.

"*Any* women," corrects the Mayor. "And no, Captain Morgan and Captain Tate supervised the transfer of the rest of the women last night."

"What are you gonna do with 'em?" I say, my knuckles gripping so hard on the saddle horn they're turning white.

He looks back at me. "Nothing, Todd. They will be treated with the care and dignity that befits their importance to the future of New World." He turns away. "But for now, separate is best."

"You put the bitches in their place," Davy sneers.

"You will not speak that way in front of me, David," the Mayor says, calmly but in a voice that ain't joking. "Women will be respected at all times and given every comfort. Though in a non-vulgar sense you are correct. We all have places. New World made men forget theirs, and that means men must be away from women until we all remember who we are, who we were meant to be."

His voice brightens a little. "The people will welcome this. I offer clarity where before there was only chaos."

"Is Viola with the women?" I ask. "Is she okay?"

He looks back at me again. "You made a promise, Todd Hewitt," he says. "Need I remind you once more? *Just save her and I'll do anything you want*, I believe were your exact words."

I lick my lips nervously. "How do I know yer keeping yer end of the bargain?"

"You don't," he says, his eyes on mine, like he's peering right past every lie I could tell him. "I want your faith in me, Todd, and faith with proof is no faith at all."

He turns back down the road and I'm left with Davy snickering to my side so I just whisper "Whoa, girl," to my horse. Her coat is dark brown with a white stripe down her nose and a mane brushed so nice I'm trying not to grab onto it less it make her mad. ᗷ૦ᶌ ᥴᵒᶅᵗ, she thinks.

She, I think. She. Then I think an asking I ain't never

had a chance to ask before. Cuz the ewes I had back on the farm had Noise, too, and if women ain't got Noise–

"Because women are not animals," the Mayor says, reading me. "No matter what anyone claims I believe. They are merely naturally Noiseless."

He lowers his voice. "Which makes them different."

It's mostly shops that line this part of the road, dotted twixt all the trees, closed, re-opening who knows when, with houses stretching back from side streets both towards the river on the left and the hill of the valley on the right. Most of the buildings, if not all, are built a fair distance from one another, which I spose is how you'd plan a big town before you found a cure for the Noise.

We pass more soldiers marching in groups of five or ten, more men heading west with their belongings, still no women. I look at the faces of the men going by, most of them pointed to the road at their feet, none of them looking ready to fight.

"Whoa, girl," I whisper again cuz riding a horse is turning out to be powerfully uncomfortable on yer private bits.

"And there's Todd," Davy says, pulling up next to me. "Moaning already."

"Shut it, Davy," I say.

"You will address each other as Mr Prentiss Jr and Mr Hewitt," the Mayor calls back to us.

"*What?*" Davy says, his Noise rising. "He ain't a man yet! He's just–"

The Mayor silences him with a look. "A body was discovered in the river in the early hours of this morning," he says. "A body with many terrible wounds to its flesh and a large knife sticking out of its neck, a body dead not more than two days."

He stares at me, looking into my Noise again. I put up the pictures he wants to see, making my imaginings seem like the real thing, cuz that's what Noise is, it's everything you think, not just the truth, and if you think hard enough that you did something, well, then, maybe you actually did.

Davy scoffs. "*You* killed Preacher Aaron? I don't believe it."

The Mayor don't say nothing, just gees Morpeth along a little faster. Davy sneers at me, then kicks his own horse to follow.

"Follow," Morpeth nickers.

"Follow," Davy's horse whinnies back.

Follow, thinks my own horse, taking off after them, bouncing me even worse.

As we go, I'm on the constant look out for her, even tho there's no chance of seeing her. Even if she's still alive, she'd still be too sick to walk, and if she weren't too sick to walk, she'd be locked up with the rest of the women.

But I keep looking–

(cuz maybe she escaped–)

(maybe she's looking for me–)

(maybe she's–)

And then I hear it.

I AM THE CIRCLE AND THE CIRCLE IS ME.

Clear as a bell, right inside my head, the voice of the Mayor, twining around my own voice, like it's speaking direktly into my Noise, so sudden and real I sit up and nearly fall off my horse. Davy looks surprised, his Noise wondering what I'm reacting to.

But the Mayor just rides on down the road, like nothing happened at all.

The town gets less shiny the farther east we get from the cathedral and soon we're riding on gravel. The buildings get plainer, too, long wooden houses set at distances from each other like bricks dropped into clearings of trees.

Houses that radiate the silence of women.

"Quite correct," the Mayor says. "We're entering the new Women's Quarter."

My heart starts to clench as we go past, the silence rising up like a grasping hand.

I try to sit up higher on my horse.

Cuz this is where she'd be, this is where she'd be healing.

Davy rides up next to me again, his pathetic, half-there moustache bending into an ugly smile. **I'll tell you where yer whore is**, his Noise says.

Mayor Prentiss spins round in his saddle.

And there's the weirdest flash of sound from him, like a shout but quiet and away from me, not in the world at all, like a million words all said together, so fast I swear I feel my hair brush back like in a wind.

But it's Davy who reacts—

His head jerks back like he's been hit, and he has to catch his horse's reins so he don't fall off, spinning the horse round, his eyes wide and dazed, his mouth open, some drool dripping out.

What the hell–?

"He doesn't know, Todd," the Mayor says. "Anything his Noise tells you about her is a lie."

I look at Davy, still dazed and blinking with pain, then back to the Mayor. "Does that mean she's safe?"

"It means he doesn't know. Do you, David?"

No, Pa, says Davy's Noise, still shaky.

Mayor Prentiss raises his eyebrows.

I see Davy clench his teeth. "No, Pa," he says out loud.

"I know my son is a liar," the Mayor says. "I know he is a bully and a brute and ignorant of the things I hold dear. But he is my son." He turns back down the road. "And I believe in redemption."

Davy's Noise is quiet as we follow on but there's a dark red seething in it.

New Prentisstown fades in the distance and the road becomes almost free of buildings. Farm fields start showing up red and green thru the trees and up the hills, with crops I reckernize and others I don't. The silence of the women starts to ease a little and the valley becomes a wilder place, flowers growing in the ditches and waxy squirrels chattering insults to each other and the sun shining clear and cool like nothing else was going on.

At a bend in the river, we curve round a hill and I see a

large metal tower poking out the top of it, stretching up into the sky.

"What's that?" I say.

"Wouldn't you like to know?" Davy says, tho it's obvious he don't know neither. The Mayor don't answer.

Just past the tower, the road bends again and follows a long stone wall emerging outta the trees. Down a little farther, the wall connects to a big arched gate with a huge set of wooden doors. It's the only opening in the long, long wall I see. The road beyond is dirt, like we've come to the end.

"New World's first and last monastery," the Mayor says, stopping at the gate. "Built as a refuge of quiet contemplation for our holiest of men. Built when there was still faith we could beat the Noise germ through self-denial and discipline." His voice goes hard. "Abandoned before it was even properly finished."

He turns to face us. I hear a strange spark of happiness rising in Davy's Noise. Mayor Prentiss gives him a warning look.

"You are wondering," he says to me, "why I appointed my son as your overseer."

I cast a look over to Davy, still smiling away.

"You need a firm hand, Todd," the Mayor says. "Your thoughts even now are of how you might escape at the first opportunity and try to find your precious Viola."

"Where is she?" I say, knowing I won't get no answer.

"And I have no doubt," the Mayor continues, "that David here will be quite a firm hand for you indeed."

Davy's face and Noise both smirk.

"And in return, David will learn what real courage looks

55

like." Davy's smirk vanishes. "He will learn what it's like to act with honour, what it's like to act like a real man. What it's like, in short, to act like you, Todd Hewitt." He gives his son a last glance and then turns Morpeth in the road. "I shall be exceedingly eager to hear how your first day together went."

Without another word, he sets off back to New Prentisstown. I wonder now why he came in the first place. Surely he's got more important things to do.

"Surely I do," the Mayor calls, not turning back. "But don't underestimate yourself, Todd."

He rides off. Davy and I wait till he's well outta hearing distance.

I'm the one who speaks first.

"Tell me what happened to Ben or I'll rip yer effing throat out."

"I'm yer boss, boyo," Davy says, smirking again, jumping off his horse and throwing his rucksack to the ground. "Best treat me with respect or pa ain't gonna—"

But I'm already off Angharrad and hitting him as hard as I can in the face, aiming right for that sad excuse for a moustache. He takes the punch but comes back fast with his own. I ignore the pain, he does, too, and we fall to the ground in a heap of fists and kicks and elbows and knees. He's still bigger than me but only just, only in a way that don't feel like much of a difference no more, but still enough so that after a bit he's got me on my back with his forearm pressed into my throat.

His lip's bleeding, so's his nose, the same as my own poor

face but that ain't concerning me now. Davy reaches behind him and pulls a pistol from a holster strapped to his back.

"Ain't no way yer pa's gonna let you shoot me," I say.

"Yeah," he says, "but I still got a gun and you don't."

"Ben beat you," I grunt, underneath his arm. "He stopped you on the road. We got away from you."

"He didn't stop me," Davy sneers. "I took him prisoner, didn't I? And I took him back to Pa and Pa let me torture him. Let me torture him right to *death*."

And Davy's Noise—

I—

I can't say what's in Davy's Noise (he's a liar, he's a *liar*) but it makes me strong enough to push him away. We fight more, Davy fending me off with the butt of the gun till finally, with an elbow to his throat, I knock him down.

"You remember *that*, boy," Davy says, coughing, gun still gripped. "When my pa says all those nice things about you. He's the one who had me torture yer Ben."

"Yer a liar," I say. "Ben beat you."

"Oh, yeah?" Davy says. "Where is he now then? Coming to rescue you?"

I step forward, my fists up, cuz of course he's right, ain't he? My Noise surges with the loss of Ben, like it's happening all over again right here.

Davy's laughing, scrambling back away from me till he's against the huge wooden door. "My pa can read you," he says, then his eyes widen into a taunt. "Read you like a *book*."

My Noise gets even louder. "You *give* me that book! Or I swear, I'll kill you!"

"You ain't gonna do nothing to me, *Mr Hewitt*," Davy says, rising, his back still against the door. "You wouldn't wanna put yer beloved bitch at risk now, would you?"

And there it is.

They know they got me.

Cuz I won't put her in no more danger.

My hands are ready to do more damage to Davy Prentiss, like they did before when he hurt her, when he *shot* her–

But they won't now–

Even tho they *could*–

Cuz he's weak.

And we both know it.

Davy's smile drops. "Think yer special, do you?" he spits. "Think Pa's got a treat for you?"

I clench my fists, unclench them.

But I keep my place.

"Pa knows you," Davy says. "Pa's *read* you."

"He don't know," I say. "You don't neither."

Davy sneers again. "That so?" His hand reaches for the cast iron handle of the door. "Come and meet yer new flock then, Todd Hewitt."

His weight opens the door behind him and he steps into the paddock and outta the way, giving me a clear view.

Of a hundred or more Spackle staring right back at me.

4

THE MAKING OF
A NEW WORLD

[TODD]

MY FIRST THOUGHT is to turn and run. Run and
run and run and never stop.

"I'd like to see *that*," Davy says, standing inside the gate,
smiling like he just won a prize.

There's so many of 'em, so many long white faces looking
back at me, their eyes too big, their mouths too small and
toothy and high on their faces, their ears looking nothing like
a man's.

But you can still see a man's face in there, can't you?
Still see a face that feels and fears—

And suffers.

It's hard to tell which are male and which are female
cuz they all got the same lichen and moss growing right on
their skins for clothing but there seem to be whole Spackle
families in there, larger spacks protecting their spack children and what must be spack husbands protecting spack
wives, arms wrapped round each other, heads pressed

close together. All of them silently–

Silently.

"I *know*!" Davy says. "Can you believe they gave the cure to these *animals*?"

They look at Davy now and a weird clicking starts passing twixt 'em all with glances and nods moving along the crowd. Davy raises his pistol and steps further into the monastery grounds. "Thinking of trying something?" he spits. "Give me a reason! Go on! GIVE ME A REASON!"

The Spackle huddle closer together in their little groups, backing away from him where they can.

"Get in here, Todd," Davy says. "We got work to do."

I don't move.

"I said, get in here! They're animals. They ain't gonna do *nothing*."

I still don't move.

"He murdered one of y'all," Davy says to the Spackle.

"*Davy!*" I shout.

"Cut its head right off with a knife. Sawed and sawed–"

"Stop it!" I run at him to get him to shut his effing mouth. I don't know how he knows but he knows and he's gotta shut up right *effing now*.

The Spackle nearest the gate scoot way back at my approach, getting outta my way as fast as they can, looking at me with frightened faces, parents getting their children behind them. I push Davy hard but he just laughs and I realize I'm inside the monastery walls now.

And I see just how many Spackle there are.

* * *

The stone wall of the monastery surrounds a *huge* bit of land but only one little building, some kind of storehouse. The rest is divided up into smaller fields, separated by old wooden fences with low gates. Most of 'em are badly overgrown and you can see heavy grass and brambles stretching all the way to the back walls a good hundred metres away.

But mostly you can see Spackle.

Hundreds and hundreds of 'em spread out over the grounds.

Maybe even more than a thousand.

They're pushing themselves against the monastery wall, huddling behind the rotting fences, sitting in groups or standing in rows.

But all watching me, silent as the grave, as my Noise spills out all over the place.

"He's a liar!" I say. "It weren't like that! It weren't like that at all!"

But what was it like? What was it like that I can explain?

Cuz I *did* do it, didn't I?

Not how Davy said but nearly as bad and completely as big in my Noise, too big to cover with all their eyes looking back at me, too big to surround with lies and confuse the truth, too big to not think about as a crowd of Spackle faces just stare.

"It was an accident," I say, my voice trailing off, looking from face to weird face, not seeing no pictures of Spackle Noise, not understanding the clicking they make, so doubly not knowing what's happening. "I didn't mean it."

But not one of 'em says a thing back. They don't do nothing but stare.

* * *

There's a creak as the gate behind us opens up again. We turn to look.

It's Ivan from Farbranch, the one who joined the army rather than fight it.

And look how right he was. He's wearing an officer's uniform and he's got a group of soldiers with him.

"Mr Prentiss Jr," he says, nodding at Davy, who nods back. Ivan turns to me, a look in his eye I can't read and no Noise to be heard. "It's good to see you well, Mr Hewitt."

"You two *know* each other?" Davy says, sharp-like.

"We've had past acquaintance," Ivan says, still looking at me.

But I ain't saying a word to him.

I'm too busy putting up pictures in my Noise.

Pictures of Farbranch. Pictures of Hildy and Tam and Francia. Pictures of the massacre that happened there. The massacre that didn't include him.

A look of annoyance crosses his face. "You go where the power is," he says. "That's how you stay alive."

I put up a picture of his town burning, men and women and children burning with it.

He frowns harder. "These men will stay here as guards. Your orders are to set the Spackle a-clearing the fields and make sure they're fed and watered."

Davy rolls his eyes. "Well, we know *that—*"

But Ivan's already turning and heading out the gate, leaving behind ten men with rifles. They take up stayshuns standing on top of the monastery wall, already getting to work unrolling coils of barbed wire along its edge.

"Ten men with rifles and us against all these Spackle," I say, under my breath but all over my Noise.

"Ah, we'll be okay," Davy says. He raises his pistol at the Spackle nearest him, maybe a female, holding a Spackle baby. She turns the baby away so her body's protecting it. "They ain't got no fight in 'em anyway."

I see the face of the Spackle protecting her baby.

It's defeated, I think. They all are. And they know it.

I know how they feel.

"Hey, pigpiss, check it out," Davy says. He raises his arms in the air, getting all the Spackle eyes on him. "People of New Prentisstown!" he shouts, waving his arms about. "I read to you yer *dooooooooom!*"

And he just laughs and laughs and laughs.

Davy decides to oversee the Spackle clearing the fields of scrub but that's only cuz that means I'm the one who'll have to shovel out the fodder from the storehouse for all of 'em to eat and then fill troughs for 'em to drink from.

But it's farm work. I'm used to it. All the chores Ben and Cillian set me to doing every day. All the chores I used to complain about.

I wipe my eyes and get on with it.

The Spackle keep their distance from me as best they can while I work. Which, I gotta say, is okay by me.

Cuz I find I can't really look 'em in the eyes.

I keep my head down and carry on shovelling.

Davy says his pa told him the Spackle worked as servants

or cooks but one of the Mayor's first orders was for everyone to keep 'em locked away in their homes till the army collected 'em last night while I slept.

"People had 'em living in their back *gardens*," Davy says, watching me shovel as the morning turns to afternoon, eating what's sposed to be lunch for both of us. "Can you believe that? Like they're effing members of the *family*."

"Maybe they were," I say.

"Well they ain't no more," Davy says, rising and taking out his pistol. He grins at me. "Back to work."

I empty most of the storehouse of fodder but it still don't look like nearly enough. Plus, three of the five water pumps ain't working and by sunset, I've only managed to fix one.

"Time to go," Davy says.

"I ain't done," I say.

"Fine," he says, walking towards the gate. "Stay here on yer own then."

I look back at the Spackle. Now that the work day's thru, they've pushed themselves as far away from the soldiers and the front gates as possible.

As far away from me and Davy as possible, too.

I look back and forth twixt them and Davy leaving. They ain't got enough food. They ain't got enough water. There ain't no place to go to the toilet and no shelter of any kind at all.

I hold out my empty hands towards 'em but that don't do no kind of explaining that'll make anything okay. They just stare at me as I drop my hands and follow Davy out the gate.

"So much for being a man of courage, eh, pigpiss?" Davy says, untying his horse, which he calls Deadfall but which only seems to answer to Acorn.

I ignore him cuz I'm thinking bout the Spackle. How I'll treat them well. I will. I'll see that they get enough water and food and I'll do everything I can to protect 'em.

I *will*.

I promise that to myself.

Cuz that's what she'd want.

"Oh, I'll tell you what she *really* wants," Davy sneers.

And we fight again.

New bedding's been put in the tower when I get back, a mattress and a sheet spread out on one side for me and another on the other side for Mayor Ledger, already sitting on his, Noise jangling, eating a bowl of stew.

The bad smell's gone, too.

"Yes," says Mayor Ledger. "And guess who had to clean it up?"

It turns out he's been put to work as a rubbish man.

"Honest labour," he says to me, shrugging, but there are other sounds in his greyish Noise that make me think he don't believe it's very honest at all. "Symbolic, I suppose. I go from the top of the heap to the bottom. It'd be poetic if it weren't so obvious."

There's stew for me by my bed, too, and I take it to the window to look out over the town.

Which is starting to buzz.

As the cure leaves the systems of the men of the town,

you begin to hear it. From inside the houses and buildings, from down the side streets and behind the trees.

Noise is returning to New Prentisstown.

It was hard for me to even walk thru *old* Prentisstown and that only ever had 146 men in it. New Prentisstown's gotta have ten times that many. And boys, too.

I don't know how I'm gonna be able to bear it.

"You'll get used to it," Mayor Ledger says, finishing his stew. "Remember, I lived here for twenty years before we found a cure."

I close my eyes but all I see is a herd of Spackle, looking back at me.

Judging me.

Mayor Ledger taps me on the shoulder and points at my bowl of stew. "Are you going to eat that?"

That night I dream—

About her—

The sun's shining behind her and I can't see her face and we're on a hillside and she's saying something but the roar of the falls behind us is too loud and I say "What?" and when I reach for her, I don't touch her but my hand comes back covered in blood—

"Viola!" I say, sitting up on my mattress in the dark, breathing heavy.

I look over to Mayor Ledger on his mattress, facing away from me, but his Noise ain't sleeping Noise, it's the grey-type Noise he has when he's awake.

"I know yer up," I say.

"You dream quite loud," he says, not looking back. "She someone important?"

"Never you mind."

"We just have to get through it, Todd," he says. "That's all any of us has to do now. Just stay alive and get through it."

I turn to the wall.

There ain't nothing I can do. Not while they got her.

Not while I don't know.

Not while they could still hurt her.

Stay alive and get thru it, I think.

And I think of her out there.

And I whisper it, whisper it to her, wherever she is. "Stay alive and get thru it."

Stay alive.

PART II

HOUSE OF HEALING

5

VIOLA WAKES

{ VIOLA }

"CALM YOURSELF, MY GIRL."

A voice–

In the brightness–

I blink open my eyes. Everything is a pure white so bright it's almost a sound and there's a voice out there in it and my head is groggy and there's a pain in my side and it's too bright and I can't think–

Wait–

Wait–

He was carrying me down the hill–

Just *now* he was carrying me down the hill into Haven after–

"Todd?" I say, my voice a rasp, full of cotton and spit, but I run at it as hard as I can, forcing it out into the bright lights blinding my eyes. "*TODD?*"

"I said to calm yourself, now."

I don't recognize the voice, the voice of a woman–

A woman.

"Who are you?" I ask, trying to sit up, pushing out my hands to feel what's around me, feeling the coolness of the air, the softness of–

A bed?

I feel panic begin to rise.

"*Where is he?*" I shout. "*TODD?*"

"I don't know any Todd, my girl," the voice says as shapes start to come together, as the brightness separates into lesser brightnesses, "but I do know you're in no shape to be demanding information."

"You were *shot*," says another voice, another woman, younger than the first, off to my right.

"Hush your mouth, Madeleine Poole," says the first woman.

"Yes, Mistress Coyle."

I keep on blinking and I start to see what's right in front of me. I'm in a narrow white bed in a narrow white room. I'm wearing a thin white gown, tied at the back. A woman both tall and plump stands in front of me, a white coat with a blue outstretched hand stitched into it draped over her shoulders, her mouth set in a line, her expression solid. Mistress Coyle. Behind her at the door holding a bowl of steaming water is a girl not much older than me.

"I'm Maddy," says the girl, sneaking a smile.

"Out," says Mistress Coyle, without even turning her head. Maddy catches my eye as she leaves, another smile sent my way.

"Where am I?" I ask Mistress Coyle, my breath still fast.

"Do you mean the room, my girl? Or the *town*?" She holds my eyes. "Or indeed the planet?"

"Please," I say and my eyes suddenly start to fill with water and I'm angry about that but I keep talking. "I was with a boy."

She sighs and looks away for a second, then she purses her lips and sits down in a chair next to the bed. Her face is stern, her hair pulled back in plaits so tight you could probably climb them, her body solid and big and not at all someone who you'd mess around.

"I'm sorry," she says, almost tenderly. Almost. "I don't know anything about a boy." She frowns. "I'm afraid I don't know anything about anything except that you were brought to this house of healing yesterday morning so close to death I wasn't at all sure we would be able to bring you back. Except that we were informed in no uncertain terms that *our* survival rather depended upon *yours*."

She waits to see how I take this.

I have no idea how I take this.

Where *is* he? What have they done with him?

I turn away from her to try and *think* but I'm wrapped so tight in bandages around my middle I can't properly sit up.

Mistress Coyle runs a couple of fingers across her brow. "And now that you're back," she says, "I'm not at all sure you're going to thank us for the world to which we've returned you."

She tells me of Mayor Prentiss arriving in Haven in front of the rumour of an army, a big one, big enough to crush the town without effort, big enough to set the whole world ablaze. She tells me of the surrender of someone called Mayor Ledger, of how he shouted down the few people who wanted to fight, of how most people agreed to let him "hand over the town on a plate with a bow tied round it".

"And then the houses of healing," she says, real anger coming off her voice, "suddenly became prisons for the women inside."

"So you're a doctor, then?" I ask, but all I can feel is my chest pulling in on itself, sinking as if under an enormous weight, sinking because we failed, sinking because outrunning the army proved to be of no use at all.

Her mouth curls in a small smile, a secret one, like I just let something go. But it's not cruel and I'm finding myself less afraid of her, of what this room might mean, less afraid for myself, more afraid for *him*.

"No, my girl," she says, cocking her head. "As I'm sure you know, there are no women doctors on New World. I'm a healer."

"What's the difference?"

She runs her fingers across her brow again. "What's the difference indeed?" She drops her hands in her lap and looks at them. "Even though we're locked up," she says, "we still hear rumours, you see. Rumours of men and women being separated all over town, rumours of the army arriving perhaps this very day, rumours of slaughter coming over the hill to vanquish us all no matter how well we *surrendered*."

She's looking at me hard now. "And then there's you."

I look away from her. "I'm not anyone special."

"Are you not?" She looks unconvinced. "A girl whose arrival the whole town has to be cleared for? A girl whose life I am ordered to save on pain of my own? A girl," she leans forward to make sure I'm listening, "fresh from the great black beyond?"

I stop breathing for a second and hope she doesn't notice. "Where'd you get an idea like that?"

She grins again, not unkindly. "I'm a healer. The first thing I ever see is skin and so I know it well. Skin tells the story of a person, where they've been, what they've eaten, who they are. You've got some surface wear, my girl, but the rest of your skin is the softest and whitest I've seen in my twenty years of doing the good work. Too soft and white for a planet of farmers."

I'm still not looking at her.

"And then there are the rumours, of course, brought in by the refugees, of more settlers on the way. Thousands of them."

"Please," I say quietly, my eyes welling up again. I try to force them to stop.

"And no girl from New World would ever ask a woman if she was a doctor," she finishes.

I swallow. I put a hand to my mouth. Where is he? I don't care about any of this because *where is he?*

"I know you're frightened," Mistress Coyle says. "But we're suffering from an *excess* of fright here in this town and there's nothing I can do about that." She reaches out a rough hand to touch my arm. "But maybe you can do something to help *us*."

I swallow but I don't say anything.

There's only one person I can trust.

And he's not here.

Mistress Coyle leans back in her chair. "We did save your life," she says. "A little knowledge could be a large comfort."

I breathe in deep, looking around the room, around at the sunlight streaming in from a window looking out onto trees and a river, *the* river, the one we followed into what was supposed to be safety. It seems impossible that anything bad could be happening anywhere on a day so bright, that there's any danger on the doorstep, that there's an army coming.

But there *is* an army coming.

There *is*.

And it won't be any friend to Mistress Coyle, no matter what's happened to–

I feel a little pain in my chest.

But I take a breath.

And I start to talk.

"My name," I say, "is Viola Eade."

"More settlers, huh?" Maddy says with a smile. I'm lying on my side as she unwraps the long bandage around my middle. The underside is covered in blood, my skin dusty and rust-coloured where it's dried. There's a little hole in my stomach, tied up with fine string.

"Why doesn't this hurt?" I say.

"Jeffers root on the bandages," Maddy says. "Natural opiate. You won't feel any pain but you won't be able to go to the toilet for a month either. Plus, you'll be sound asleep in about five minutes."

I touch the skin around the bullet wound, gently, gently. There's another on my back where the bullet went in. "Why aren't I dead?"

"Would you rather be dead?" She smiles again, which

changes to the smiliest frown I've ever seen. "I shouldn't joke. Mistress Coyle's always saying I lack the *proper serious-ness* to be a healer." She dips a cloth in a basin of hot water and starts washing the wounds. "You aren't dead because Mistress Coyle is the best healer in all of Haven, better than any of those so-called *doctors* they've got in this town. Even the bad guys know that. Why do you think they brought you here instead of a clinic?"

She's wearing the same long white coat as Mistress Coyle but she's also got on a short white cap with the blue out-stretched hand stitched on it, which she told me is something apprentices wear. She can't be more than a year or two older than me, whatever way they measure age on this planet, but her hands are sure, gentle and firm all around the wounds.

"So," she says, her voice deceptively light. "How bad *are* these bad guys?"

The door opens. A short girl in another apprentice cap leans in, young as Maddy but with dark brown skin and a storm cloud hanging over her head. "Mistress Coyle says you need to finish up right now."

Maddy doesn't look up from taping new bandages to my front. "Mistress Coyle knows I've only had time to get halfway done."

"We've been summoned," says the girl.

"You say that like we get *summoned* all the time, Corinne." The bandages are almost as good as the ones I had from my ship, the medicine on them already cooling my torso, already making my eyelids heavy. Maddy finishes on the front and turns to cut another set for my back. "I am in the middle of a healing."

"A man came by with a gun," Corinne says.

Maddy stops bandaging.

"Everyone's been called to the town square," Corinne continues. "Which includes you, Maddy Poole, healing or not." She crosses her arms hard. "I'll bet it's the army coming."

Maddy looks me in the eyes. I look away.

"We'll finally see what our end looks like," Corinne says.

Maddy rolls her eyes. "Always so cheerful, you," she says. "Tell Mistress Coyle I'll be out in two ticks."

Corinne gives her a sour look but leaves. Maddy finishes up the bandages on my back, by which time I can barely stay awake.

"You sleep now," Maddy says. "It'll be all right, you just watch. Why would they save you if they were going to..." She doesn't finish the thought, just scrunches her lips and then smiles. "I'm always *saying* Corinne's got enough proper seriousness in her for all of us put together."

Her smile is the last thing I see before I sleep.

"TODD!"

I jolt awake again, the nightmare dashing away, Todd slipping from me–

I hear a clunk and I see a book drop from Maddy's lap as she blinks herself awake in the chair by the bed. Night's fallen, and the room is dark, just a little lamp on where Maddy was meant to have been reading.

"Who's Todd?" she asks, yawning, already smiling through it. "Your *boyfriend?*" The look on my face makes her drop the tease immediately. "Someone important?"

I nod, still breathing heavily from the nightmare, my hair plastered to my forehead with sweat. "Someone important."

She pours me a glass of water from a pitcher on the bedside table. "What happened?" I say, taking a drink. "You were summoned."

"Ah, yes, that," Maddy says, sitting back. "*That* was interesting."

She tells me about how everyone in the entire town – not Haven any more, New Prentisstown, a name that makes my stomach sink – gathered to watch the army march in and watch the new Mayor execute the old one.

"Except he didn't," Maddy says. "He spared him. Said he would spare all of us, too. That he was taking away the Noise cure, which the men weren't too happy about and good Lord it's been nice not to hear it yammering for the past six months, but that we should all know our place and remember who we were and that we would make a new home together in preparation for all the settlers that were coming."

She widens her eyes, waits for me to say something.

"I didn't understand half of that," I say. "There's a cure?"

She shakes her head but not to say no. "Boy, you really aren't from around here, are you?"

I set down the glass of water, leaning forward and lowering my voice to a whisper. "Maddy, is there a communications hub near here?"

She looks at me like I just asked her if she'd like to move with me to one of the moons. "So I can contact the ships," I say. "It might be a big, curved dish? Or a tower, maybe?"

She looks thoughtful. "There's an old metal tower up in the hills," she says, also whispering, "but I'm not even sure it *is* a communications tower. It's been abandoned for ages. Besides, you won't be able to get to it. There's a whole army out there, Vi."

"How big?"

"Big enough." We're both still whispering. "People are saying they're separating out the last of the women tonight."

"To do what?"

Maddy shrugs. "Corinne said a woman in the crowd told her they rounded up the Spackle, too."

I sit up, pressing against the bandages. "Spackle?"

"They're the native species here."

"I know who they are." I sit up even more, straining against the bandage. "Todd told me things, told me what happened before. Maddy, if the Mayor's separating out women and Spackle, then we're in danger. We're in the *worst kind* of danger."

I push back my sheets to get up but a sudden bolt of lightning rips through my stomach. I call out and fall back.

"Pulled a stitch," Maddy tuts, standing right up.

"Please." I grit my teeth against the pain. "We have to get out of here. We have to *run*."

"You're in no position to run anywhere," she says, reaching for my bandage.

Which is when the Mayor walks in the door.

6

SIDES OF THE STORY

{V I O L A}

MISTRESS COYLE LEADS HIM IN. Her face is sterner than ever, her forehead creased, her jaw set. Even having only met her once I can tell she's not happy.

He stands behind her. Tall, thin but broad-shouldered, all in white with a hat he hasn't taken off.

I've never properly seen him. I was bleeding, dying when he approached us in the town square.

But it's him.

It can only be him.

"Good evening, Viola," he says. "I've been wanting to meet you for a very long time."

Mistress Coyle sees me struggling with the sheet, sees Maddy reaching for me. "Is there a problem, Madeleine?"

"Nightmare," Maddy says, catching my eye. "I think she pulled a stitch."

"We'll deal with that later," Mistress Coyle says and the calm and serious way she says it gets Maddy's full attention. "Get her 400 units of Jeffers root in the meantime."

"400?" Maddy says, sounding surprised, but seeing the look on Mistress Coyle's face, all she says is, "Yes, Mistress." She gives my hand a last squeeze and leaves the room.

They both watch me for a long moment, then the Mayor says, "That'll be all, Mistress."

Mistress Coyle gives me a silent look as she leaves, maybe to reassure me, maybe to ask me something or *tell* me something, but I'm too frightened to figure it out before she backs out of the room, closing the door behind her.

And then I'm alone with him.

He lets the silence build until it's clear I'm meant to say something. I'm gripping the sheet to my chest with a fist, still feeling the lightning pain fire up my side if I move.

"You're Mayor Prentiss," I say. My voice shakes when I say it but I say it.

"*President* Prentiss," he says, "but you would know me as Mayor, of course."

"Where's Todd?" I look into his eyes. I do not blink. "What have you done with him?"

He smiles again. "Smart in your first sentence, courageous in your second. We may be friends yet."

"Is he hurt?" I swallow away the burn rising in my chest. "Is he alive?"

For a second, it looks like he's not going to tell me, not even going to acknowledge that I asked, but then he says,

"Todd is well. Todd is alive and well and asking about you every chance he gets."

I realize I've held my breath for his answer. "Is that true?"

"Of course it's true."

"I want to see him."

"And he wants to see you," says Mayor Prentiss. "But all things in their proper order."

He keeps his smile. It's almost friendly.

Here is the man we spent all those weeks running from, here he is, standing in my very own room, where I can barely move from the pain.

And he's *smiling*.

And it's almost friendly.

If he's hurt Todd, if he's laid a *finger* on him–

"Mayor Prentiss–"

"*President* Prentiss," he says again, then his voice brightens. "But you may call me David."

I don't say anything, just press down harder onto my bandage against the pain.

There's something about him. Something I can't quite place–

"That is," he says, "if I may call you Viola."

There's a knock on the door. Maddy opens it, a phial in her hand. "Jeffers," she says, keeping her eyes firmly on the floor. "For her pain."

"Yes, of course," the Mayor says, moving away from my bed, hands behind his back. "Proceed."

Maddy pours me a glass of water and watches me swallow four yellow gel caps, two more than I've taken before. She takes the glass from me and, with her back to the Mayor, gives me a firm look, a solid one, no smile but all kinds of bravery, and it makes me feel a little bit good, a little bit stronger.

"She'll grow tired very quickly," Maddy says to the Mayor, still not looking at him.

"I understand," the Mayor says. Maddy leaves, closing the door behind her. My stomach immediately starts to grow warm but it'll take a minute just yet to make the pain start to go or take away the quivering running all through me.

"So," the Mayor says. "May I?"

"May you what?"

"Call you Viola?"

"I can't stop you," I say. "If you want."

"Good," he says, not sitting, not moving, the smile still fixed. "When you are feeling better, Viola, I would very much like to have a talk with you."

"About what?"

"Why, your ships, of course," he says. "Coming closer by the moment."

I swallow. "What ships?"

"Oh, no, no, no." He shakes his head but still smiles. "You started out with intelligence and with courage. You are frightened but that has not stopped you from addressing me with calmness and clarity. All most admirable." He bends his head down. "But to that we must add honesty. We *must* start out honestly with each other, Viola, or how may we proceed at all?"

Proceed to where? I think.

"I have told you that Todd is alive and well," he says, "and what I tell you is true." He places a hand on the rail at the end of the bed. "And he will *stay* safe." He pauses. "And you will give me your honesty."

And I understand without having to be told that one depends on the other.

The warmth is starting to spread up from my stomach, making everything seem slower, softer. The lightning in my side is fading, but it's taking wakefulness along with it. Why *two* doses when that would put me to sleep so fast? So fast I won't even be able to talk to–

Oh.

Oh.

"I need to see him to believe you," I say.

"Soon," he says. "There is much to be done in New Prentisstown first. Much to be *un*done."

"Whether anyone wants it or not." My eyelids are getting heavy. I force them up. Only then do I realize I said it out loud.

He smiles again. "I find myself saying this with great frequency, Viola. The war is over. I am not your enemy."

I lift my groggy eyes to him in surprise.

I'm afraid of him. I am.

But–

"You were the enemy of the women of Prentisstown," I say. "You were the enemy of everyone in Farbranch."

He stiffens a little, though he tries not to let me see it. "A body was found in the river this morning," he says. "A body with a knife in its throat."

I try to keep my eyes from widening, even under the Jeffers. He's looking at me close now. "Perhaps the man's death was justified," he says. "Perhaps the man had *enemies*."

I see myself doing it–

I see myself plunging the knife–

I close my eyes.

"As for me," the Mayor says, "the war is over. My days of soldiering are at an end. Now come the days of leadership, of bringing people together."

By separating them, I think, but my breathing is slowing. The whiteness of the room is growing brighter but only in a soft way that makes me want to fall down into it and sleep and sleep and sleep. I press further into the pillow.

"I'll leave you now," he says. "We will meet again."

I begin to breathe through my mouth. Sleep is becoming impossible to avoid.

He sees me starting to drift off.

And he does the most surprising thing.

He steps forward and pulls the sheet straight across me, almost like he's tucking me in.

"Before I go," he says. "I have one request."

"What?" I say, fighting to keep awake.

"I'd like you to call me David."

"*What?*" I say, my voice heavy.

"I'd like you to say, *Good night, David.*"

The Jeffers has so disconnected me that the words come out before I know I'm even saying them. "Good night, David."

Through the haze of the drug, I see him look a little surprised, even a little disappointed.

But he recovers quickly. "And to you, Viola." He nods at me and steps towards the door to leave.

And I realize what it is, what's so different about him.

"I can't hear you," I whisper from my bed.

He stops and turns. "I said, *And to–*"

"No," I say, my tongue barely able to move. "I mean I can't *hear* you. I can't hear you think."

He raises his eyebrows. "I should hope not."

And I think I'm asleep before he can even leave.

I don't wake for a long, long time, finally blinking again into the sunshine, wondering what was real and what was a dream.

(... my father, holding out his hand to help me up the ladder into the hatch, smiling, saying, "Welcome aboard, skipper...")

"You snore," says a voice.

Corinne is seated in the chair, her fingers flying a threaded needle through a piece of fabric so fast it's like it's not her doing it, like someone else's angry hands are using her lap.

"I do not," I say.

"Like a cow in oestrus."

I push back the covers. My bandages have been changed and the lightning pain is gone so the stitch must be repaired. "How long have I been asleep?"

"More than a day." She sounds disapproving. "The President's already sent men by twice to check on your condition."

I put a hand on my side, tentatively pushing on the wound. The pain is almost non-existent.

"Nothing to say to that then, my girl?" Corinne says, needle thrashing ferociously.

I furrow my forehead. "What's there to say? I'd never met him before."

"He was sure keen to know *you* though, wasn't he? Ow!" She breathes in a sharp hiss and sticks a fingertip in her mouth. "All the while he's got us trapped," she says around her finger. "All the while we can't even leave this building."

"I don't see how that's my fault."

"It isn't your fault, my girl," Mistress Coyle says, coming into the room. She looks sternly at Corinne. "And no one here thinks it is."

Corinne stands, bows slightly to Mistress Coyle and leaves without another word.

"How are you feeling?" Mistress Coyle asks.

"Groggy." I sit up more, finding it much easier to do so this time. I also notice my bladder is uncomfortably full. I tell Mistress Coyle.

"Well, then," she says, "let's see if you can stand on your own to help with that."

I take in a breath and turn to put my feet on the floor. My legs don't want to bend very fast but eventually they get there and eventually I can stand up and even walk to the door.

"Maddy *said* you were the best healer in town," I marvel.

"Maddy tells no lies."

She accompanies me down a long white hallway to a toilet. When I've finished and washed and opened the door again, Mistress Coyle is holding a heavier white gown for me to wear, longer and much nicer than the backwards robe I have on. I slip it over my head and we walk back up the hallway, a little wobbly, but walking all the same.

"The President has been asking after your health," she says, steadying me with her hand.

"Corinne told me." I look up at her out of the corner of my eye. "It's only because of the settler ships. I don't know him. I'm not on his side."

"Ah," Mistress Coyle says, getting me back through the door to my room and onto my bed. "You do recognize there are sides then?"

I lie back, my tongue pressed against the back of my teeth. "Did you give me two doses of Jeffers so I wouldn't have to speak to him for very long?" I say. "Or so I wouldn't be able to tell him very much?"

She gives a nod as if to say how clever I am. "Would it be the worst thing in the world if it was a little of both?"

"You could have asked."

"Wasn't time," she says, sitting down in the chair next to the bed. "We only know him by his history, my girl, and his history is bad, bad, bad. Whatever he might say about a new society, there is good reason to want to be better prepared if he starts a conversation."

"I don't know him," I say again. "I don't know anything."

"But, done rightly," she says, with a little smile, "you might *learn* things from a man who takes an interest."

I try to read her, read what she's trying to tell me, but of course women here don't have Noise either, do they?

"What are you saying?" I ask.

"I'm saying it's time for you to get something solid into your stomach." She stands, brushing invisible threads off her white coat. "I'll have Madeleine bring in some breakfast for you."

She walks to the door, taking hold of the handle but not turning it yet. "But know this," she says, without turning around. "If there *are* sides and our President is on one..." She glances back at me over her shoulder. "Then I am most definitely on the other."

7

MISTRESS COYLE

{VIOLA}

"THERE ARE SIX SHIPS," I say from my bed, for the third time in as many days, days where Todd is still out there somewhere, days where I don't know what's happening to him or to anyone else outside.

From the windows of my room, I see soldiers marching by all the time, but all they do is march. Everyone here at the house of healing half-expected them to come bursting through the doors at any moment, ready to do terrible things, ready to assert their victory.

But they haven't. They just march by. Other men bring us deliveries of food to the back doors, and the healers are left to their work.

We still can't leave, but the world outside doesn't seem to be ending. Which isn't what anyone expected, not least, it seems, Mistress Coyle, who's convinced it only means something worse is waiting to happen.

I can't help but think that she's probably right.

She frowns into her notes. "Just six?"

"Eight hundred sleeping settlers and three caretaker families in each," I say. I'm getting hungry, but I know by now there's no eating until she says the consultation is finished. "Mistress Coyle–"

"And you're sure there are eighty-one members of the caretaker families?"

"I should know," I say. "I was in school with their children."

She looks up. "I know this is tedious, Viola, but information is power. The information we give him. The information we learn *from* him."

I sigh impatiently. "I don't know anything *about* spying."

"It's not spying," she says, returning to her notes. "It's just finding things out." She writes something more in her pad. "Four thousand, eight hundred and eighty-one people," she says, almost to herself.

I know what she means. More people than the entire population of this planet. Enough to change everything.

But change it how?

"When he speaks with you again," she says, "you can't tell him about the ships. Keep him guessing. Keep him off the right number."

"While I'm also supposed to be finding out what I can," I say.

She closes her pad, consultation over. "Information is power," she repeats.

I sit up in the bed, pretty much sick to death of being a patient. "Can I ask you something?"

She stands and reaches for her cloak. "Certainly."

"Why do you trust me?"

"Your face when he walked into your room," she says without hesitating. "You looked as if you'd just met your worst enemy."

She snaps the buttons of the cloak under her chin. I watch her carefully. "If I could just find Todd or get to that communications tower..."

"And be taken by the army?" She's not frowning but her eyes are bright. "Lose us our one advantage?" She opens the door. "No, my girl, the President will come a-calling and when he does, what you find out from him will help us."

I call out after her as she goes, "Who do you mean by *us*?"

But she's gone.

" ... and the last thing I really remember is him picking me up and carrying me down a long, long hill, and telling me that I wasn't going to die, that he'd save me."

"Wow," breathes Maddy softly, wisps of hair sneaking out from under her cap as we walk slowly up one hallway and down another to build my strength. "And he did save you."

"But he can't kill," I say, "not even to save himself. That's the thing about him, why they wanted him so bad. He isn't like them. He killed a Spackle once and you should have seen how he suffered for it. And now they've *got* him–"

I have to stop and blink a lot and look at the floor.

"I need to get *out* of here," I say, clenching my teeth. "I'm no spy. I need to find him and I need to get to that tower and *warn* them. Maybe they can send help. They have more scout ships that could reach here. They've got weapons..."

Maddy's face looks tense, like it always does when I talk this way. "We're not even allowed outside yet."

"You can't just accept what people tell you, Maddy. You can't just *do* that if they're wrong."

"And *you* can't fight an army on your own." She turns me gently back down the hallway, giving me a smile. "Not even the great and brave Viola Eade."

"I did it before," I say. "I did with *him*."

She lowers her voice. "Vi–"

"I lost my parents," I say and my voice is husky. "And there's no way I can get them back. And now I've lost him. And if there's a chance, if there's even a chance–"

"Mistress Coyle won't allow it," she says, but there's something in her voice that makes me look up.

"But?" I say.

Maddy says no more, just walks us over to the hall window that looks out onto the road. A troop of soldiers passes by in the bright sunlight, a cart full of dusty purple grain passing by the other way, the Noise we can hear from the town coming down the road like an army all on its own.

At first it was like no Noise I'd ever heard, this weird buzzing sound of metal grinding against metal. Then it got even louder than that, like a thousand men shouting at once, which I guess is pretty much what it is, too loud and messy to be able to pick out any individual person.

Too loud to pick out one boy.

"Maybe it's not as bad as we all think." Maddy's voice is slow, weighing every word as if she's testing them out for herself. "I mean, the town looks peaceful. *Loud,* but the men who deliver the food say the stores are about to re-open. I'll bet your Todd is out there working away at a job, safe and alive and waiting to see you."

I can't tell if she's saying this because she believes it or because she's trying to get *me* to believe it. I wipe my nose with my sleeve. "That could be true."

She looks at me for a long time, obviously thinking something but not saying it. Then she turns back to the glass.

"Just listen to them roar," she says.

There are three other healers here besides Mistress Coyle. Mistress Waggoner, a short round puff of a woman with wrinkles and a moustache, Mistress Nadari, who treats cancers and who I've only seen once closing a door behind her, and Mistress Lawson, who treats children in another house of healing but who was trapped here while having a consultation with Mistress Coyle when the surrender happened and who's been fretting ever since about the ill children she left behind.

There are more apprentices, too, a dozen besides Maddy and Corinne, who – because they work with Mistress Coyle – seem to be the top two apprentices out of the whole house, maybe even all of Haven. I rarely see the others except when they're trailing behind one of the healers, stethoscopes bouncing, white coats flapping behind them, off to find something to do.

Because the truth of it is, as the days go by and the town gets on with whatever it's doing beyond our doors, most of us patients are getting better and new ones aren't arriving. All the male patients were taken out of here the first night,

Maddy told me, whether they could travel or not, and no new women have been brought here even though invasion and surrender aren't bars to getting sick.

Mistress Coyle worries about this.

"Well, if she can't heal, then who is she?" Corinne says, snapping the elastic band around my arm a little too tight. "She used to run all of the houses of healing, not just this one. Everyone knew her, everyone respected her. For a while, she was even Chair of the Town Council."

I blink. "She used to be in charge?"

"Years ago. Quit moving around." She jabs the needle into my arm harder than she needs to. "She's always saying that being a leader is making the people you love hate you a little more each day." She catches my eye. "Which is something I believe, too."

"So what happened?" I ask. "Why isn't she still in charge?"

"She made a mistake," Corinne says primly. "People who didn't like her took advantage of it."

"What kind of mistake?"

Her permanent frown gets bigger. "She saved a life," she says and snaps loose the elastic band so hard it leaves a mark.

Another day passes, and another, and nothing changes. We're still not allowed out, our food still comes, and the Mayor still hasn't asked for me. His men check on my condition but the promised talk never happens. He's just leaving me here, so far.

Who knows why?

He's all anyone ever talks about, though.

"And do you know what he's done?" Mistress Coyle says over dinner, my first one where I'm allowed out of bed and in the canteen. "The cathedral isn't just his base of operations. He's made it into his *home*."

There's a general clucking of disgust from the women around her. Mistress Waggoner even pushes her plate away. "He fancies himself *God* now," she says.

"He hasn't burned the town down, though," I say, wondering aloud from the other end of the table. Maddy and Corinne both look up from their plates with wide eyes. I carry on anyway. "We all thought he would, but he hasn't."

Mistresses Waggoner and Lawson give Mistress Coyle a meaningful look.

"You show your youth, Viola," Mistress Coyle says. "And you shouldn't challenge your superiors."

I blink, surprised. "That's not what I meant," I say. "I'm only saying it's not what we expected."

Mistress Coyle takes another bite while eyeing me. "He killed every woman in his town because he couldn't hear them, because he couldn't *know* them in the way that men could be known before the cure."

The other mistresses nod. I open my mouth to speak but she overrides me.

"What's also true, my girl," she says, "is that everything we've been through since landing on this planet – the surprise of the Noise, the chaos that followed – all of that remains unknown to your friends up there." She's watching me closely now. "Everything that happened to us is waiting to happen to them."

I don't reply, I just watch her.

"And who do you want in charge of that process?" she asks. "Him?"

She's done talking to me and returns to quieter conference with the mistresses. Corinne starts eating again, a smug grin on her face. Maddy's still staring at me wide-eyed, but all I can think of is the word left hanging in the air.

When she said *Him?*, did she also mean, *Or her?*

On our ninth day locked indoors, I'm no longer a patient. Mistress Coyle summons me to her office.

"Your clothes," she says, handing me a package over her desk. "You can put them on now, if you like. Make you feel like a real person again."

"Thank you," I say genuinely, heading behind the screen she's pointed out. I lift off the patient's robe and look for a second at my wound, almost healed both front and back.

"You really are the most amazing healer," I say.

"I do try," she says from her desk.

I unwrap the package and find all of my own clothes, freshly laundered, smelling so clean and crisp I feel a strange pull on my face and discover I'm smiling.

"You know, you're a brave girl, Viola," Mistress Coyle is saying, as I start to dress. "Despite not knowing when to keep quiet."

"Thank you," I say, a little annoyed.

"The crashing of your ship, the deaths of your parents, the amazing journey here. All faced with intelligence and resourcefulness."

"I had help," I say, sitting down to put on clean socks.

I notice Mistress Coyle's pad on a little side table, the one so full of notes from our little consultations. I look up but she's still on the other side of the screen. I reach over and flip open the cover.

"I sense big things in you, my girl," she says. "Leadership potential."

The notebook is upside down and I don't want to make a noise by moving it so I try to twist round to see what it says.

"I see a lot of myself in you."

On the first page, before her notes start, there's only a single letter, written in blue.

A.

Nothing else.

"We are the choices we make, Viola," Mistress Coyle is still talking. "And you can be so valuable to us. If you choose."

I lift up my head from the pad. "Us who?"

The door bursts open so loud and sudden I jump up and look around the screen. It's Maddy. "There was a messenger," she says, breathless. "Women can start leaving their houses."

"It's so loud out here," I say, wincing into the ROAR of all the New Prentisstown Noise twining together.

"You get used to it," Maddy says. We're sitting on a bench outside a store while Corinne and another apprentice named Thea buy supplies for the house of healing, stocking up for the expected flood of new patients.

I look around the streets. Stores are open, people pass by, mostly on foot but on fissionbikes and horses, too. If you don't look too closely, you'd almost think nothing was even wrong.

But then you see that the men who move down the road never talk to each other. And women are allowed out only in groups of four and only in daylight and only for an hour at a time. And the groups of four never interact. Even the men of Haven don't approach us.

And there are soldiers on every corner, rifles in hand.

A bell chimes as the door of the store opens. Corinne storms out, arms full of bags, face full of thunder, Thea struggling behind her. "The storekeeper says no one's heard from the Spackle since they were taken," Corinne says, practically dropping a bag in my lap.

"Corinne and her spacks," Thea says, rolling her eyes and handing me another bag.

"Don't call them that," Corinne says. "If *we* could never treat them right, what do you think *he's* going to be doing to them?"

"I'm sorry, Corinne," Maddy says before I can ask what Corinne means, "but don't you think it makes more sense to worry about us right now?" Her eyes are watching some soldiers who've noticed Corinne's raised voice. They aren't moving, haven't even shifted from the veranda of a feed store.

But they're looking.

"It was inhuman, what we did to them," Corinne says.

"Yes, but they *aren't* human," Thea says, under her breath, looking at the soldiers, too.

"*Thea Reese!*" A vein bulges out of Corinne's forehead. "How can you call yourself a healer and say–"

"Yes, yes, all right," Maddy says, trying to calm her down. "It was awful. I agree. You know we *all* agree, but what could we have done about it?"

"What are you talking about?" I say. "Did *what* to them?"

"The *cure*," Corinne says, saying it like a curse.

Maddy turns to me with a frustrated sigh. "They found out that the cure worked on the Spackle."

"By *testing* it on them," Corinne says.

"But it does more than that," Maddy says. "The Spackle don't *speak*, you see. They can click their mouths a little but it's hardly more than like when we snap our fingers."

"The Noise was the only way they communicated," Thea says.

"And it turned out we didn't really need them to talk to us to tell them what to do," Corinne says, her voice rising even more. "So who cares if they needed to talk to each *other*?"

I'm beginning to see. "And the cure..."

Thea nods. "It makes them docile."

"Better slaves," Corinne says bitterly.

My mouth drops open. "They were *slaves*?"

"Shhhh," Maddy shushes harshly, jerking her head toward the soldiers watching us, their lack of Noise among all the ROAR of the other men making them seem ominously blank.

"It's like we cut out their tongues," Corinne says, lowering her voice but still burning.

But Maddy is already getting us on our way, looking back over her shoulder at the soldiers.

Who watch us go.

* * *

We walk the short distance back to the house of healing in silence, entering the front door under the blue outstretched hand painted over the door frame. After Corinne and Thea go inside, Maddy takes my arm lightly to hold me back.

She looks at the ground for a minute, a dimple forming in the middle of her eyebrows. "The way those soldiers looked at us," she says.

"Yeah?"

She crosses her arms and shivers. "I don't know if I like this version of peace very much."

"I know," I say softly.

She waits a moment, then she looks at me square. "Could your people help us? Could they stop this?"

"I don't know," I say, "but finding out would be better than just sitting here, waiting for the worst to happen."

She looks around to see if we're being overheard. "Mistress Coyle is brilliant," she says, "but sometimes she can only hear her own opinion."

She waits, biting her upper lip.

"Maddy?"

"We'll watch out," she says.

"For what?"

"*If* the right moment arrives, and *only* if," she looks around again, "we'll see what we can do about contacting your ships."

8

THE NEWEST APPRENTICE

{VIOLA}

"BUT SLAVERY IS WRONG," I say, rolling up another bandage.

"The healers were always opposed to it." Mistress Coyle ticks off another box on her inventory. "Even after the Spackle War, we thought it inhuman."

"Then why didn't you stop it?"

"If you ever see a war," she says, not looking up from her clipboard, "you'll learn that war only destroys. No one escapes from a war. No one. Not even the survivors. You accept things that would appal you at any other time because life has temporarily lost all meaning."

"*War makes monsters of men*," I say, quoting Ben from that night in the weird place where New World buried its dead.

"And women," Mistress Coyle says. She taps her fingers on boxes of syringes to count them.

"But the Spackle War was over a long time ago, wasn't it?"

"Thirteen years now."

"Thirteen years where you could have righted a wrong."

She finally looks at me. "Life is only that simple when you're young, my girl."

"But you were in charge," I say. "You could have done something."

"And who told you I was in charge?"

"Corinne said–"

"Ah, Corinne," she says, turning back to her clipboard, "doing her best to love me no matter what the facts."

I open up another bag of supplies. "But if you were head of this Council thing," I press on, "surely you could have done *something* about the Spackle."

"Sometimes, my girl," she says, giving me a displeased look, "you can lead people where they don't want to go, but most of the time you *can't*. The Spackle weren't going to be freed, not after we'd just beaten them in an awful and vicious war, not when we needed so much labour to rebuild. But they could be treated better, couldn't they? They could be fed properly and set to work humane hours and allowed to live together with their families. All victories *I* won for them, Viola."

Her writing on the clipboard is a lot more forceful than it was. I watch her for a second. "Corinne says you were thrown off the Council for saving a life."

She doesn't answer me, just sets down her clipboard and looks on one of the higher shelves. She reaches up and takes down an apprentice hat and a folded apprentice cloak. She turns and tosses them to me.

"Who are these for?" I say, catching them.

"You want to find out about being a leader?" she says. "Then let's put you on the path."

I look at her face.

I look down at the cloak and the cap.

From then on, I barely have time to eat.

The day after women were allowed to move again, there were eighteen new patients, all female, who'd been suffering all kinds of things – appendicitis, heart problems, lapsed cancer treatments, broken bones – all trapped in houses where they'd been stuck after being separated from husbands and sons. The next day, there were eleven more. Mistress Lawson went back to the children's house of healing the second she was able, but Mistresses Coyle, Waggoner and Nadari were suddenly rushing from room to room, shouting orders and saving lives. I don't think anyone's been to sleep since.

There's certainly no time for me and Maddy to look for our moment, no time to even notice that the Mayor still hasn't come to see me. Instead, I run around a lot, getting in the way, helping out where I can, and squeezing apprentice lessons in.

I turn out not to be a natural healer.

"I don't think I'm ever going to get this," I say, failing yet again to tell the blood pressure of a sweet old patient called Mrs Fox.

"It sure feels that way," Corinne says, glancing up at the clock.

"Patience, pretty girl," Mrs Fox says, her face wrinkling up in a smile. "A thing worth learning is worth learning well."

"You're right there, Mrs Fox," Corinne says, looking back at me. "Try it again."

I pump up the armband to inflate it, listen through the stethoscope for the right kind of *whoosh, whoosh* in Mrs Fox's blood and match that up to the little dial. "Sixty over twenty?" I guess weakly.

"Well, let's find out," Corinne says. "Have you died this morning, Mrs Fox?"

"Oh, dearie me, no," Mrs Fox says.

"Probably not sixty over twenty then," Corinne says.

"I've only been doing this for three days," I say.

"I've been doing it for six years," Corinne says, "since I was *way* younger than you, my girl. And here you are, can't even work a blood pressure sleeve, yet suddenly an apprentice just like me. Funny how life works, huh?"

"You're doing fine, sweetheart," Mrs Fox says to me.

"No, she isn't, Mrs Fox," Corinne says. "I'm sorry to contradict you, but some of us regard healing as a sacred duty."

"I regard it as a sacred duty," I say, almost as a reflex.

This is a mistake.

"Healing is more than a *job*, my girl," Corinne says, making *my girl* sound like the worst insult. "There is nothing more important in this life than the preservation of it. We're God's hands on this world. We are the opposite of your friend the tyrant."

"He's not my–"

"To allow someone, *anyone*, to suffer is the greatest sin there is."

"Corinne–"

"You don't understand anything," she says, her voice low

and fierce. "Quit pretending that you do."

Mrs Fox has shrunk down nearly as far as I have.

Corinne glances at her and back at me, then she straightens her cap and tugs the lapels on her cloak, stretching out her neck from right to left. She closes her eyes and lets out a long, long breath.

Without looking at me, she says, "Try it again."

"The difference between a clinic and a house of healing?" Mistress Coyle asks, ticking off boxes on a sheet.

"The main difference is that clinics are run by male doctors, houses of healing by female healers," I recite, as I count out the day's pills into separate little cups for each patient.

"And why is that?"

"So that a patient, male or female, can have a choice between knowing the thoughts of their doctor or not."

She raises an eyebrow. "And the real reason?"

"Politics," I say, returning her word.

"Correct." She finishes the paperwork and hands it to me. "Take these and the medicines to Madeleine, please."

She leaves and I finish filling up the tray of medicines. When I come out with it in my hands, I see Mistress Coyle down at the end of the hallway, passing by Mistress Nadari.

And I swear I see her slip Mistress Nadari a note, without either of them pausing.

We can still only go out for an hour at a time, still only in groups of four, but that's enough to see how New Prentisstown is putting itself together. As my first week as an apprentice comes to an end, we hear tell that some women are even being sent out into fields to work in women-only groups.

We hear tell that the Spackle are being kept somewhere on the edge of town, all together as one group, awaiting "processing", whatever that might mean.

We hear tell the old Mayor is working as a dustman.

We hear nothing about a boy.

"I missed his birthday," I tell Maddy, as I practise tying bandages around a rubber leg so ridiculously realistic everyone calls it Ruby. "It was four days ago. I lost track of how long I was asleep and–"

I can't say any more, just pull the bandage tight–

And think of when he put a bandage on me–

And when I put bandages on him.

"I'm sure he's fine, Vi," Maddy says.

"No, you're not."

"No," she says, looking back out the window to the road, "but against all odds the city's not at war. Against all odds, we're still alive and still working. So, against all odds, Todd could be alive and well."

I pull tighter on the bandage. "Do you know anything about a blue *A*?"

She turns to me. "A what?"

I shrug. "Something I saw in Mistress Coyle's notebook."

"No idea." She looks back out the window.

"What are you looking for?"

"I'm counting soldiers," she says. She looks back again at me and Ruby. "It's a good bandage." Her smile makes it almost seem true.

* * *

I head down the main hallway, Ruby kicking from one hand. I have to practise injecting shots into her thigh. I already feel sorry for the poor woman whose thigh gets my first real jab.

I come round a corner as the hallway reaches the centre of the building, where it turns ninety degrees down the other wing, and I nearly collide with a group of mistresses, who stop when they see me.

Mistress Coyle and four, five, *six* other healers behind her. I recognize Mistress Nadari and Mistress Waggoner, and there's Mistress Lawson, too, but I've never seen the other three before and didn't even see them come into the house of healing.

"Have you no work, my girl?" Mistress Coyle says, some edge in her voice.

"Ruby," I stammer, holding out the leg.

"Is this her?" asks one of the healers I don't recognize.

Mistress Coyle doesn't introduce me.

She just says, "Yes, this is the girl."

I have to wait all day to see Maddy again, but before I can ask her about it, she says, "I've figured it out."

"Did one of them have a scar on her upper lip?" Maddy whispers in the dark. It's well past midnight, well past lights out, well past when she should be in her own room.

"I think so," I whisper back. "They left really quickly."

We watch another pair of soldiers march down the road. By Maddy's reckoning, we've got three minutes.

"That would have been Mistress Barker," she says. "Which means the others were probably Mistress Braithwaite and Mistress Forth." She looks back out the window. "This is crazy, you know. If she catches us, we'll get it good."

"I hardly think she's going to fire you under the circumstances."

Her face goes thoughtful. "Did you hear what the mistresses were saying?"

"No, they shut up the second they saw me."

"But you were *the girl*?"

"Yeah," I say. "And Mistress Coyle avoided me the rest of today."

"Mistress Barker..." Maddy says, still thinking. "But how could that accomplish anything?"

"How could what accomplish what?"

"Those three were on the Council with Mistress Coyle. Mistress Barker still *is*. Or was, before all this. But why would they be—" She stops and leans closer to the window. "That's the last foursome."

I look out and see four soldiers marching up the road.

If the pattern Maddy's spotted is right, the time is now.

If the pattern's right.

"You ready?" I whisper.

"Of *course* I'm not ready," Maddy says, with a terrified smile. "But I'm going."

I see how she's flexing her hands to keep them from shaking. "We're just going to look," I say. "That's all. Out and back again before you know it."

Maddy still looks terrified but nods her head. "I've never done anything like this before in my whole life."

"Don't worry," I say, lifting the sash on my window all the way up. "I'm an expert."

The **ROAR** of the town, even when it's sleeping, covers our footsteps pretty well as we sneak across the dark lawn. The only light is from the two moons, shining down on us, half-circles in the sky.

We make it to the ditch at the side of the road, crouching in the bushes.

"What now?" Maddy whispers.

"You said two minutes, then another pair."

Maddy nods in the shadows. "Then another break of seven minutes."

In that break, Maddy and I will start moving down the road, sticking to the trees, staying under cover, and see if we can get to the communications tower, if that's even what it *is*.

See what's there when we do.

"You all right?" I whisper.

"Yeah," she whispers back. "Scared but excited, too."

I know what she means. Out here, crouching in a ditch under the cover of night, it's crazy, it's dangerous, but I finally feel like I'm *doing* something, finally feel like I'm taking charge of my own life for the first time since being stuck in that bed.

Finally feel like I'm doing something for Todd.

We hear the crunch of gravel on the road and crouch a

little lower as the expected pair of soldiers march past us and away.

"Here we go," I say.

We stand up as much as we dare and move quickly down the ditch, away from the town.

"Do you still have family on the ships?" Maddy whispers. "Someone besides your mother and father?"

I wince a little at the sound she's making but I know she's only talking to cover her nerves. "No, but I know everyone else. Bradley Tench, he's lead caretaker on the *Beta*, and Simone Watkin on the *Gamma* is really smart."

The ditch bends with the road and there's a crossroads coming up that we'll have to negotiate.

Maddy starts up again. "So Simone's the one you'd–"

"Shh," I say because I think I heard something.

Maddy comes close enough to press against me. Her whole body is shaking and her breath is coming in short little puffs. She has to come this time because she knows where the tower is, but I can't ask her to do it again. When I come back, I'll come on my own.

Because if anything goes wrong–

"I think we're okay," I say.

We step slowly out from the ditch to cross the crossroads, looking all around us, stepping lightly in the gravel.

"Going somewhere?" says a voice.

Maddy takes in a sharp breath behind me. There's a soldier

leaning against a tree, his legs crossed like he couldn't be more relaxed.

Even in the moonlight I can see the rifle hanging lazily from his hand.

"Little late to be out, innit?"

"We got lost," I sputter. "We were separated from–"

"Yeah," he interrupts. "I'll bet."

He strikes a match against the zip of his uniform jacket. In the flare of light, I see SERGEANT HAMMAR written across his pocket. He uses the match to light a cigarette in his mouth.

Cigarettes were banned by the Mayor.

But I guess if you're an officer.

An officer without Noise who can hide in the dark.

He takes a step forward and we see his face. He's got a smile on over the cigarette, an ugly one, the ugliest I've ever seen.

"You?" he says, recognition in his voice as he gets nearer.

As he raises his rifle.

"Yer the girl," he says, looking at me.

"Viola?" Maddy whispers, a step behind me and to my right.

"Mayor Prentiss knows me," I say. "You won't harm me."

He inhales on the cigarette, flashing the ember, making a streak against my vision. "*President* Prentiss knows you."

Then he looks at Maddy, pointing at her with the rifle.

"I don't reckon he knows you, tho."

And before I can say anything–

Without giving any kind of warning–

As if it was as natural to him as taking his next breath–

Sergeant Hammar pulls the trigger.

9

WAR IS OVER

[TODD]

"YOUR TURN TO DO THE BOG," Davy says, throwing me the canister of lime.

We never see the Spackle use the corner where they've dug a bog to do their business but every morning it's a little bit bigger and stinks a little bit more and it needs lime powdered over it to cut down on the smell and the danger of infeckshun.

I hope it works better on infeckshun than it does on smell.

"Why ain't it never *yer* turn?" I say.

"Cuz Pa may think yer the *better man*, pigpiss," Davy says, "but he still put me in charge."

And he grins at me.

I start walking to the bog.

The days passed and they kept passing, till there was two full weeks of 'em gone and more.

I stayed alive and got thru.

(did she?)

(*did* she?)

Davy and I ride to the monastery every morning and he "oversees" the Spackle tearing down fences and pulling up brambles and I spend the day shovelling out not enough fodder and trying and failing to fix the last two water pumps and taking every turn to do the bog.

The Spackle've stayed silent, still not doing nothing that could save themselves, fifteen hundred of 'em when we finally got 'em counted, crammed into an area where I wouldn't herd two hundred sheep. More guards came, standing along the top of the stone wall, rifles pointed twixt rows of barbed wire, but the Spackle don't do nothing that even comes close to threatening.

They've stayed alive. They've got thru it.

And so has New Prentisstown.

Every day, Mayor Ledger tells me what he sees out on his rubbish rounds. Men and women are still separated and there are more taxes, more rules about dress, a list of books to be surrendered and burned, and compulsory church attendance, tho not in the cathedral, of course.

But it's also started to act like a real town again. The stores are back open, carts and fissionbikes and even a fissioncar or two are back on the roads. Men've gone back to work. Repairmen returned to repairing, bakers returned to baking, farmers returned to farming, loggers returned to logging, some of 'em even signing up to join the army itself, tho you can tell who the new soldiers are cuz they ain't been given the cure yet.

"You know," Mayor Ledger said one night and I could see it in his Noise before he said it, see the thought forming, the thought I hadn't thought myself, the thought I hadn't *let* myself think. "It's not nearly as bad as I thought," he said. "I expected slaughter. I expected my own death, certainly, and perhaps the burning of the entire town. The surrender was a fool's chance at best, but maybe he's not lying."

He got up and looked out over New Prentisstown. "Maybe," he said, "the war really is over."

"Oi!" I hear Davy call as I'm halfway to the bog. I turn round. A Spackle has come up to him.

It's holding its long white arms up and out in what may be a peaceful way and then it starts clicking, pointing to where a group of Spackle have finished tearing down a fence. It's clicking and clicking, pointing to one of the empty water troughs, but there ain't no way of understanding it, not if you can't hear its Noise.

Davy steps closer to it, his eyes wide, his head nodding in sympathy, his smile dangerous. "Yeah, yeah, yer thirsty from the hard work," he says. "Course you are, course you are, thank you for bringing that to my attenshun, thank you very much. And in reply, let me just say this."

He smashes the butt of his pistol into the Spackle's face. You can hear the crack of bone and the Spackle falls to the ground clutching at his jaw, long legs twisting in the air.

There's a wave of clicking around us and Davy lifts his pistol again, bullet end facing the crowd. Rifles cock on the fence-top, too, soldiers pointing their weapons. The Spackle slink back, the broken-jawed one still writhing and writhing in the grass.

"Know what, pigpiss?" Davy says.

"What?" I say, my eyes still on the Spackle on the ground, my Noise shaky as a leaf about to fall.

He turns to me, pistol still out. "It's *good* to be in charge."

Every minute I've expected life to blow apart.

But every minute, it don't.

And every day I've looked for her.

I've looked for her from the openings outta the top of the bell tower but all I ever see is the army marching and men working. Never a face I reckernize, never a silence I can feel as hers.

I've looked for her when Davy and I ride back and forth to the monastery, seeking her out in the windows of the Women's Quarter, but I never see her looking back.

I've even half-looked for her in the crowds of Spackle, wondering if she's hiding behind one, ready to pop out and yell at Davy for beating on 'em and then saying to me, like everything's okay, "Hey, I'm here, it's me."

But she ain't there.

She ain't there.

I've asked Mayor Prentiss bout her every time I've seen him and he's said I need to trust him, said he's not my enemy, said if I put my faith in him that everything will be all right.

But I've looked.

And she ain't there.

"Hey, girl," I whisper to Angharrad as I saddle her up at the end of our day. I've got way better at riding her, better at talking to her, better at reading her moods. I'm less nervous about being on her back and she's less nervous about being underneath me. This morning after I gave her an apple to eat, she clipped her teeth thru my hair once, like I was just another horse.

Boy colt, she says, as I climb on her back and me and Davy set off back into town.

"Angharrad," I say, leaning forward twixt her ears, cuz this is what horses like, it seems, constant reminders that everyone's there, constant reminders that they're still in the herd.

Above anything else, a horse hates to be alone.

Boy colt, Angharrad says again.

"Angharrad," I say.

"Jesus, pigpiss," Davy moans, "why don't you marry the effing—" He stops. "Well, goddam," he says, his voice suddenly a whisper, "would you look at this?"

I look up.

There are women coming out of a store.

Four of 'em, together in a group. We knew they were being let out but it's always daylight hours, always while me and Davy are at the monastery, so we always return to a city of men, like the women are just phantoms and rumour.

It's been ages since I even seen one more than just thru a window or from up top of the tower.

They're wearing longer sleeves and longer skirts than I saw before and they each got their hair tied behind their heads the same way. They look nervously at the soldiers that line the streets, at me and Davy, too, all of us watching 'em come down the store's front steps.

And there's still the silence, still the pull at my chest and I have to wipe my eyes when I'm sure Davy ain't looking.

Cuz none of 'em is her.

"They're late," Davy says, his voice so quiet I guess he ain't seen a woman for weeks neither. "They're all sposed to be in way before sundown."

Our heads turn as we watch 'em pass by, parcels held close, and they carry on down the road back to the Women's Quarter and my chest tightens and my throat clenches.

Cuz *none* of 'em is *her*.

And I realize–

I realize all over again how much–

And my Noise goes all muddy.

Mayor Prentiss has used her to control me.

Duh.

Any effing idiot would know it. If I don't do what they say, they kill her. If I try to escape, they kill her. If I do anything to Davy, they kill her.

If she ain't dead already.

My Noise gets blacker.

No.

No, I think.

Cuz she might not be.

She mighta been out here, on this very street, in another group of four.

Stay alive, I think. *Please please please stay alive.*

(*please be alive*)

I stand at an opening as me and Mayor Ledger eat our dinners, looking for her again, trying to close my ears against the **ROAR**.

Cuz Mayor Ledger was right. There's so many men that once the cure left their systems, you stopped being able to hear individual Noise. It'd be like trying to hear one drop of water in the middle of a river. Their Noise became a single loud wall, all mushed together so much it don't say nothing but

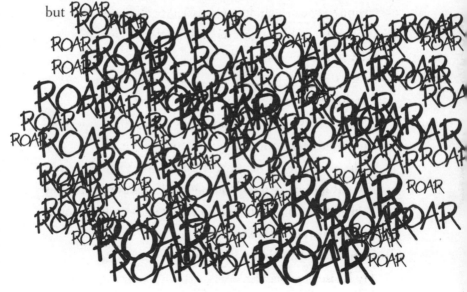

But it's actually something you can sorta get used to. In a way, Mayor Ledger's words and thoughts and feelings bubbling round his own personal grey Noise are more distracting.

"Quite correct," he says, patting his stomach. "A man is capable of thought. A crowd is not."

"An army is," I say.

"Only if it has a general for a brain."

He looks out the opening next to mine as he says it. Mayor Prentiss is riding across the square, Mr Hammar, Mr Tate, Mr Morgan and Mr O'Hare riding behind him, listening to the orders he's giving.

"The inner circle," Mayor Ledger says.

And for a second, I wonder if his Noise sounds jealous.

We watch the Mayor dismount, hand his reins to Mr Tate and disappear into the cathedral.

Not two minutes later, *ker-thunk*, Mr Collins opens our door.

"The President wants you," he says to me.

"One moment, Todd," the Mayor says, opening up one of the crates and looking inside.

We're in the cellar of the cathedral, Mr Collins having pushed me down the stairs at the back of the main lobby. I stand there waiting, wondering how much of my dinner Mayor Ledger will eat before I can get back.

I watch Mayor Prentiss look thru another crate.

"*President* Prentiss," he says, without looking up. "Do try to remember that." He stands up straight. "Used to be wine stored down here. Far more than was ever needed for communion."

I don't say nothing. He looks at me, curious. "You aren't going to ask, are you?"

"Bout what?" I say.

"The cure, Todd," he says, thumping one of the crates with his fist. "My men have retrieved every last trace of it from every home in New Prentisstown and here it all is."

He reaches in and takes out a phial of the cure pills. He pops the lid off and takes out a small white pill twixt his finger and thumb. "Do you never wonder why I haven't given the cure to you or David?"

I shift from foot to foot. "Punishment?"

He shakes his head. "Does Mr Ledger still fidget?"

I shrug. "Sometimes. A little."

"They made the cure," the Mayor says. "And then they made themselves *need* it." He indicates row after row of crates and boxes. "And if I have *all* of what they need…"

He puts the pill back in the phial and turns more fully to me, smiling wider.

"You wanted something?" I mumble.

"You really don't know, do you?" he asks.

"Know what?"

He pauses again, and then he says, "Happy birthday, Todd."

I open my mouth. Then I open it wider.

"It was four days ago," he says. "I'm surprised you didn't mention it."

I don't believe it. I completely forgot.

"No celebrations," the Mayor says, "because of course we both know you are *already* a man, now, aren't you?"

And again I raise the pictures of Aaron.

"You have been very impressive these past two weeks," he says, ignoring them. "I know it's been a great struggle for you, not knowing what to believe about Viola, not knowing exactly how you should behave to keep her safe." I can feel his voice buzzing in my head, searching around. "But you have worked hard nonetheless. You have even been a good influence on David."

I can't help but think of the ways I'd like to beat Davy Prentiss into a bloody pulp but Mayor Prentiss just says, "As a reward, I bring you two belated birthday presents."

My Noise rises. "Can I see her?"

He smiles like he expected it. "You may not," he says, "but I will promise you this. On the day that you can bring yourself to trust me, Todd, truly bring yourself to understand that I mean good for this town and good for you, then on that day, you will see that I am indeed trustworthy."

I can hear myself breathing. It's the closest he's come to saying she's all right.

"No, your first birthday present is one you've earned," he says. "You'll have a new job starting tomorrow. Still with our Spackle friends, but added responsibility and an important part of our new process." He looks me hard in the eye again. "It's a job that could take you far, Todd Hewitt."

"All the way up to be a leader of men?" I say, my voice a bit more sarcastic than he'd probably like.

"Indeed," he says.

"And the second present?" I say, still hoping it might be her.

"My second present to you, Todd, surrounded by all this cure." He gestures at the crates again. "Is not to give you any at all."

I screw up my mouth. "Huh?"

But he's already walking towards me as if we're thru talking.

And as he passes me—

I AM THE CIRCLE AND THE CIRCLE IS ME.

Rings thru my head, just the once, coming right from the centre of me, of who I am.

I jump from the surprise of it.

"Why can I hear it if yer taking the cure?" I say.

But he just gives me a sly smile and disappears up the staircase, leaving me there.

Happy late birthday to me.

I am Todd Hewitt, I think, as I lie in bed, staring up into the dark. *I am Todd Hewitt and four days ago I was a man.*

Sure don't feel no different, tho.

All that reaching for it, all that importance on the date, and I'm still the same ol' stupid effing Todd Hewitt, powerless to do anything, powerless to save myself much less her.

Todd effing Hewitt.

And lying here in the dark, Mayor Ledger snoring away over on his mattress, I hear a faint *pop* outside, somewhere in the distance, some stupid soldier firing off his gun at who knows what (or who knows who) and that's when I think it.

That's when I think getting thru it ain't enough.

Staying alive ain't enough if yer barely living.

They'll play me as long as I let 'em.

And she coulda been out there.

She coulda been out there *today*.

I'm gonna find her—

First chance I get, I'm gonna take it and I'm gonna find her—

And when I do—

And then I notice Mayor Ledger ain't snoring no more.

I raise my voice into the dark. "You got something to say?"

But then he's snoring again and his Noise is grey and muzzy and I wonder if I imagined it.

10

IN GOD'S HOUSE

{VIOLA}

"I CAN'T TELL YOU HOW SORRY I AM."

I don't take the cup of root coffee he offers.

"Please, Viola," he says, holding it out towards me.

I take it. My hands are still shaking.

They haven't stopped since last night.

Since I watched her fall.

First to her knees, then onto her side down to the gravel, her eyes still open.

Open, but already unseeing.

I watched her fall.

"Sergeant Hammar will be punished." The Mayor takes a seat across from me. "He was by no means and under no circumstances following my orders."

"He killed her," I say, hardly any sound to my voice. Sergeant Hammar dragged me back to the house of healing, pounding on the door with the butt of his rifle, waking everyone up, sending them out after Maddy's body.

125

I couldn't speak, I could barely even cry.

They wouldn't look at me, the mistresses, the other apprentices. Even Mistress Coyle refused to meet my eye.

What did you think you were doing? Where did you think you were taking her?

And then Mayor Prentiss summoned me here this morning to his cathedral, to his home, to God's house.

And then they *really* wouldn't look at me.

"I'm sorry, Viola," he says. "Some of the men of Prentisstown, *old* Prentisstown, still bear grudges against women over what happened all those years ago."

He sees my look of horror. "The story you think you know," he says, "is not the story that's true."

I'm still gaping at him. He sighs. "The Spackle War was in Prentisstown, too, Viola, and it was a terrible thing, but women and men fought side by side to save ourselves." He puts his fingertips together in a triangle, his voice still calm, still gentle. "But there was division in our little outpost even as we were victorious. Division between men and women."

"I'll say there was."

"They made their own army, Viola. They splintered off, not trusting men whose thoughts they could read. We tried to reason with them, but eventually, they wanted war. And I'm afraid they got it."

He sits up, looking at me sadly. "An army of women is still an army with guns, still an army that can defeat you."

I can hear myself breathing. "You killed every single one."

"I did not," he says. "Many of them died in battle, but when they saw the war was lost, they spread the word that we were their murderers and then they killed themselves so that the remaining men would be doomed either way."

"I don't believe you," I say, remembering that Ben told us a different version. "That's not how it happened."

"I was there, Viola. I remember it all far more clearly than I want to." He catches my eye. "I am also the one most keen that history doesn't repeat itself. Do you understand me?"

I think I do understand him and my stomach sinks and I can't help it – I start to cry, thinking of how they brought Maddy's body back, how Mistress Coyle insisted I be the one to help her prepare the body for burial, how she wanted me to see up close the cost of trying to find the tower.

"Mistress Coyle," I say, fighting to control myself. "Mistress Coyle wanted me to ask if we can bury her this afternoon."

"I've already sent word that she can," the Mayor says. "Everything Mistress Coyle requires is being delivered to her as we speak."

I set the coffee down on a little table next to my chair. We're in a huge room, bigger than any place indoors I've ever seen except for the launch hangars of my ship. Too large for just a pair of comfortable chairs and a wooden table. The only light shines down through a round window of coloured glass showing this world and its two moons.

Everything else is in shadow.

"How are you finding her?" the Mayor asks. "Mistress Coyle."

The weight on my shoulders, the weight of Maddy being gone, the weight of Todd still out there, sits so heavily I'd forgotten for a minute he was even there. "What do you mean?"

He shrugs a little. "How is she to work with? How is she as a teacher?"

I swallow. "She's the best healer in Haven."

"And now the best healer in New Prentisstown," he corrects. "People tell me she used to be quite powerful around here. A force to be reckoned with."

I bite my lip and look back at the carpet. "She couldn't save Maddy."

"Well, let's forgive her for that, shall we?" His voice is low, soft, almost kind. "Nobody's perfect."

He sets down his cup. "I'm sorry about your friend," he says again. "And I'm sorry it has taken this long for us to speak again. There has been much work to do. I look to *stop* the suffering on this planet, which is why your friend's death grieves me so. That's been my whole mission. The war is over, Viola, it truly is. Now is the time for healing."

I don't say anything to that.

"But your mistress doesn't see it that way, does she?" he asks. "She sees me as the enemy."

In the early hours of this morning, as we dressed Maddy in her white burial cloths, she said, *If he wants a war, he's got a war. We haven't even* started *fighting.*

But then when I was summoned here, she said to tell him no such thing, to ask only about the funeral.

And to find out what I could.

"You see me as the enemy, too," he says, "and I truly wish that weren't the case. I am so disappointed that this terrible incident has made you even more suspicious of me."

I feel Maddy rising again in my chest. I feel Todd rising, too. I have to breathe through my mouth for a minute.

"I know how appealing it seems that there should be sides, that you should be on *her* side," he says. "I don't blame you. I haven't even asked you about your ships because I know you would lie to me. I know she would have asked you to. If I were in Mistress Coyle's position, I would do exactly the same thing. Push you to help me. Use an asset that's fallen into my lap."

"She's not using me," I say quietly.

You can be so valuable to us, I remember, *if you choose.*

He leans forward. "Can I tell you something, Viola?"

"What?" I ask.

He cocks his head. "I really do wish you would call me David."

I look back down to the carpet. "What is it, David?"

"Thank you, Viola," he says. "It really does mean something to me." He waits until I look up again. "I've met the Council that ran Haven as was. I've met the former Mayor of Haven. I've met the former police chief and the chief medical officer and the head of education. I've met everyone of any importance in this town. Some of them now work for me. Some of them don't fit into the new administration and that's fine, there's plenty of work to be done rebuilding this city, making it ready for *your* people, Viola, making it the proper paradise that they need and want and expect."

He's still looking right into my eyes. I notice how dark blue his own are, like water running over a slate.

"And of all the people I've met in New Prentisstown, your Mistress Coyle is the only one who truly knows what leading is like. Leadership isn't grown, Viola. It's *taken,* and she may be the only person on this entire planet besides myself who has enough strength, enough *will* to take it."

I keep looking at his eyes and a thought comes.

His Noise is still silent as the black beyond and his face and eyes give away nothing either.

But I do begin to wonder–

Right there, just at the back of my thinking–

Is he *afraid* of her?

"Why do you think I had you taken to her for your gunshot wound?" he asks.

"She's the best healer. You said it yourself."

"Yes, but she's far from the only one. Bandages and medicine do most of the work. Mistress Coyle just applies them especially skilfully."

My hand goes unconsciously to my front scar. "It's not just that."

"It is not, you're correct." He leans even farther forward. "I want her on my side, Viola. I *need* her on my side if I'm going to make this new society any kind of success. If we worked together, Mistress Coyle and I," he leans back, "well, what a world we could make."

"You locked her up."

"But I wasn't going to *keep* her locked up. The borders between men and women had become blurred, and the reintroduction of those borders is a slow and painful process. The formation of mutual trust takes time, but the important thing to remember is, as I've said, the war is *over*, Viola. It truly is. I want no more fighting, no more bloodshed."

For something to do, I pick up the cooling cup of coffee. I put it to my lips but I don't drink it.

"Is Todd okay?" I ask, not looking at him.

"Happy and healthy and working in the sun," the Mayor says.

130

"Can I see him?"

He's silent, as if he's considering it. "Will you do something for me?" he asks.

"What?" Another idea begins to form in my head. "You want me to spy on her for you."

"No," he says. "Not *spying*, not at all. I just want your help in convincing her that I'm not the tyrant she thinks, that history isn't as she knows it, that if we work together, we can make this place into the home we *both* wanted when our people left Old World all those many years ago. I am not her enemy. And I am not yours."

He seems so sincere. He really does.

"I'm asking for your help," he says.

"You're in complete control," I say. "You don't need my help."

"I do," he says insistently. "You've grown closer to her than I ever possibly could."

Have I? I think.

This is the girl, I remember.

"I also know that she drugged you that first night so you would fall asleep before you told me anything."

I sip my cold coffee. "Wouldn't you have done the same?"

He smiles. "So you agree we're not that different, her and I?"

"How can I trust you?"

"How can you trust her if she drugged you?"

"She saved my life."

"After I delivered you to her."

"She's not keeping me locked up in the house of healing."

"You came here unchaperoned, didn't you? The restrictions are being lessened this very day."

"She's training me as a healer."

"And who are all those other healers she's been meeting with?" He folds his fingers back into a tent. "What are they up to, do you suppose?"

I look down into the coffee cup and swallow, wondering how he knows.

"And what do they have planned for *you*?" he asks.

I still don't look at him.

He stands. "Come with me, please."

He leads me out of the huge room and across the short lobby at the front of the cathedral. The doors are wide open onto the town square. The army is doing marching exercises out there and the *pound pound pound* of their feet pours in and the ROARof the men who no longer have the cure floods in right behind it.

I wince a little.

"Look there," says the Mayor.

Past the army, in the centre of the square, some men are assembling a small platform of plain wood, a bent pole up on the top.

"What's that?"

"It's where Sergeant Hammar is going to be hanged tomorrow afternoon for his terrible, terrible crime."

The memory of Maddy, of her lifeless eyes, rises in my chest again. I have to press my hand to my mouth to hold it back.

"I spared the old Mayor of this town," he says, "but I will not spare one of my most loyal and long-standing sergeants."

He looks at me. "Do you honestly think I would go to such lengths just to please one girl who has information I could use? Do you honestly think I would go to that much trouble when, as you say, I'm in complete control?"

"Why are you doing it then?" I ask.

"Because he broke the law. Because this is a civilized world and acts of barbarity will not be tolerated. Because the *war* is *over*." He turns to me. "I would very much like you to convince Mistress Coyle of that." He steps closer. "Will you do that? Will you at least tell her the things I'm doing to remedy this tragic sítuation?"

I look down at my feet. My mind is whirling, spinning like a meteor.

The things he says could be true.

But Maddy is dead.

And it's my fault.

And Todd's still gone.

What do I do?

(what do I do?)

"Will you, Viola?"

At least, I think, *it's information to give to Mistress Coyle.*

I swallow. "I'll try?"

He smiles again. "Wonderful." He touches me gently on the arm. "Run along back now. They'll be needing you for the funeral service."

I nod and step out onto the front steps and away from him, moving into the square a little bit, the ROAR of it all beating down on me as hard as the sun. I stop and try to catch the breath that seems to have run away from me.

"Viola." He's still watching me, watching me from the

steps of his house, the cathedral. "Why don't you have dinner with me here tomorrow night?"

He grins, seeing how I try to hide how much I don't want to come.

"Todd will be there, of course," he says.

I open my eyes wide. Another wave rises from my chest, bringing the tears again and surprising me so much I hiccup. "Really?"

"Really," he says.

"You mean it?"

"I mean it," he says.

And then he opens his arms to me for an embrace.

11

SAVED YER LIFE

[TODD]

"WE GOTTA NUMBER 'EM," Davy says, getting out a heavy canvas bag that's been left in the monastery storeroom and dropping it loudly to the grass. "That's our new job."

It's the morning after the Mayor wished me a late happy birthday, the morning after I vowed I'd find her.

But ain't nothing's changed.

"Number 'em?" I ask, looking out at the Spackle, still staring back at us in the silence that don't make no sense. Surely the cure shoulda worn off by now? "Why?"

"Don't you *never* listen to Pa?" Davy says, getting out some of the tools. "Everyone's gotta know their place. Besides, we gotta keep track of the animals somehow."

"They ain't animals, Davy," I say, not too heated cuz we've had this fight before a coupla times. "They're just aliens."

"Whatever, pigpiss," he says and pulls out a pair of bolt cutters from the bag, setting them on the grass. He reaches

135

in the bag again. "Take these," he says, holding out a handful of metal bands, strapped together with a longer one. I take them from him.

Then I reckernize what I'm holding.

"We're not," I say.

"Oh, yes, we are." He holds up another tool, which I also reckernize.

It's how we marked sheep back in Prentisstown. You take the tool Davy's holding and you wrap a metal band around a sheep's leg. The tool bolts the ends together tight, too tight, so tight it cuts into the skin, so tight it starts an infeckshun. But the metal's coated with a medicine to fight it so what happens is that the infeckted skin starts to heal around the band, grow *into* it, replacing that bit of skin with the metal band itself.

I look up again at the Spackle, looking back at us.

Cuz the catch is, it don't heal if you take it off. The sheep'll bleed to death if you do. You put on a band and it's yers till it dies. There ain't no going back from it.

"Then all you gotta do is think of 'em as sheep," Davy says, standing up with the bolting tool and looking out over the Spackle. "Line up!"

"We'll do one field at a time," he shouts, gesturing at the Spackle with the bolting tool in one hand and the pistol in the other. The soldiers on the stone walls keep their rifles pointed into the herd. "Once you get yer number, you stay in that field and you don't leave it, unnerstand?"

And they seem to unnerstand.

That's the thing.

They unnerstand way more than a sheep would.

I look at the packet of metal bands I'm holding. "Davy, this is—"

"Just get a move on, pigpiss," he says impayshuntly. "We're meant to get thru two hundred today."

I swallow. The first Spackle in line is watching the metal bands as well. I think it's female cuz sometimes you can tell by the colour of the lichen they've got growing for their clothes. She's shorter than usual, too, for a Spackle. My height or less.

And I'm thinking, if I don't do it, if I'm not the one who does this, then they'll just get someone else who won't care if it hurts. Better they have me who'll treat 'em right. Better than just Davy on his own.

Right?

(right?)

"Just wrap the effing band round its arm or we'll be here all effing morning," Davy says.

I gesture for her to hold out her arm. She does, staring at my eyes, not blinking. I swallow again. I unwrap the packet of bands and peel off the one marked 0001. She's still staring, still not blinking.

I take hold of her outstretched hand.

The flesh is warm, warmer than I expected, they look so white and cold.

I wrap the band round her wrist.

I can feel her pulse beating under my fingertips.

She still looks into my eyes.

"I'm sorry," I whisper.

Davy steps up, takes the loose ends of the bands in the bolting tool, gives it a twist so sharp and hard the Spackle lets out a pained hiss, and then he slams the bolting tool together, locking the metal strip into her wrist, making her 0001 for ever and ever.

She bleeds from under the band. 0001 bleeds red.

(which I already knew)

Holding her wrist with her other hand, she moves away from us, still staring, still unblinking, silent as a curse.

None of 'em fight. They just line up and stare and stare and stare. Once in a while they make their clicking sounds to one another but no Noise, no struggles, no resistance.

Which makes Davy angrier and angrier.

"Damn things," he says, holding the twist for a second before he bolts it off just to see how long he can make 'em hiss. And a second or two longer than that.

"How d'you like *that*, huh?" he yells at a Spackle as it walks away, holding its wrist, staring back at us.

0038 is next in line. It's a tall one, probably male, skinny as anything and getting skinnier cuz even a fool can see that the fodder we put out every morning ain't enough for fifteen hundred Spackle.

"Put the band round its neck," Davy says.

"What?" I say, my eyes widening. "*No!*"

"Put it round its effing neck!"

"I'm not—"

He lunges forward suddenly, clonking me on the head with the bolting tool and ripping the metal bands outta my hand. I fall to one knee, clutching at my skull and the pain keeps me from looking up for a few seconds.

And when I do, it's too late.

Davy's got the Spackle kneeling in front of him, the 0038 band twisted tight around its neck, and is using the bolting tool to twist it tighter. The soldiers on the top of the wall are laughing and the Spackle's gasping for air, clawing at the band with its fingers, blood coming from round its neck.

"Stop it!" I shout, struggling to get to my feet.

But Davy slams the bolting tool shut and the Spackle tumbles over into the grass, making loud gagging sounds, its head starting to turn a cruel-looking pink. Davy stands above it, not moving, just watching it choke to death.

I see the bolt cutters Davy set on the grass and I stumble to 'em, grabbing 'em and rushing back over to 0038. Davy tries to stop me but I swing the bolt cutters at him and he jumps back and I kneel beside 0038 and try to get to the metal band but Davy's twisted it so tight and the Spackle's thrashing so much from suffocating that I finally have to force him down with one fist.

I cut the band free. It flies off in a mess of blood and skin. The Spackle takes in a rake of air so loud it hurts yer ears and I lean back away from him, bolt cutters still in my hand.

And as I watch the Spackle struggle to breathe again and possibly fail and as Davy hovers behind me, bolting tool in his hand, I realize how much *clicking* I'm hearing running thru the Spackle and it's now, of all times, of all moments, of all reasons—

It's *right now* they decide to attack.

The first punch glances lightly off the crown of my head. They're thin and they're light so there's not much weight behind the punch.

But there are fifteen hundred of 'em.

And they come in a wave, so thick it's like being plunged under water–

More fists, more punching, scratches across my face and the back of my neck and I'm knocked farther to the ground and the weight of 'em presses down on me, grabbing at my arms and legs, grabbing at my clothes and hair, and I'm calling out and yelling and one of 'em's taken the bolt cutters from my hand and swings it hard into my elbow and the pain of it is more than I can actually stand–

And my only thought, my only stupid thought is–

Why are they attacking *me*? I tried to *save* 0038.

(but they know, they know–)

(they know I'm a killer–)

Davy cries out as I hear the first gunshots from the top of the stone walls. More punches and more scratches but more gunshots, too, and the Spackle start to scatter which is something I can hear more than see cuz of the pain radiating up from my elbow.

And there's still one on top of me, scratching at me from behind as I lie face-down on the grass and I manage to turn myself over and tho the guns are still firing and the smell of cordite is filling the air and Spackle are running and running, this one stays on me, scratching and slapping away.

And the same second I realize it's 0001, the first one in line, the first one I touched, there's a bang and she spins and falls to the grass beside me. Dead.

Davy's standing over me with his pistol, smoke still coming from its barrel. His nose and lip are bleeding, he's got as many scratches as I do, and he's leaning heavily to one side.

But he's smiling.

"Saved yer life, didn't I?"

The firing of rifles carries on. The Spackle keep running but there's nowhere to go. They fall and they fall and they fall.

I look down at my elbow. "I think my arm's broke."

"I think my *leg's* broke," Davy says, "but you go back to Pa. Tell him what's happened. Tell him I *saved yer life*."

Davy's not looking at me, still raising his pistol, firing it, keeping his weight all weird on his legs.

"Davy–"

"Go!" he says and there's a grim kinda joy coming from him. "I got me a job to finish here." He fires the gun again. Another Spackle falls. They're falling all over the place.

I take a step towards the gate. And another.

And then I'm running.

My arm throbs with every step but Angharrad says **bOy cOlt** when I get to her and snuffles my face with a wet nose. She kneels down so I can flop forward onto her saddle. When she takes off down the road, she waits till I'm upright before she hits the fastest gallop I ever seen from her. I'm hanging onto her mane with one hand, my hurt arm curled under me, and I'm trying not to throw up from the pain.

I look up now and then to see women watch me ride past from their windows, quiet and distant. I see men watch the horse run by, looking at my face all bloody and injured.

And I wonder who they think they're seeing.

Are they seeing one of them?

Or are they seeing their enemy?

Who do they think I am?

I close my eyes but I nearly lose my balance so I open them again.

Angharrad takes me down the road on the side of the cathedral, her shoes striking sparks on the cobbles as she turns the corner to go round to the entrance. The army's in the square doing marching exercises. Most of them still ain't got Noise but the pounding of their feet is loud enough to bend the air.

I wince at it all and look up to where we're going, to the front door of the cathedral–

And my Noise gives such a shock, Angharrad stops up short, scrabbling on the cobbles, flanks foaming from getting me here so fast.

I barely notice–

My heart has stopped beating–

I've stopped breathing–

Cuz there she is.

In front of my eyes, walking up the steps of the cathedral–
    There she *is*.

And my heart jump-starts again and my Noise is ready to
scream her name and my pain is disappearing–
    Cuz she's alive–
    She's *alive*–
    But then I'm seeing more–
    I'm seeing her walking up the steps–
    Towards Mayor Prentiss–

Into his open arms–

And he's *embracing* her–

And she's *letting* him–

And all I can think–
    All I can say–
    Is–

"Viola?"

PART
III

WAR IS
OVER

12

BETRAYAL

{VIOLA}

MAYOR PRENTISS STANDS THERE.

The leader of this town, this world.

Arms wide.

As if this is the price.

Do I pay it?

It's just one hug, I think.

(isn't it?)

One hug to see Todd.

I step forward–

(just one hug)

– and he puts his arms around me.

I try not to go rigid at his touch.

"I never told you," he says into my ear. "We found your ship in the swamp as we marched here. We found your parents."

I let out a little gasp of tears and try to swallow them back.

"We gave them a decent burial. I'm so sorry, Viola. I know how lonely you must be, and nothing would please me more than if, one day, maybe, you could consider me as your–"

There's a sudden sound above the ROAR–

One bit of Noise flying higher than the rest, clear as an arrow–

An arrow fired directly at me–

Viola! it screams, knocking the words right out of the Mayor's mouth–

I step back from his embrace, his arms falling away–

I turn–

And there, in the afternoon sunshine, in the square, on the back of a horse not ten metres away–

There he is.

It's him.

It's *him*.

"TODD!" I yell and I'm already running.

He's standing where he slid off the horse, holding his arm at a bad angle, and I hear Viola! roaring through his Noise but I can also hear the pain in his arm and confusion lacing through everything but my own mind is racing too fast and my heart is pounding too loud for me to hear any of it clearly.

"TODD!" I yell again and I reach him and his Noise opens even farther and wraps around me like a blanket and I'm grabbing him to me, grabbing him to me like I'll never let him go and he calls out in pain but his other arm is grabbing me back, it's grabbing me back, it's grabbing me back–

"I thought you were dead," he's saying, his breath on my neck. "I thought you were dead."

"Todd," I say and I'm crying and the only thing I can say is his name. "*Todd*."

He gasps sharply again and the pain flashes so loud in his Noise I'm almost blinded by it. "Your arm," I say, pulling back.

"Broken," he pants, "broken by–"

"Todd?" the Mayor says, right behind us, staring hard into him. "You're back early."

"My arm," Todd says. "The Spackle–"

"The *Spackle*?" I say.

"That looks bad, Todd," the Mayor says, talking over us. "We need to get you healed right away."

"He can come to Mistress Coyle!"

"Viola," the Mayor says and I hear Todd think **"Viola"?**, wondering all over how the Mayor speaks to me like this. "Your house of healing is too far for Todd to walk with an injury this bad."

"I'll come with you!" I say. "I'm training as an apprentice!"

"Yer what?" Todd says. His pain is wailing like a siren but he's still looking back and forth between me and the Mayor. "What's going on? How do you know–"

"I'll explain everything," the Mayor says, taking Todd's free arm, "after we get you healed." He turns to me. "The invitation is still on for tomorrow. You have a funeral to get to just now."

"Funeral?" Todd says. "What funeral?"

"Tomorrow," the Mayor says to me again firmly, pulling Todd away.

"Wait–" I say.

"Viola!" Todd shouts, jerking away from the Mayor's grasp but the movement shakes his broken arm and he falls to one knee with the pain of it, pain so sharp, so loud and clear in his Noise that soldiers from the army stop to hear it. I jump forward to help but the Mayor holds out a hand to stop me.

"Go," he says and it's not a voice that's asking for discussion. "I'll help Todd. You go to your funeral and mourn your friend. You'll see Todd tomorrow night, good as new."

Viola? Todd's Noise says again, choking back a weep from pain so heavy now I don't think he can speak.

"Tomorrow, Todd," I say loudly, trying to get through his Noise. "I'll see you tomorrow."

Viola! he calls again but the Mayor is already leading him away.

"You promised!" I call after them. "Remember that you promised!"

The Mayor gives me a smile. "Remember you promised, too."

Did I? I think.

And then I'm watching them go, so fast it's like it didn't even happen.

But Todd–

Todd is alive.

I have to bend down close to the ground for a minute and just let it be true.

* * *

"And with burdened hearts, we commit you to the earth."

"Here." Mistress Coyle takes my hand after the priestess finishes speaking and puts some loose dirt into it. "We sprinkle it over the coffin."

I stare at the dirt in my hand. "Why?"

"So that she's been buried by the efforts of all of us." She directs me to a place with her in the line of healers gathering by the graveside. We pass by the hole one by one, each of us throwing our handful of dry soil onto the wooden box where Maddy now rests. Everyone stands as far away from me as they can.

No one but Mistress Coyle will even speak to me.

They blame me.

I blame me, too.

There are more than fifty women here, healers, apprentices, patients. Soldiers are spread out in a circle around us, more than you'd think necessary for a funeral. Men, including Maddy's father, are kept separate on the other side of the grave. Maddy's father's weeping Noise is the saddest thing I think I've ever heard.

And in the middle of everything, I can only feel even more guilty because what I'm mostly thinking about is Todd.

Now that I'm away from it, I can see the confusion in his Noise more clearly, see how it must have looked to find me in the arms of the Mayor, how friendly we must have seemed together.

Even though I can explain it all, I still feel ashamed.

And then he was gone.

I throw my dirt on Maddy's coffin, then Mistress Coyle takes me by the arm. "We need to talk."

* * *

"He wants to *work* with me?" Mistress Coyle says, over a cup of tea in my small bedroom.

"He says he admires you."

Her eyebrows raise. "Does he now?"

"I know," I say. "I know how it sounds, but maybe if you *heard* him—"

"Oh, I think I've heard enough from our President to last me a good while."

I lean back on my bed. "But he could have, I don't know, *forced* me to tell him about the ships. And he's not forcing me to do anything." I look away. "He's even letting me see my friend tomorrow."

"Your Todd?"

I nod. Her expression is solid as stone.

"And I suppose that makes you grateful to him, does it?"

"No," I say, rubbing my face with my hands. "I saw what his army did as they marched. I saw it with my own two eyes."

There's a long silence.

"But?" Mistress Coyle finally says.

I don't look at her. "But he's hanging the man who shot Maddy. He's executing him tomorrow."

She makes a dismissive sound with her lips. "What's one more killing to a man like him? What's one more life to take? Typical that he should think that solves the problem."

"He seemed genuinely sorry."

She looks at me sideways. "I'm sure he did. I'm sure that's exactly how he *seemed*." She lowers her voice. "He's the

President of Lies, my girl. He will lie so well you'll believe it's the truth. The Devil tells the best stories. Didn't your mama teach you that?"

"He doesn't think he's the Devil," I say. "He thinks he's just a soldier who won a war."

She looks at me carefully. "Appeasement," she says. "That's what it's called. Appeasement. It's a slippery slope."

"What does it mean?"

"It means you want to work with the enemy. It means you'd rather join him than beat him, and it's a sure-fire way to stay beaten."

"I don't want *that*!" I yell. "I just want this all to *stop*! I want this to be a home for all the people on their way, the home that we were all looking forward to. I want there to be peace and happiness." My voice starts to thicken. "I don't want anyone else to die."

She sets down her teacup, puts her hands on her knees and looks hard at me. "Are you sure that's what you want?" she says. "Or is it your boy you'll do anything for?"

And I wonder for a minute if she can read my mind.

(because, yes, I want to see Todd–)

(I want to *explain* to him–)

"Clearly your loyalty doesn't lie with *us*," Mistress Coyle says. "After your little stunt with Maddy, there are those of us who aren't so sure you're not more of a danger than an asset."

Asset, I think.

She sighs, long and hard. "For the record," she says, "I don't blame you for Maddy's death. She was old enough to make her own decisions and if she chose to help you, well, then." She runs her fingers across her forehead. "I see so much of myself in you, Viola. Even when I'd rather not." She stands to leave. "So please know, I don't blame you. Whatever happens."

"What do you mean, *whatever happens*?"

But she doesn't say anything more.

That night, they have something called a wake, where everyone at the house of healing drinks lots of weak beer and sings songs that Maddy liked and tells stories about her. There are tears, including my own, and they're not happy tears but they're not as sad as they could be.

And I'm going to see Todd again tomorrow.

And that's as close as I can feel to all right about anything just now.

I wander around the house of healing, around the other healers and apprentices and patients talking to one another. None of them will talk to me. I see Corinne sitting by herself in a chair by the window, looking especially stormy. She's refused to speak to anyone since Maddy's death, even declining to say something over the grave. You'd have to have been sitting right next to her to see how many tear tracks were on her cheeks.

It must be the beer working in me, but she looks so upset I go over and sit down next to her.

"I'm sorry–" I start to say but she stands up before I can even finish and walks away, leaving me there.

Mistress Coyle comes over, two glasses of beer in her hands. She hands one to me. We both watch Corinne as she leaves the room. "Don't be too bothered about her," Mistress Coyle says, sitting down.

"She's always hated me."

"She hasn't. She's just had a hard time of it, that's all."

"How hard?"

"It's her place to tell you, not mine. Drink up."

I take a drink. It's sweet and wheaty-tasting, the bubbles sharp against the roof of my mouth but not in a bad way. We sit and drink for a minute or two.

"Have you ever seen an ocean, Viola?" Mistress Coyle asks.

I cough away a little of the beer. "An ocean?"

"There's oceans on New World," she says, "big as anything."

"I was born on the settler ship," I say, "but I saw them from orbit as we flew in on the scout."

"Ah, well, then you've never stood on a beach as the waves came crashing in, the water stretching out from you until it's beyond sight, moving and blue and alive and so much bigger than even the black beyond seems because the ocean hides what it contains." She shakes her head in a happy way. "If you ever want to see how small you are in the plan of God, just stand at the edge of an ocean."

"I've only ever been to a river."

She puffs out her bottom lip, regarding me. "This river goes to the ocean, you know. It's not even all that far. Two days on horseback at most. A long morning in a fissioncar, though the road's not that great."

"There's a road?"

"Not much left of it any more."

"Is there something there?"

"Used to be my home," she says, shifting in her chair. "When we first landed, going on twenty-three years ago now. Meant to be a fishing settlement, boats and everything. In a hundred years' time, it might have even been a port."

"What happened?"

"What happened all over this planet, all our grand plans just sort of falling by the wayside in the first couple of years in the face of difficulty. It was harder to start a new civilization than we thought. You have to crawl before you can walk." She takes a sip of her beer. "And then sometimes you go back to crawling." She smiles to herself. "Probably for the best, though. Turns out New World's oceans aren't really for fishing."

"Why not?"

"Oh, the fish are the size of your boat and they swim up alongside and look you in the eye and tell you how they're going to eat you." She laughs a little. "And then they eat you."

I laugh a little, too. And then I remember all that's happened.

She looks at me again, catching my eye. "It's beautiful, though, the ocean. Like nothing you've ever seen."

"You miss it." I drink the last of my beer.

"To see the ocean once is to learn how to miss it," she says, taking my glass. "Let me get you another."

That night, I dream.

I dream of oceans and of fish that will eat me. I dream of armies that swim by and of Mistress Coyle leading them. I dream of Maddy taking my hand and holding me up from the water.

I dream of thunder making a single loud *BOOM!* that almost breaks the sky in two.

Maddy smiles when I jump at the sound of it. "I'm going to see him," I tell her.

She glances over my shoulder and says, "There he is."

I turn to look.

I wake but the sun's all wrong. I sit up, my head feeling like it's a boulder, and I have to close my eyes to make everything stop spinning.

"Is this what a hangover feels like?" I say out loud.

"There was no alcohol in that beer," Corinne says.

I snap my eyes open, which is a mistake as black spots form everywhere in my vision. "What are you doing here?"

"Waiting for you to wake up so the President's men can take you."

"What?" I say, as she stands. "What's going on?"

"She drugged you. Jeffers in your beer, plus bandy root to disguise the taste. She left you this." She holds out a small piece of paper. "You're to destroy it after you read it."

I take the paper. It's a note from Mistress Coyle.

Forgive me, my girl, it says, *but the President is wrong. The war is not over. Keep to the side of right, keep gathering information, keep leading him astray. You'll be contacted.*

"They blew up a storefront and left in the confusion," Corinne says.

"They did *what*?" My voice starts to rise. "Corinne, *what's going on*?"

But she's not even looking at me. "I told them they were

abandoning their sacred trust, that *nothing* was more important than saving lives."

"Who else is here?"

"Just you and me," she says. "And the soldiers waiting outside to take you to your President." She looks down at her shoes and for the first time I notice the anger, the *rage* burning off her. "I expect I'll be interrogated by someone less *handsome*."

"Corinne—"

"You'll have to start calling me Mistress Wyatt now," she says, turning towards the door. "That is, in the unlikely event that both of us get back here alive."

"They're gone?" I say, still not believing it.

Corinne just glares at me, waiting for me to rise.

They're gone.

She left me here alone with Corinne.

She *left* me here.

To go off and start a war.

13

SPLINTERS

[TODD]

"FISSION FUEL, SIR, soaked into clay powder to make a paste–"

"I know how to make a bush bomb, Corporal Parker," says the Mayor, surveying the damage from his saddle. "What I do not know is how a group of unarmed women managed to *plant* one in full view of soldiers under your command."

We see Corporal Parker swallow, actually see it move in his throat. He's not a man from old Prentisstown, so he musta been picked up along the way. *You go where the power is*, Ivan said. But what about when the power wants answers you ain't got? "It may not have been just women, sir," Parker says. "People are talking about something called–"

"Look at this, pigpiss," Davy says to me. He's ridden Deadfall/Acorn over to a tree trunk, near where we've stopped across the road from the blown-out storefront.

I chirrup to Angharrad, using my one good hand to tap

159

the reins. She picks her feet lightly over the bits of wood and plaster and glass and foodstuffs that are scattered everywhere, like the store finally let go of a sneeze it was holding in. We get over to Davy, who's pointing at a bunch of light-coloured splinters sticking straight outta the tree trunk.

"Explozhun so big it rammed 'em straight into the tree," he says. "Those bitches."

"It was late at night," I say, readjusting my arm in the sling. "They didn't hurt no one."

"Bitches," Davy repeats, shaking his head.

"You'll turn in your supply of cure, Corporal," we hear the Mayor say, loud enough so Corporal Parker's men hear the punishment, too. "All of you will. Privacy is a privilege for those who've earned it."

The Mayor ignores Corporal Parker's mumbled, "Yes, sir," and turns to have a short, quiet word with Mr O'Hare and Mr Morgan, who then ride off in different direkshuns. The Mayor comes over to us next, not saying nothing, face frowning like a slap. Morpeth stares viciously at our mounts, too. **Submit**, says his Noise. **Submit. Submit**. Deadfall and Angharrad both lower their heads and step back.

All horses are a little bit crazy.

"Want me to go hunting for 'em, Pa?" Davy says. "The bitches who did this?"

"Mind your language," the Mayor says. "You both have work to be getting on with."

Davy gives me a sideways glance and holds out his left leg. The whole bottom half is covered in a cast. "Pa?" he says. "If you ain't noticed, I can barely walk and pigpiss here's in a sling and—"

He don't even finish the sentence before there's that *whoosh* of sound, flying from the Mayor faster than thought, like a bullet made of Noise. Davy flinches back in his saddle, yanking the reins so hard Deadfall rears up, nearly dumping Davy to the ground. Davy recovers, breathing heavy, eyes unfocused.

What the hell *is* that?

"Does this look like a day you can take off?" the Mayor says, indicating all the wreckage of the store stretched around us, the husk of the building still smoking in some parts.

Blown up.

(I've been hiding it in my Noise, doing my best to keep it down—)

(but it's there, hidden away, bubbling below the surface—)

(the thought of a bridge that blew up once—)

I look back to see the Mayor staring at me so hard I'm blurting it out before I can barely think. "It wasn't her," I say. "I'm sure it wasn't."

He keeps on staring. "I never thought it might be, Todd."

Fixing my arm didn't take very long yesterday once he'd dragged me cross the square to a clinic where men in white coats set it and gave me two injeckshuns of bone-mending that hurt more than the break but by then he was already gone, promising I'd see Viola the next night (tonight, tonight) and already outta reach of a million and one askings about how he came to be embracing her and calling her all friendly-like by her first name and how she's working as a doctor or something and how she had to leave to go to a funeral and–

(and how my heart just exploded from my chest when I saw her–)

(and how it hurt all over again when she left–)

And then off she went somehow to a life of her own already being lived out there somewhere without me in it and then there was just me and my arm going back to the cathedral with the painkillers making me so sleepy I barely had time to fall on my mattress before blinking right out.

I didn't wake when Mayor Ledger came back in with his grey day-of-rubbish-collecting Noise complaints. I didn't wake when dinner came and Mayor Ledger ate both servings. I didn't wake when we were locked inside for the night *ker-thunk*.

But I surely did wake when a *BOOM!* shook the entire city.

And even as I sat up in the darkness and felt the queasy of the painkillers in my stomach, even without knowing what the *BOOM* was or where it had come from or what it meant, even then I knew things had changed again, that the world had suddenly become different one more time.

And sure enough, out we came with the Mayor and his men at first light, injuries or no, straight to the bombsite. I look at him on Morpeth. The morning sun's shining behind him, casting his shadow over everything.

"Will I still see her tonight?" I ask.

There's a long, quiet moment where he just stares.

"Mr President?" calls Corporal Parker, as his men take away a long plank of wood that was blown against another tree.

Something's been drawn onto the trunk underneath.

Even with not knowing how to–

Well, even with not knowing much, I can tell what it is.

A single letter, smeared on the trunk in blue.

A, it says. Just the letter **A**.

"I can't believe he's making us effing go back there one day after we fought off the attack," Davy grumbles as we make our way down the long road to the monastery.

I can't believe it neither, frankly. Davy can barely walk and even with the bone-mending doing its work on my arm, it'll be a coupla days before everything's back to normal. I can start to bend it already but I sure as hell can't fight off a Spackle army with it.

"Did you tell him I saved yer life?" Davy asks, looking both angry and shy.

"Didn't *you* tell him?" I say.

Davy's mouth flattens, pulling his sad little moustache fluff even thinner. "He don't believe me when I tell him stuff like that."

I sigh. "I told him. He saw it in my Noise anyway."

We ride in silence for a bit before Davy finally says, "Did he say anything?"

I hesitate. "He said, *Good for him.*"

"That all?"

"He said it was good for me, too."

Davy bites his lip. "That's it?"

"That's it."

"I see." He don't say no more, just jigs Deadfall along a bit faster.

Even tho it was only one building that got blown up in the night, the whole city looks different as we ride. The patrols of soldiers are suddenly larger and there's more of 'em, marching up and down the roads and side streets so fast it's like they're running. There are soldiers on rooftops now, too, here and there, holding rifles, watching watching watching.

The only non-soldier men out are hustling as fast as they can from place to place, staying outta the way, not looking up.

I ain't seen no women this morning. Not one.

(not her)

(what was she *doing* with him?)

(is she lying to him?)

(is he believing her?)

(did she have something to do with the explozhun?)

"Did *who* have something to do with it?" Davy asks.

"Shut up."

"Make me," he says. But his heart ain't in it.

We ride past a group of soldiers escorting a beat-up look-ing man with his wrists bound. I press my slinged arm closer to my chest and we keep on riding. The morning sun's high in the sky by the time we pass the hill with the metal tower and come round the final bend to the monastery.

Ain't no putting off getting there any longer.

"What happened after I left?" I say.

"We beat 'em," Davy says, huffing a little with the rising pain in his leg, pain I can see in his Noise. "We beat 'em back good and proper."

Something lands on Angharrad's mane. I brush it away and something else lands on my arm. I look up.

"What the hell?" Davy says.

It's snowing.

I only ever seen snow once in my whole life, back when I was too young to really know how I'd hardly never see it again.

Flakes of white fall thru the trees and onto the road, catching on our clothes and hair. It's a silent fall and it's weird how it makes everything else seem quiet, too, like it's trying to tell you a secret, a terrible, terrible secret.

But the sun is blazing.

And this ain't snow.

"Ash," Davy spits when a flake lands near his mouth. "They're burning the bodies."

They're burning the bodies. The men are still on the tops of the stone walls with their rifles, making the Spackle that lived pile up the bodies of the ones that died. The burning pile is huge, taller than the tallest living Spackle, and more bodies are being brought to it by Spackle with their heads down and their mouths shut.

I watch a body get thrown up to the top of the pile. It lands askew and tumbles down the side, rolling over other bodies, thru the flames, till it reaches the mud below and comes to a stop facing straight up, holes in its chest, blood dried on its wounds–

(a dead-eyed Spackle, face up in a campsite–)

(a Spackle with a knife in its chest–)

I breathe a heavy breath and I look away.

Apart from some of the clicking, the living Spackle still ain't got no Noise. No sounds of mourning nor anger nor nothing at all bout the mess they're having to clean up.

It's like someone cut out their tongues.

Ivan's there waiting for us, rifle in the crook of his arm. He's quieter this morning and his face ain't happy.

"You're to be a-carrying on with the numbers," he says, kicking over the bag with the numbering bands and tools. "Though there's less to do now."

"How many'd we get?" Davy says, smiling.

Ivan shrugs, annoyed. "Three hundred, three-fifty, can't say for sure."

I feel another greasy twist in my stomach at that but Davy's grin gets even higher. "That's hot stuff, right there."

"I'm to give you this," Ivan says, holding out the rifle to me.

"Yer *arming* him?" Davy says, his Noise rising right up.

"President's orders," Ivan snaps. He's still holding out the rifle. "You're to give it to the night watch when you leave. It's only for your protection while you're in here." He looks at me, frowning. "The President says to tell you he knows you'll do the right thing."

I'm just staring at the rifle.

"I don't effing believe this," Davy says, under his breath and shaking his head.

I know how to use a rifle. Ben and Cillian taught me how to use one so I didn't blow my own head off, how to hunt safely with it, how to use it only when necessary.

The right thing.

I look up. Most of the Spackle are back and away in the far fields, as far as they can get from the entrance. The rest are dragging broken and torn bodies to the fire that's burning in the middle of the next field over.

But the ones that can see me are watching me.

And they're watching me watch the rifle.

And they ain't thinking nothing I can hear.

So who knows what they're planning?

I take the rifle.

It don't mean nothing. I won't use it. I just take it.

Ivan turns and walks back to the gate to leave and as he goes, I notice it.

A low *buzz*, just barely beyond hearing, but there. And growing.

No wonder he looked so pissed off.

The Mayor took away *his* cure, too.

We spend the rest of the morning shovelling out the fodder, refilling the troughs and putting lime on the hogs, me one-handed, Davy one-legged, but taking more time than even that would allow for cuz brag tho he may I don't think Davy wants to get back to the numbering just yet either. We may both have guns now but touching an enemy that almost killed you, well, that takes a bit of leading up to.

Morning turns to early afternoon. For the first time, instead of taking both our lunches for himself, Davy throws a sandwich at me, hitting me in the chest with it.

So we eat and watch the Spackle watching us, watch the pile of bodies burn, watch the eleven hundred and fifty Spackle left over from the attack that went wrong, wrong, wrong. They're gathered round the edges of the fields we opened up and along the wall of the monastery, as far from us and from the burning pile as they can be.

"The bodies should go in a swamp," I say, eating my sandwich with one tired arm. "That's what Spackle bodies are for. You put 'em in water and then—"

"Fire's good enough for 'em," Davy says, leaning against the bag of numbering tools.

"Yeah, but—"

"There's no buts here, pigpiss." He frowns. "And what're you moaning for their sakes anyway? All yer blessed kindness didn't stop 'em from trying to rip yer arm off, now did it?"

He's right but I don't say nothing to that, just keep on watching them, feeling the rifle at my back.

I could take it. I could shoot Davy. I could run from here.

"You'd be dead before you got to the gate," Davy mumbles, looking at his sandwich. "And so would yer precious girl."

I don't say nothing to that neither, just finish my lunch. Every pile of food is out, every trough has been refilled, every bog has been limed up. There ain't nothing left to do except the thing we gotta do.

Davy sits up from where he was leaning against the bag. "Where were we?" he says, opening it up.

"0038," I say, keeping my gaze on the Spackle.

He sees from the metal bands that I'm right. "How'd you remember that?" he says, amazed.

"I just do."

They're looking back at us now, all of 'em. Their faces are hollowed-out, bruised, blank. They know what we're doing. They know what's coming. They know what's in the bag. They know there ain't nothing they can do about it except die if they resist us.

Cuz I got a rifle on my back to make that happen.

(what's the right thing?)

"Davy," I start to say but it's all that comes out cuz—

BOOM!

– in the distance, almost not a sound at all, more like the faraway thunder of a storm you know is gonna get here quick and do its best to knock yer house down.

We turn, as if we could see over the walls, as if the smoke's already rising over the treetops outside the gates.

We can't and it ain't yet.

"Those bitches," Davy whispers.

But I'm thinking—

(is it her?)

(is it her?)

(what is she *doing*?)

14

THE SECOND BOMB

{VIOLA}

THE SOLDIERS WAIT until midday to take me and
Corinne. They practically have to tear her away from treating the remaining patients and they march us down the road,
eight soldiers to guard two small girls. They won't even look
at us, the one next to me so young he's barely older than
Todd, so young he's got a large angry spot on his neck that
for some stupid reason I can't keep my eyes off.

Then I hear Corinne gasp. They've marched us past the
storefront where the bomb went off, the front of the building collapsed on itself, soldiers guarding what's left of it. Our
escort slows to take a look.

And that's when it happens.

BOOM!

A sound so big it makes the air as solid as a fist, as a
wave of bricks, as if the world's dropped out beneath you and

you're falling sideways and up and down all at once, like the weightlessness of the black beyond.

There's a blankness where I can't remember anything and then I open my eyes to find myself lying on the ground with smoke twirling around me in spinning, floating ribbons and bits of fire drifting down from the sky here and there and for a minute it seems almost peaceful, almost beautiful, and then I realize I can't hear anything except a high-pitched whine that's drowning out all the sounds the people around me are making as they stagger to their feet or open their mouths in what must be shouting and I sit up slowly, the world still gone in whining silence and there's the soldier with the spot on his neck, there he is on the ground next to me, covered in wooden splinters, and he must have shielded me from the blast because I'm mostly okay but he's not moving.

He's not moving.

And sound begins to return and I start to hear the screaming.

"This is exactly the kind of history I did *not* want to repeat," the Mayor says, staring up thoughtfully into the shaft of light coming down from the coloured-glass window.

"I didn't know anything about a bomb," I say for a second time, my hands still shaking and my ears ringing so loud it's hard to hear what he's saying. "Neither one."

"I believe you," he says. "You were very nearly killed yourself."

"A soldier blocked most of it for me," I stutter out,

remembering his body, remembering the blood from it, the splinters that were stuck in nearly every part of him–

"She drugged you again, didn't she?" he asks, staring back up into the coloured window, as if the answers might be there. "She drugged you and abandoned you."

This hits me like a punch.

She did abandon me.

And set off a bomb that killed a young soldier.

"Yes," I finally say. "She left. They all did."

"Not all." He walks behind me, becoming just a voice in the room, talking loud and clear enough so I can hear. "There are five houses of healing in this city. One remains fully staffed, three others are partially depleted of their healers and apprentices. It's only yours where there's been complete desertion."

"Corinne stayed," I whisper and then I'm suddenly pleading. "She tended the soldiers who were hurt in the second bomb. She didn't hesitate. She went right to the worst injured and tied tourniquets and cleared airways and–"

"Duly noted," he interrupts, even though it's true, even though she called me over to help her and we did the best we could until other stupid soldiers who couldn't or *wouldn't* see what we were doing grabbed us and dragged us away. Corinne struggled against them but they hit her in the face and she stopped.

"Please don't hurt her," I say again. "She has nothing to do with this. She stayed behind out of choice. She tried to help those–"

"I'm not going to *hurt* her!" he shouts suddenly. "Enough of this *cowering*! There will be no harm to women as long as I am President! Why is that so difficult for you to understand?"

I think of the soldiers hitting Corinne. I think of Maddy falling to the ground.

"Please don't hurt her," I whisper again.

He sighs and lowers his voice. "We just need answers from her, that's all. The same answers I'll be needing from you."

"I don't know where they went," I say. "She didn't tell me. She didn't mention anything."

And I stop myself and he notices. Because she did mention something, didn't she?

She told me a story about–

"Something you'd like to share, Viola?" the Mayor asks, coming around to face me, looking suddenly interested.

"Nothing," I say quickly. "Nothing, just..."

"Just what?" His eyes are keen on me, flitting over my face, trying to read me, even though I have no Noise, and I realize briefly how much he must *hate* that.

"Just that she spent her first years on New World in the hills," I lie, swallowing. "Out west of town past the waterfall. I thought it was just idle talk."

He's still staring deep into me and there's a long silence while he looks and looks before starting his walk again.

"The most important issue," he says, "is whether the second bomb was a mistake, part of the first bomb that went off later by accident?" He comes round again to read my face. "Or was it on purpose? Was it set to go off later deliberately so that my men would be surrounding a crime scene, so that there would be maximum loss of life?"

"No," I say, shaking my head. "She wouldn't. She's a healer. She wouldn't kill–"

"A general would do anything to win a war," he says. "That's why it's war."

"No," I keep saying. "No, I don't believe–"

"I know you don't believe it." He steps away from me again, turning his back. "That's why you were left behind."

He goes to the small table next to his chair and picks up a piece of paper. He holds it up so I can see it.

There's a blue A written across it.

"Does this mean anything to you, Viola?"

I try to keep any look off my face.

"I've never seen that before." I swallow again, cursing myself as I do. "What is it?"

He looks at me long and hard again, then he puts the paper back down on the table. "She will contact you." He watches my face. I try to give him nothing. "Yes," he says, as if to himself. "She will, and when she does, pass along one message in particular, please."

"I don't–"

"Tell her that we can stop this bloodshed at once, that we can end all this before it even begins, before more people die and peace is for ever put aside. Tell her that, Viola."

He's staring so hard at me, I say, "Okay."

He's not blinking, his eyes black holes I can't turn away from. "But also tell her that if she wants war, she can have her war."

"Please–" I start to say.

"That'll be all," he says, gesturing me to my feet and towards the door. "Go back to your house of healing. Treat what patients you can."

"But–"

He opens the door for me. "There'll be no hanging this afternoon," he says. "Some civic functions will have to be curtailed in light of recent terrorist activities."

"*Terrorist*–?"

"And I'm afraid I'll be far too busy sweeping up the mess your mistress has made to host the dinner I promised you tonight."

I open my mouth but nothing comes out.

He closes the door on me.

My head spins as I stagger back down the main road. Todd is out here somewhere and all I can think of is how I can't see him and won't be able to tell him anything about what's happened or explain myself or anything.

And it's her fault.

It is. I hate to say it but it's her fault. All of this. Even if it was for reasons she thought were right, it's all her fault. Her fault that I won't see Todd tonight. Her fault that war is coming. Her fault–

I come upon the wreckage again.

There are four bodies lying in the road, covered in white sheets that don't quite conceal the pools of blood beneath them. Nearest to me but behind a cordon of soldiers guarding the site is the sheet covering the soldier who accidentally saved me.

I didn't even know his name.

And then all of a sudden he was dead.

If she'd just waited, if she'd just seen what the Mayor wanted her to do–

But then I think, *Appeasement, my girl, it's a slippery slope–*

But the bodies here in the road–

But Maddy dying–

But the boy soldier who saved me–

But Corinne being hit to stop her from helping–

(oh, Todd, where are you?)

(what do I do? what's the right thing?)

"Move along there," a soldier barks at me, making me jump.

I hurry along the road and before I even realize it, I'm running.

I return to the nearly empty house of healing out of breath and slam the front door behind me. There were yet more soldiers on the road, more patrols, men on rooftops with rifles who watched me run very closely, one of them even whistling rudely as I went by.

There'll be no getting to the communications tower now, not any more.

Another thing she screwed up.

As I catch my breath, it sinks in that I'm the only thing even resembling a healer here now. Many of the patients were well enough to follow Mistress Coyle out to wherever she's gone and, who knows, might have even been the ones to plant the bombs, but there's still at least two dozen in beds here, with more coming in every day.

And I'm just about the worst healer New Prentisstown has ever seen.

"Oh, help," I whisper to myself.

"Where'd everybody go?" Mrs Fox asks as soon as I open the door to her room. "There's been no food, no medicine–"

"I'm sorry," I say, bustling up her bedpan. "I'll get you food as soon as I can."

"Good heavens, dear!" she says as I turn, her eyes widening. I look at the back of my white coat where her eyes have gone. There's a dirty smear of the young soldier's blood all the way down to the hem.

"Are you all right?" Mrs Fox asks.

I look at the blood, and all I can say is, "I'll get your food."

The next hours pass in a blur. The help staff are all gone, too, and I do my best to cook for the remaining patients, serving them and asking at the same time which medicines they take and when and how much and though they're all wondering what's going on, they see how I must look and try to be as helpful as they can.

It's well past nightfall when I come round a corner with a tray full of dirty dinner dishes and there's Corinne, just inside the entrance, pressing on the wall with one hand to hold herself up.

I throw the tray on the floor and run to her. She holds up her other hand to stop me before I reach her. She winces as I get close.

And I see the swelling around her eyes.

And the swelling in her lower lip.

And the way she's holding her body up too straight, like it hurts, like it really hurts.

"Oh, Corinne," I say.

"Just," she says, taking a breath. "Just help me to my room."

I take her hand to help her along and feel something hidden in her palm, pressed into mine. She holds up a finger to her lips to shush the wonderings about to come from my open mouth.

"A girl," she whispers. "Hidden in the bushes by the road." She shakes her head angrily. "No more than a girl."

I don't look at it until I've got Corinne to her room and left again to get bandages for her face and compresses for her ribs. I wait until I'm alone in the supply room and open my palm.

It's a note, folded, with V written on the outside. Inside, it's only a few lines, saying almost nothing at all.

My girl, it says. *Now is the time you must choose.*

And then there's a single asking.

Can we count on you?

I look up.

I swallow.

Can we count on you?

I fold the note into my pocket and I take up the bandages and compresses and I go to help Corinne.

Who was beaten by the Mayor's men.

But who wouldn't have been beaten if she hadn't had to speak for Mistress Coyle.

But who was beaten even though the Mayor said she wouldn't be hurt.

Can we count on you?

And it wasn't signed with a name.

It just said, The Answer.

And Answer was spelled with a bright blue *A*.

15

LOCKED IN

[TODD]

BOOM!

– and the sky tears open behind us and a rush of wind comes up the road and Angharrad rears back in terror and I tumble off her to the ground and there's dust and screaming and a throbbing in my ears as I lay there and wait to see if I'm dead or not.

Another bomb. The third this week since the first two. Not two hundred metres away from us this time.

"Bitches," I hear Davy spit, getting to his own feet and looking back down the road.

My ears are ringing and my body's shaking as I get to my feet. The bombs've come at different times of day and night, at different spots in the city. Once it was an aqueduct that fed water to the western part of town, once it was the two main bridges to the farmlands north of the river. Today, it's–

"That's that caff," Davy says, trying to stop Deadfall/ Acorn from bolting. "Where the soldiers eat."

He gets Deadfall to heel and climbs back up on the saddle. "Come on!" he barks. "We'll go see if they need help."

I put my hands on Angharrad who's still frightened, still saying **bəy cəlt bəy cəlt** over and over again. I say her name a buncha times and finally get back up on her.

"Don't you go getting no funny ideas," Davy says. He takes out his pistol and points it at me. "You ain't sposed to leave my sight."

Cuz that's also how life's gone since the bombs started.

Davy with a gun on me, every waking minute of every waking day.

So I can't never go looking for her.

"The women certainly aren't helping their own cause any," says Mayor Ledger, mouth filled with chook.

I don't say nothing, just eat my own dinner and field off the asking marks coming from his Noise. The caff was bombed at a time when it was closed, like everything else this Answer thing bombs, but just cuz it's sposed to be empty don't mean it always is. Davy and I found two dead soldiers when we got there and one other dead guy who probably mopped the floors or something. Three more soldiers have died in the other bombs.

It's all really pissing off Mayor Prentiss.

I don't hardly see him no more, not since the day of my arm break, not since the day I sorta got to see Viola again. Mayor Ledger says he's arresting people and stuffing 'em in prisons west of town but not getting the knowledge he wants out of 'em. Mr Morgan, Mr O'Hare and Mr Tate are leading parts of the army off into the hills west of town looking for the camps of the bomb-planters, who are all these women who disappeared the night of the first bombs.

But the army ain't finding nothing and the Mayor just gets madder and madder, making more and more curfews, taking away more and more cure from his soldiers.

New Prentisstown gets louder by the day.

"The Mayor's denying the Answer even exists," I say.

"Well, the *President* can say anything he likes." Mayor Ledger pokes at his dinner with a fork. "But people talk." He takes another bite. "Oh, yes, they do."

In addishun to the mattresses wedged in on the tower ledges, they've put in a basin with fresh water every morning and a little chemical toilet back in the darkest corner. We're also getting better food, brought to us by Mr Collins, who then locks us back inside.

Ker-thunk.

That's where I am, locked up here every minute I'm not with Davy. The Mayor obviously don't want me out looking for Viola, despite what he says about *trust.*

"We don't know it's just women," I say, trying to keep her outta my Noise. "We don't know for sure."

"A group calling themselves the Answer played a role in the Spackle War, Todd. Covert bombing, night-time operations, that sort of thing."

"And?"

"And it was all women. No Noise to be heard by the enemy, you see." He shakes his head. "But they got out of hand at the end, became a law unto themselves. After the

181

peace, they even attacked our own city. We were finally forced to execute some of them. A nasty business."

"But if you executed them, how can it be them?"

"Because an idea lives on after the death of the person." He burps quietly. "I don't know what they think they're going to accomplish, though. It's only a matter of time before the President finds them."

"Men have gone missing, too," I say, cuz it's true but what I'm thinking is—

(did she go with 'em?)

I lick my lips. "These healing houses where women work," I say, "are they marked somehow? Some way to tell what they are?"

He takes a sip of his water, watching me over his cup. "Why do you want to know a thing like that?"

I rustle my Noise a little to hide anything that might give me away. "No reason," I say. "Never mind." I set my dinner on the little table they've given us, our agreed sign that he can eat the rest of mine. "I'm gonna sleep."

I lay back on my bed and face the wall. The last of the setting sun's coming thru the openings in the tower. There ain't no glass in the openings and winter's coming. I don't know how we're gonna get thru the cold. I put my arm under my pillow and pull my legs up to me, trying not to think too loud. I can hear Mayor Ledger eating the rest of my dinner.

But then a picture comes floating from his Noise, floating right over to me, a picture of an outstretched hand, painted in blue.

I turn to look at him. I've seen the hand on at least two different buildings on the way to the monastery.

"There are five of them," he says, his voice low. "I can tell you where they are. If you want."

I look into his Noise. He looks into mine. We're both covering something, hiding something beneath all the other strands of our thoughts. All these days locked together and we're still wondering if we can trust each other.

"Tell me," I say.

"1017," I read out to Davy as he spins the bolting tool around, latching the band to a Spackle who instantly becomes 1017.

"That's enough for today," Davy says, tossing the bolting tool in the bag.

"We've still got—"

"I said that's enough." He limps back over to our bottle of water and takes a swig. His leg should be healed by now. My *arm* is, but he still limps.

"We were sposed to be done with this in a week," I say. "We're going on *two* now."

"I don't see no one hurrying us along." He spits out some water. "Do you?"

"No, but—"

"And no further instruckshuns and no new jobs…" He trails off, takes another swig of water and spits some more. He glares to my left. "What're you looking at?"

1017 is still standing there, holding the band with one hand and staring at us. I think it's a male and I think it's young, not quite an adult. It clicks at us once and then once again and even tho it ain't got Noise the click sure sounds like something rude.

Davy thinks so, too. "Oh, yeah?" He reaches for the rifle slung on his back, his Noise firing it again and again at fleeing Spackle.

1017 stands his ground. He looks me in the eye and clicks again.

Yeah, definitely rude.

He backs off, walking away but still staring at us, one hand rubbing his metal band. I turn to Davy, who's got his rifle up and pointed at 1017 as he goes.

"Don't," I say.

"Why not?" Davy says. "Who's gonna stop us?"

I don't got the answer, cuz it seems there's nobody.

The bombs have come every third or fourth day. No one knows where they'll be or how they're planted, but *BOOM! BOOM! BOOM!* The evening of the sixth bomb, a small fission reactor this time, Mayor Ledger comes in with a blackened eye and a swollen nose.

"What happened?" I ask.

"Soldiers," he spits. He takes up his dinner plate, stew again, and winces as he takes the first bite.

"What did you do?"

His Noise rises a little and he turns an angry eye on me. "I didn't *do* anything."

"You know what I mean."

He grumbles some, eats some more stew, then says, "Some of them got the brilliant idea that *I* was the Answer. *Me.*"

"You?" I say, maybe a bit too surprised.

184

He stands, setting down his stew, mostly uneaten, so I know he must be *really* sore. "They can't find the women responsible and the soldiers are looking for someone to blame." He stares outta one of the openings, watching night fall across the town that was once his home. "And did our President do anything to stop my beating?" he says, almost to himself. "No, he did not."

I keep eating, trying to keep my Noise quiet of things I don't wanna think.

"People are talking," Mayor Ledger says, keeping his voice low, "about a new healer, a young one no one's ever seen before, going in and out of this very cathedral a while back, now working at the house of healing Mistress Coyle used to run."

Viola, I think, loud and clear before I can cover it.

Mayor Ledger turns to me. "That's one you won't have seen. It's off the main road and down a little hill towards the river about halfway to the monastery. There are two barns together on the road where you need to turn." He looks out the opening again. "You can't miss it."

"I can't get away from Davy," I say.

"I'm sure I don't know what you're talking about," Mayor Ledger says, lying back down on his bed. "I'm merely telling you idle facts about our fair city."

My breathing gets heavier, my mind and Noise racing thru possibilities about how I can get there, how I can get away from Davy to find the house of healing.

(to find her)

It isn't till later that I think to ask, "Who's Mistress Coyle?"

Even tho it's dark, I can feel Mayor Ledger's Noise get a little redder. "Ah, well," he says, into the night. "She'd be your Answer, wouldn't she?"

"That's the last of 'em," I say, watching Spackle 1182 slink away, rubbing her wrist.

"About effing time," Davy says, flopping down onto the grass. There's a crispness to the air but the sun is out and the sky is mostly clear.

"What are we sposed to do now?" I say.

"No effing idea."

I stand there and watch the Spackle. If you didn't know no better, you really wouldn't think they were much smarter than sheep.

"They *ain't*," Davy says, closing his eyes to the sun.

"Shut up," I say.

But I mean, *look* at 'em, tho.

They just sit on the grass, still no Noise, not saying nothing, half of 'em staring at us, half of 'em staring at each other, clicking now and then but hardly ever moving, not doing nothing with their hands or their time. All these white faces, looking drained of life, just sitting by the walls, waiting and waiting for *something*, whatever that something's gonna be.

"And the time for that something is now, Todd," booms a voice behind us. Davy scrambles to his feet as the Mayor comes in thru the main opening, his horse tied up outside.

But he looks at me, only me. "Ready for your new job?"

* * *

"Ain't barely talked to me for weeks," Davy's fuming as we ride home. Things didn't go so well twixt him and his pa. "Just *keep watch on Todd* this and *hurry up with the Spackle* that." His hands're gripped tightly round the reins. "Do I even get a *thank you*? Do I even get a *nice job, David*?"

"We were sposed to band the Spackle in a week," I say, repeating what the Mayor told him. "It took us more'n twice that."

He turns to me, his Noise really rising red. "We got *attacked*! How's that sposed to be *my* fault?"

"I ain't saying it was," I say back but my Noise is remembering the band around 0038's neck.

"So you blame me, *too*, do you?" He's stopped his horse and is glaring at me, leaning forward in the saddle, ready to jump off.

I open my mouth to answer but then I glance down the road behind him.

There's two barns by a turning in the road, a turning that heads down to the river.

I look back to Davy quickly.

He's got an evil smile. "What's down there?"

"Nothing."

"Yer girl, ain't it?" he sneers.

"Eff you, Davy."

"No, pigpiss," he says, sliding off his saddle to the ground, his Noise rising even redder. "Eff *you*."

There ain't nothing for it but to fight.

* * *

"Soldiers?" Mayor Ledger asks, seeing my bruises and blood as I come into the tower for dinner.

"Never you mind," I growl. It was me and Davy's worst fight in ages. I'm so sore I can barely reach my bed.

"You going to eat that?" Mayor Ledger asks.

A certain word in my Noise lets him know that no, I ain't gonna eat that. He picks it up and starts chomping away without even a thank you.

"You trying to eat yer way to freedom?" I say.

"Says a boy who's always had food provided for him."

"I ain't a boy."

"The supplies we brought when we landed only lasted a year," he says, twixt mouthfuls, "by which time our hunting and farming wasn't quite up to where it should have been." He takes another bite. "Lean times make you appreciate a hot meal, Todd."

"What is it about men that makes them need to turn everything into a lesson?" I cover my face with my arm, then take it away cuz of how much my blackening eye hurts.

Night falls again. The air is even cooler and I leave most of my clothes on as I get under the blanket. Mayor Ledger starts to snore, dreaming about walking in a house with endless rooms and not being able to find the exit.

This is the safest time I got to think about her.

Cuz is she really out there?

And is she part of this Answer thing?

And other things, too.

Like what would she say if she saw me?

If she saw what I did every day?

And with *who*?

I swallow the cool night air and blink away the wet in my eyes.

(are you still with me, Viola?)

(are you?)

An hour later and I'm still not asleep. Something's nagging at me and I'm turning in my sheets, trying to clear my Noise of whatever it is, trying to calm down enough so I can be ready for the new job the Mayor's got planned for us tomorrow, one which don't sound all that bad, if I'm honest.

But it's like I'm missing something, something obvious, right in front of my face.

Something–

I sit up, listening to the snoring Noise of Mayor Ledger, the sleeping roar of New Prentisstown outside, the night birds chirping, even the river rushing by in the distance.

There was no *ker-thunk* sound after Mr Collins let me in.

I think back.

Definitely not.

I look thru the darkness towards the door.

He forgot to lock it.

Right now, right this second.

It's unlocked.

16

WHO YOU ARE

{VIOLA}

"I HEAR NOISE OUTSIDE," Mrs Fox says as I refill her water jug for the night.

"It'd only be remarkable if you *didn't*, Mrs Fox."

"Just by the window–"

"Soldiers smoking their cigarettes."

"No, I'm sure it was–"

"I'm really very busy, Mrs Fox, if you don't mind."

I replace her pillows and empty her bedpan. She doesn't speak again until I'm almost ready to go.

"Things aren't like they used to be," she says quietly.

"You can say that again."

"Haven used to be better," she says. "Not perfect. But better than this."

And she just looks out of her window.

I'm dying with tiredness at the end of my rounds but I sit

down on my bed and take out the note that hasn't left my pocket. I read it for the hundredth, thousandth time.

My girl,

Now is the time you must choose.

Can we count on you?

The Answer

Not even a name, not even *her* name.

Almost three weeks I've had this note. Three weeks and nothing, so maybe that's how much they think they can count on me. Not another note, not another sign, just stuck here in this house with Corinne – or Mistress Wyatt, as I have to call her now – and the patients. Women who've fallen sick in the normal course of things, yes, but also women who've returned from "interviews" with the Mayor's men about the Answer, women with bruises and cuts, women with broken ribs, broken fingers, broken arms. Women with burns.

And those are the lucky ones, the ones who aren't in prison.

And every third or fourth day, *BOOM! BOOM! BOOM!*

And more are arrested and more are sent here.

And there's no word from Mistress Coyle.

And no word from the Mayor.

No word about why I'm being left alone. You'd think I'd be the one who'd be taken in first, the one who'd have interview after interview, the one who'd be sitting rotting in a prison cell.

"But nothing," I whisper. "Nothing at all."

And no word from Todd.

I close my eyes. I'm too tired to feel anything. Every day, I look for ways to get to the communications tower but there are soldiers *everywhere* now, way too many to find a pattern, and it only gets worse with each new bomb.

"I've got to do *something*," I say out loud. "I have to or I'll go crazy." I laugh. "I'll go crazy and start talking to myself."

I laugh some more, a lot more than how funny it actually is.

And there's a knock at my window.

I sit up, my heart pumping.

"Mistress Coyle?" I say.

Is this it? Is it now?

Is this where I have to choose?

Can they count on me?

(but is that *Noise* I can hear...?)

I get to my knees on the bed and pull the curtains back just far enough to look through a slit outside, expecting that frown, those fingers going over her forehead–

But it's not her.

It's not her at all.

"Todd!"

And I'm throwing back the sash and lifting up the glass and he's leaning in and his Noise is saying my name and I'm putting my arms around him and dragging him inside, actually *lifting* him off the ground and pulling him through my window and he's climbing up and we fall onto my bed and I'm on my back and he's lying on top of me and my face is close to his and I remember how we were like this after we'd jumped under the waterfall with Aaron right behind us and I looked right into his eyes.

And I knew we'd be safe.

"*Todd.*"

In the light of my room, I see his eye is blacked and there's blood on his nose and I'm saying, "What happened? Are you hurt? I can–"

But he just says, "It's you."

I don't know how much time passes with us just lying there, just feeling that the other is really there, really true, really *alive*, feeling the safety of him, his weight against mine, the roughness of his fingers touching my face, his warmth and his smell and the dustiness of his clothes, and we barely speak and his Noise is roiling with feeling, with complicated things, with memories of me being shot, of how he felt when he thought I was dying, of how I feel now at his fingertips, but at the front of it all, he's just saying, Viola, Viola, Viola.

And it's Todd.

Bloody hell, it's *Todd*.

And everything's all right.

And then there are footsteps in the hall.

Footsteps that stop right outside my room.

We both look towards the door. A shadow is cast underneath it, two legs of someone standing just on the other side.

I wait for the knock.

I wait for the order to get him out of here.

I wait for the fight I'll put up.

But then the feet walk away.

"Who was that?" Todd asks.

"Mistress Wyatt," I say, and I can hear the surprise in my own voice.

"And then the bombs started going off," I finish, "and he only called for me twice, early on, to ask me if I knew anything and I didn't, I truly didn't, and then that was it. Nothing. That's all I know about him, I swear."

"He ain't barely spoken to me since the bombs neither," Todd says, looking down at his feet. "I was worried it was you setting 'em off."

I see the bridge blowing up in his Noise. I see me being the one to do it. "No," I say, thinking of the note in my pocket. "It wasn't me."

Todd swallows, then he says simply, clearly, "Should we run?"

"Yes," I say, betraying Corinne so fast I feel a red blush of shame already coming over me, but yes, we should run, we should run and run.

"Where, tho?" he asks. "Where is there to go?"

I open my mouth to answer–

But I hesitate.

"Where are the Answer hiding?" he asks. "Can we go there?"

And I notice some tension in his Noise, disapproval and reluctance.

The bombs. He doesn't like the bombs either.

I see a picture of some dead soldiers in the wreckage of a cafe.

But there's more, too, isn't there?

I hesitate again.

I'm wondering, just for the briefest moment, just as if it's a fly I'm brushing away, I'm wondering–

I'm wondering if I can tell him.

"I don't know," I say. "I really don't. They didn't tell me in case I couldn't be trusted."

Todd looks up at me.

And for a second, I see the doubt on his face, too.

"You don't trust me," I say, before I think to stop.

"You don't trust me neither," he says. "Yer wondering if I'm working for the Mayor right now. And yer wondering what took me so long to find you." He looks down sadly at the floor again. "I can still read you," he says. "Nearly as well as my own self."

I look at him, into his Noise. "*You* wonder if I'm part of the Answer. You think it's something I'd do."

He doesn't look at me, but he nods. "I was just trying to stay alive, looking for ways to find you, hoping you hadn't left me behind."

"Never," I say. "Not ever."

He looks back up at me. "I'd never leave you neither."

"You promise?"

"Cross my heart, hope to die," he says, grinning shyly.

"I promise, too," I say and I smile at him. "I ain't never leaving you, Todd Hewitt, not never again."

He smiles harder when I say *ain't* but it fades and then I see him gathering his Noise to tell me something, something difficult, something he's ashamed of, but before he does, I want him to *know*, I want him to know for *sure*.

"I think they're at the ocean," I say. "Mistress Coyle told me a story about it before she left. I think she was trying to tell me that's where they were going."

He looks back up at me.

"Now tell me I don't trust you, Todd Hewitt."

And then I see my mistake.

"What?" he says, seeing the look on my face.

"It's in your Noise," I say, standing up. "Todd, it's all *over* your Noise. *Ocean*, over and over and over again."

"It ain't on purpose," he says but his eyes are widening and I see the door of his cell left unlocked and I see a man in the cell with him telling him where I am and I see asking marks rising–

"I'm so *stupid*," Todd says, standing, too. "Such an effing *idiot!* We need to go. Now!"

"Todd–"

"How far away is the ocean?"

"Two days' ride–"

"Four days' walk then." He's pacing now. His Noise says Ocean again, clear as a bomb itself. He sees me looking at him, sees me seeing it. "I'm not spying on you," he says. "I'm *not*, but he musta left the door open so I'd–" He pulls his hair in frustration. "I'll hide it. I hid the truth about Aaron and I can hide this."

My stomach flutters, remembering what the Mayor said to me about Aaron.

"But we have to go," Todd's saying. "Do you have any food we can take?"

"I can get some," I say.

"*Hurry.*"

As I turn to leave, I hear my name in his Noise. V̌íol̄a, it says, and it's covered in worry, worry that we've been set up, worry that I think he was sent here on purpose, worry that I think he's lying, and all I can do is just look at him and think his name.

Todd.

And hope he knows what I mean.

I burst into the canteen and run to the cabinets. I leave most of the lights off, trying to keep quiet as I grab meal-packs and loaves of bread.

"That fast, huh?" Corinne says.

She's sitting at a table far back in the darkness, cup of coffee in front of her. "Your friend shows up and you just leave." She stands and walks over to me.

"I have to," I say. "I'm sorry."

"You're sorry?" she says, eyebrows raised. "And what happens here, then? What happens to all the patients who need you?"

"I'm a *terrible* healer, Corinne, all I do is wash and feed them-"

"So that I can have time to do the very little healing that I'm capable of."

"Corinne-"

Her eyes flash. "*Mistress Wyatt.*"

I sigh. "Mistress Wyatt," I say and then I think and say it at the same time. "Come with us!"

She looks startled, threatened almost. "What?"

"Can't you see where this is all headed? Women in prison, women with injuries. Can't you see this isn't going to get any better?"

"Not with bombs going off every day, it isn't."

"It's the President who's the enemy," I say.

She crosses her arms. "You think you can have just one enemy?"

"Corinne–"

"A healer doesn't take life," she says. "A healer *never* takes life. Our first oath is to do no harm."

"The bombs are set for empty targets."

"Which aren't always empty, are they?" She shakes her head, her face looking suddenly sad, sadder than I've ever seen it. "I know who I am, Viola. In my *soul*, I know it. I heal the sick, I heal the wounded, that's who I am."

"If we stay here, they'll eventually come for us."

"If we leave, patients will die." She doesn't even sound angry any more, which is scarier than before.

"And if you're taken in?" I say, my voice getting challenging. "Who'll heal them then?"

"I was hoping you would."

I just breathe for a second. "It's not that simple."

"It is to me."

"Corinne, if I can get away, if I can contact my people–"

"Then what? They're still five months away, you said. Five months is a long time."

I turn back to the cabinets, continue filling the sack with food. "I have to try," I say. "I have to do *something*." I turn back to her, bag full. "That's who *I* am." I think of Todd, waiting for me, and my heart races faster. "That's who I've become, anyway."

She regards me quietly and then she quotes something Mistress Coyle once said to me. "We are the choices we make."

It takes me a second to realize she's just said goodbye.

"What took so long?" Todd says, anxiously looking out of the window.

"Nothing," I say. "I'll tell you later."

"You got the food?"

I hold up the bag.

"And I'm guessing we just follow the river again?" he says.

"I guess so."

He takes a second to look at me awkwardly, trying not to smile. "Here we go again."

And I feel this funny rush and I know that however much danger we're in, the rush is *happiness* and he feels it, too, and we clasp hands hard for just a second and then he stands on the bed, puts a leg on the sill and jumps through.

I pass the bag of food to him and climb out, my shoes thudding on the hard mud. "Todd," I whisper.

"Yeah?"

"Someone told me there's a communications tower somewhere outside of town," I say. "It's probably surrounded by soldiers but I was thinking if we could find it—"

"Big metal tower?" he interrupts. "Higher than the trees?"

I blink. "Probably," I say and my eyes open wide. "You know where it is?"

He nods. "I pass it every day."

"*Really?*"

"Yes, really," he says and I see it in his Noise, I see the road–

"And I think finally that's enough," says a voice from the darkness.

A voice we both recognize.

The Mayor steps out of the blackness, a row of soldiers behind him.

"Good evening to you both," he says.

And I hear a flash of Noise from the Mayor.

And Todd collapses.

17

HARD LABOUR

IT'S A SOUND but it's not a sound and it's louder than anything possible and it would burst yer eardrums if you were hearing it with yer ears rather than the inside of yer head and everything goes white and it's not just like I'm blind but deaf and dumb and frozen, too, and the pain of it comes from right deep down within so there's no part of yerself you can grab to protect it, just a stinging, burning slap right into the middle of who you are.

This is what Davy felt, every time he got hit with the Mayor's Noise.

And it's words–

All it is is *words*–

But it's *every* word, crammed into yer head all at once, and the whole world is shouting at you that YER NOTHING YER NOTHING YER NOTHING and it rips away every word of yer own, like pulling yer hair out at the roots and taking skin with it–

A flash of words and I'm nothing–

I'm nothing–

YER NOTHING–

And I fall to the ground and the Mayor can do whatever he wants with me.

I don't wanna talk about what happens next.

The Mayor leaves some soldiers behind to guard the house of healing and the others drag me back to the cathedral and he don't say nothing as we go, not a word as I beg him not to hurt her, as I promise and scream and cry (shut up) that I'll do anything he wants as long as he don't hurt her.

(shut up, shut up)

When we get back, he ties me to the chair again.

And lets Mr Collins go to town.

And–

And I don't wanna talk about it.

Cuz I cry and I throw up and I beg and I call out her name and I beg some more and it all shames me so much I can't even say it.

And all thru it, the Mayor says nothing. He just walks round me, over and over again, listening to me yell, listening to me plead.

Listening to my Noise beneath it all.

And I tell myself that I'm doing all this yelling, all this begging, to hide in my Noise what she told me, to keep her safe, to keep him from knowing. I tell myself I have to cry and beg as loud as I can so he won't hear.

(shut up)

That's what I tell myself.

And I don't wanna say no more about it.

(just effing shut the hell up)

By the time I get back in the tower, it's nearly morning and Mayor Ledger's waiting up for me and even tho I'm in no fitness to do anything, I'm wondering if maybe he played a part in all this somehow but his instant concern for me, his horror at the shape I'm in, it all sounds true in his Noise, so true that I just lay slowly down on the mattress and don't know what to think.

"They barely even came in," he says, standing behind me. "Collins just opened the door, took a look, then locked me in again. It's like they knew."

"Yeah," I say into my pillow. "It sure is like they knew."

"I had nothing to do with it, Todd," he says, reading me. "I swear to you. I'd never help that man."

"Just leave me be," I say.

And he does.

I don't sleep.

I burn.

I burn with the stupidity of how easy they trapped me, how easy it was to use her against me. I burn with the shame of crying at the beating (shut *up*). I burn with the ache of being taken from her again, the ache of her promise to me, the ache of not knowing what's going to happen to her now.

I don't care nothing bout what they do to me.

Eventually, the sun rises and I find out my punishment.

"Put yer back into it, pigpiss."

"Shut it, Davy."

Our new job is putting the Spackle to work in groups, digging up foundayshuns for new buildings in the monastery grounds, new buildings that'll house the Spackle for the coming winter.

My punishment is, I'm working right down there with 'em.

My punishment is, Davy's in complete charge.

My punishment is, he's got a new whip.

"C'mon," he says, slashing it against my shoulders. "Work!"

I spin round, every bit of me sore and aching. "You hit me with that again, I'll tear yer effing throat out."

He smiles, all teeth, his Noise a joyous shout of triumph. "Like to see you try, *Mr Hewitt*."

And he just *laughs*.

I turn back to my shovel. The Spackle in my group are all staring at me. I ain't had no sleep and my fingers are cold in the sharp, morning sun and I can't help myself and I shout at 'em. "Get back to work!"

They make a few clicking sounds one to another and start digging at the ground again with their hands.

All except one, who looks at me a minute longer.

I stare him out, seething, my Noise riled and raging right at him. He just takes it silently, his breath steaming from his mouth, his eyes daring me to do something. He holds up his wrist, like he's identifying himself, as if I don't know which one he is, then he returns to working the cold earth as slowly as he can.

1017 is the only one who ain't afraid of us.

I take my shovel and stab it hard into the ground.

"Enjoying yerself?" Davy calls.

I put something in my Noise, rude as I can think of.

"Oh, my mother's long dead," he says. "Just like yers." Then he laughs. "I wonder if she talked as much in real life as she wrote in her little book."

I straighten up, my Noise rising red. "Davy–"

"Cuz boy, don't she go on for *pages*."

"One of these days, Davy," I say, my Noise so fierce I can almost see it bending the air like a heat shimmer. "One of these days, I'm gonna–"

"You're going to what, dear boy?" the Mayor says, riding thru the entrance on Morpeth. "I can hear you two arguing from out on the road." He turns his gaze to Davy. "And arguing is not working."

"Oh, I got 'em working, Pa," Davy says, nodding out to the fields.

And it's true. Me and the Spackle are all separated into teams of ten or twenty, spread out among the whole enclosed bit of the monastery, removing stones from the low internal walls and pulling up the sod in the fields. Others are piling the dug-up dirt in other fields and my group here near the front have already dug parts of the trenches for the foundayshuns of the first building. I've got a shovel. The Spackle have to use their hands.

"Not bad," the Mayor says. "Not bad at all."

Davy's Noise is so pleased it's embarrassing. Nobody looks at him.

"And you, Todd?" The Mayor turns to me. "How is your morning progressing?"

"Please don't hurt her," I say.

"*Please don't hurt her*," Davy mocks.

"For the last time, Todd," the Mayor says, "I'm not going to hurt her. I'm just going to *talk* with her. In fact, I'm on my way to speak with her right now."

My heart jumps and my Noise raises.

"Oh, he don't like *that*, Pa," Davy says.

"Hush," the Mayor says. "Todd, is there anything you'd like to tell me that might make my visit with her go more quickly, more pleasantly for everyone?"

I swallow.

And the Mayor's just *staring* at me, staring into my Noise, and words form in my brain, PLEASE DON'T HURT HER said in my voice and his voice all twisted together, pressing down on the things I think, the things I know and it's different from the Noise slap, this voice pokes around where I don't want him, trying to open locked doors and turn over stones and shine lights where they shouldn't never be shone and all the while saying PLEASE DON'T HURT HER and I can feel myself starting to *want* to tell (*ocean*), starting to *want* to unlock those doors (*the ocean*), starting to *want* to do just exactly what he says, cuz he's right, he's right about everything and who am I to resist–

"She don't know nothing," I say, my voice wobbly, almost gasping.

He arches an eyebrow. "You seem distressed, Todd." He angles Morpeth to approach. **Submit**, Morpeth says. Davy watches the Mayor's attenshuns on me and even from here I can hear him getting jealous. "Whenever my passions need calming, Todd, there's something I like to do."

He looks into my eyes.

I AM THE CIRCLE AND THE CIRCLE IS ME.

Hatched right in the middle of my brain, like a worm in an apple.

"Reminds me who I am," the Mayor says. "Reminds me of how I can control myself."

"What does?" Davy says and I realize he's not hearing it.

I AM THE CIRCLE AND THE CIRCLE IS ME.

Again, right on the inside of me.

"What does it mean?" I almost gasp cuz it's sitting so heavy in my brain I'm finding it hard to speak.

And then we hear it.

A whining in the air, a buzzing that ain't Noise, a buzz more like a fat purple bee coming in to sting you.

"What the–?" Davy says.

And then we're all turning, looking at the far end of the monastery, looking up over the heads of the soldiers along the top of the wall.

Buzzzz–

It's in the sky, a shape making an arc, high and sharp, coming up thru some trees behind the monastery, trailing smoke behind it, but the buzzing is getting louder and the smoke is starting to thicken into black.

And then the Mayor pulls Viola's binos out of his shirt pocket to get a closer look.

I stare at them, my Noise churning, slopping out with asking marks that he ignores.

Davy musta brought them back down the hill, too.

I clench my fists.

"Whatever it is," Davy says, "it's coming this way."

I look back round. The thing has reached the high point of its arc and is heading back down to earth.

Down towards the monastery where we're all standing.

Buzzzz–

"I'd get out of the way if I were you," the Mayor says. "That's a bomb."

Davy runs so fast back to the gate he drops the whip. The soldiers on the wall start jumping off to the outside. The Mayor readies his horse but he don't move yet, waiting to see where the bomb's gonna land.

"Tracer," he's saying, his voice full of interest. "Antiquated, practically useless. We used them in the Spackle War."

The *buzzzzzz* is getting louder. The bomb's still falling, but picking up speed.

"Mayor Prentiss?"

"President," he corrects but he's still looking thru the binos almost like he's hypnotized. "The sound and the smoke," he says. "Far too obvious for covert use."

"Mayor Prentiss!" My Noise is getting higher with nerves.

"The city's all been bush bombs, so why–"

"RUN!" I yell.

Morpeth starts and the Mayor looks at me.

But I ain't talking to him.

"RUN!" I'm yelling and waving my hands and the shovel at the Spackle nearest me, the Spackle in my field.

The field the bomb is heading right for.

Buzzzzz–

They don't understand. Most of 'em are just watching the bomb coming right for them. "RUN!" I keep shouting and I'm sending explozhuns out in my Noise, showing 'em what'll happen when that bomb lands, imagining blood and guts and the **BOOM** that's on its way. "*RUN*, GODDAMMIT!"

It finally gets thru and some start to scatter, maybe just to get away from me screaming and waving my shovel, but they run and I chase them further up the field. I look back. The Mayor's moved to the entrance of the monastery, ready to ride further if necessary.

But he's watching me.

"RUN!" I keep yelling, getting the Spackle to move up and away, fleeing from the centre of this field. The last few hop over the nearest internal wall and I hop over with 'em, gasping for breath and turning round again to watch it land–

And I see 1017, still there in the middle of the field, just staring up at the sky.

At the bomb that's gonna kill him where he stands.

I'm jumping back over the internal wall before I even know it–

My feet pounding over the grass–

Leaping over the trenches we've dug–

Running so hard there ain't nothing in my Noise–

Just the *BUZZ* of the bomb–

Getting louder and lower–

And 1017 raising up his hand to shield his eyes from the sun–

Why ain't he running?
And *pound pound* go my feet–
And I'm chanting *"Damn you, damn you"* –
BUZZZZZZZZZZZZZZZZZZZ–
And 1017 don't see me coming–

I slam into him hard enough to lift him off his feet, feeling the air punched from his lungs as we fly across the grass, as we hit the ground rolling, as we go end over end across the dirt and into a shallow trench, as one titanic–

BOOM

eats the entire planet in a single bite of sound

blasting away every thought and bit of Noise

picking up yer brain and shattering it into pieces

and every bit of air is sucked up and blown past us
and dirt and grass hits us in hard, heavy clods
and smoke fills our lungs

And then there's silence.

Loud silence.

"Are you hurt?" I hear the Mayor shout, as if he's miles and miles away and deep under water.

I sit back up in the trench, see the huge smoking crater in the middle of the field, smoke already thinning cuz there's nothing to burn, row upon row of Spackle watching huddled from the far fields.

I'm breathing but I can't hear it.

I turn back to 1017, still mostly under me in the trench, scrabbling to get up, and I'm opening my mouth to ask him if he's all right even tho there's no way for him to answer–

And he hits me in a hard slap that leaves a rake of scratches across my face.

"Hey!" I shout, tho I can barely hear myself–

He's twisting out from under me and I reach out a hand to hold him there-

And he bites it hard with his rows of little sharp teeth–

And I pull it back, already bleeding–

And I'm ready to punch him, ready to *pound* him–

And he's out from under me, running away across the crater, back towards the other Spackle–

"Hey!" I shout again, my Noise rising into red.

He's just running and staring back and the rows of Spackle are all looking back at me, too, their stupid silent faces with less expresshun than the dumbest sheep I ever had back on the farm and my hand is bleeding and my ears are ringing and my face is stinging from the scratches and I saved his stupid life and this is the thanks I get?

Animals, I think. *Stupid, worthless, effing animals.*

"Todd?" says the Mayor again, riding over to me. "Are you hurt?"

I turn my face up towards him, not even sure if I'm calm enough to answer, but when I open my mouth–

The ground heaves.

My hearing's still gone so I feel it more than hear it, feel the rumble thru the dirt, feel the air pulse with three hard vibrayshuns, one right after the other, and I see the Mayor turn his head suddenly back towards town, see Davy and all the Spackle do the same.

More bombs.

In the distance, towards the city, the biggest bombs that've ever exploded in the history of this world.

18

TO LIVE IS TO FIGHT

{VIOLA}

I'M SO STUPIDLY UNDONE after the Mayor and his soldiers take Todd away Corinne finally has to give me something for it, though I feel the prick of the needle in my arm as little as I feel her hand on my back, not moving, not caressing, not doing anything to make it feel better, just holding me there, keeping me to earth.

I'm sorry to say, I'm not grateful.

When I wake in my bed, it's only just dawn, the sun so low it's not quite over the horizon yet, everything else in morning shadow.

Corinne is in the chair next to me.

"As much as it would do you good to sleep longer," she says, "I'm afraid you can't."

I lean forward in the bed until I'm almost bent in half. There's a weight in my chest so heavy, it's like I'm being pulled into the ground. "I know," I whisper. "I know."

I don't even know why he collapsed. He was dazed,

nearly unconscious, foam coming from his mouth, and then the soldiers lifted him to his feet and dragged him away.

"They'll come for me," I say, having to swallow away the tightness in my throat. "After they're done with Todd."

"Yes, I expect they will," Corinne says simply, looking at her hands, at the cream-coloured calluses raised on her fingertips, at the ash-coloured skin that flakes off the top of her hands because of so much time under hot water.

The morning is cold, surprisingly, harshly so. Even with my window closed, I can feel a shiver coming. I wrap my arms around my middle.

He's gone.

He's gone.

And I don't know what'll happen now.

"I grew up in a settlement called the Kentish Gate," Corinne suddenly says, keeping her eyes off mine, "on the edge of a great forest."

I look up. "Corinne?"

"My father died in the Spackle War," she presses on, "but my mother was a survivor. From the time I could stand, I worked with her in our orchards, picking apples and crested pine and roisin fruit."

I stare at her, wondering why now, why this story now?

"My reward for all that hard work," she continues, "was a camping trip every year after final harvest, just me and my mother, as deep in the forest as we dared to go." She looks out into the dark dawn. "There's so much life here, Viola. So much, in every corner of every forest and stream and river and mountain. This planet just *hums* with it."

She runs a fingertip over her calluses. "The last time we

went, I was eight. We walked south for three whole days, a present for how grown-up I was getting. God only knows how many miles away we were, but we were alone, just me and her and that was all that mattered."

She lets a long pause go by. I don't break it.

"She was bitten by a Banded Red, on her heel, as she cooled her feet in a stream." She's rubbing her hands again. "It's fatal, red snake venom, but slow."

"Oh, Corinne," I say, under my breath.

She stands suddenly, as if my sympathy is almost rude. She walks over to my window. "It took her seventeen hours to die," she says, still not looking at me. "And they were awful and painful and when she went blind, she grabbed onto me and begged me to save her, begged me over and over to save her life."

I remain silent.

"What we know now, what the healers have discovered, is that I *could* have saved her life just by boiling up some Xanthus root." She crosses her arms. "Which was all around us. In abundance."

The ROAR of New Prentisstown is only just starting to rise with the sun. Light shoots in from the far horizon, but we stay silent for a moment longer.

"I'm sorry, Corinne," I finally say. "But why–?"

"Everyone here is someone's daughter," she says quietly. "Every soldier out there is someone's son. The only crime, the *only* crime is to take a life. There is nothing else."

"And that's why you don't fight," I say.

She turns to me sharply. "To live *is* to fight," she snaps. "To preserve life is to fight *everything* that man stands for."

She takes an angry huff of air. "And now her, too, with all the bombs. I fight them every time I bandage the blackened eye of a woman, every time I remove shrapnel from a bomb victim."

Her voice has raised but she lowers it again. "That's my war," she says. "That's the war I'm fighting."

She walks back to her chair and picks up a bundle of cloth sat next to it. "And to that end," she says, "I need you to put these on."

She doesn't give me time to argue or even ask about her plan. She takes my apprentice robes and my own few much-washed clothes and has me put on poorer rags, a long-sleeved blouse, a long skirt, and a headscarf that completely covers my hair.

"Corinne," I say, tying up the scarf.

"Shut up and hurry."

When I'm dressed, she takes me down to the end of the long hallway leading out to the riverside by the house of healing. There's a heavy canvas bag of medicines and bandages loaded up by the door. She hands it to me and says, "Wait for the sound. You'll know it when you hear it."

"Corinne—"

"Your chances aren't very good, you have to know that." She's looking me in the eye now. "But if you get to wherever they're hiding, you put these supplies to use as a *healer*, do you hear me? You've got it in you whether you know it or not."

My breathing is heavy, nervous, but I look at her and I say, "Yes, Mistress."

"*Mistress* is right," she says and looks out of the window in the door. We can see a single bored soldier at the corner of the building, picking his nose. Corinne turns to me. "Now. Strike me, please."

I blink. "What?"

"Strike me," she says again. "I'll need a bloody nose or a split lip at least."

"Corinne–"

"Quickly or the streets will grow too crowded with soldiers."

"I'm not going to *hit* you!"

She grabs me by the arm, so fiercely I flinch back. "If the President comes for you, do you honestly think you'll return? He's tried to get the truth from you by asking and then by trapping your friend. Do you honestly think the patience of a man like that lasts forever?"

"Corinne–"

"He will eventually hurt you," she says. "If you refuse to help him, he will kill you."

"But I don't *know*–"

"He doesn't *care* what you don't know!" she hisses through her teeth. "If I can prevent the taking of a life, I will do so, even one as irritating as yours."

"You're hurting me," I say quietly, as her fingers dig into my arm.

"Good," she says. "Get angry enough to strike me."

"But why–"

"Just do it!" she shouts.

I take in a breath, then another, then I hit her across the face as hard as I can.

* * *

I wait, crouched by the window in the door, watching the soldier. Corinne's footsteps fade down the corridor as she runs to the reception room. I wait some more. The soldier is one of the many now who have had the cure taken from them and in the relative quiet of the morning I can hear what he thinks. Thoughts of boredom, thoughts of the village he lived in before the army invaded, thoughts of the army he was forced to join.

Thoughts of a girl he knew who died.

And then I hear the faint shout of Corinne coming from the front. She'll be screaming that the Answer snuck in during the night, beat her senseless and kidnapped me under their very noses but that she saw us all flee in the opposite direction I'm going to be running.

It's a poor story, there's no way it's going to work, how could anyone sneak in with guards everywhere?

But I know what she's counting on. A legend that's been rising, a legend about the Answer.

How can the bombs be planted with no one seeing?

With no one being caught?

If the Answer can do that, could they sneak past armed guards?

Are they invisible?

I hear thoughts just like this as soon as I see the soldier's head snap up when he hears the ruckus. It grows louder in his Noise as he runs around the corner and out of view.

And as fast as that, it's time.

I hoist the bag of medicines up onto my shoulder.

I open the door.

I run.

I run towards a line of trees and down to the river. There's a path along the riverbank but I stick to the trees beside it and as the bag bashes my shoulders and back with heavy corners, I can't help but think of me and Todd running down this same river, this same riverbank, running from the army, running and running and running.

I have to get to the ocean.

As much as I want to save Todd, my only chance is to find her first.

And then I'll come back for him.

I will.

I ain't never leaving you, Todd Hewitt.

My heart aches as I remember saying it.

As I break my promise.

(you hold on, Todd)

(you stay alive)

I run.

I make my way downriver, avoiding patrols, cutting across back gardens, running behind back fences, staying as far clear of houses and housing blocks as I can.

The valley is narrowing again. The hills approach the road and the houses begin to thin out. Once, I hear marching and I have to dive deep into the undergrowth as soldiers pass, holding my breath, crouching as low to the ground as

I can. I wait until there's only bird call (**Where's my safety?**) and the now-distant **ROAR** of the town, wait for a breath or two more, then I raise my head and look down the road.

The river bends in the distance and the road is lost from view behind further rolling hills and forests. Across the road here, this far from town, there are mostly farms and farmhouses, working their way up sloping hillsides, back towards more forest. Directly across, there's a small drive leading to a farmhouse with a little stand of trees in the front garden. The farming fields spread out to the right, but above and beyond the farmhouse, thicker forest begins again. If I can get up the drive, that'll be the safest place for me. If I have to, I'll hide until nightfall and make my way in the dark.

I look up and down the road again and once more. I listen out for marching, for stray Noise, for the rattle of a cart.

I take in a breath.

And I bolt across the road.

I keep my eyes on the farmhouse, the bag banging into my back, my arms pumping the air, my lungs gasping as I run faster and faster and faster–

Up the drive–

Nearly to the trees–

Nearly there–

And a farmer steps out from behind them.

I skid to a stop, sliding in the dirt and nearly falling. He jumps back, obviously surprised to see me appearing suddenly in front of him.

We stare at each other.

His Noise is quiet, disciplined, almost gentlemanly, which is why I didn't hear it from a distance. He's holding a basket under one arm and a red pear in his free hand.

He looks me up and down, sees the bag on my back, sees me alone out on the road in a break of the law, sees from the heaviness of my breath that I've obviously been running.

And it comes in his Noise, fast and clear as morning.

The Answer, he thinks.

"No," I say. "I'm not–"

But he holds a finger up to his lips.

He cocks his head in the direction of the road.

And I hear the distant sound of soldiers marching down it.

"That way," the farmer whispers. He points up a narrow path, a small entrance to the woods above that would be easy to miss if you didn't know it was there. "Quickly now."

I look at him again, trying to see a trap, trying to *tell* but there's no time. There's no time.

"Thank you," I say and I take off running.

The path leads almost immediately into thicker woods, all uphill. It's narrow and I have to push back vines and branches to make my way. The trees swallow me and I can only go forward and forward, hoping that I'm not being led into a trap. I get to the top of the hill only to find a small slope down and then another hill to climb. I run up that, too. I'm still heading east but I can't see enough over anything to tell where the road is or the river or which way I'm–

I nearly stumble out into a clearing.

Where there's a soldier not ten metres from me.

His back is to me (thank god, thank god) and it's not until my heart has leapt out of my chest and I've caught myself and fallen back into the bushes that I see what he's guarding.

There it is.

In the middle of a clearing cresting the hill, stretching up on three metal legs almost fifty metres into the sky. The trees around it have been felled, and across the clearing underneath it I can see a small building and a road that leads back down the other side of the hill to the river.

I've found the communications tower.

It's here.

And there aren't that many soldiers around it. I count five, no, six.

Just six. With big gaps.

My heart rises.

And rises.

I've found it.

And a *BOOM!* echoes in the distance beyond the tower.

I flinch, along with the soldiers. Another bomb. Another statement from the Answer. Another–

The soldiers are leaving.

They're running, running towards the sound of the explosion, running away from me and down the other side of the hill, towards where I can already see a white pillar of smoke rising.

The tower stands in front of me.

All of a sudden, it's completely unguarded.

I don't even wait to think how stupid I'm being–
    I'm just running–
    Running towards the tower–
    If this is my chance to save us then–
    I don't know–
    I'm just running–
    Across the open ground–
    Towards the tower–
    Towards the building underneath–
    I can save us–
    Somehow I can save all of us–

And out of the corner of my eye, I see someone else break
cover from the trees to my left–
    Someone running straight towards me–
    Someone–
    Someone saying my name–

"Viola!" I hear. "Get back!"

    "Viola, *NO!*" Mistress Coyle is screaming at me.

I don't stop–
    Neither does she–

"GET BACK!" she's yelling–
And she's crossing the clearing in front of me–
Running and running and running–
And then I realize–
Like a blow to the stomach–
The reason why she's yelling–
No–
Even as I'm skidding to a stop–
No, I think–
No, you can't–
And Mistress Coyle reaches me–
You CAN'T–
And pushes us both to the ground–
NO!

And the legs of the tower explode in three blinding flashes of light.

PART IV

NIGHT FALLING

19

WHAT YOU DON'T KNOW

{VIOLA}

"GET OFF ME!"

She slaps her hand over my mouth, holding it there, holding *me* there with the weight of her body as clouds of dust billow around us from the rubble of the communications tower. "*Quit shouting,*" she hisses.

I bite her hand.

She makes a pained face, fierce and angry, but she doesn't let go, just takes the bite and doesn't move.

"You can scream and shout all you want later, my girl," she says, "but in two seconds, this place is going to be swarming with soldiers and do you honestly think they're going to believe you just *happened by?*"

She waits to see my reaction. I glare at her but finally nod. She takes away her hand.

"Don't you call me *my girl,*" I say, keeping my voice low but just as fierce as hers. "Don't you call me that ever again."

*　*　*

I follow her down a steep slope, heading back towards the road, sliding on fallen leaves and gathered dew but always down and down. I hop over logs and roots, the canvas bag like a stone around my shoulders.

I have no choice but to go with her.

I'd be captured and god knows what else if I went back to town.

And she took my other choice away.

She reaches a stand of bushes at the bottom of a steepening in the slope. She ducks fast under them and beckons for me to follow. I slide down next to her, my breath almost gone, and she says, "Whatever you do, don't scream."

Before I can even open my mouth, she's jumped out through the bushes. They close up behind her and I have to fight my way through leaves and branches to follow. I'm still pushing them back when I practically tumble out the other side.

Onto the road.

Where two soldiers stand by a man with a cart, all of them looking straight at me and Mistress Coyle.

The soldiers look more astonished than angry, but they have no Noise, so there's no way to know.

But they're carrying rifles.

And they're raising them at us.

"And who the hell is *this*?" one barks, a middle-aged man with a shaved head and a scar down his jaw line.

"Don't shoot!" Mistress Coyle says, hands out and up.

"We heard the explosion," says the other soldier, a younger one, not much older than me, with blond, shoulder-length hair.

Then the older soldier says something else, something unexpected.

"You're *late*."

"That's enough, Magnus," Mistress Coyle says, lowering her hands and stepping forward to the cart. "And put your rifles down, she's with me."

"What?" I say, still frozen to my spot.

"The tracer malfunctioned completely," the younger soldier says to her. "We're not even sure where it came down."

"I told you they were too old," Magnus says.

"It did its job," Mistress Coyle says, bustling around the cart, "wherever it landed."

"Hey!" I say. "What's going on?"

And then I hear, "Hildy?"

Mistress Coyle stops in her tracks, the two soldiers do, too, and stare at the man driving the cart.

"Iss you, ain it?" he says. "Hildy hoo's also called Viola."

My mind's been racing so fast, so completely focused on the soldiers, that I barely took in the man driving the cart, the nearly expressionless face, the clothes, the hat, the voice, the Noise flat and calm as the far horizon.

The man that once drove me and Todd across a sea of things.

"*Wilf*," I gasp.

Now everyone looks at *me*, Mistress Coyle's eyebrows so high it's like they're trying to crawl into her hair.

"Hey," Wilf says, in greeting.

"Hey," I say back, too stunned to say any more.

He touches two fingers to the brim of his hat. "Ah'm glad to see yoo mayde it."

Mistress Coyle's mouth is moving but no sound comes out for a second or two. "There'll be time for that later," she finally says. "We have to go *now*."

"Will there be room for two?" the younger soldier asks.

"There'll have to be." She ducks down under the cart and removes a panel from the underside. She motions to me. "Get in."

"In where?" I bend down and see a compartment hidden like a trick of the eye in the width of the cart, narrow and thin as a cot above the rear axle.

"Pack won't fit," Wilf says, pointing at the bag on my back. "Ah'll take it."

I slip it off and hand it to him. "Thank you, Wilf."

"*Now*, Viola," Mistress Coyle says.

I give Wilf a last nod, duck under the cart and crawl in, forcing my way across the compartment until my head's nearly touching the far side. Mistress Coyle doesn't wait and forces herself in after me. The younger soldier was right. There isn't enough room. She's pressed right up against me, face to face, her knees digging into my thighs, our noses less than a centimetre apart. She's barely drawn her feet inside when the panel is replaced, plunging us into almost complete darkness.

"Where are we–" I start to say but she shushes me harshly.

And outside I hear soldiers marching fast up the road, led by the clopping of horse's hooves.

"Report!" one of them shouts as they stop by the cart.

His voice–

It's up high and I hear the horse whinnying beneath it–

But his voice–

"Heard the explosion, sir," the older of our soldiers replies. "This man says he saw women heading past him down the river road about an hour ago."

We hear the real soldier spit. "Bitches."

I recognize his voice–

It's Sergeant Hammar.

"Whose unit you two in?" he says.

"First, sir," says our younger soldier, after the briefest of pauses. "Captain O'Hare."

"*That* pansy?" Sergeant Hammar spits. "You wanna do some *real* soldiering, transfer to the Fourth. I'll show you what's what."

"Yes, sir," says our older soldier, sounding more nervous than I'd want him to.

I can hear the Noise of the soldiers in Sergeant Hammar's unit. They're thinking of the cart. They're thinking of the explosions. They're thinking about shooting women.

But there's no Noise coming from Sergeant Hammar.

"Arrest this man," Sergeant Hammar finally says, meaning Wilf.

"We were just doing that, sir."

"Bitches," Sergeant Hammar says again, and we hear him spur his horse (**Yield**, it thinks) and he and his men march off at speed.

I let out the breath I didn't realize I was holding. "He wasn't even *punished*," I whisper, more to myself than to Mistress Coyle.

"Later," she whispers back.

I hear Wilf snap the reins and we rock as the cart plods slowly forward.

So the Mayor was a liar. All along.

Of course he was, you *idiot*.

And Maddy's killer walks free to kill again, his cure still in place.

And I'm bumping and juddering against the woman who destroyed the only hope of contacting the ships that might save us.

And Todd is out there. Somewhere. Being left behind.

I've never felt so lonely in my life.

The compartment is hellishly small. We share too much of each other's air, elbows and shoulders bruising away as we ride along, the heat soaking our clothes.

We don't speak.

Time passes. And then more. And more after that. I fall into a kind of doze, the close warmth sucking the life right out of me. The rocking of the cart eventually flattens all my worries and I close my eyes against it.

I'm awakened by the older soldier knocking on the wood and I think we're going to finally get out, but he just says, "We're at the rough bit. Hold on."

"To what?" I say, but I don't say any more as the cart feels like it drops off a cliff.

Mistress Coyle's forehead smacks into my nose and I smell blood almost at once. I hear her gasp and choke as my stray hand is shoved into her neck and still the cart tumbles and bumps and I wait for the moment where we topple end over end.

And then Mistress Coyle is working both arms around me, pulling me close to her and bracing us in the compartment with one hand and one foot pressed against the opposite side. I resist her, resist the implied comfort, but there's wisdom in it as almost immediately we stop knocking each other about, even though the cart lurches and stutters.

And so it's in Mistress Coyle's arms that the last bit of my journey is taken. And it's in Mistress Coyle's arms that I enter the camp of the Answer.

Finally the cart stops and the panel is removed almost immediately.

"We're here," says the younger soldier, the blond one. "Everyone okay?"

"Why wouldn't we be?" Mistress Coyle says sourly. She lets go of me and scoots her way out of the compartment, extending a hand to help me out, too. I ignore it, getting myself out and looking at my surroundings.

We've come down a steep rocky path that's barely fit for a cart and into what looks like a gash of rocks in the middle of a forest. Trees press in on every side, a row of them on the level ground in front of us.

The ocean must be beyond them. Either I dozed off for longer than I thought or she lied and it's closer than she said.

Which wouldn't surprise me.

The blond soldier whistles when he sees our faces, and I can feel caked blood under my nose. "I can get you something for that," he says.

"She's a healer," Mistress Coyle says. "She can do it herself."

"I'm Lee," he says to me, a grin on his face.

For a brief second, I'm completely aware of how terrible I must look with my bloody nose and this ridiculous outfit.

"I'm Viola," I say to the ground.

"'Ere's yer bag," Wilf says, suddenly next to me, holding out the canvas sack of medicines and bandages. I look at him for a second and then I pretty much throw myself at him in a hug, pulling him tight to me, feeling the big, safe bulk of him. "Ah'm glad to see yoo, Hildy," he says.

"You, too, Wilf," I say, my voice thick. I let him go and take the bag.

"Corinne pack that?" Mistress Coyle asks.

I fish out a bandage and start cleaning the blood from my nose. "What do you care?"

"You can accuse me of many things," she says, "but not caring isn't one of them, my girl."

"I told you," I say, catching her eye, "never call me that again."

Mistress Coyle licks her teeth. She makes a quick glance to Lee and to the other soldier, Magnus, and they leave, quickly, disappearing into the trees ahead of us. "You, too, Wilf."

Wilf looks at me. "Yoo gone be all right?"

"I think so, Wilf," I say, swallowing, "but don't you go far."

He nods, touching the brim of his hat again and walking after the soldiers. We watch him go.

"All right." Mistress Coyle turns to me, crossing her arms. "Let's hear it."

I look at her, at her face full of defiance, and I feel my breath quicken, the anger rising up again so fast, so easily, it feels like I might crack in two. "How *dare you*–"

But she's interrupting, *already*. "Whoever contacts your ships first has the advantage. If he's first, he tells them all about the nasty little terrorist organization he's got on his hands and can they please use their guidance equipment to track us down and blow us off the face of New World."

"Yes but if we–"

"If we got to them first, yes, of course, we could have told them all about our local tyrant, but that was never going to happen."

"We could have tried–"

"Did you know what you were doing when you ran towards that tower?"

I clench my fists. "*No*, but at least I could have–"

"Could have what?" Her eyes challenge me. "Sent out a message to the very coordinates the President's been searching for? Don't you think he was counting on you *trying*? Just why exactly do you think you haven't been arrested yet?"

I dig my nails into my palms, forcing myself not to hear what she's saying.

"We were running out of time," she says. "And if *we* can't

235

use it to contact help, then at the very least we prevent him from doing the same."

"And when they land? What's your brilliant plan then?"

"Well," she says, uncrossing her arms and taking a step towards me, "if we haven't overthrown him, then there's a race to get to them first, isn't there? At least this way, it's a fair fight."

I shake my head. "You had no right."

"It's a war."

"That you started."

"*He* started it, my girl."

"And you escalated it."

"Hard decisions have to be made."

"And who put you in charge of making them?"

"Who put *him* in charge of locking away half the population of this planet?"

"You're blowing people up!"

"Accidents," she says. "Deeply regrettable."

Now it's my turn to take a step towards her. "That sounds exactly like something *he* would say."

Her shoulders rise and if she had Noise, it would be taking the top of my head off. "Have you *seen* the women's prisons, my girl? What you don't know could fill a *crater*–"

"Mistress Coyle!" A voice calls from the trees. Lee steps back into the rocky gash. "There's a report just come in."

"What is it?" Mistress Coyle says.

He looks from her to me. I look at the ground again.

"Three divisions of soldiers marching down the river road," he says, "full out for the ocean."

*   *   *

I look up sharply. "They're coming *here?*"

Both Mistress Coyle and Lee look at me.

"No," Lee says. "They're going to the ocean."

I blink back and forth between them. "But aren't we–?"

"Of course not," Mistress Coyle says, her voice flat, mocking. "Whatever made you think we were? And whatever, I wonder, makes the *President* think we are?"

I feel an angry chill, despite the sun, and I notice I'm shaking inside these big stupid puffy sleeves.

She was *testing* me.

As if I would tell the Mayor where–

"How *dare* you–" I start to say again.

But the anger suddenly fades as it comes flooding back.

"Todd," I whisper.

O¢eaη all over his Noise.

How he promised to hide it.

And how I know he'd keep that promise–

If he could.

(oh, Todd, did he–?)

(are you–?)

Oh, *no.*

"I have to go back," I say. "I have to *save* him–"

She's already shaking her head. "There's nothing we can do for him right now–"

"He'll kill him."

She looks at me, not without pity. "He's probably dead already, my girl."

I feel my throat closing up but I fight it. "You don't know that."

"If he's not dead, then he must have told the President

voluntarily." She cocks her head. "Which would you rather be true?"

"No," I say, shaking my head. "No–"

"I'm sorry, my girl." Her voice is a little calmer than before, a little softer, but still strong. "I truly am, but there are thousands of lives at stake. And like it or not, you've picked a side." She looks over to where Lee stands. "So why don't you let me show you your army?"

20

RUBBLE

[TODD]

"BITCHES," Mr Hammar says from atop his horse.

"Your analysis was not asked for, Sergeant," says the Mayor, riding Morpeth thru the smoke and the twisted metal.

"They've left the mark, tho," Mr Hammar says, pointing at the trunk of a large tree at the edge of the clearing.

The blue *A* of the Answer is smeared across it.

"Your concern for my eyesight does you credit," says the Mayor, sharply enough that even Mr Hammar shuts up.

We rode up here straight from the monastery, meeting Mr Hammar's squadron coming up the hill, looking ready for battle. When we got to the top, we found Ivan and the soldiers who were meant to be guarding the tower. Ivan got promoted here, I guess, after all the Spackle were rounded up, but now he's looking like he wishes he never *heard* of a tower.

Cuz it ain't here no more. It's just a heap of smoking metal, mostly in a long line where it fell, like a drunk man tipping forward onto the ground and deciding to just stay there and sleep.

(and I do my damnedest not to think about her asking me how to get here)

(saying we should go here first)

(oh, Viola, you didn't–)

"If they got enough to blow up something this big…" Davy says to my right, looking across the field. He don't finish his sentence cuz it's the same thing we're all thinking, the thing that's in everyone's Noise.

Everyone that's *got* Noise, that is, cuz Mr Hammar seems to be one of the lucky ones. "Hey, boy," he sneers at me. "You a man yet?"

"Don't you have somewhere you need to be heading, Sergeant?" the Mayor asks, not looking at him.

"With haste, sir," Mr Hammar says again, giving me an evil wink, then spurring his horse and shouting for his men to follow. They speed down the hill in the fastest march I've seen, leaving us with Ivan and his soldiers, all of their Noise regretting to a man how they ran towards the monastery after hearing the tracer bomb hit.

It's obvious, tho, when you look back. A smaller bomb in one place to get people running away from where you want to plant yer bigger bomb.

But what the hell were they doing bombing the monastery?

Why attack the Spackle?

Why attack *me*?

"Private Farrow," the Mayor says to Ivan.

"It's *Corporal* Farrow, actually–" Ivan says.

240

The Mayor turns his head slowly and Ivan stops talking as he comes to understand. "Private Farrow," the Mayor says again. "You will salvage what metal and scrap you can and then report to your commanding officer to relinquish your supply of cure–"

He stops. We can all hear Ivan's Noise clear as day. The Mayor looks round. Every soldier in the squadron has Noise. Every one of 'em's already been punished for one thing or another.

"You will submit yourselves to your commanding officer for appropriate punishment."

Ivan don't reply but his Noise rumbles.

"Is something unclear, Private?" the Mayor says, his voice dangerously bright. He looks into Ivan's eyes, holding his gaze. "You will submit yourselves to your commanding officer for appropriate punishment," he says again, but there's something in his voice, some weird vibrayshun.

I look at Ivan. His eyes are going foggy, unfocused, his mouth a little slack. "I will submit to my commanding officer for appropriate punishment," he says.

"Good," the Mayor says, looking back at the wreckage.

Ivan slumps a little when the eye contact is broken, blinking as if he's just woken up, forehead furrowing.

"But, sir," he says to the Mayor's back.

The Mayor turns round again, looking *very* surprised at still being spoken to.

Ivan presses on. "We were coming to your aid when–"

The Mayor's eyes flash. "When the Answer watched you do exactly what it wanted you to do and then blew up *my* tower."

"But, sir—"

Without changing his expresshun, the Mayor pulls out a pistol from his holster and shoots Ivan in the leg.

Ivan tumbles over, wailing. The Mayor looks at the other soldiers.

"Anyone else care to contribute before you get to work?"

As the rest of the soldiers ignore Ivan's screams and start clearing up the wreckage, the Mayor moves Morpeth right in front of that **A**, loud and clear like the announcement it is. "The Answer," he says, in a low voice like he's talking to himself. "The Answer."

"Let *us* go after 'em, Pa," Davy says.

"Hmm?" The Mayor turns his head slowly, like he forgot we were there.

"We can fight," Davy says. "We proved that. And instead you got us babysitting animals that are already beat."

The Mayor considers us for a minute, tho I don't know how or when Davy turned him and me into an *us*. "If you think they're already beaten, David," he finally says, "then you know very little about the Spackle."

Davy's Noise ruffles a little. "I think I've learnt a thing or two by now."

And as much as I hate to, I have to agree with him.

"Yes," says the Mayor. "I suppose you have. Both of you." He looks me in the eye and I can't help thinking of me saving 1017 from the bomb, risking my own life to get him outta the way.

242

And him biting and scratching me by way of thanks.

"Then how about a new project?" the Mayor says, steering Morpeth over to us. "One where you can put all your expertise to work."

Davy's Noise ain't sure of this. There's pride but doubt, too.

All I got in mine is dread.

"Are you ready to lead, Todd?" the Mayor asks lightly.

"*I'm* ready, Pa," Davy says.

The Mayor still looks only at me. He knows I'm thinking about her but he's ignoring all my askings.

"The Answer," he says, turning back to the **A**. "If that's who they want to be, then let them." He looks back at us. "But if there's an Answer, then someone must first…"

He lets his voice fade and he gets a faraway smile on his face, like he's laughing at his own private joke.

Davy unfolds the big white scroll onto the grass, not caring that it's getting wet in the cold morning dew. There's words written across the top and diagrams and squares and things drawn in below it.

"Measurements mostly," Davy reads. "Too effing many. I mean, *look* at that."

He holds the scroll up to me, trying to get me to agree.

And, well—

Yeah, okay, I—

Whatever.

"Too effing many," I say, feeling sweat come up under my arms.

It's the day after the tower fell and we're back at the monastery, back to putting teams of Spackle to work. My escape seems to be forgotten, like it was part of another life and now we've all got new things to think about. The Mayor won't talk to me about Viola and I'm back working for Davy, who ain't too happy.

So it's like old times.

"There's fighting to be done and he's got us building an effing *palace*," Davy frowns, looking over the plans.

It ain't a palace but he's got a point. Before it was just gonna be rough shacks to shelter the Spackle for the winter but this looks like a whole new building for men, taking up most of the inside of the monastery.

It's even got a name written across the top.

A name my eye stumbles over, trying to—

Davy turns to me, his eyes widening. I make my Noise as Noisy as possible.

"We should get started," I say, standing up.

But Davy's still looking at me. "What do you think about what it says right here?" he asks, putting his finger on a block of words. "Ain't that something amazing what it says?"

"Yeah," I shrug. "I guess."

His eyes get even wider with delight. "It's a list of materials, pigpiss!" His voice is practically celebrating. "You can't read, can you?"

"Shut up," I say, looking away.

"You can't even *read*!" Davy's smiling up into the cold sun and around at all the Spackle watching us. "What kinda idiot gets thru life—"

"I said, *shut up*!"

244

Davy's mouth drops open as he realizes.

And I know what he's gonna say before he says it.

"Yer ma's book," he says. "She wrote it for you and you can't even–"

And what can I do but hit him across his stupid lughole of a mouth?

I'm getting taller and bigger and he comes off worst in the fight but he don't seem to mind all that much. Even when we get back to work, he's still giggling and making a big show outta reading the plans.

"Mighty complicated, these instruckshuns," he says, a big smile across his bloody lips.

"Just effing get on with it!"

"Fine, fine," he says. "First step is what we were already doing. Tearing down all the internal walls." He looks up. "I could write it down for you."

My Noise rages red at him but Noise is useless as a weapon.

Unless yer the Mayor.

I didn't think life could turn more to crap but it always does, don't it? Bombs and towers falling and having to work with Davy and the Mayor paying me special attenshun and–

(and I don't know where she is)

(and I don't know what the Mayor's gonna do to her)

(and did she plant the bombs?)

(did she?)

I turn back round to the work site.

1150 pairs of Spackle eyes are watching us, watching *me*, like they're just effing farm animals looking up from their grazing cuz they heard a loud noise.

Stupid effing *sheep*.

"GET TO WORK!" I shout.

"You look like hell," Mayor Ledger says, as I fall onto my bed.

"Stuff it," I say.

"Working you hard, is he?" He brings me over the dinner that's already waiting for us. It don't even look like he ate too much of mine before I got here.

"Ain't he working *you* hard?" I say, digging in to the food.

"I think he's forgotten about me, truth to tell." He sits back on his own bed. "I haven't spoken to him in I don't know how long."

I look up at him. His Noise is grey, like he's hiding something, tho that ain't unusual.

"I've just been doing my rubbish duties," he says, watching me eat. "Listening to people talk."

"And what're they saying?" I ask, cuz it seems like he wants to talk.

"Well," he says. His Noise shifts uncomfortably.

"Well what?"

And then I see the reason his Noise is so flat is cuz there's something he don't wanna tell me but feels like he has to, so here it comes.

"That house of healing," he says. "That one in particular."

"What about it?" I say, trying not to make it sound important, failing.

"It's closed down," he says. "Empty."

I stop eating. "What do you mean, empty?"

"I mean *empty*," he says gently, cuz he knows it's bad news. "There's no one there, not even the patients. Everyone's gone."

"Gone?" I whisper.

Gone.

I stand up tho there ain't nowhere to go, my stupid plate of dinner still in my hand.

"Gone where? What's he done with her?"

"He hasn't done anything," Mayor Ledger says. "Your friend ran. That's what I heard. Ran off with the women just before the tower fell." He rubs his chin. "Everyone else was arrested and taken to the prisons. But your friend ... got away."

He says *got away* like that's not what he means, like what he means is she was planning to get away all along.

"You can't know that," I say. "You can't know that's true about her."

He shrugs. "Maybe not," he says. "But I heard it from one of the soldiers who was guarding the house of healing."

"No," I say, but I don't know what I mean. "No."

"How well did you really know her?" Mayor Ledger says.

"You shut up."

I'm breathing hard, my chest rising and falling.

It's good that she ran, ain't it?

Ain't it?

She was in danger and now—
(but)
(but did she blow up the tower?)
(why didn't she tell me she was going to?)
(did she lie to me?)
And I shouldn't think it, I shouldn't think it, but here it
comes—
She promised.
And she left.
She left *me*.
(Viola?)
(did you leave me?)

21

THE MINE

{VIOLA}

I OPEN MY EYES to the sound of wings flapping outside the door, something I already know in the few days I've been here means that the bats have returned to the caves after their night's hunting, that the sun is about to rise, that it's almost time to get myself out of bed.

Some women start to stir, stretching in their cots. Others are still dead to the world, still snoring, still farting, still drifting on in the empty nothing of sleep.

I spend a second wishing I was still there, too.

The sleeping quarters is basically just a long shack, swept earth floor, wood walls, wood door, barely any windows and only an iron stove in the centre for not enough heat. The rest is just a row of cots stretched from one end to the other, full of sleeping women.

As the newest arrival, I'm at one end.

And I'm watching the occupant of the bed at the other end. She sits up straight, body fully under her command, like she never actually sleeps, just puts herself on pause until she can start work again.

Mistress Coyle turns in her cot, sets her feet on the floor, and looks over the other sleepers straight at me.

Checking on me first.

To see, no doubt, if I've run off sometime in the night to find Todd.

I don't believe he's dead. And I don't believe he told the Mayor on us, either.

There must be another answer.

I look back at Mistress Coyle, unmoving.

Not gone, I think. *Not yet*.

But mainly because I don't even know where we are.

We're not by the ocean. Not even close, as far as I can tell, though that's not saying much because secrecy is the watchword of the camp. No one gives information out unless it's absolutely necessary. That's in case anyone gets captured on a bombing raid or, now that the Answer has started running out of things like flour and medicine, raids for supplies as well.

Mistress Coyle guards information as her most valuable resource.

All I know is that the camp is at an old mine, started up – like so many other things seem to have been on this planet – with great optimism after the first landings but abandoned after just a few years. There are a number of shacks around the openings to a couple of deep caves. The shacks, some new, some from the mining days, serve as sleeping quarters and meeting rooms and dining halls and so on.

The caves – the ones where there aren't bats, anyway – are the food and supply stores, always worryingly low, always guarded fiercely by Mistress Lawson, still fretting over the children she left behind and taking out her fretting on anyone who requests another blanket for the cold.

Deeper in the caves are the mines, originally sunk to find coal or salt and then when none were found, diamonds and then gold, which weren't found either, as if they'd do anyone any good in this place anyway. The mines are now where the weapons and explosives are hidden. I don't know how they got here or where they came from, but if the camp is found, they'll be detonated, probably wiping us all off the map.

But for now it's a camp that's near a natural well and hidden by the forest around it. The only entrance is through the trees at the bottom of the path Mistress Coyle and I bumped our way down, and it's so steep and hard you'd hear intruders come from a long way away.

"And they'll come," Mistress Coyle said to me on my first day. "We'll just have to make sure we're ready to meet them."

"Why haven't they come already?" I asked. "People must know there's a mine here."

All she did was wink at me and touch the side of her nose.

"What's *that* supposed to mean?" I asked.

But that was all I got, because information is her most valuable resource, isn't it?

At breakfast, I get my usual snubbing by Thea and the other apprentices I recognize, none of whom will say a word to me, still blaming me for Maddy's death, blaming me for somehow being a traitor, blaming me for this whole sodding war, for all I know.

Not that I care.

Because I don't.

I leave them to the dining hall, and I take my plate of grey porridge out in the cold morning to some rocks near the mouth of one of the caves. As I eat, I watch the camp start to wake itself, start to put itself together for the things that terrorists spend their days doing.

The biggest surprise is how few people there are. Maybe a hundred. That's all. That's the big Answer causing all the fuss in New Prentisstown by blowing things up. One hundred people. Mistresses and apprentices, former patients and others, too, disappearing in the night and returning in the morning, or keeping the camp running for those that come and go, tending to the few horses the Answer has and the oxes that pull the carts and the hens we get our eggs from and a million other things that need doing.

But only a hundred people. Not enough to have a whisper of a prayer if the Mayor's *real* army comes marching down towards us.

"All right, Hildy?"

"Hi, Wilf," I say, as he comes up to me, a plate of porridge in his hands, too. I scoot over so he can sit near me. He doesn't say anything, just eats his porridge and lets me eat mine.

"Wilf?" we both hear. Jane, Wilf's wife, is coming for us, two steaming mugs in her hands. She picks her way over the rocks towards us, stumbling once, spilling some coffee and causing Wilf to rise halfway up, but she recovers. "Here ya go!" she practically shouts, thrusting the mugs at us.

"Thank you," I say, taking mine.

She shoves her hands under her armpits against the cold and smiles, eyes wide and searching around, like she eats with them. "Awful cold to be eating outside," she says, like an overly friendly demand that we explain ourselves.

"Yup," Wilf says, going back to his porridge.

"It's not too bad," I say, also going back to eating.

"Didja hear they got a grain store last night?" she says, lowering her voice to a whisper but somehow making it louder at the same time. "We can have *bread* again!"

"Yup," Wilf says again.

"D'you like bread?" she asks me.

"I do."

"Ya gotta have bread," she says, to the ground, to the sky, to the rocks. "Ya gotta have bread."

And then she's back off to the dining hall, not another word, though Wilf doesn't seem to much mind or even notice. But I know, I *definitely* know that Wilf's clear and even Noise, his lack of words, his seeming blankness doesn't describe all of him, not even close.

Wilf and Jane were refugees, fleeing into Haven as the army swept behind them, passing us on the road as Todd slept off his fever in Carbonel Downs. Jane fell ill on the trip and, after asking directions, Wilf took her straight to Mistress Forth's house of healing, where Jane was still recovering when the army invaded. Wilf, whose Noise is as free of deception as anyone's on this planet, was assumed by the soldiers to be an idiot and so allowed to visit his wife when no other man was.

When the women ran, Wilf helped. When I asked him why, all he did was shrug and say, "They were gone take Jane." He hid the less able women on his cart as they fled, built a hidey-hole in it so others could return for missions, and for weeks on end has risked his life taking them to and fro because the soldiers have always assumed a man so transparent couldn't be hiding anything.

All of which has been a surprise to the leaders of the Answer.

But none of which is a surprise to me.

He saved me and Todd once when he didn't have to. He saved Todd again when there was even more danger. He was even ready the first night I was here to turn right back around to help me find him, but Sergeant Hammar knows Wilf's face now, knows that he should have been arrested, so any trip back is pretty much a death sentence.

I take a last spoonful of my porridge and sigh heavily as I pop it into my mouth. I could be sighing at the cold, sighing at the boring porridge, sighing at the lack of anything to do in camp.

But, somehow, Wilf knows. Somehow, Wilf always knows.

"Ah'm shur he's okay, Hildy," he says, finishing up his own porridge. "He survives, does our Todd."

I look up into the cold morning sun and I swallow again, though there's no porridge left in my throat.

"Keep yerself strong," Wilf stays, standing. "Strong for what's comin."

I blink. "What's coming?" I ask as he walks on towards the dining hall, drinking his mug of coffee.

He just keeps on going.

I finish my coffee, rubbing my arms to gather some heat, thinking I'll ask her again today, no, I'll *tell* her I'm coming on the next mission, that I need to find–

"You're sitting out here all by yourself?"

I look up. Lee, the blond soldier, is standing there, smiling all toothy.

I immediately feel my face go hot.

"No, no," I say, standing straight up, turning away from him and picking up the plate.

"You don't have to leave–" he's saying.

"No, I'm finished–"

"Viola–"

"All yours–"

"That's not what I meant–"

But I'm already stomping back to the dining hall, cursing myself for the redness of my face.

Lee isn't the only man. Well, he's hardly a *man*, but like Wilf, he and Magnus can no longer pretend to be soldiers and go to the city, now that their faces are known.

But there are others who can. Because that's the biggest secret of all about the Answer.

At least a third of the people here are men, men who pretend to be soldiers to shuttle women in and out of the city, men who help Mistress Coyle with the planning and targets, men with expertise on handling explosives, men who believe in the cause and want to fight against the Mayor and all he stands for.

Men who've lost wives and daughters and mothers and who are fighting to save them or fighting to avenge their memories.

Mostly it's memories.

I suppose it's useful if everyone thinks it's only women; it allows men to come and go, even if the Mayor surely knows what's what, which is probably why he's denying the cure to so much of his own army, why the Answer's own supply of cure is becoming more burden than blessing.

I cast a glance quickly back to Lee behind me and forward again.

I'm not sure of his reason for being here.

I haven't been able–

I haven't had the *chance* to ask him yet.

I'm not paying attention as I reach the dining room door and don't really notice when it opens before I can take the handle.

I look up into Mistress Coyle's face.

I don't even greet her.

"Take me with you on the next raid," I say.

Her expression doesn't change. "You know why you can't."

"Todd would join us," I say. "In a *second*."

"Others aren't so sure about that, my girl." I open my mouth to reply but she interrupts. "If he's even still alive.

Which matters not, because we can't afford to have you captured. You're the most valuable prize of all. The girl who can help the President when the ships land."

"I–"

She holds up her hand. "I won't have this fight with you again. There is too much important work to do."

The camp feels silent now. The people behind her have stopped moving as we stare at one another, no one willing to ask her to get out of the way, not even Mistresses Forth and Nadari, who wait there patiently. Like Thea, they've barely spoken to me since my arrival, all these acolytes of Mistress Coyle, all these people who wouldn't dare to dream of speaking to her the way I'm speaking to her now.

They treat me as if I'm a little dangerous.

I'm slightly surprised to find I kind of like it.

I look into her eyes, into the unyieldingness of them. "I won't forgive you," I say quietly, as if I'm only talking to her. "I won't. Not now, not ever."

"I don't want your forgiveness," she says, equally quietly. "But one day, you *will* understand."

And then her eyes glint and she pulls her mouth into a smile. "You know," she says, raising her voice. "I think it's time you had some employment."

22

1017

[TODD]

"CAN'T YOU EFFING THINGS move any faster?"

The four or five Spackle nearest to me flinch away, tho I ain't even spoken that loud.

"Get a *move* on!"

And as ever, no thoughts, no Noise, no nothing.

They can only be getting the cure in the fodder I still have to shovel out. But why? Why when no one else is? It makes them a sea of silent clicking and white backs bent into the cold and white mouths sending out puffs of steam and white arms pulling up handfuls of dirt and when yer looking out across the monastery grounds, all those white bodies working, well, they could be a herd of sheep, couldn't they?

Even tho if you look close you can see family groups and husbands and wives and fathers and sons. You can see older ones lifting smaller amounts more slowly. You can see younger ones helping 'em, trying to keep us from seeing that the older ones can't work too hard. You can see a baby strapped to its mother's chest with an old piece of cloth. You can see an especially tall one directing others along a faster work chain. You can see a small female packing mud around the infected number band of a larger female. You can see 'em working together, keeping their heads down, trying not to be the one who gets seen by me or Davy or the guards behind the barbed wire.

You can see all that if you look close.

But it's easier if you don't.

We can't give 'em shovels, of course. They could use 'em against us as weapons and the soldiers on the walls get twitchy if a Spackle even stretches its arms up too high. So there they all are, bending to the ground, digging, moving rocks, silent as clouds, suffering and not doing nothing about it.

I got a weapon, tho. They gave me the rifle back.

Cuz where am I gonna go?

Now that she's gone.

"Hurry it *up*!" I shout at the Spackle, my Noise rising red at the thought of her.

I catch Davy looking over at me, a surprised grin on his face. I turn away and cross the field to another group. I'm halfway there when I hear a louder click.

I look round till I find the source.

But it's only ever the same one.

1017, staring at me again, with that look that ain't forgiveness. He moves his eyes to my hands.

It's only then I realize I've got them both clenched hard around my rifle.

I can't even remember taking it off my shoulder.

Even with all this Spackle labour, it's still gonna take a coupla months to even come close to finishing this building, whatever it is, and by that time it'll be mid-winter and the Spackle won't have the shelter they were sposed to be building for themselves and I know they live outside more than men do but I don't think even they can live unsheltered in the winter frost and I ain't heard of nowhere else they're gonna be going yet.

Still, we had all the internal walls torn down in seven days, two ahead of schedule, and no Spackle even died, tho we did have a few with broken arms. Those Spackle were taken away by soldiers.

We ain't seen 'em since.

By the end of the second week after the tower bomb, we've nearly dug all the trenches and blocks for the foundayshuns to be poured, something Davy and I are sposed to supervize even tho it's gonna be the Spackle who know how to do it.

"Pa says they were the labour that rebuilt the city after the Spackle War," Davy says. "Tho you wouldn't know it from this bunch."

He spits out a shell from the seeds he's eating. Food's getting a bit scarce what with the Answer adding supply raids to the ongoing bombs but Davy always manages to scrounge up something. We're sitting on a pile of rocks, looking out over the one big field, now dug up with square holes and ditches and so full of rock piles there's barely any room for the Spackle to crowd into.

But they do, cramming onto the edges and huddling together in the cold. And they don't say nothing about it.

Davy spits out another shell. "You ever gonna talk again?"

"I talk," I say.

"No, you scream at yer workforce and you grunt at me. That ain't talking." He's spits out another shell, high and long, hitting the nearest Spackle in the head. It just brushes it away and keeps on digging out the last of a trench.

"She left ya," Davy says. "Get over it."

My Noise rises. "*Shut up.*"

"I don't mean it in a bad way."

I turn to look at him, eyes wide.

"*What?*" he says. "I'm just saying, you know? She left, don't mean she's dead or nothing." Spit. "From what I remember, that filly can take plenty care of herself."

There's a memory in his Noise of being electrocuted on the river road. It should make me smile, but it don't, cuz she's standing right there in his Noise, standing right there and taking him down.

Standing right there and not standing right here.

(where'd she go?)

(where'd she effing *go*?)

Mayor Ledger told me just after the tower bombs that the army had gone straight for the ocean cuz they'd got a tip-off that that's where the Answer were hiding–

(was it me? did he hear it in me? I burn at the thought–)

But when Mr Hammar and his men got there, they didn't find nothing but long-abandoned buildings and half-sunken boats.

Cuz the informayshun turned out to be false.

And I burn at that, too.

(did she lie to me?)

(did she do it on purpose?)

"Jesus, pigpiss." Davy spits again. "It's not like any of the *rest* of us got girlfriends. They're all in ruddy *jail* or setting off bombs every week or walking around in groups so big you can't even talk to 'em."

"She ain't my girlfriend," I say.

"Not the point," he says. "All it means is that yer just as alone as the rest of us, so get over it."

There's a sudden, ugly strength of feeling in his Noise, which he wipes away in an instant when he sees me watching him. "What're you looking at?"

"Nothing," I say.

"Damn right." He stands, takes his rifle and stomps back into the field.

Somehow 1017 keeps ending up in my part of the work. I'm mainly in the back part of the fields, finishing up digging the trenches. Davy's near the front, getting Spackle to snap together the pre-formed guide walls we'll be using once the concrete gets poured. 1017's sposed to be doing that, but every time I look up, there he is, nearest me again no matter how many times I send him back.

He's working, sure, digging up his handfuls of dirt or piling up the sod in even rows, but always looking for me, always trying to catch my eye.

Clicking at me.

I walk towards him, my hand up on the stock of my rifle, grey clouds starting to move in overhead. "I sent you over to Davy," I bark. "What're you doing here?"

Davy, hearing his name, calls from far across the field. "What?"

I call back, "Why do you keep letting this one back over here?"

"What the hell are you talking about?" Davy yells. "They all look the same!"

"It's 1017!"

Davy gives an exaggerated shrug. "*So?*"

I hear a click, a rude and sarcastic one, from behind me.

I turn and I swear 1017 is *smiling* at me.

"You little piece of–" I start to say, reaching my rifle round my front.

Which is when I see a flash of Noise.

Coming from 1017.

Quick as anything but clear, too, me standing in front of him, reaching for my rifle, nothing more than what he's seeing with his eyes–

Except a flash as he grabs the rifle from me–

And then it's gone.

I've still got the rifle in my hands, 1017 still knee-deep in the ditch.

No Noise at all.

I look him up and down. He's skinnier than he used to be, but they *all* are, they never get quite enough fodder of a day, and I'm wondering if 1017's been skipping meals altogether.

So he don't take no cure.

"What're you playing at?" I ask him.

But he's back at work, arms and hands digging for more dirt, ribs showing thru the side of his white, white skin.

And he don't say nothing.

"Why do we keep giving 'em the cure if yer pa's taking it away from everyone else?"

Me and Davy are lunching the next day. The clouds are heavy in the sky and it'll probably start raining soon, the first rain in a good long while, and it'll be cold rain, too, but we've got orders to keep working no matter what so we're spending the day watching the Spackle pour out the first concrete from the mixer.

Ivan brought it in this morning, healed but limping, his Noise raging. I wonder where he thinks the power is *now*.

"Well, it keeps 'em from plotting, don't it?" Davy says. "Keeps 'em from passing along ideas to each other."

"But they can do that with the clicking." I think for a second. "Can't they?"

Davy just gives a *who cares, pigpiss* shrug. "Got any of that sandwich left?"

I hand him my sandwich, keeping an eye out over the Spackle. "Shouldn't we know what they're thinking?" I say. "Wouldn't that be a good thing to know?"

I look out over the field for 1017 who, sure enough, is looking back at me.

Plick. The first drop of rain hits me on the eyelash.

"Aw, crap," Davy says, looking up.

* * *

It don't let up for three days. The site gets muckier and muckier but the Mayor still wants us to keep on somehow so those three days are spent slipping and sliding thru mud and putting up huge tarpaulins on frames to cover big parts of the field.

Davy's got the inside work, bossing Spackle around to keep the tarpaulin frames in place. I spend most of my time out in the rain, trying to keep the edges of the tarpaulin pinned to the ground with heavy stones.

It's ruddy *stupid* work.

"Hurry up!" I shout to the Spackle helping me get one of the last edges pinned to the ground. My fingers are freezing cuz no one's given us gloves and there ain't been no Mayor round to ask. "Ow!" I put a bloodied knuckle up to my lips, having scraped my hand for the millionth time.

The Spackle keep at it with the rocks, seeming oblivious to the rain, which is good cuz there ain't room under the tarpaulins for all of 'em to shelter.

"Hey," I say, raising my voice. "Watch the edge! Watch that—"

A gust of wind rips away the whole sheet of tarpaulin we just pinned down. One of the Spackle keeps hold of it as it flies up, taking him with it and tumbling him hard down to the ground. I leap over him as I chase after the tarpaulin, twisting and rolling away across the muddy field and up a little slope, and I've just about got a hand on it—

And I slip badly, skidding right down the other side of the slope on my rump—

And I realize where I've run, where I've slipped—

I'm heading right down into the bog.

I grab at the mud to stop myself but there's nothing to hold on to and I drop right in with a *splat*.

"Gah!" I shout and try to stand. I'm up to my thighs in lime-covered Spackle shit, splattered all up my front and back, the stink of it making me retch–

And I see another flash of Noise.

Of me standing in the bog.

Of a Spackle standing right over me.

I look up.

There's a wall of Spackle staring.

And right in front of 'em all.

1017.

Above me.

With a huge stone in his hands.

He don't say nothing, just stands there with the stone, more'n big enough to do a lot of harm if thrown right.

"Yeah?" I say up to him. "That's what you want, ain't it?"

He just stares back.

I don't see the Noise again.

I reach up for my rifle, slowly.

"What's it gonna be?" I ask and he can see in my Noise just how ready I am, how ready I am to fight him.

How ready I am to–

I've got the rifle stock in my hand now.

But he's just staring at me.

And then he tosses the rock down on the ground and turns back towards the tarpaulin. I watch him go, five steps, then ten, and my body relaxes a bit.

It's when I'm pulling myself outta the bog that I hear it.

The click.

His rude click.

And I lose it.

I'm running towards him and I'm yelling but I don't know what I'm saying and Davy's turning round in shock as I reach the shelter of the tarpaulin just after 1017 and I'm running in with the rifle up above my head like I'm some stupid madman and 1017's turning to me but I don't give him a chance to do nothing and I knock him hard in the face with the butt of the rifle and he falls back on the ground and I lift the rifle again and bring it down and he raises his hands to protect himself and I hit him again and again and again–

In the hands–

And the face–

And in those skinny ribs–

And my Noise is raging–

And I hit–

And I hit–

And I hit–

And I'm screaming–

I'm screaming out–

"WHY DID YOU LEAVE?"

"WHY DID YOU LEAVE ME?"

And I hear the cold, crisp *snick* of his arm breaking.

* * *

It fills the air, louder than the rain or the wind, turning my stomach upside down, making a thick lump in my throat.

I stop, mid-swing.

Davy's staring at me, his mouth open.

All the Spackle are edging back, terrified.

And from the ground, 1017 is looking back up at me, red blood pouring from his weird nose and the corner of his too-high eyes but there's no sound coming from him, no Noise, no thoughts, no clicks, no nothing–

(and we're in the campsite and there's a dead Spackle on the ground and Viola's looking so scared and she's backing away from me and there's blood everywhere and I've done it again I've done it again and why did you go oh jesus dammit Viola why did you *leave–*)

And 1017 just looks at me.

And I swear to God, it's a look of triumph.

23

SOMETHING'S COMING

{VIOLA}

"WATER PUMP'S workin agin, Hildy."

"Thank you, Wilf." I hand him a tray of bread, the heat still coming off it. "Could you take these to Jane, please? She's setting the tables for breakfast."

He takes the tray, a flat little tune coming from his Noise. As he leaves the kitchen shack, I hear him call out, "Wife!"

"Why does he call you Hildy?" Lee says, appearing at the back door with a basket of flour he just pounded. He's wearing a sleeveless shirt and the skin up to his elbows is dusty white.

I look at his bare arms for a second and look away quickly.

Mistress Coyle put us to work together since he can't go back to New Prentisstown any more either.

No, I will certainly *not* forgive her.

"Hildy was the name of someone who helped us," I say. "Someone worth being called after."

"And by *us*, you mean–"

"Me and Todd, yes." I take the basket of flour from him and thump it down heavily on the table.

There's a silence, as there always seems to be when Todd's name comes up.

"No one's seen him, Viola," Lee says gently. "But they mostly go in at night so that doesn't–"

"She wouldn't tell me even if she did." I start separating the flour into bowls. "She thinks he's dead."

Lee shifts from foot to foot out. "But you say different."

I look at him. He smiles and I can't help but smile back. "And you believe me, do you?"

He shrugs. "Wilf believes you. And you'd be surprised how far the word of Wilf goes around here."

"No." I look out the window to where Wilf disappeared. "No, actually I wouldn't."

That day passes like the others and still we cook. That's our new employment, Lee and me, cooking. All of it, for the entire camp. We've learned how to make bread from a starting point of *wheat*, not even flour. We've learned how to skin squirrels, de-shell turtles and gut fish. We've learned how much base you need for soup to feed a hundred. We've learned how to peel potatoes and pears faster than possibly anyone on this whole stupid planet.

Mistress Coyle swears this is how wars are won.

"This isn't really why I signed up," Lee says, pulling another handful of feathers off the sixteenth forest fowl of the afternoon.

"At least signing up was your idea," I say, fingers cramping on my own fowl. The feathers hover in the air like a swarm of sticky flies, catching everywhere they touch. I've got little green puffs under my fingernails, in the crooks of my elbows, glopped in the corner of my eyes.

I know this because Lee's got them all over his face, too, all through his long golden hair and in the matching golden hair on his forearms.

I feel my face flush again and pull out a furious rip of feathers.

A day turned into two, turned into three, turned into a week, turned into the week after and the week after that, cooking with Lee, washing up with Lee, sitting out three days of solid rain stuck in this shack with Lee.

And still. And *still*.

Something's coming, something's being prepared for, no one's telling me anything.

And I'm still stuck *here*.

Lee tosses a plucked fowl onto the table and picks up another one. "We're going to make this species extinct if we're not careful."

"It's the only thing Magnus can shoot," I say. "Everything else is too fast."

"A whole animal lost," Lee says, "because the Answer lacked for an optician."

I laugh, too loud. I roll my eyes at myself.

I finish my own fowl and pick up a new one. "I'm doing three of these for every two of yours," I say. "*And* I did more loaves this morning *and*–"

"You burnt half of them."

"Because *you* stoked the oven too hot!"

"I'm not made for cooking," he says, smiling. "I'm made for soldiering."

I gasp. "And you think *I'm* made for cooking–"

But he's laughing and keeps laughing even when I throw a handful of wet feathers at him, smacking him straight on the eye. "Ow," he says, wiping it away. "You got some aim, Viola. We really need to get a gun in your hands."

I turn my face quickly back down to the millionth fowl in my lap.

"Or maybe not," he says, more quietly.

"Have you–?" I stop.

"Have I what?"

I lick my lips, which is a mistake because then I have to spit out a mouthful of feathery puffs, so when I do finally say it, it comes out more exasperated than I meant. "Have you ever shot someone?"

"No." He sits up straighter. "Have you?"

I shake my head and see him relax, which makes me immediately say, "But I've *been* shot."

He sits back up. "No way!"

I say it before I mean to, before I even know it's coming, and then I'm saying it and I realize I've never said it, not out loud, not to myself, not ever, not since it happened, and yet here it is, tumbling out in a room full of floating feathers.

"And I've stabbed someone." I stop plucking. "To death."

My body feels suddenly twice as heavy in the silence that follows.

When I start to cry, Lee just hands me a kitchen towel and lets me, not crowding me or saying anything stupid or even asking about it, though he must be dying of curiosity. He just lets me cry.

Which is exactly right.

"Yes, but we're gaining sympathy," Lee says near the end of dinner with Wilf and Jane. I'm putting off finishing because as soon as I do, we have go back to the kitchens to start preparing the yeasts to cook *tomorrow's* bread. You wouldn't believe how much bloody bread a hundred people can eat.

I take half of my last bite. "I'm just saying there aren't very many of you."

"Of *us*," Lee says, looking at me seriously. "And we've got spies working throughout the city and people join us when they can. Things are only getting worse there. They're rationing *food* now and no one's getting the cure any more. They're going to have to start turning against him."

"And so many in prisons," Jane adds. "Hundreds of women, all locked up, all chained together underground, starving and dying by the dozen."

"Wife!" Wilf snaps.

"Ah'm only sayin what Ah heard!"

"Yoo din't hear nothin of the sort."

Jane looks sullen. "Don't mean it's not true."

"There are a lot of people who'd support us in prison, though," Lee says. "And so that might turn out–"

He stops.

"What?" I ask, looking up. "Turn out what?"

He doesn't answer me, just looks over to another table where Mistress Coyle is sitting with Mistresses Braithwaite,

Forth, Waggoner and Barker, and Thea, too, like they always do, discussing things, whispering in low voices, devising secret orders for other people to carry out.

"Nothing," Lee says, seeing Mistress Coyle stand and come towards us.

"I'm going to need the cart hitched up for tonight, Wilf, please," she says, approaching our table.

"Yes, Mistress," he says, getting to his feet.

"Eat a little longer," she says, stopping him. "This isn't forced labour."

"Ah'm happy to do it," Wilf says, brushing off his trousers and leaving us.

"Who are you blowing up tonight?" I ask.

Mistress Coyle pulls her lips tight. "I think that's enough for now, Viola."

"I want to come," I say. "If you're going back into the city tonight, I want to come with you."

"Patience, my girl," she says. "You'll have your day."

"Which day?" I ask as she walks off. "*When?*"

"Patience," she says again.

But she says it impatiently.

It gets dark earlier and earlier every day. I sit outside on a pile of rocks as night falls, watching tonight's mission-takers head on out to the carts, their bags packed with secret things. Some of the men have Noise now, taking reduced amounts of cure from our own dwindling supply stashed in the cave. They take enough to blend in with the city but not enough to give anything away. It's a tricky balance, and it's getting more and more dangerous for our men to be on city streets, but still they go.

And as the people of New Prentisstown sleep tonight, they'll be stolen from and bombed, all in the name of what's right.

"Hey," Lee says, hardly more than a shadow in the twilight as he sits down next to me.

"Hey," I say back.

"You okay?"

"Why wouldn't I be?"

"Yeah." He picks up a stone and tosses it into the night. "Why wouldn't you be?"

Stars start to appear in the sky. My ships are up there somewhere. People who might've been able to help us, no, who *would* have helped us if I could've contacted them. Simone Watkin and Bradley Tench, good people, *smart* people who would have stopped all this stupidity and the explosions and–

I feel my throat clench again.

"You really killed someone," Lee says, tossing another stone.

"Yeah," I say, pulling my knees up to my chest.

Lee waits a moment. "With Todd?"

"*For* Todd," I say. "To save him. To save *us*."

Now that the sun's gone, the real cold moves in swiftly. I hold my knees tighter.

"She's afraid of you, you know," he says. "Mistress Coyle. She thinks you're powerful."

I look over at him, trying to see him in the dark. "That's stupid."

"I heard her say it to Mistress Braithwaite. Said you could lead whole armies if you put your mind to it."

I shake my head but of course he can't see. "She doesn't even know me."

"Yeah, but she's smart."

"And everyone here follows her like little lambs."

"Everyone but you." He bumps me with his shoulder in a friendly way. "Maybe that's what she's talking about."

We start to hear the low rumble from the caves that means the bats are readying themselves.

"Why are *you* here?" I ask. "Why do you follow her?"

I've asked before but he's always changed the subject.

But maybe tonight's different. It sure *feels* different.

"My father died in the Spackle War," he says.

"Lots of fathers did," I say and I think of Corinne, wondering where she is, wondering if–

"I don't really remember him," Lee's saying. "It was just me and my mother and my older sister growing up, really. And my sister–" he laughs. "You'd like her. All mouth and fire and we had some fights you wouldn't believe."

He laughs again but more quietly. "When the army came, Siobhan wanted to fight but Mum didn't. I wanted to fight, too, but Siobhan and Mum really went at it, Siobhan ready to take up arms and Mum practically having to bar the door to keep her from running out into the streets when the army came marching in."

The rumbling is getting louder and the bats' Noise starts to echo through the cave opening. **Fly, fly**, they say. **Away, away**.

"And then it was out of our hands, wasn't it?" he says.

"The army was here and that night they took all the women away to the houses east of town. Mum said to cooperate, you know, 'just for now, just to see where it goes, maybe he's not all that bad.' That sort of thing."

I don't respond and I'm glad it's dark so he can't see my face.

"But Siobhan wasn't going to go without a fight, was she? She shouted and screamed at the soldiers and refused to go along and Mum's just begging for her to stop, to not make them angry, but Siobhan–" He stops and makes a clicking sound with his tongue. "Siobhan punched the first soldier who tried to move her by force."

He takes a deep breath. "And then it was uproar. I tried to fight and the next thing I know I'm on the ground with my ears ringing and a soldier's knee in my back and Mum is screaming but there's nothing from Siobhan and I black out and when I wake up, I'm alone in my house."

F₃y, f₃y, we hear, just inside the cave mouth. Away, away, away.

"I looked for them when the restrictions eased," he says, "but I never found them. I looked in every cabin and dormitory and at every house of healing. And finally, at the last one, Mistress Coyle answered."

He pauses and looks up. "Here they come."

The bats swarm out of the caves, like the world's been tipped on its side and they're being poured out over the top of us, a flood of greater darkness against the night sky. The sheer *whoosh* of them makes it impossible to talk for a minute so we just sit and watch them.

Each is at least two metres across, with furred wings and

short stubby ears and a green glowing dot of phosphorus on each outstretched wingtip which they use somehow to confuse and stun the moths and bugs they eat. The dots glow in the night, making a blanket of temporary fluttering stars above us. We sit, surrounded by the slapping of wings, the cheeping of their Noise, the **fly fly away away away**.

And in five minutes they're gone, out into the surrounding forest, not to return until just before dawn.

"Something's coming," Lee says in the quiet that follows. "You know that. I can't say what but I'm going along because there's one more place to look for them."

"Then I'll go, too," I say.

"She won't let you." He turns to me. "But I promise you, I'll look for Todd. With the same eyes I look for Siobhan and my mother, I'll look for him."

A bell chimes out over the camp, signalling all raiding teams are off into town and all remaining people in camp are to go to bed. Lee and I sit in the dark for a while longer, his shoulder brushed up against mine, and mine brushed up against his.

24

PRISON WALLS

[TODD]

"NOT BAD," says the Mayor from atop Morpeth, "for an unskilled workforce."

"There'd be more," Davy says, "but it rained and then everything was just *mud*."

"No, no," the Mayor says, casting his eyes around the field. "You've done admirably, both of you, managing so much in just a month."

We all take a minute to look at what we've managed admirably. We've got all the concrete foundayshuns poured for a single long building. Every guide wall is up, some have even started to be filled in by the stones we took from the monastery's internal walls, and the tarpaulin makes a kind of roof. It already looks like a building.

He's right, we have done admirably.

Us and 1150 Spackle.

"Yes," says the Mayor. "Very pleasing."

Davy's Noise is taking on a pinkish glow that's

uncomfortable to look at.

"So what is it?" I ask.

The Mayor looks my way. "What's what?"

"This." I gesture at the building. "What's it sposed to be?"

"You finish building it, Todd, and I promise to invite you to the grand opening."

"It's not for the Spackle, tho, is it?"

The Mayor frowns slightly. "No, Todd, it's not."

I rub the back of my neck with my hand and I can hear some clanking in Davy's Noise, clanks that are gonna get louder if he thinks I'm messing up his moment of praise. "It's just," I say, "there's been frost the past three nights and it's only getting colder."

The Mayor turns Morpeth to face me. **BOy colt**, he thinks. **BOy colt steps back**.

I step back without even thinking.

The Mayor's eyebrows raise. "Are you wanting heaters for your workforce?"

"Well," I look at the ground and at the building and at the Spackle who are doing their best to stay at the far end, as much away from the three of us as is possible to do when there are so many crowded into such a limited space. "Snow might come," I say. "I don't know that they'll survive."

"Oh, they're tougher than you think, Todd." The Mayor's voice is low and full of something I can't put my finger on. "A lot tougher."

I look down again. "Yeah," I say. "Okay."

"I'll have Private Farrow bring in some small fission heaters if that will make you feel better."

280

I blink. "Really?"

"*Really?*" Davy says.

"They've done good work," the Mayor says, "under your direction, and you've shown real dedication these past weeks, Todd. Real *leadership.*"

He smiles, almost warmly.

"I know you're the kind of soul who hates to see others suffer." He keeps hold of my eye, almost daring me to break it. "Your tenderness does you credit."

"*Tenderness,*" Davy snickers.

"I'm proud of you." The Mayor gathers up his reins. "*Both* of you. And you will be rewarded for your efforts."

Davy's Noise beams again as the Mayor rides outta the monastery gates. "Didja hear that?" he says, waggling his eyebrows. "Rewards, my tender pigpiss."

"Shut up, Davy." I'm already walking down the guide wall and towards the back of the building where there's the last of the clear ground and so that's where all the Spackle are having to crowd themselves. They get outta my way as I move thru them. "Heaters're coming," I say, putting it in my Noise, too. "Things'll be better."

But they just keep doing all they can not to touch me.

"I *said* things'll be better!"

Stupid ungrateful—

I stop. I take in a breath. I keep walking.

I get to the back of the building where we've leaned a few unused guide walls against the building frame, forming a nook. "You can come out now," I say.

281

There's no sound for a minute, then a bit of rustling and 1017 emerges, his arm in a sling made up from one of my few shirts. He's skinnier than ever, some redness still creeping up his arm from the break but it seems to be finally fading. "I managed to scrounge some painkillers," I say, taking 'em outta my pocket.

He snatches 'em from my hand with a slap, scratching my palm.

"Watch it," I say, thru clenched teeth. "You wanna be taken away to whatever they do with lame Spackle?"

There's a burst of Noise from him, one I've grown to expect, and it's the usual thing, him standing over me with a rifle, him hitting me and hitting me, me pleading for him to stop, him breaking *my* arm.

"Yeah," I say. "Whatever."

"Playing with yer pet?" Davy's come round, too, leaning against the building with his arms crossed. "You know, when horses break their legs, they shoot 'em."

"He ain't a horse."

"Nah," Davy says. "He's a sheep."

I puff out my lips. "Thanks for not telling yer pa."

Davy shrugs. "Whatever, pigpiss, as long as it don't screw up our reward."

1017 makes his rude clicking at both of us, but mostly at me.

"He don't seem too grateful, tho," Davy says.

"Yeah, well, I saved him twice now." I look at 1017, look right into eyes that never leave mine. "I ain't doing it again."

"You say that," Davy says, "but everyone knows you will." He nods at 1017. "Even him." Davy's eyes widen in a mock.

"It's cuz yer *tender*."

"Shut up."

But he's already laughing and leaving and 1017 just stares at me and stares at me.

And I stare back.

I saved him.

(I saved him for her)

(if she was here, she could see, see how I saved him)

(if she was here)

(but she ain't)

I clench my fists and then force myself to unclench them.

New Prentisstown has changed in the past month, I see it every day as we ride home.

Part of it's winter coming. The leaves on the trees have turned purple and red and dropped to the ground, leaving the tall winter skeletons behind them. The evergreens have kept their needles but dropped their cones and the reachers have pulled their branches tight into their trunks, leaving naked poles to sit out the cold. All of it plus the constant darker skies makes it look like the town's going hungry.

Which it is. The army invaded at the end of harvest, so there were food stocks, but there's no one left in the outer settlements to bring in food to trade and the Answer are keeping up their bombs and food raids. One night a whole storehouse of wheat was taken, so completely and success-fully it's obvious now there's people in the town and the army who've been helping 'em.

Which is bad news for the town and the army.

The curfew got lowered two weeks ago and again last week till no one's allowed out after dark at all except for a few patrols. The square in front of the cathedral has become a place for bonfires, of books, of the wordly belongings of people found to have helped the Answer, of a bunch of healer uniforms from when the Mayor closed the last house of healing. And practically no one takes the cure no more, except some of the Mayor's closest men, Mr Morgan, Mr O'Hare, Mr Tate, Mr Hammar, men from old Prentisstown who've been with him for years. Loyalty, I guess.

Me and Davy ain't never been given it in the first place so there weren't never a chance for him to take it away.

"Maybe that's our reward," Davy says as we ride. "Maybe he'll get some outta the cellar and we'll finally see what it's like."

Our *reward*, I think. *We*.

I run my hand along Angharrad's flank, feeling the chill in her skin. "Almost home, girl," I whisper twixt her ears. "Nice warm barn."

Warm, she thinks. **Boy colt**.

"Angharrad," I say back.

Horses ain't pets and they're half-crazy all the time but I've been learning if you treat 'em right, they get to know you.

Boy colt, she thinks again and it's like I'm part of her herd.

"Maybe the reward is women!" Davy says suddenly. "Yeah! Maybe he's gonna give us some women and finally make a real man outta you."

"Shut up," I say, but it don't turn into a fight. Come to think of it, we ain't had a fight in a good long while.

We're just used to each other, I guess.

We don't hardly see women no more neither. When the communicayshuns tower fell, they were all confined to their houses again, except when teams of 'em are working the fields, readying for next year's planting, under guard from armed soldiers. The visits from husbands and sons and fathers are now once a week at most.

We hear stories about soldiers and women, stories about soldiers getting into dormitories at night, stories about awful things going on that no one gets punished for.

And that don't even count the women in the prisons, prisons I've only seen from the cathedral tower, a group of converted buildings in the far west of town down near the foot of the waterfalls. Who knows what goes on inside? They're way far away, outta sight of everyone 'cept for those that guard 'em.

Kinda like the Spackle.

"Jesus, Todd," Davy says, "the racket you make by *thinking* all the time."

Which is exactly the kinda thing I've learned to ignore from Davy. Except this time, he called me *Todd*.

We leave our horses in the barn near the cathedral. Davy walks me back to the cathedral, tho I don't really need a guard no more.

Cuz where would I go?

I go in the front door and I hear, "Todd?"

The Mayor's waiting for me.

"Yes, sir?" I say.

"Always so polite," he smiles, walking towards me, boots clicking on the marble. "You seem better lately, calmer." He stops a metre away. "Have you been using the tool?"

Huh?

"What tool?" I ask.

He sighs a little. And then–

I AM THE CIRCLE AND THE CIRCLE IS ME.

I put a hand up to the side of my head. "How do you do that?"

"Noise can be used, Todd," he says. "If you're disciplined enough. And the first step is using the tool."

"I am the Circle and the Circle is me?"

"It's a way of centring yourself," he nods, "a way of aligning your Noise, of reining it in, *controlling* it, and a man who can control his Noise is a man with an advantage."

I remember him chanting away back in his house in old Prentisstown, how sharp and scary his Noise sounded compared to other men's, how much it felt like–

Like a weapon.

"What's the Circle?" I ask.

"Your destiny, Todd Hewitt. A circle is a closed system. There's no way of getting out, so it's easier if you don't fight it."

I AM THE CIRCLE AND THE CIRCLE IS ME.

But this time, my voice is in there, too.

"There's so much I look forward to teaching you," he says and leaves without saying good night.

* * *

I pace the walls of the bell tower, looking out towards the falls in the west, the hill with the notch on it in the south, and to the east, the hills that lead towards the monastery, tho you can't see it from here. All you can see is New Prentisstown, indoors and huddled together as a cold night settles in.

She's out there somewhere.

A month and she ain't come.

A month and—

(shut up)

(just effing shut up your effing whiny *mouth*)

I start pacing again.

We've got glass in the openings now and a heater to protect us from the autumn nights. More blankets, too, and a light and approved books for Mayor Ledger to read.

"Still a prison, though, isn't it?" he says behind me, mouth full. "You'd think he'd have at least found a better place for *you* by now."

"I sure wish everyone would stop thinking it's okay to read me all the damn time," I say, without turning around.

"He probably wants you out of the town," he says, finishing up his meal, which is just over half what we used to get. "Wants you away from all the rumours."

"What rumours?" I say, tho I'm barely interested.

"Oh, rumours of the great mind-control powers of our Mayor. Rumours of weapons made from Noise. Rumours he can fly, I don't doubt."

I don't look back at him and I keep my Noise quiet.

I am the Circle, I think.

And then I stop.

* * *

It's after midnight when the first one goes off.

Boom!

I jump a little on my mattress but that's all.

"Where do you think that was?" Mayor Ledger asks, also not rising from his bed.

"Sounded near east," I say, looking up into the dark of the tower bells. "Maybe a food store?"

We wait for the second. There's always a second now. As the soldiers rush to the first, the Answer take the chance for a second–

Boom!

"There it is," Mayor Ledger says, sitting up in bed and looking out of an opening. I get up, too.

"Damn," he says.

"What?" I say, moving next to him.

"I think that was the water plant down by the river."

"What does that mean?"

"It means we'll have to boil every stupid cup of–"

BOOM!

There's a huge flash that causes me and Mayor Ledger to flinch back from the window. The glass shakes in its frames.

And every light in New Prentisstown goes off.

"The power station," Mayor Ledger says, unbelieving. "But that's guarded every hour of the day. How could they possibly get to *that*?"

"I don't know," I say, my stomach sinking. "But there's gonna be hell to pay."

Mayor Ledger runs a tired hand over his face as we hear sirens and soldiers shouting down in the city below. He's shaking his head. "I don't know *what* they think they're accomp–"

BOOM!

BOOM!

BOOM!

BOOM!

BOOM!

Five huge explosions, one right after the other, shaking the tower so much that me and Mayor Ledger are thrown to the floor and a bunch of our windows shatter, busting inwards, covering us in shards and powdery glass.

We see the sky light up.

The sky to the west.

A cloud of fire and smoke shooting so high above the prisons it's like a giant's flinging it there.

Mayor Ledger is breathing heavy beside me.

"They've done it," he says, gasping. "They've really done it."

They've really done it, I think.

They've started their war.

And I can't help it–

I can't help but think it–

Is she coming for me?

25

THE NIGHT IT HAPPENS

{VIOLA}

"I NEED YOUR HELP," Mistress Lawson says, standing in the doorway of the kitchen.

I hold up my hands, covered in flour. "I'm kind of in the middle of–"

"Mistress Coyle specifically asked me to fetch you."

I frown. I don't like the word *fetch*. "Then who's going to finish these loaves for tomorrow? Lee's out getting firewood–"

"Mistress Coyle said you had experience in medical supplies," Mistress Lawson interrupts. "We've brought a lot more in and the girl I have now is hopeless at sorting them out."

I sigh. It's better than cooking, at least.

I follow her out into the dusk, into the mouth of a cave and through a series of passages until we get to the large cavern where we keep our most valuable supplies.

"This might take a while," Mistress Lawson says.

We spend most of the evening and into the night counting just how many medicines, bandages, compresses, bed linens, ethers, tourniquets, diagnostic bands, blood pressure straps, stethoscopes, gowns, water purification tablets, splints, cotton swabs, clamps, Jeffers root pills, adhesives, and everything else we have, sorting them out into smaller piles and spreading them across the supply cavern, right up the lip of the main tunnel.

I wipe cold sweat from my forehead. "Shouldn't we be stacking these up already?"

"Not just yet," Mistress Lawson says. She looks around at the neat piles of everything we've done. She rubs her hands together, a worried frown creasing her face. "I hope it's enough."

"Enough for what?" I follow her with my eyes as she goes from pile to pile. "Enough for *what*, Mistress Lawson?"

She looks up at me, biting her lip. "How much of your healing do you remember?"

I stare at her for a second, suspicions rising and rising, then I take off running out of the cavern. "Wait!" she calls after me, but I'm already out into the central tunnel, running out of the main mouth of the cave and shooting into the camp.

Which is deserted.

"Don't be angry," Mistress Lawson says after I've searched every cabin.

I stand there, stupidly, hands on my hips, staring around at the empty camp. Having found a distraction for me, Mistress Coyle left, along with all the other mistresses except for Mistress Lawson. Thea and the apprentices are gone, too.

And everyone else. Every cart, horse and ox.

291

And Lee.

Wilf's gone, too, though Jane is here, the only other one who stayed behind.

Tonight's the night.

Tonight's the night it happens.

"You know why she couldn't take you," Mistress Lawson says.

"She doesn't trust me," I say. "None of you do."

"That's neither here nor there right now," she says, her voice taking on that stern mistress tone I've grown to hate. "What matters is that when they come back, we're going to need all the healing hands we can get."

I'm about to argue but I see how much she's still wringing her hands, how worried her face looks, how much is going on beneath the surface.

And then she says, "If any of them make it back at all."

There's nothing left to do but wait. Jane makes us coffee, and we sit in the increasing cold, watching the path out of the woods, watching to see who returns down it.

"Frost," Jane says, digging her toe across the small breath of ice frozen on a stone near her foot.

"We should have done it earlier," Mistress Lawson says into her cup, face over the rising steam. "We should have done it before the weather turned."

"Done *what*?" I ask.

"Rescue," Jane says simply. "Wilf tole me when he was leavin."

"Rescue of who?" I say, though of course it can only be–

We hear rocks fall on the path. We're already on our feet when Magnus comes barrelling over the hill. "Hurry!" he's shouting. "Come on!"

Mistress Lawson grabs some of the most urgent of the medical supplies and starts running after him up the path. Jane and I do the same.

We're halfway up when they start to come out of the forest.

On the backs of carts, across the shoulders of others, on stretchers, on horseback, with more people pouring down the path behind them and more cresting the hill behind *them*.

All the ones who needed rescuing.

The prisoners locked away by the Mayor and his army.

And the *state* of them–

"Oh, m'Gawd," Jane says, quietly, next to me, both of us stopped, stunned.

Oh, my God.

The next hours are a blur, as we rush to bring the wounded into camp, though some of them are hurt so bad we have to treat them where they are. I'm ordered from one healer to another and another, racing from wound to wound, running back for more supplies, going so fast it's only after a while that I start to realize that most of the wounds being treated aren't from fighting.

"They've been beaten," I say.

"And starved," Mistress Lawson says angrily, setting up a fluid injection into the arm of a woman we've carried into the cave. "And tortured."

The woman is just one of a growing number that threatens

never to stop. Most of them too shocked to speak, staring at you in the most horrible silence or keening at you without words, burn scars on their arms and faces, old wounds left untreated, the sunken eyes of women who haven't eaten for days and days and days.

"He did this," I say to myself. "He did this."

"Hold it together, my girl," Mistress Lawson says. We rush back outside, arms full of bandages that don't begin to cover what's needed. Mistress Braithwaite waves me over with a frantic hand. She tears the bandages from me, furiously wrapping up the leg of a woman screaming beneath her. "Jeffers root!" Mistress Braithwaite snaps.

"I didn't bring any," I say.

"Then bloody well get some!"

I go back to the cave, twisting around healers and apprentices and fake soldiers crouched over patients everywhere, up the hillsides, on backs of carts, everywhere. It's not just women injured either. I see male prisoners, also starved, also beaten. I see people from the camp wounded in the fighting, including Wilf with a burn bandage up the side of his face, though he's still helping carry patients on stretchers into the camp.

I run into the cave, grab more bandages and Jeffers root, and run back to the gully for the dozenth time. I cross the open ground and look up the path, where a few more people are still arriving.

I stop a second and check the new faces before running back to Mistress Braithwaite.

Mistress Coyle hasn't returned yet.

Neither has Lee.

*   *   *

"He was right in the thick of it," Mistress Nadari says, as I help her get a freshly-drugged woman to her feet. "Like he was looking for someone."

"His mother and sister," I say, taking the woman's weight against me.

"We didn't get everyone," Mistress Nadari says. "There was a whole other building where the bomb didn't go off–"

"Siobhan!" we hear someone shout in the distance.

I turn, my heart racing a lot faster and bigger than I expect, a smile breaking my cheeks. "He's found them!"

But you can see right away it's not true.

"Siobhan?" Lee is coming down the path from the forest, the arm and shoulder of his uniform blackened, his face covered in soot, his eyes looking everywhere, this way and that through all the people in the gully as he walks through them. "Mum?"

"Go," Mistress Nadari says to me. "See if he's hurt."

I let the woman lean onto Mistress Nadari and I run towards Lee, ignoring the other mistresses calling my name.

"Lee!" I call.

"Viola?" he says, seeing me. "Are they here? Do you know if they're here?"

"Are you hurt?" I reach him, taking the blackened sleeve and looking at his hands. "You're burned."

"There were fires," he says, and I look into his eyes. He's looking at me but he's not seeing me, he's seeing what he saw at the prisons, he's seeing the fires and what was behind them, he's seeing the prisoners they found, maybe he's seeing guards he had to kill.

He's not seeing his sister or his mother.

"Are they *here*?" he pleads. "Tell me they're here."

"I don't know what they look like," I say quietly.

Lee stares at me, his mouth open, his breath heavy and raspy, like he's breathed in a lot of smoke. "It was..." he says. "Oh, God, Viola, it was..." He looks up and past me, over my shoulder. "I've got to find them. They've got to be here."

He steps past me and down the gully. "Siobhan? *Mum*?"

I can't help it and I call after him. "Lee? Did you see Todd?"

But he keeps on walking, stumbling away.

"Viola!" I hear and at first I think it's just another mistress calling for my help.

But then a voice beside me says, "Mistress Coyle!"

I turn and look up. At the top of the path is Mistress Coyle, on horseback, clopping down the rocks of the path as fast as she can make the horse go. She's got someone in the saddle behind her, someone tied to her to keep them from falling off. I feel a jolt of hope. Maybe it's Siobhan. Or Lee's mum.

(or him, maybe it's him, maybe–)

"Help us, Viola!" Mistress Coyle shouts, working the reins.

And as I start to run up the hill towards them, the horse turns to find its footing and I see who it is, unconscious and leaning badly.

Corinne.

"No," I keep saying, under my breath, hardly realizing it. "No, no, no, no, no," as we get her down onto a flat of rock and as Mistress Lawson runs towards us with armfuls of bandages and medicines. "No, no, no," as I take her head in my hands to cradle it from the hard rock and Mistress Coyle tears off Corinne's sleeve to prepare for injections. "No," as Mistress

Lawson reaches us and gasps as she sees who it is.

"You found her," Mistress Lawson says.

Mistress Coyle nods. "I found her."

I feel Corinne's skull under my hands, feel how the skin burns with fever. I see how sharp her cheeks look, how the bruising that discolours her eyes is against skin sagging and limp. And the collarbones that jut up from above the neckline of her torn and dirty mistress cloak. And the circles of burns against her neck. And the cuts on her forearms. And the tearing at her fingernails.

"Oh, Corinne," I whisper and wet from my eyes drops onto her forehead. "Oh, no."

"Stay with us, my girl," Mistress Coyle says, and I don't know whether she's talking to me or Corinne.

"Thea?" Mistress Lawson asks, not looking up.

Mistress Coyle shakes her head.

"Thea's dead?" I ask.

"And Mistress Waggoner," Mistress Coyle says, and I notice the smoke on her face, the red angry burns on her forehead. "And others." Her mouth draws thin. "But we got some of *them*, too."

"Come on, my girl," Mistress Lawson says to Corinne, still unconscious. "You were always the stubborn one. We need that now."

"Hold this," Mistress Coyle says, handing me a bag of fluid connected to a tube injected into Corinne's arm. I take it in one hand, keeping Corinne's head in my lap.

"Here it is," Mistress Lawson says, peeling away a strap of crusted cloth on Corinne's side. A terrible smell hits all of us at the same time.

It's worse than how sickening it stinks. It's worse because of what it means.

"Gangrene," Mistress Coyle says pointlessly, because we can all see that it's way past infection. The smell means the tissue's dead. It means it's started to eat her alive. Something I wish I didn't remember that Corinne taught me herself.

"They didn't even give her basic bloody treatment," grunts Mistress Lawson, getting to her feet and running back towards the cave to get the heaviest medicines we've got.

"Come on, my difficult girl," Mistress Coyle says quietly, stroking Corinne's forehead.

"You stayed until you found her," I say. "That's why you were last."

"She'd never yield, this one," Mistress Coyle says, her voice rough and not just because of smoke. "No matter what they did to her."

We look down at Corinne's face, her eyes still closed, her mouth dropped open, her breath faltering.

Mistress Coyle's right. Corinne would never yield, would never give names or information, would take the punishment to keep other daughters, other mothers, from feeling it themselves.

"The infection," I say, my throat swelling. "The smell, it means–"

Mistress Coyle just bites her lips hard and shakes her head.

"Oh, Corinne," I say. "Oh, no."

And right there, right there in my hands, in my lap, her face turned up to mine–

She dies.

*   *   *

There's only silence when it happens. It isn't loud or struggled against or violent or anything at all. She just falls quiet, a
certain type of quiet you know is endless as soon as you hear
it, a quiet that muffles everything around it, turning off the
volume of the world.

The only thing I *can* hear, in fact, is my own breathing,
wet and heavy and like I'll never feel lightness again. And in
the silence of my breath I look down the hillside, I see the rest
of the wounded around us, their mouths open to cry out in
pain, their eyes blank with horrors still being seen even after
rescue. I see Mistress Lawson, running towards us with medicine, too late, too late. I see Lee, coming back up the path,
calling out for his mother and sister, not willing to believe yet
that in all this mess, they're still not here.

I think of the Mayor in his cathedral, making promises,
telling lies.

(I think of Todd in the Mayor's hands)

I look down at Corinne in my lap, Corinne who never liked
me, not ever, but who gave her life for mine anyway.

We are the choices we make.

When I look up at Mistress Coyle, the wet in my eyes
makes everything shine with pointed lights, makes the first
peek of the rising sun a smear across the sky.

But I can see her clearly enough.

My teeth are clenched, my voice thick as mud.

"I'm ready," I say. "I'll do anything you want."

26

THE ANSWER

[TODD]

"OH, GOD," Mayor Ledger keeps saying under his breath. "Oh, God."

"What're *you* so upset about?" I finally snap at him.

The door ain't unlocked at its usual time. Morning's come and gone with no sign of anyone remembering that we're here. Outside the city burns and ROARs but a sour part of me can't help thinking he's moaning cuz they're late with our breakfast.

"The surrender was supposed to bring *peace*," he says. "And that bloody woman has ruined *everything*."

I look at him strangely. "It's not like it's paradise here or nothing. There's curfews and prisons and–

But he's shaking his head. "Before she started her little *campaign*, the President was relaxing the laws. He was easing the restrictions. Things were going to be okay."

I stand and look out the windows to the west, where smoke still rises and fires still rage and the Noise of men

300

don't show no sign of stopping.

"You've got to be *practical*," Mayor Ledger says, "even in the face of tyrants."

"Is that what you are then?" I say. "Practical?"

He narrows his eyes. "I don't know what you're getting at, *boy*."

I don't really know what I'm getting at neither but I'm frightened and I'm hungry and we're stuck in this stupid tower while the world falls to bits around us and we can *watch* it but we can't do nothing to *change* it and I don't know what Viola's part in all this is or *where* she is and I don't know where the future's heading and I don't know how any good can possibly come outta any of this but what I *do* know is that Mayor Ledger telling me how *practical* he's been is kinda pissing me off.

Oh, yeah, and one more thing.

"Don't you call me boy."

He takes a step towards me. "A man would understand that things are more complicated than just right or wrong."

"A man trying to save his own skin surely would." And my Noise is saying *Try it, come on, try it.*

Mayor Ledger clenches his fists. "What you don't know, Todd," he says, nostrils flaring. "What you don't know."

"*What* don't I know?" I say but then the door goes *ker-thunk*, making us both jump.

Davy comes busting in, rifles in hand. "Come on," he says, shoving one at me. "Pa wants us."

I go without another word, leaving Mayor Ledger shouting "Hey!" behind us as Davy locks the door.

* * *

"Fifty-six soldiers killed," Davy says as we trundle down the stairs on the inside of the tower. "We killed a dozen of 'em and captured a dozen more but they got away with almost two hundred prisoners."

"*Two hundred*?" I say, stopping for a second. "How many people were in prison?"

"Come on, pigpiss, Pa's waiting."

I run to catch up. We cross the lobby of the cathedral and head out the front door. "Those bitches," Davy's saying, shaking his head. "You wouldn't believe the things they're capable of. They blew up a bunkhouse. A *bunkhouse*! Where men were *sleeping*!"

We exit the cathedral to chaos in the square. Smoke is still blowing in from the west, making everything hazy. Soldiers, both by themselves and in squads, run this way and that, some of them pushing people before them, beating them with their rifles. Others are standing guard around groups of terrified-looking women and separate smaller groups of terrified-looking men.

"But we showed them, tho," Davy says, grimacing.

"You were there?"

"No." He looks down at his rifle. "But I will be next time."

"David!" we hear. "Todd!" The Mayor's riding towards us from across the square, moving so heavy and fast Morpeth's shoes are striking sparks from the bricks.

"Something's happened at the monastery," he's shouting. "Get there. *Now!*"

*   *   *

The chaos is city-wide. We see soldiers everywhere as we ride, herding townspeople before them, forcing them into bucket-lines to help put out the smaller fires from the first three bombs of last night, the ones that *did* take out the power stayshun, the water plant and a food store, all still burning cuz New Prentisstown's fire hoses are busy trying to put out the prisons.

"They won't know what hit 'em," Davy says as we ride, fast.

"Who won't?"

"The Answer and any man who helps them."

"There ain't gonna be no one *left*."

"There'll be us," Davy says, looking at me. "That'll be a start."

The road gets quieter as we get away from the city, till you can almost believe things are still normal, unless you look back and see the columns of smoke rising in the air. There ain't no one on the roads down this far and it starts to get so quiet it's like the world's ended.

We ride past the hill where the tower rubble lies but don't see no soldiers going up the path towards it. We turn the last corner and come round to the monastery.

And pull back hard on our reins.

"Holy shit," Davy says.

The whole front wall of the monastery has been blown open. There ain't any guards on the walls, just a gaping hole in the masonry where the gate used to be.

"Those bitches," Davy says. "They set them *free*."

I feel a weird smile in my stomach at the thought of it.

(is this what she did?)

"Now we're gonna have to bloody fight them, *too*," Davy whines.

But I'm hopping off Angharrad, my stomach all funny and light. *Free*, I think. *They're free.*

(is this why she joined them?)

I feel so–

So *relieved*.

I pick up the pace as I near the opening, my hands gripping my rifle but I have a feeling I ain't gonna need it.

(ah, Viola, I knew I could count–)

Then I reach the opening and stop.

Everything stops.

My stomach falls right thru my feet.

"They all gone?" Davy says, coming up beside me.

Then he sees what I see.

"What the–?" Davy says.

The Spackle ain't all gone.

They're still here.

Every single one.

All 1150 of them.

Dead.

"I don't unnerstand this at all," Davy says, looking round.

"Shut up," I whisper.

The guide walls have all been knocked down till it's just a field again and bodies are piled everywhere, thrown on top of each another and tumbled across the grass, too, like someone tossed 'em away, males and females and children and babies, tossed away like they were trash.

Something's burning somewhere and white smoke twists thru the field, circling the piles, pushing at them with smoky fingers, finding nothing alive.

And the quiet.

No clicking, no shuffling, no *breathing*.

"I gotta tell Pa," Davy says, already turning back. "I gotta tell Pa."

And he's off back out the front, hopping on Deadfall and riding back up the road.

I don't follow.

My feet will only go forward, thru them all, my rifle dragging behind me.

The piles of bodies are higher than my head. I have to look up to see the dead faces flung back, the eyes still open, grassflies already picking at the bullet wounds in their heads. Looks like all of 'em were shot, most of 'em in the middle of their high foreheads, but some of the bodies look slashed, too, cut across the throat or the chest and I start to see ripped-off limbs and heads twisted all the way round and–

I drop my rifle to the grass. I barely even notice.

I keep walking, not blinking, mouth open, not believing what I'm seeing, not taking in the scale of it–

Cuz I have to step over bodies with arms flung out, arms with hands round 'em that *I* put there, twisted mouths that I fed, broken backs that I–

That I–

Oh, God.

Oh, God, no, I hated 'em –
I tried not to but I couldn't help it–
(no, I could–)
I think of all the times I cursed 'em–
All the times I imagined 'em as sheep–
(a knife in my hand, plunging down–)
But I didn't want *this*–
Never, I–
And I come round the biggest pile of bodies, stacked
near the east wall–
And I see it.
And I fall to my knees in the frozen grass.

Written on the wall, tall as a man–
The *A*.
The *A* of the Answer.
Written in blue.

I lean my head forward slowly till it's touching the ground,
the cold sinking into my skull.
(no)
(no, it can't be her)
(it *can't* be)
My breath comes up around mc as steam, melting a
little spot of mud. I don't move.
(have they done this to you?)
(have they changed you?)
(Viola?)

(*Viola?*)

The blackness starts to overwhelm me, starts to fall over me like a blanket, like water rising above my head, no Viola no, it can't be you, it can't be you (can it?) no no no it can't–

No–

No–

And I sit up–

And I lean back–

And I strike myself in the face.

I punch myself hard.

Again.

And again.

Not feeling nothing as I hit.

As my lips crack open.

As my eyes swell.

No–

God no–

Please–

And I reach back to punch myself again–

But I switch off–

I feel it go cold inside me–

Deep down inside–

(where are you to save me?)

I switch off.

I go numb.

I look at the Spackle, dead, everywhere dead.

And Viola gone–

Gone in ways that I can't even say–

(you did *this*?)

(you did *this* instead of finding me?)
And inside I just *die*.

And a body tumbles from the pile, knocking right into me.

I scoot back fast, rolling over other bodies, scrambling to my feet, wiping my hands on my trousers, wiping the dead away.

And then another body falls.

I look up at the pile.

1017 is working his way out.

He sees me and freezes, his head and arms sticking out from the rest of the bodies, bones showing thru his skin, thin as the dead.

Course he survived. *Course* he did. If any of 'em is spiteful enough to find a way to live, it's him.

I run to the pile and I start pulling on his shoulders to get him out, to get him out from under the dead, all the dead.

We fall back as he pops free, tumbling to the ground, rolling apart and then staring at each other across the ground.

Our breaths are heavy, clouds of steam huffing into the air.

He don't look injured, tho the sling's gone from his arm. He's just staring, eyes probably open as wide as mine.

"Yer alive," I say stupidly. "Yer alive."

He just stares back, no Noise this time, no clicking, nothing. Just the silence of us in the morning, the smoke sneaking thru the air like a vine.

"How?" I say. "How did–?"

But there ain't no answer from him, just staring and staring.

"Did you–?" I say, then I have to clear my throat. "Did you see a girl?"

And then I hear, *Thump budda-thump–*

Hoofbeats down the road. Davy musta caught his pa coming the other way.

I look hard at 1017.

"Run," I say. "You gotta get outta here."

Thump budda-thump–

"Please," I whisper. "Please, I'm so sorry, I'm *so* sorry, but please, just run, just run, just get outta here–"

I stop cuz he's getting to his feet. He's still eyeing me, not blinking, his face almost dead of expresshun.

Thump budda-THUMP–

He takes one step away, then two, then faster, heading for the blown open gate.

And then he stops and looks back.

Looks back at me.

A clear flash of Noise coming right at me.

Of me, alone.

Of 1017 with a gun.

Of him pulling the trigger.

Of me dying at his feet.

Then he turns and runs out the gate and into the woods beyond.

* * *

"I know how hard this must be for you, Todd," says the Mayor, looking at the blown out gate. We've come outside. No one wanted to see the bodies any more.

"But *why?*" I say, trying to keep the tightness outta my voice. "Why would they do it?"

The Mayor looks at the blood on my face from where I hit myself but he don't say nothing about it. "They thought we would have used them as soldiers, I expect."

"But to kill them *all?*" I look up at him on his horse. "The Answer never killed no one before except by accident."

"Fifty-six soldiers," Davy says.

"Seventy-five," the Mayor corrects. "And three hundred escaped prisoners."

"They tried to bomb us here before, remember?" Davy adds. "The bitches."

"The Answer have stepped up their campaign," the Mayor says, looking mainly at me. "And we will respond in kind."

"Damn right, we will," Davy says, cocking his rifle for no reason.

"I'm sorry about Viola," the Mayor says to me. "I'm as disappointed as you are that she's a part of this."

"We don't know that," I whisper.

(is she?)

(are you?)

"Regardless," the Mayor says. "The time for your boyhood is well and truly past. I need leaders now. I need *you* to be a leader. Are you ready to lead, Todd Hewitt?"

"*I'm* ready," Davy says, his Noise feeling like it's being left out.

"I already know I can count on you, son."

And there's the pink Noise again.

"It's Todd I need to hear from." He comes a bit closer to me. "You're no longer my prisoner, Todd Hewitt. We're beyond that now. But I need to know if you'll join *me*–" he nods his head towards the opening in the wall "– or them. There is no other choice."

I look into the monastery, at all those bodies, all those shocked and dead faces, all that pointless end.

"Will you help me, Todd?"

"Help you how?" I say to the ground.

But he just asks it again. "Will you help me?"

I think of 1017, alone now, alone in the entire world.

His friends, his family for all I know, piled like rubbish, left for the flies.

I can't stop seeing it, even when I close my eyes.

I can't stop seeing that bright blue *A*.

Oh don't deceive me, I think.

Oh never leave me.

(but she's gone)

(she's gone)

And I'm dead.

Inside, I'm dead dead dead.

There ain't nothing left.

"I will," I say. "I'll help."

"Excellent," the Mayor says, with feeling. "I knew you'd be special, Todd. I've known it all along."

Davy's Noise squeaks at this but the Mayor ignores it.

He turns Morpeth to face the killing grounds of the monastery.

"As to how you'll help me," he says. "Well, we have met the Answer, have we not?" He turns back to look at us, his eyes glinting. "It is time for them to meet the Ask."

PART V

THE OFFICE OF THE ASK

27

THE WAY WE LIVE NOW

[TODD]

"DON'T LET THIS period of quiet fool you," says the Mayor, standing atop the platform, voice booming thru the square from speakers set at every corner, extra loud to be heard above the ROAR. The people of New Prentisstown stare up at him in the cold morning, the men gathered in front of the platform, surrounded by the army, with the women back on the side streets.

Here we all are again.

Davy and I are behind the platform on our horses, directly behind the Mayor.

Kinda like an honour guard.

Wearing our new uniforms.

I think, *I am the Circle and the Circle is me.*

Cuz when I think it, I don't gotta think about nothing else at all.

"Even now our enemies move against us. Even now they plot our destruction. Even now we have reason to believe an

315

attack is imminent."

The Mayor takes a long sweeping look across the crowd. It's easy to forget how many people are still here, still working, still trying to eat, still getting on with their daily lives. They're tired-looking, hungry, many of 'em dirty, but still staring, still listening.

"The Answer could strike in any place, at any time, against any*one*," he says, tho the Answer ain't done no such thing, not for almost a month now. The prison break was the last we heard from 'em before they disappeared into the wild, the soldiers who woulda chased 'em killed while sleeping in their bunkers.

But that just means they're out there, gloating on their victory and planning the next.

"Three hundred escaped prisoners," the Mayor says. "Almost two hundred soldiers and civilians dead."

"Up they go again," Davy mutters under his breath, talking about the numbers. "Next time he gives this speech, the whole *city'll* be dead." He looks to me to see if I'll laugh. I don't. I don't even look at him. "Yeah, whatever," he says, turning back.

"And not to mention the genocide," says the Mayor.

The crowd murmurs at this and the **ROAR** gets a bit louder and redder.

"The very same Spackle who served in your homes so peacefully for the past decade, the ones we had all grown to admire for their pluck under duress, the ones we had come to regard as our partners on New World."

He pauses again. "All dead, all gone."

The crowd **ROAR**s some more. The deaths of the Spackle

really did affect the people, even more than the deaths of the soldiers or the townspeople caught up in the attack. Men even started joining the army again. Then the Mayor let some of the women who remained in prison out, some of 'em even back with their families and not even in dormitories. He upped everyone's food rashuns, too.

And he started holding these rallies. Explaining things.

"The Answer says it fights for freedom. But are these the people in whom you put your faith for salvation? The ones who would kill an entire *unarmed* population?"

I feel a choke rising and I make my Noise empty space, make it a wasteland, thinking nothing, *feeling* nothing, except—

I am the Circle and the Circle is me.

"I know these past weeks have been difficult. The food and water shortages, the necessary curfews, the power cuts, especially during the cold nights. I applaud your fortitude. The only way we're going to get thru this is by pulling together against those who would destroy us."

And people have pulled together, ain't they? They obey the curfew and take their assigned amounts of water and food without fuss and stay inside when they're sposed to and turn off their lights after a certain hour and generally keep getting on with things even as it gets colder. You ride thru the town, you even see stores open, big lines of people outside 'em, waiting to get what they need.

Their eyes looking at the ground, waiting it out.

At night, Mayor Ledger tells me the townsfolk still grumble against Mayor Prentiss, but now there's even louder grumbles against the Answer, for blowing up the water plant, for blowing up the power stayshun, and specially for killing all the Spackle.

Better the devil you know, Mayor Ledger says.

We're still up in that tower, me and Mayor Ledger, for some reason best known to Mayor Prentiss, but I got a key now and I lock him in when I ain't there. He don't like it but what's he gonna do?

Better the devil you know.

I wonder why the only choice is twixt two devils, tho.

"I also want to express my thanks," says the Mayor to the people, "for your continued help in coming forward with information. It is only eternal vigilance that will lead us into the light. Let your neighbour know he is watched. Only then are we truly safe."

"How long is this gonna go *on*?" Davy says, accidentally spurring Deadfall/Acorn, who has to be reined back when he steps forward. "I'm effing freezing over here."

Angharrad moves from foot to foot below me. **Go?** her Noise asks, her breath heavy and white in the cold. "Almost," I say, rubbing my hand against her flank.

"Effective tonight," says the Mayor, "curfew is pushed back by two hours and visiting times for wives and mothers is extended by thirty minutes."

There's some nodding in the crowd of men, some relieved crying from the crowd of women.

They're grateful, I think. *Grateful* to the Mayor.

Ain't that something.

"Finally," says the Mayor. "It is my pleasure to announce that building work has been completed on a new Ministry, one that will keep us safe from the threat of the Answer, a building where no secret may be kept, where anyone who tries to undermine our way of life will be re-educated into understanding our ideals, where our future will be secured against those who would steal it from us."

The Mayor pauses, to give his words maximum impact.

"Today we launch the Office of the Ask."

Davy catches my eye and taps the sharp, silver **A** sewn on the shoulders of our new uniforms, the **A** that the Mayor picked special cuz it's got all kinda associashuns, don't it?

Me and Davy are now Officers of the Ask.

I don't share his excitement.

But that's cuz I don't feel nothing much at all no more.

I am the Circle and the Circle is me.

"Good speech, Pa," Davy says. "Long."

"It wasn't for you, David," the Mayor says, not looking at him.

The three of us are riding down the road to the monastery.

Tho it ain't the monastery no more.

"Everything *is* ready, I trust?" the Mayor says, barely turning his head. "I'd hate to be made a liar of."

"It ain't gonna get less ready if you keep asking," Davy mumbles.

The Mayor turns to him, a deep frown on his face, but I speak before anyone gets slapped with Noise.

"It's as ready as it can be," I say, my voice flat. "The walls and roof are up but the inside–"

"No need to sound so morose, Todd," the Mayor says.

"The inside can follow in due course. The building is up, that's all that's important. They can look at the outside and they can tremble."

He's got his back to us now, riding on ahead, but I can *feel* him smile at *they can tremble*.

"Are we gonna have a part in it?" Davy asks, Noise still stormy. "Or are you just gonna find a way for us to be babysitters again?"

The Mayor turns Morpeth in the road, blocking our way. "Do you ever hear Todd complain this much?" he asks.

"No," Davy says, sullen. "But he's just, you know, *Todd*."

The Mayor raises his eyebrows. "And?"

"And I'm yer *son*."

The Mayor walks Morpeth towards us, making Angharrad step back. **Submit**, Morpeth says. **Lead**, Angharrad says in answer, lowering her head. I stroke her mane, untangling a bit with my fingers, trying to calm her down.

"Let me tell you something interesting, David," the Mayor says, looking hard at him. "The officers, the army, the townspeople, they see the two of you riding together, in your new uniforms, with all your new authority, and they know that *one* of you is my son." He's almost side on to Davy now, pushing him back down the road. "And as they watch you ride by, as they watch you go about your business, do you know? They often guess wrong. They often guess wrong as to which one of you is my own flesh and blood."

The Mayor looks over to me. "They see Todd with his devotion to duty, with his modest brow and his serious face, with his calm exterior and mature handling of his Noise, and they never even consider that his loud, sloppy, *insolent* friend is the one who's actually my son."

Davy's looking at the ground, his teeth clenched, his Noise boiling. "He don't even *look* like you."

"I know," says the Mayor, turning Morpeth back down the road. "I just thought it was interesting. How often it happens."

We keep on riding, Davy in a silent, red storm of Noise, lagging behind. I keep Angharrad in the middle with the Mayor clopping on ahead.

"Good girl," I murmur to her.

Boy colt, she says back, and then she thinks **Todd**.

"Yeah, girl," I whisper twixt her ears. "I'm here."

I've taken to hanging round her stables at the end of the day, taken to unsaddling her myself and brushing her mane and bringing her apples to eat. The only thing she needs from me is assurance that I'm there, proof I haven't left the herd, and as long as that's true, she's happy and she calls me **Todd** and I don't have to explain myself to her and I don't have to ask her nothing and she don't need nothing from me.

Except that I don't leave her.

Except that I don't never *leave*.

My Noise starts getting cloudy and I think it again, *I am the Circle and the Circle is me.*

The Mayor looks back at me. And he smiles.

* * *

Even tho we got uniforms, we ain't in the army, the Mayor was particular about that. We don't got ranks except Officer but the uniform and the *A* on its sleeve is enough to keep people outta our way as we ride towards the monastery.

Our job till now has been guarding the men and women who're still in prison, tho it's mostly women. After the prisons were busted into and burnt down, the prisoners left over were moved to a former house of healing down by the river.

Guess which one?

For the past month, Davy and I've been escorting work crews of prisoners back and forth from the house of healing to the monastery to finish the work the Spackle started, women and men working faster than Spackle, I guess. The Mayor didn't ask us to supervise the building this time, something I'm grateful for.

When everyone's in for the night back at the house of healing, Davy and I ain't got much to do except ride our horses round the building, doing what we can so as not to hear the screams coming from inside.

Some of the ones still in prison, see, are from the Answer, the ones the Mayor caught the night of the prison break. We don't never see them, they don't get sent out with the work parties, they just get Asked all day long till they answer with something. So far, all the Mayor's got from 'em is the locayshun of a camp around a mine, which was deserted by the time the soldiers got there. Anything else useful is slow in coming.

There are others in there, too, found guilty of helping the Answer or whatever, but the ones who said they saw the Answer kill the Spackle and saw women writing the *A* on the wall, those prisoners are the ones who've been set free and sent back to their families. Even tho there ain't really no way they coulda been there to see it.

The others, well, the others keep being Asked till they answer.

Davy talks loud to cover the sounds we hear while the Asking's going on inside, trying to pretend it don't bother him when any fool could see it does.

I just keep myself in myself, closing my eyes, waiting for the screaming to stop.

I have an easier time than Davy.

Cuz like I say, I don't feel nothing much, not no more.

I am the Circle and the Circle is me.

But today, everything's sposed to change. Today, the new building is ready, or ready enough, and Davy and I are gonna guard it instead of the house of healing, while sposedly learning the business of Asking.

Fine. It don't matter.

Nothing matters.

"The Office of the Ask," the Mayor says as we round the final corner.

The front wall of the monastery has been rebuilt and you can see the new building sticking over the top, a big stone block that looks like it'd happily knock yer brains out if you stood too close. And on the newly built gate, there's a great, shiny silver *A* to match the ones on our uniforms.

There are guards in army uniforms on either side of the door. One of them is Ivan, still a Private, still sour-faced as anything. He tries to catch my eye as I ride up, his Noise clanging loud with things he don't want the Mayor to hear, I reckon.

I ignore him. So does the Mayor.

"Now we find out when the real war begins," the Mayor says.

The gate opens and out walks the man in charge of all the Asking, the man charged with finding out where the Answer are hiding and how best to track them down.

Our newly promoted boss.

"Mr President," he says.

"Captain Hammar," says the Mayor.

28

SOLDIER

{VIOLA}

"QUIET," Mistress Coyle says, a finger to her lips.

The wind has died and you can hear our footsteps snapping the twigs on the ground at the foot of the trees. We stop, ears open for the sounds of soldiers marching.

Nothing.

More nothing.

Mistress Coyle nods and continues moving down the hill and through the trees. I follow her. It's just the two of us.

Me and her and the bomb strapped to my back.

The rescue saved 132 prisoners. 29 of them died either on the way to or back in the camp. Corinne was number 30. There are others unrescued, like poor old Mrs Fox, whose fates I'm probably never going to know. But Mistress Coyle estimates we killed at least twenty of their soldiers. Miraculously, only six members of the Answer on the original raid were killed, including Thea and Mistress Waggoner, but another five were captured and there was no possibility they wouldn't be tortured for information about where the Answer was hiding.

So we moved. In a hurry.

Even before many of the injured could walk for themselves, we loaded up supplies and weapons, anything and everything we could carry on carts, horses, the backs of the able-bodied, and we fled into the woods, keeping moving all through the night, the next day, and the night after that until we came to a lake at the base of a rock cliff, where at least we might have water and some shelter.

"It'll do," Mistress Coyle said.

We pitched camp along the shore.

And then we began our preparations for war.

She makes a movement with the palm of her hand and I instantly duck below some shrubs. We've reached a narrow drive up from the main road and I can hear a troop of soldiers Noisily moving away from us in the distance.

Our own supply of cure is getting lower by the day, and Mistress Coyle has set up a rationing system, but since the raid, it's too dangerous for any man, with or without Noise, to go into town anyway, which means they can no longer ferry us in hidden compartments to easy targets. We have to take a cart to a certain point outside of town and walk the rest of the way.

Escaping will be more difficult, so we'll just have to be more careful.

"Okay," Mistress Coyle whispers.

I stand. The moons are our only light.

We cross the road, keeping low.

After we moved to the lake, after the rescue of all those people, after the death of Corinne–

After I joined the Answer–

I began to learn things.

"Basic training," Mistress Coyle called it. Led by Mistress Braithwaite and done not only for me but for every patient who improved enough to join in, which was most of them, more than you'd think, we were taught how to load a rifle and fire it, basics of infiltration, night-time manoeuvres, tracking, hand communications, code words.

How to wire and set a bomb.

"How do you know how to do this?" I asked one night at dinner, my body weary and aching from the running and diving and carrying we'd done all throughout the day. "You're healers. How do you know how–"

"To run an army?" Mistress Coyle said. "You forget about the Spackle War."

"We were our own division," Mistress Forth said, down the table, snuffling up some broth.

The mistresses talked to me, now that they could see how hard I was training.

"We weren't very popular," giggled Mistress Lawson, across from her.

"We didn't like how some of the generals were waging the war," Mistress Coyle said to me. "We thought an underground approach would be more effective."

"And since we didn't have Noise," said Mistress Nadari, down the table, "we could sneak into places, couldn't we?"

"The men in charge didn't think we were the answer to their problem, though," Mistress Lawson said, still giggling.

"Hence the name," Mistress Coyle said.

"And when the new government was formed and the city rebuilt, well," Mistress Forth said, "it wouldn't have been sensible not to keep important materials available should the need ever arise."

"The explosives in the mine," I said, realizing. "You hid them there years ago."

"And what a good decision it turned out to be," Mistress Lawson said. "Nicola Coyle always was a woman of foresight."

I blinked at the name Nicola, as if it was hardly possible that Mistress Coyle had a first name.

"Yes, well," said Mistress Coyle. "Men are creatures of war. It's only prudent to remember that."

Our target is deserted, as we expect it to be. It's small, but symbolic, a well above a tract of farmland east of the city. The well and the apparatus above it only bring water for the field below, not any huge system or set of buildings. But if the city goes on allowing the Mayor to Imprison, torture and kill, then the city won't eat.

It's also a good way away from the city centre, so no chance of me seeing Todd.

Which I won't argue about. For now.

We've come up the cut-off road, keeping to the ditch

beside it, holding our breaths as we move past the sleeping farmhouse, a light still on in the upper floor but it's so late it can only be for security.

Mistress Coyle makes another hand signal and I move past her, ducking under a wire carriage of laundry, hung outside to dry. I trip on a child's toy scooter but manage to keep my balance.

The bomb's supposed to be safe, supposed to be impervious to any kind of jostling or shaking.

But.

I let out a breath and keep on towards the well.

Even in the weeks when we hid, when we didn't approach the city at all, the weeks where we laid low and kept quiet, training and preparing, even then a few escapees from the city found us.

"They're saying *what*?" Mistress Coyle said.

"That you killed all the Spackle," the woman said, pressing the poultice against her bleeding nose.

"Wait," I said. "*All* the Spackle are dead?"

The woman nodded.

"And they're saying we did it," Mistress Coyle repeated.

"Why would they say that?" I asked.

Mistress Coyle stood and looked out across the lake. "Turn the city against us. Make us look like the bad guys."

"That's exactly what he's saying," the woman said. I found her on a training run through the woods. She'd tripped down a rocky embankment, managing to break only her nose. "There's rallies every other day," she said. "People are listening."

"I'm not surprised," Mistress Coyle said.

I looked up at her. "You didn't do it, did you? You didn't kill them?"

Her face could've lit a match. "Exactly what sort of people do you think we are, my girl?"

I kept her gaze. "Well, I don't know, do I? You blew up a bunker. You killed soldiers."

But she just shook her head, though I didn't know if that was an answer.

"You're sure you weren't followed?" she asked the woman.

"I was wandering in the woods for three days," she said. "I didn't even find you." She pointed at me. "*She* found *me*."

"Yes," Mistress Coyle said, eyeing me. "Viola's useful that way."

There's a problem at the well.

"It's too close to the house," I whisper.

"It's not," Mistress Coyle whispers back, going behind me and unzipping my pack.

"Are you sure?" I say. "The bombs you blew up the tower with were–"

"There are bombs and there are bombs." She makes a few adjustments to the contents of my pack, then turns me around to face her. "Are you ready?"

I look over to the house, where anyone could be sleeping inside, women, innocent men, children. I won't kill anyone, not unless I have to. If I'm doing this for Todd and Corinne, well, then. "Are you sure?" I ask.

330

"Either you trust me, Viola, or you do not." She tilts her head. "Which will it be?"

The breeze has picked up again and it blows a bit of the sleeping Noise of New Prentisstown down the road. One indefinable, snuffling, snoring ROAR, almost quiet, if such a thing could be.

Todd somewhere in it all.

(not dead, no matter what she says)

"Let's get this done," I say, taking off the pack.

The rescue wasn't a rescue for Lee. His sister and his mother weren't among the prisoners saved or the prisoners who died. It's possible they were in the one prison the Answer didn't manage to break.

But.

"Even if they're dead," he said, one night as we sat on the shore of the lake, throwing in stones, aching again after yet another long day's training. "I just want to know."

I shook my head. "If you don't know, then there's still a chance."

"Knowing or not knowing doesn't keep them alive." He sat down, close to me again. "I think they're dead. I *feel* like they're dead."

"Lee–"

"I'm going to kill him." His voice was that of a man making a promise, not a threat. "If I get close enough, I swear to you."

The moons rose over us, making two more of themselves in the surface of the lake. I threw in another stone, watching it skip across the moons' reflections. The camp gave a low bustle in the trees behind us and up the bank. You could hear Noise here and there, including a growing buzz from Lee, not lucky enough to qualify for Mistress Coyle's ration.

"It's not what you think it's going to be like," I said quietly.

"Killing someone?"

I nodded. "Even if it's someone who deserves it, someone who will kill you if you don't kill them, even then it's not what you think."

There was more silence, until he finally said. "I know."

I looked over at him. "You killed a soldier."

He didn't answer, which was its own answer.

"Lee?" I said. "Why didn't you tell−?"

"Because it's not what you think it's going to be like, is it?" he said. "Even if it's someone who deserves it."

He threw another stone into the lake. We weren't resting our shoulders on each other. We were a space apart.

"I'm still going to kill him," he said.

. I peel off the backing paper and press the bomb into the side of the well, sticking it there with a glue made from tree sap. I take two wires out of my pack and twist the ends on two more wires already sticking out of the bomb, hooking two together and leaving one end dangling.

The bomb is now armed.

I take a small green number pad from the front pocket of my pack and twist the end of the dangling wire around a point at the end of the pad. I press a red button on the pad and then a grey one. The green numbers light up.

The bomb is now ready for timing.

I click a silver button until the digits count up to 30:00. I press the red button again, flip over the green pad, slide one metal flap into another, then press the grey button one more time. The green numbers immediately change to 29:59, 29:58, 29:57.

The bomb is now live.

"Nicely done," Mistress Coyle whispers. "Time to go."

And then after almost a month of hiding in the forest, waiting for the prisoners to recuperate, waiting for the rest of us to train, waiting for a real army to have life breathed into it, there came a night when that waiting was over.

"Get up, my girl," Mistress Coyle said, kneeling at the foot of my cot.

I blinked myself awake. It was still pitch black. Mistress Coyle's voice was low so as not to wake the others in the long tent.

"Why?" I whispered back.

"You said you'd do anything."

I got up and went out into the cold, hopping to get my boots on while Mistress Coyle readied a pack for me to wear.

"We're going into town, aren't we?" I said, tying my laces.

"She's a genius, this one," Mistress Coyle muttered into the pack.

"Why tonight? Why now?"

She looked up at me. "Because we need to remind them that we're still here."

* * *

The pack rests empty against my back. We cross the yard and sidle up to the house, stopping to listen for anyone stirring.

No one does.

I'm ready to go but Mistress Coyle is leaning back from the outer wall of the house, looking at the white expanse of it.

"This should do fine," she says.

"For what?" I look around us, spooked now that there's a timer running.

"Have you forgotten who we are?" She reaches into a pocket of her long healer's skirt, still worn even though trousers are so much more practical. She pulls out something and tosses it to me. I catch it without even thinking.

"Why don't you do the honours?" she says.

I look in my hand. It's a crumbling piece of blue charcoal, pulled from our wood fires, the remains of the reacher trees we burn to keep warm. It smears dusty blue across my hand, across my skin.

I look at it for a moment longer.

"Tick tock," says Mistress Coyle.

I swallow. Then I raise the charcoal and make three quick slashes against the white wall of the house.

A, looking back at me, by my hand.

I find myself breathing heavily.

When I look round, Mistress Coyle's already off down the ditches of the drive. I hurry after her, keeping my head low.

Twenty-eight minutes later, just as we reach our cart, deep in the woods, we hear the *Boom*.

"Congratulations, soldier," Mistress Coyle says, as we set off back to camp. "You have just fired the first shot of the final battle."

29

THE BUSINESS OF ASKING

[TODD]

THE WOMAN IS STRAPPED against a metal frame, her arms out behind her and up, each tied at the wrist to a bar of the frame.

It looks like she's diving into a lake.

Except for the watery blood on her face.

"She's gonna get it now," Davy says.

But his voice is oddly quiet.

"One more time, my female friend," Mr Hammar says, walking behind her. "Who set the bomb?"

The first bomb since the prison break went off last night, taking out a well and pump on a farm.

It's begun.

"I don't know," says the woman, her voice strangled and coughing. "I haven't even left Haven since–"

"Haven't left *where*?" Mr Hammar says. He grabs a handle on the frame and tips the whole thing forward, plunging the woman face first into a tub of water, holding her there as she thrashes against her bindings.

I look down at my feet.

"Raise your head, please, Todd," the Mayor says, standing behind us. "How else will you learn?"

I raise my head.

We're on the other side of a two-way mirror, in a small room looking in on the Arena of the Ask, which is just a room with high concrete walls and similar mirrored rooms off of each side. Davy and I sit next to each other on a short bench.

Watching.

Mr Hammar pulls up the frame. The woman rises outta the water, gasping for air, straining against where her arms are tied.

"*Where* do you live?" Mr Hammar's got his smile on, that nasty thing that hardly ever leaves his face.

"New Prentisstown," the woman gasps. "New Prentisstown."

"Correct," says Mr Hammar, then watches as the woman coughs so hard she throws up down her front. He takes a towel from a side table and gently wipes the woman's face, cleaning as much of the vomit off her as he can.

The woman's still gasping but her eyes don't leave Mr Hammar as he cleans her.

She looks even more frightened than before.

"Why's he doing that?" Davy says.

"Doing what?" the Mayor says.

Davy shrugs. "Being, I don't know, *kind*."

I don't say nothing. I keep my Noise clear of the Mayor putting bandages on me.

All those months ago.

I hear the Mayor shift his stance, rustling himself to cover up my Noise so Davy don't hear it. "We're not inhuman, David. We don't do this for our own joy."

I look out at Mr Hammar, look at his smile.

"Yes, Todd," the Mayor says, "Captain Hammar does show a certain *glee* that is perhaps unseemly, but you have to admit, he does get results."

"Are you recovered?" Mr Hammar asks the woman. We can hear his voice over a microphone system, pumped into the room. It separates it oddly from his mouth, making it seem like we're watching a vid rather than a real thing.

"I'm sorry to have to keep Asking you," Mr Hammar says. "This can end as quick as you want."

"Please," says the woman in a whisper. "Please, I don't know anything."

And she starts to weep.

"Christ," Davy says, under his breath.

"The enemy will try many tricks to win our sympathy," says the Mayor.

Davy turns to him. "So this is a trick?"

"Almost certainly."

I keep watching the woman. It don't look like a trick.

I am the Circle and the Circle is me, I think.

"Just so," says the Mayor.

"Yer in control here," says Mr Hammar, starting round the woman again. Her head turns to try and follow him but there ain't much movement from where she's strapped to the frame. He hovers just outside of her vision. To keep her off balance, I'm guessing.

Cuz of course Mr Hammar ain't got no Noise.

Me and Davy do, tho.

"Only muffled sounds, Todd," the Mayor says, reading my asking. "Do you see the metal rods coming out of the frame by the sides of her head?"

He points. Davy and I see them.

"They play a whining buzz into her ears at all times," the Mayor says. "Muffles any Noise she might hear from the observation rooms. Keeps her focused on the Officer of the Ask."

"Wouldn't want 'em hearing what we already know," Davy says.

"Yes," the Mayor says, sounding a little surprised. "Yes, that's it exactly, David."

Davy smiles and his Noise glows a bit.

"We saw the **A** written in blue on the side of the farm-house," Mr Hammar says, still hovering behind the woman. "The bomb was the same as all the others planted by your organizayshun–"

"It's not *my* organization!" says the woman but Mr Hammar continues like she didn't even speak.

"And we know you've worked in that field for the past month."

"So have other women!" she yells, sounding more and more desperate. "Milla Price, Cassia MacRae, Martha Sutpen–"

"So they were in on it, too?"

"No! No, just that–"

"Cuz Mrs Price and Mrs Sutpen have already been Asked."

The woman stops, her face suddenly even more frightened.

Davy chuckles next to me. "Got you," he whispers.

But I can hear a weird sense of relief in him.

I wonder if the Mayor hears it, too.

"What did–" the woman says, stopping and then having to go on. "What did they say?"

"They said you tried to get 'em to help," Mr Hammar says calmly. "Said you tried to enlist 'em as terrorists and when they refused, you said you'd carry on alone."

The woman goes pale, her mouth falling open, her eyes wide in disbelief.

"That's not true, is it?" I say, my voice level. *I am the Circle and the Circle is me.* "He's trying to make her confess by pretending he don't need her to."

"Excellent, Todd," says the Mayor. "You may end up having a flair for this."

Davy looks first at me, then at his pa, then at me again, askings left unsaid.

"We already know yer responsible," Mr Hammar says. "We already have enough to stick you in prison for the rest of yer life." He stops in front of her. "I stand before you as yer friend," he says. "I stand before you as the one who can save you from a fate worse than prison."

The woman swallows and looks like she's going to vomit again.

"But I don't *know* anything," she says weakly. "I just don't *know*."

Mr Hammar sighs. "Well, that's a real disappointment, I must say."

He walks behind her again, grabs the frame and plunges her into the water.

And holds her there–

And holds her there–

He looks up to the mirror where he knows we're watching–

He smiles at us–

And still holds her there–

The water churns with the limited thrashing she can do–

I am the Circle and the Circle is me, I think, closing my eyes–

"Open them, Todd," the Mayor says–

I do–

And still Mr Hammar holds her there–

The thrashing gets worse–

So hard the binds on her wrists start to bleed–

"Jesus," Davy says, under his breath–

"He's gonna kill her," I say, voice still low–

It's only a vid–

It's only a vid–

(except it ain't–)

(feeling nothing–)

(cuz I'm dead–)

(I'm dead–)

The Mayor leans past me and presses a button on the wall. "I should think that's enough, Captain," he says, his voice carrying into the Arena of the Ask.

Mr Hammar raises the frame outta the water. But he does it slowly.

The woman hangs from it, chin down on her chest, water pouring from her mouth and nose.

"He killed her," Davy says.

"No," says the Mayor.

"Tell me," Mr Hammar says to the woman, "and this will all stop."

There's a long silence, longer still.

And then a croaking sound from the woman.

"What was that?" Mr Hammar says.

"I did it," croaks the woman.

"*No way!*" says Davy.

"What did you do?" Mr Hammar asks.

"I set the bomb," the woman says, her head still down.

"And you tried to get yer worksisters to join you in a terrorist organizayshun."

"Yes," the woman whispers. "Anything."

"Ha!" Davy says, and again there's relief, relief that he tries to cover. "She confessed! She did it!"

"No, she didn't," I say, still looking at her, still not moving on the bench.

"*What?*" Davy says to me.

"She's making it up," I say, still looking thru the mirror. "So he'll stop drowning her." I move my head just slightly to show I'm talking to the Mayor. "Ain't she?"

The Mayor waits before answering. Even without Noise, I can tell he's impressed. Ever since I started with *the Circle*, things have taken on the worst kinda clarity.

Maybe that's the point.

"Almost certainly she's making it up," he finally says. "But now we've got her confession, we can use it against her."

Davy's eyes are still rocketing back and forth twixt me and his pa. "You mean, yer gonna … Ask her some more?"

"All women are part of the Answer," the Mayor says, "if only in sympathy. We need to know what she thinks. We need to know what she *knows*."

Davy looks back at the woman, still panting against the frame.

"I don't get it," he says.

"When they send her back to prison," I say, "all the other women will know what happened to her."

"Quite," says the Mayor, putting a hand briefly on my shoulder. Almost like affecshun. When I don't move, he takes it away. "They'll know what's in store for them if they don't answer. And that way, we'll find out what we need to know from whoever knows it. The bomb last night was a resumption of aggressions, the start of something larger. We need to know what their next move is going to be."

Davy's still looking at the woman. "What about her?"

"She'll be punished for the crime she confessed to, of course," the Mayor says, carrying on talking when Davy tries to interrupt with the obvious. "And who knows? Maybe she really *does* know something." He looks back up thru the mirror. "There's only one way to find out."

"I want to thank you for yer help today," Mr Hammar says, putting his hand under the woman's chin to lift it. "You've been very brave and can be proud of the fight you put up." He smiles at her but she won't meet his eye. "You've shown more spirit than many a man I've seen under Asking."

He steps away from her, going to a little side table and removing a cloth that's lying on top. Underneath are several shiny bits of metal. Mr Hammar picks one up.

"And now for the second part of our interview," he says, approaching the woman.

Who starts to scream.

"That was," Davy says, pacing around as we wait outside but it's all he can get out. "That was." He turns to me. "Holy crap, Todd."

I don't say nothing, just take the apple I been saving outta my pocket. "Apple," I whisper to Angharrad, my head close to hers. **Apple**, she says back, clipping at it with her teeth, lips back. **Todd**, she says, munching it and then she makes an asking of it, **Todd?**

"Nothing to do with you, girl," I whisper, rubbing her nose.

We're down from the gate where Ivan's still guarding, still trying to catch my eye. I can hear him calling quietly to me in his Noise.

I still ignore him.

"That was effing intense," Davy says, trying to read my Noise, trying to see what I might think about it all, but I'm keeping it as flat as I can.

Feeling nothing.

Taking nothing in.

"Yer a cool customer these days," Davy says, voice scornful, ignoring Deadfall, who's wanting an apple, too. "You didn't even flinch when he–"

"Gentlemen," the Mayor says, coming outta the gate, a long, heavy sack in one hand.

Ivan stands up straight as a board, back at attenshun.

"Pa," Davy says in greeting.

"Is she dead?" I say, looking into Angharrad's eyes.

"She's no use to us dead, Todd," the Mayor says.

"She sure *looked* dead," Davy says.

"Only when she lost consciousness," the Mayor says. "Now, I've got a new job for the two of you."

There's a beat as we take in the words, *a new job*.

I close my eyes. *I am the Circle and the Circle is me.*

"Would you quit effing *saying* that?" Davy shouts at me.

But we can all hear the horror in his own Noise, the anxiety that's rising, the fear of his pa, of the *new job*, fear he won't be able to–

"You won't be leading the Askings, if that's what you're afraid of," says the Mayor.

"I ain't afraid," Davy says, too loud. "Who's saying I'm afraid?"

The Mayor drops the bag at our feet.

I reckernize its shape.

Feeling nothing, taking nothing in.

Davy's looking down at the bag, too. Even *he's* shocked.

"Just the prisoners," says the Mayor. "So we can fight against enemy infiltration on the inside."

"You want us to–?" Davy looks up at his pa. "On *people*?"

"Not people," says the Mayor. "Enemies of the state."

I'm still looking at the bag.

The bag that we all know carries a bolting tool and a supply of numbered bands.

10

THE BAND

{VIOLA}

I'VE JUST SET THE TIMER running and turned to Mistress Braithwaite to tell her we can leave when a woman comes tumbling out of the bushes behind us.

"Help me," she says, so gently it's almost as if she doesn't know we're there and is just asking the universe to help her somehow.

Then she collapses.

"What *is* this thing?" I say, taking another bandage from the too-small first aid kit we keep hidden in the cart, trying to tend her wound as we rock back and forth. There's a metal band encircling the middle of her forearm, so tight it seems like the skin around it is trying to grow *into* it. It's also so red with infection I can almost feel the heat coming off it.

"It's for branding livestock," Mistress Braithwaite says, angrily snapping the reins on the oxes, bumping us along paths that we aren't meant to take this fast. "That vicious *bastard*."

"Help me," the woman whispers.

"I'm helping you," I say. Her head is in my lap to cushion it from the bumps in the road. I wrap a bandage around the metal band but not before I see a number etched into the side.

1391.

"What's your name?" I ask.

But her eyes are half-closed and all she says is, "Help me."

"And we're sure she's not a spy?" Mistress Coyle says, arms crossed.

"Good *God*," I snap. "Is there a stone where your heart should be?"

Her brow darkens. "We have to consider all manner of tricks—"

"The infection is so bad we're not going to be able to save her arm," Mistress Braithwaite says. "If she's a spy, she's in no position to return with information."

Mistress Coyle sighs. "Where was she?"

"Near that new Office of the Ask we've been hearing about," Mistress Braithwaite says, frowning even harder.

"We planted a device on a small storehouse nearby," I say. "It was as close as we could get."

"*Branding* strips, Nicola," Mistress Braithwaite says, anger puffing out of her like the steam of her breath.

Mistress Coyle rubs her fingers along her forehead. "I know."

"Can't we just cut it off?" I ask. "Heal the wound?"

Mistress Braithwaite shakes her head. "Chemicals make it so the banded skin never heals, that's the point. You can never remove it unless you want to bleed to death. They're permanent. *Forever*."

"Oh, my God."

"I need to talk to her," Mistress Coyle says.

"Nadari's treating her," Mistress Braithwaite says. "She might be lucid before the surgery."

"Let's go then," Mistress Coyle says and they head off towards the healing tent. I move to follow, but Mistress Coyle stops me with a look. "Not you, my girl."

"Why not?"

But off they keep walking, leaving me standing in the cold.

"Y'all right, Hildy?" Wilf asks as I wander among the oxes. He's brushing them down where they strained against the harnesses. **Wilf**, they say.

That's pretty much all they ever say.

"Rough night," I say. "We rescued a woman who'd been branded with some kind of metal band."

Wilf looks thoughtful for a minute. He points to a metal band around the right front leg of each ox. "Like these 'ere?"

I nod.

"On a person?" He whistles in amazement.

"Things are turning, Wilf," I say. "Turning for the worse."

"Ah know," he says. "We'll make a move soon and that'll be it, one way or t'other."

I look up at him. "Do you know exactly what she's planning?"

He shakes his head and runs his hand around the metal band on one of the oxes. **Wilf**, says the ox.

"Viola!" I hear, called across the camp.

Wilf and I both see Mistress Coyle treading through the darkened camp towards us. "She's gone wake everyone up," Wilf says.

"She's a little delirious," Mistress Nadari says as I kneel down by the cot of the rescued woman. "You've got a minute, tops."

"Tell her what you told us, my girl," Mistress Coyle says to the woman. "Just once more and we'll let you sleep."

"My arm?" says the woman, her eyes cloudy. "It don't hurt no more."

"Just tell her what you said, my love," Mistress Coyle says, her voice as warm as it ever gets. "And everything'll be all right."

The woman's eyes focus briefly on mine and widen slightly. "You," she says. "The girl who was there."

"Viola," I say, touching her non-banded arm.

"We haven't got much time, Jess." Mistress Coyle's voice gets a little sterner, even as she says what must be the woman's name. "Tell her."

"Tell me what?" I say, getting a little annoyed. It's cruel to keep her awake like this and I'm about to say as much when Mistress Coyle says, "Tell her who did this to you."

Jess's eyes grow frightened. "Oh," she says. "Oh, oh."

"Just this one thing and we'll leave you be," Mistress Coyle says.

"Mistress Coyle–" I start to say, getting angry.

"*Boys*," the woman says. "Boys. Not even men."

I take in a breath.

"Which boys?" Mistress Coyle asks. "What were their names?"

"Davy," says the woman, her eyes not seeing the inside of the tent any more. "Davy was the older one."

Mistress Coyle catches my eye. "And the other?"

"The quiet one," the woman says. "Didn't say nothing. Just did his job and didn't say nothing."

"What was his name?" Mistress Coyle insists.

"I need to go," I say, standing up, not wanting to hear. Mistress Coyle grabs my hand and holds me there firmly.

"What was his name?" she says again.

The woman is breathing harshly now, almost panting.

"That's enough," Mistress Nadari says. "I didn't want this in the first–"

"One second more," Mistress Coyle says.

"Nicola–" Mistress Nadari warns.

"Todd," says the woman on the cot, the woman I saved, the woman with the infected arm she's going to lose, the woman I now wish was at the bottom of the ocean I've never seen. "The other one called him Todd."

"Get away from me," I say, as Mistress Coyle follows me out of the tent.

"He's alive," she's saying, "but he's one of them."

"Shut up!" I say, stomping across the camp, not caring how loud I'm being.

Mistress Coyle races forward and grabs my arm. "You've lost him, my girl," she says. "If you ever really had him in the first place."

I slap her face so fast and hard she doesn't have time to defend herself. It's like smacking a tree trunk. The solid weight of her staggers back and my arm rings with pain.

"You don't know what you're talking about," I say, my voice blazing.

"How *dare* you," she says, her hand to her face.

"You haven't even *seen* me fight yet," I say, standing my ground. "*I* knocked down a bridge to stop an army. *I* put a knife through the neck of a crazy murderer. *I* saved the lives of others while you just ran around at night blowing them up."

"You ignorant child–"

I step towards her.

She doesn't step back.

But she stops her sentence.

"I hate you," I say slowly. "Everything you do makes the Mayor respond with something *worse*."

"I did *not* start this war–"

"But you *love* it!" I take another step towards her. "You love everything about it. The bombs, the fighting, the rescues."

Her face is so angry I can even see it in the moonlight.

But I'm not afraid of her.

And I think she can tell.

"You want to see it as simple good and evil, my girl," she says. "The world doesn't work that way. Never has, never will, and don't forget," she gives me a smile that could curdle milk, "you're fighting the war *with* me."

I lean in close to her face. "He needs to be overthrown, so I'm helping you do it. But when it's done?" I'm so close I can feel her breath. "Are we going to have to overthrow you next?"

She doesn't say anything.

But she doesn't back down either.

I turn on my heels and I walk away from her.

"He's gone, Viola!" Mistress Coyle shouts after me.

But I just keep walking.

"I need to go back to the city."

"Now?" Wilf says, looking up at the sky. "Be dawn soon. T'ain't safe."

"It's *never* safe," I say, "but I have no choice."

He blinks at me. Then he starts gathering ropes and bindings to get the cart ready again.

"No," I say, "you'll have to show me how to do it. I can't ask you to risk your life."

"Yer goin for Todd?"

I nod.

"Then Ah'll take yoo."

"Wilf–"

"Still early," he says, backing the oxes into position. "Ah'll at least get yoo close."

He doesn't say another word as he re-harnesses the oxes to his cart. They ask him **Wilf? Wilf?** in surprise at being used so quickly again after thinking their night of work was finished.

I think about what Jane would say. I think about putting her Wilf into danger.

But all I say is, "Thank you."

"I'm coming, too." I turn around. Lee is there, rubbing sleep out of his eyes but dressed and ready.

"What are you doing up?" I ask. "And no, you're not."

"Yes, I am," he says, "and who can sleep with all that shouting?"

"It's too dangerous," I say. "They'll hear your Noise–"

He keeps his mouth shut and says to me, Then they can just hear it.

"Lee–"

"You're going to look for him, aren't you?"

I sigh in frustration, beginning to wonder if I should abandon the idea altogether before I put anyone else in danger.

"You're going to the Office of the Ask," Lee says, lowering his voice.

I nod.

And then I understand.

Siobhan and his mum might be there.

I nod again, and this time he knows I've agreed.

No one tries to stop us, though half the camp must know we're going. Mistress Coyle must have her reasons.

We don't talk much as we go. I just listen to Lee's Noise and its thoughts of his family, of the Mayor, of what he'll do if he ever gets his hands on him.

Thoughts of me.

"You'd better say something," Lee says. "Listening that close is rude."

"So I've heard," I say.

But my mouth is dry and I find I don't have much to say.

The sun rises before we get to the city. Wilf pushes the oxes as fast as they'll go, but even so, it's going to be a dangerous trip back, with the city awake, with Noisy men on our cart. We're taking a terrible risk.

But on Wilf drives.

I've explained what I want to see, and he says he knows a place. He stops the cart deep in some woods and directs us up a bluff.

"Keep yer heads down now," he says. "Don't be seen."

"We won't," I say. "But if we're not back in an hour, don't walt for us."

Wilf just looks at me. We all know how likely him leaving us is.

Lee and I make our way up the bluff, keeping down in the cover of the trees, until we reach the top and see why Wilf chose the place. It's a hill near where the tower fell, one where we've got a clear view of the road coming down towards the Office of the Ask, which we've heard is some kind of prison or torture chamber or something like that.

I don't even want to know.

We lie on our stomachs, side by side, looking out from some bushes.

"Keep your ears open," Lee whispers.

As if we need to. As soon as the sun rises, New Prentisstown

ROARs to life. I begin to wonder if Lee even needs to hide his Noise so much. How could it not be possible to drown in it?

"Because drowning is the right word," Lee says when I ask. "If you disappeared into it, you'd suffocate."

"I can't imagine what it's like growing up inside it all," I say.

"No," he says. "No, you can't."

But he doesn't say it in a mean way.

I squint down the road as the sun brightens. "I wish I had some binos."

Lee reaches into a pocket and pulls out a pair.

I give him a look. "You were just waiting for me to ask so you could look all impressive."

"I don't know what you're talking about," he says, smiling, putting the binos to his eyes.

"C'mon." I push him with my shoulder. "Give them to me."

He stretches away to keep them out of my grabbing range. I start to giggle, so does he. I grab onto him and try to hold him down while I snatch at the binos but he's bigger than me and keeps twisting them away.

"I'm not afraid to hurt you," I say.

"I don't doubt that," he laughs, turning the binos back to the road.

His Noise spikes, loud enough to make me afraid someone'll hear us.

"What do you see?" I say, not giggling any more.

He hands the binos to me, pointing. "There," he says. "Coming down the road."

But I'm already seeing them in the binos.

Two people on horseback. Two people in shiny new uniforms, riding their horses. One of them talking, gesturing with his hands.

Laughing. Smiling.

The other keeping his eyes on his horse, but riding along to work.

Riding along to his job at the Office of the Ask.

In a uniform with a shiny *A* on the shoulder.

Todd.

My Todd.

Riding next to Davy Prentiss.

Riding to work with the man who shot me.

31

NUMBERS AND LETTERS

[TODD]

THE DAYS KEEP PASSING. They keep getting worse.

"*All* of 'em?" Davy asks, his Noise ringing with badly hidden alarm. "Every single one?"

"This is a vote of confidence, David," the Mayor says, standing with us at the door of the stables while our horses are made ready for the day's work. "You and Todd did such an excellent job with permanently identifying the female prisoners, who else would I want to be in charge of expanding the programme?"

I don't say nothing, not even acknowledging Davy's looks at me. His Noise is confused with the pink of his pa's praise.

But then there's also his thoughts about banding all the women.

Every single one.

Cuz banding the ones in the Office of the Ask was even worse than we thought.

"They keep leaving," the Mayor says. "In the dead of night, they slip away and cast their lot with the terrorists."

Davy's watching Deadfall get saddled in a small paddock, his Noise clanking with the faces of the women who get banded, the cries of pain they make.

The words they speak to us.

"And if they keep getting out," the Mayor says, "they obviously keep getting in, too."

He means the bombs. One every night for the past two weeks nearly, so many they must be increasing for a reason, they must be leading up to something bigger, and no women have been caught planting 'em except once when a bomb blew up while the woman was still putting it in place. They didn't find much left of her except bits of clothing and flesh.

I close my eyes when I think of it.

Feeling nothing, taking nothing in.

(was it her?)

Feeling *nothing*.

"You want us to number *all* the women," Davy says again quietly, looking away from his pa.

"I've said it before," the Mayor sighs. "*Every* woman is part of the Answer, if only because she is a woman and therefore sympathetic to other women."

The groomsmen bring Angharrad into a nearby paddock. She sticks her head over the rail to bump me with her nose. **Todd**, she says.

"They'll resist," I say, stroking her head. "The men won't like it neither."

"Ah, yes," says the Mayor. "You missed yesterday's rally, didn't you?"

Davy and I look at each other. We were at work all day yesterday and didn't hear nothing bout no rally.

"I spoke to the men of New Prentisstown," the Mayor says. "Man to man. I explained to them the threat the Answer poses us and how this is the next prudent step forward to ensure safety for all." He rubs a hand down Angharrad's neck. I try and hide how prickly my Noise gets at the sight. "I encountered no resistance."

"There weren't no women at this rally," I say, "were there?"

He turns to me. "I wouldn't want to encourage the enemy among us, now would I?

"But there's effing *thousands* of 'em!" Davy says. "Banding 'em all will take forever."

"There will be other teams working, David," the Mayor says calmly, making sure he's got his son's full attenshun. "But I'm sure the two of you will outwork any of them."

Davy's Noise perks up a bit at this. "You bet we will, Pa," he says.

He looks at me, tho.

And there's worry there.

I stroke Angharrad's nose again. The groomsmen bring out Morpeth, freshly brushed and shiny with oil. **Submit**, he says.

"If you're worried," the Mayor says, taking Morpeth's reins. "Ask yourselves this." He hoists himself up in the saddle in one smooth movement, like he's made of liquid. He looks down at us.

"Why would any innocent woman object to being identified?"

"You won't get away with this," the woman says, her voice almost steady.

Mr Hammar cocks his rifle behind us and aims it at her head.

"You blind?" Davy says to the woman, voice a little too squeaky. "I'm getting away with it *right now*."

Mr Hammar laughs.

Davy twists the bolting tool with a hard turn. The band snaps into the woman's skin halfway up her forearm. She calls out, grabbing the band and falling forward, catching herself on the floor with her unbanded arm. She stops there a minute, panting.

Her hair is pulled back into a severe knot, blondy and brown mixed together, like the wire filaments in the back of a vid player. There's a small patch on the back where the hair is grey, all growing together, a river across a dusty land.

I stare at the grey patch, letting my eyes blur a little.

I am the Circle and the Circle is me.

"Get up," Davy says to the woman. "So the healers can treat you." He looks back at the line of women staring at us down the hall to the front of the dormitory, waiting their turn.

"The boy said get up," Mr Hammar says, waving his rifle.

"We don't need you here," Davy snaps, his voice tight. "We're doing just fine without no babysitter."

"I ain't babysitting," Mr Hammar smiles. "I'm protecting."

The woman stands, her eyes on me.

My own expresshun is dead, removed, not here if it don't have to be.

I am the Circle and the Circle is me.

"Where's your heart?" she asks. "Where is your heart if you can do these things?" And then she turns to where the healers, who we've already banded, wait to give her treatment.

I watch her go.

I don't know her name.

Her number, tho, is 1484.

"1485!" Davy calls out.

The next woman in line steps forward.

We spend the day riding from one women's dormitory to another, getting thru almost three hundred bands, much faster than we ever did the Spackle. We start for home when the sun begins to set, as New Prentisstown turns its thoughts to curfew.

We ain't saying much.

"What a day, eh, pigpiss?" Davy says, after a while.

I don't say nothing but he don't want an answer.

"They'll be all right," he says. "They got the healers to take away the pain and stuff."

Clop, clop, along we go.

I hear what he's thinking.

Dusk is falling. I can't see his face.

Maybe that's why he ain't covering it up.

"When they cry, tho," he says.

I keep quiet.

"Ain't you got nothing to say?" Davy's voice gets a little harder. "All silent now, like you don't wanna talk no more, like I ain't worth talking to."

His Noise starts to crackle.

"Not like I got anyone *else* to talk to, pigpiss. Not like I got any *choice* in the situashun. Not like no matter what I effing *do* can I get moved up for it, given the good work, the *fighting* work. All that stupid Spackle babysitting crap. Then we turn right around and do the same thing to the women. And for what? For *what*?"

His voice gets low.

"So they can cry at us," he says. "So they can look at us like we ain't even human."

"We ain't," I say, surprised to find I said it out loud.

"Yeah, that's the new you, ain't it?" he says, sneering. "All Mister No-Feeling I-Am-The-Circle Tough Guy. You'd put a bullet thru yer own *ma*'s head if Pa told you to."

I don't say nothing but I grind my teeth together.

Davy's quiet for a minute, too. Then he says, "Sorry."

Then he says, "Sorry, Todd," using my name.

Then he says, "What the hell am *I* saying sorry for? Yer the stupid can't-read pigpiss all getting on my pa's good side. Who cares about you?"

I still don't say nothing and *clop, clop*, along we go.

"Forward," Angharrad neighs to Deadfall, who nickers back, "Forward."

Forward, I hear in her Noise and then **Boy colt, Todd**.

"Angharrad," I whisper twixt her ears.

"Todd?" Davy says.

"Yeah?" I say.

I hear him breathe out thru his nose. "Nothing." Then he changes his mind. "How d'you *do* it?"

"Do what?"

I see him shrug in the dusk. "Be so calm bout it all. Be so, I don't know, *unfeeling*. I mean…" He drifts off and says, almost too quietly to hear, one more time, "when they cry."

I don't say nothing cuz how can I help him? How can he not know about *The Circle* unless his pa don't want him to?

"I *do* know," he says, "but I tried that crap and it don't work for me and he won't–"

He stops abruptly, like he's said too much.

"Ah, screw it," he says.

We keep riding, letting the **ROAR** of New Prentisstown enfold us as we enter the main part of town, the horses calling their orders to each other, reminding theirselves of who they are.

"Yer the only friend I got, pigpiss," Davy finally says. "Ain't that the biggest tragedy you ever heard?"

"Tiring day?" Mayor Ledger says to me when I come into our cell. His voice is oddly light and he keeps his eyes on me.

"What do you care?" I sling my bag on the floor and flop down on the bed without taking my uniform off.

"I suppose it must be exhausting torturing women all day."

I blink in surprise. "I don't torture 'em," I growl. "You shut yer mouth about that."

"No, of *course* you don't torture them. What was I

thinking? You just strap a corrosive metal band into their skin that can never be removed without them bleeding to death. How could that possibly be construed as *torture*?"

"Hey!" I sit up. "We do it fast and without fuss. There are lots of ways to make it worse and we don't do that. If it's gotta be done, then it's best that it's done by *us*."

He crosses his arms, his voice still light. "That excuse going to help you sleep tonight?"

My Noise roars up. "Oh, yeah?" I snap. "Was that you the Mayor didn't hear shouting at the rally yesterday? Was that you who weren't making that brave stand against him?"

His face goes stormy and I hear a flash of grey resentment in his Noise. "And get shot?" he says. "Or dragged away to be Asked? How would that help anything?"

"And that's what yer doing?" I say. "*Helping*?"

He don't say nothing to that, just turns to look out one of the windows, out over the few lights that come on only in essenshul places, out over the ROAR of a town wondering when the Answer are gonna make their big move and from where and how bad it'll be and who's gonna save 'em.

My Noise is raised and red. I close my eyes and take in a deep, deep breath.

I am the Circle and the Circle is me.

Feeling nothing, taking nothing in.

"They were getting used to him again," Mayor Ledger says out the window. "They were uniting behind him because what're a few curfews against being blown up? But this is a tactical mistake."

I open my eyes at *tactical* cuz it seems a weird word to choose.

"The men are terrified now," he's still saying. "Terrified they're going to be next." He looks down at his own forearm, rubbing a spot where a band might go. "Politically, he's made a mistake."

I squint at him. "What do you care if he's made a mistake?" I ask. "Whose side are you on?"

He turns to me as if I've insulted him, which I guess I have. "The *town's*," he steams. "Whose side are *you* on, Todd Hewitt?"

There's a knock on the door.

"Saved by the dinner bell," Mayor Ledger says.

"The dinner bell don't knock," I say, getting to my feet. I unlock the door with my key *ker-thunk* and open it.

It's Davy.

He don't say nothing at first, just looks nervous, eyes here and there. I figure there's a problem at the dormitories so I sigh and move back to my bed to get my few things. I ain't even had time to get my boots off.

"It'll take a minute," I say to him. "Angharrad'll still be eating. She won't like being saddled up again so soon."

He still ain't said nothing so I turn to look at him. He's still nervous, not meeting my eye. "*What?*" I say.

He chews on his upper lip and all I can see in his Noise is embarrassment and asking marks and anger at Mayor Ledger being there and more asking marks and there behind it all, a weird strong feeling, almost guilty, almost *clear*—

Then he covers it up fast and the anger and embarrassment come foremost.

"Effing pigpiss," he says to himself. He pulls angrily at a strap on his shoulder and I see he's carrying a bag. "Effing…" he says again but don't finish the thought. He unsnaps the flap on it and takes something out.

"*Here*," he practically shouts, thrusting it at me.

My ma's book.

He's giving me back my ma's book.

"Just take it!"

I reach out slowly, taking it twixt my fingers and pulling it away from him like it was a fragile thing. The leather of the cover is still soft, the gash still cut thru the front where Aaron stabbed me and it was stopped by the book. I run my hand over it.

I look up at Davy but he won't meet my eye.

"Whatever," he says and turns again, stomping back down the stairs and out into the night.

32

FINAL PREPARATIONS

{VIOLA}

I HIDE BEHIND THE TREE, my heart pounding.

I have a gun in my hand.

I listen hard for the snap of twigs, the sound of any footsteps, any sign that'll tell me where the soldier is. I know he's there because I can hear his Noise but it's so flat and wide I only get a general idea of the direction he's going to come after me.

Because he *is* coming for me. There's no doubt about that.

His Noise grows louder. My back is to the tree and I hear him off to my left.

I'm going to have to leap at just the right second.

I ready my gun.

I see the trees around me in his Noise, along with asking marks wondering which one I'm hiding behind, narrowing it down to two, the one that I'm actually using and one a few feet away to my left.

If he chooses that one, I've got him.

I hear his steps now, quiet against the damp forest floor. I close my eyes and try to concentrate solely on his Noise, on exactly where he's standing, where he's placing his feet.

Which tree he's approaching.

He steps. He hesitates. He steps again.

He makes his choice–

And I make mine–

I jump and I'm ducking and twisting and sweeping my leg at his feet and I'm catching him by surprise and he's falling to the ground, trying to aim his rifle at me, but I'm leaping on him and pinning his rifle arm down with my leg and throwing my weight on his chest and holding the barrel of my gun under his chin.

I've got him.

"Well done," Lee says, smiling up at me.

"Indeed, well done," Mistress Braithwaite says, stepping out of the darkness. "And now comes the moment, Viola. What do you do with the enemy under your mercy?"

I look down into Lee's face, breathing hard, feeling his warmth underneath me.

"What do you do?" Mistress Braithwaite asks again.

I look down at my gun.

"I do what I have to do," I say.

I do what I have to do to save him.

I do what I have to do to save Todd.

"You're *sure* you want to do this?" Mistress Coyle asks for the hundredth time as we leave the breakfast area the next morning, shaking off Jane's last insistences that we have more tea.

"I'm sure," I say.

"You've got one chance before we make our move. *One.*"

"He came for me once," I say. "When I was captive, he came for me and made the biggest sacrifice he could make to do it."

She frowns. "People change, Viola."

"He deserves the same chance he gave me."

"Hmm," Mistress Coyle hmms. She's still not convinced.

But I haven't given her any choice.

"And when he joins us," I say, "think of the information he can provide."

"Yes." She looks away, looks out at the camp of the Answer preparing itself. Preparing itself for war. "Yes, so you keep saying."

Even with how well I know Todd, I can also see how anyone else would see him on horseback, would see him in that uniform, would see him riding with Davy, and they would think he's a traitor.

And in the dead of night, when I'm under my blankets, unable to sleep.

I think it, too.

(what's he doing?)

(what's he doing with *Davy*?)

And I try to put it out of my mind as best I can.

Because I'm going to save him.

She's agreed that I can. She's agreed I can risk myself and go to the cathedral the night before the Answer makes its final attack and try one last time to save him.

She agreed because I said if she didn't, I wouldn't help her with anything more, not with the bombs, not with the final attack, not with the ships when they land, now eight weeks away and counting. Nothing, if I couldn't try for Todd.

Even with all that, I think the only reason she agreed is for what he could tell us when he got here.

Mistress Coyle *likes* to know things.

"You're brave to try," Mistress Coyle says. "Foolish, but brave." She looks me up and down once more, her face unknowable.

"What?" I ask.

She shakes her head. "Just how much of myself I see in you, you exasperating girl."

"Think I'm ready to lead my own army?" I say, almost smiling.

She just gives me a last look and starts walking off into the camp, ready to give more orders, make more preparations, put the final touches to the plans for our attack.

Which happens tomorrow.

"Mistress Coyle," I call after her.

She turns.

"Thank you," I say.

She looks surprised, her forehead furrowed. But she nods, accepting it.

"Got it?" Lee calls over the top of the cart.

"Got it," I say, twisting the final knot and locking the clamp into place.

"'At's all of 'em," Wilf says, smacking some dust off his

hands. We look at the carts, eleven of them now, packed to bursting with supplies, with weapons, with explosives. Almost the entire stash of the Answer.

Eleven carts doesn't seem like much against an army of a thousand or more, but that's what we have.

"Bin done before," Wilf says, quoting Mistress Coyle, but he's always so dry you never know if he's making fun. "Only a matter a tactics."

And then he smiles the same mysterious smile Mistress Coyle always gives. It's so funny and unexpected, I laugh out loud.

Lee doesn't, though. "Yes, her top secret plan." He pulls a rope on the cart to test that it holds.

"I expect it has to do with him," I say. "*Getting* him, somehow, and then once he's gone–"

"His army will fall apart and the town will rise up against his tyranny and we'll save the day," Lee says, sounding unconvinced. He looks at Wilf. "What do you think?"

"She says it'll be the end," Wilf shrugs. "Ah want it to be done."

Mistress Coyle does keep saying that, that this could end the whole conflict, that the right blow in the right place right *now* could be all we need, that if even just the women of the town join us we could topple him before winter comes, topple him before the ships land, topple him before he finds us.

And then Lee says, "I know something I shouldn't."

Wilf and I both look at him.

"She passed by the kitchen window with Mistress Braithwaite," he says. "They were talking about where the attack will come from tomorrow."

"Lee–" I say.

"Don't say it," Wilf says.

"It's from the hill to the south of town," he presses on, opening his Noise so we can't *not* hear it, "the one with the notch in it, the one with the smaller road that leads right into the town square."

Wilf's eyes bulge. "Yoo shouldn'ta *said*. If Hildy gets caught–"

But Lee's only looking at me. "If you get into trouble," he says. "You come running toward that hill. You come running and that's where you'll find help."

And his Noise says, That's where you'll find me.

"And with burdened hearts, we commit you to the earth."

One by one, we throw a handful of dirt on the empty coffin that doesn't contain anything of the body of Mistress Forth, blown to pieces when a bomb went off too early as she was planting it on a grain house.

The sun is setting when we finish, dusk shining cold across the lake, a lake that had a layer of ice around the edges this morning that didn't melt all day. People start to spread out for the night's work, last minute packing and orders to be received, all the women and men who will soon be soldiers, marching with weapons, ready to strike the final blow.

All they look like now are ordinary people.

I'll leave tonight as soon as it's fully dark.

They'll leave tomorrow at sunset, no matter what happens to me.

"It's time," Mistress Coyle says, coming to my side.

She doesn't mean it's time to leave.

There's something else that has to happen first.

"Are you ready?" she asks.

"As I'll ever be," I say, walking along with her.

"This is a huge risk we're taking, my girl. *Huge*. If you're caught–"

"I won't be."

"But if you are." She stops us. "If you are, you know where the camp is, you know when we're attacking and I'm going to tell you now that we're attacking from the east road, the one by the Office of the Ask. We're going to march into town and ram it down his throat." She takes both my hands and stares hard into my eyes. "Do you understand what I'm telling you?"

I do understand. I do. She's telling me wrong on purpose, she's telling me so I can truthfully give the wrong information if I'm caught, like she did before about the ocean.

It's what I'd do if I were her.

"I understand," I say.

She pulls her cloak further shut against a freezing breeze that's come up. We walk in silence for a few steps, heading towards the healing tent.

"Who did you save?" I ask.

"What?" She looks at me, genuinely confused.

We stop again. Which is fine with me. "All those years ago," I say. "Corinne said you were kicked off the Council for saving a life. Who did you save?"

She looks at me thoughtfully and rubs her fingers across her forehead.

"I may not return," I say. "You may never see me again. It'd be nice to know something good about you so I don't die thinking you're just a huge pain in my ass."

She almost grins but it disappears quickly, her eyes looking troubled again. "Who did I save?" she says to herself. She takes a deep breath. "I saved an enemy of the state."

"You *what*?"

"The Answer was never exactly authorized, you see." She walks us off in a different direction, towards the shore of the freezing lake. "The men fighting the Spackle War didn't really approve of our methods, effective as they might have been." She looks back at me. "And they were *very* effective. Effective enough to get the heads of the Answer onto the ruling Council when Haven was being put back together."

"That's why you think it'll work now. Why you think it'll work against a bigger force."

She nods and rubs her forehead again. I'm surprised she hasn't built a callus up there. "Haven restarted itself," she continues, "using the captured Spackle to rebuild and so on. But some people weren't happy with the new government. Some people didn't have as much power as they thought they should." She shivers under her cloak. "Some people in the Answer."

She lets me realize what this might mean. "Bombs," I say.

"Quite so. Some people get so caught up in warfare, they start doing it for its own sake."

She turns away, so that maybe I can't see her face or that maybe she can't see mine, see the judgement on it.

"Her name was Mistress Thrace." She's talking to the lake now, to the cold night sky. "Smart, strong, respected, but with a liking for being in charge. Which was exactly the reason no one wanted her on the Council, including the Answer, and why she reacted so strongly to being left off."

She turns back to me. "She had her supporters. And she had her bombing campaign. Not unlike the one we're giving the Mayor now, except of course, that was meant to be peacetime." She glances up at the moons. "She specialized in what we took to calling a Thrace bomb. She'd leave it somewhere soldiers were gathered and it would look like an innocent package. Wouldn't arm itself until it felt the heartbeat in the skin of the hand picking it up. Your own pulse would make it dangerous, and at that point, you knew it was a bomb and that it would only go off when you let it go. So if you dropped it or couldn't disarm it." She shrugs. "Boom."

We watch a cloud pass between the two rising moons. "Meant to be bad luck, that is," Mistress Coyle murmurs.

She loops her arm in mine again and we start walking back towards the healing tent. "And so there wasn't another war exactly," she says. "More of a skirmish. And to the delight of everyone, Mistress Thrace was mortally wounded."

There's a silence where you can only hear our footsteps and the Noise of the men, crisp in the air.

"But not mortally wounded after all," I say.

She shakes her head. "I'm a very good healer." We reach the opening of the healing tent. "I'd known her since we were girls together on Old World. As far as I saw it, I had no choice." She rubs her hands together. "They kicked me off the Council for it. And then they executed her anyway."

I look at her now, trying to understand her, trying to understand all that's good in her and all that's difficult and conflicted and all the things that went into making her the person that she is.

We are the choices we make. And *have* to make. We aren't anything else.

"Are you ready?" she says again, finally this time.

"I'm ready."

We go into the tent.

My bag is there, packed by Mistress Coyle herself, the one I'll carry on the cart with Wilf, the one I'll carry into town. It's full of food, completely innocent food which, if all goes according to plan, will be my entry into town, my entry past the guards, my entry into the cathedral.

If all goes well.

If it doesn't, there's a pistol in a secret pouch at the bottom.

Mistresses Lawson and Braithwaite are also in the tent, healing materials at the ready.

And Lee is there, as I'd asked him to be.

I sit down on the chair facing him.

He takes my hand and squeezes it and I feel a note in the palm of his hand. He looks at me, his Noise filled with what's about to happen.

I open the note, keeping its contents out of view of all three mistresses around me, who no doubt think it's something romantic or stupid like that.

Don't react, it reads. *I've decided I'm coming with you. I'll meet your cart in the woods. You want to find your family, I want to find mine, and neither of us should do it alone.*

I don't react. I refold the note and look back up at him, giving him the smallest of nods.

"Good luck, Viola," Mistress Coyle says, words echoed rapidly by everyone else there, ending with Lee.

I wanted him particularly to do this. I couldn't stand for it to have been Mistress Coyle, and I know Lee will take the best care.

Because there's only one way I'm going to be able to move around New Prentisstown without getting caught. Only one way based on the intelligence we've gathered.

Only one way I can find Todd.

"Are you ready?" Lee asks, and it feels different coming from him, so much so that I don't mind being asked yet again.

"I'm ready," I say.

I hold out my arm and roll up my sleeve.

"Just make it quick." I look into Lee's eyes. "Please."

"I will," he says.

He reaches into the bag at his feet and takes out a metal band marked 1391.

33

FATHERS AND SONS

[TODD]

"DID HE TELL YOU what he wanted?" Davy asks.

"When would I have talked to him when you weren't there?" I say.

"Duh, pigpiss, you live in the same *building*."

We're riding to the Office of the Ask, the sun setting on the end of our day. Two hundred more women labelled. It goes faster with Mr Hammar watching over it all with a gun. With the other teams around town led by Mr Morgan and Mr O'Hare, word is we've got nearly every one of 'em, tho the bands don't seem to be healing as fast on women as they do on sheep or Spackle.

I look up at the dusky sky as we move along the road and I realize something. "Where do *you* live?"

"Oh, *now* he asks." Davy slaps the reins on Deadfall/ Acorn, causing him to canter for about two steps and then drop back into a trot. "Five months we're working together almost."

"I'm asking now."

Davy's Noise is buzzing a little. He don't wanna answer, I can tell.

"You don't have to–"

"Above the stables," he says. "Little room. Mattress on a floor. Smells like horseshit."

We keep on riding. "Forward," Angharrad nickers. "Forward," Deadfall nickers back. Todd, Angharrad thinks. "Angharrad," I say.

Davy and I ain't talked about my ma's book since he brought it to me four nights back. Not a word. And any sign of it in either of our Noises gets ignored.

But we're talking more.

I begin to wonder what sort of man I'd be if I'd had the Mayor as a father. I begin to wonder what sort of man I'd be if I'd had the Mayor as a father and wasn't the son he wanted. I wonder if I'd be sleeping in a room over the stables.

"I try," Davy says, quiet. "But who knows what he effing *wants*?"

I don't know so I don't say nothing.

We tie up our horses at the front gates. Ivan tries to catch my eye again as I go inside but I don't let him.

"Todd," he says as we pass, trying harder.

"That's Mr Hewitt to you, *Private*," Davy spits at him.

I keep on walking. We take the short path from the gates to the front doors of the Office of the Ask building. Soldiers guard those doors, too, but we walk on past 'em into the entryway, across the cold concrete floor, still uncovered, still unheated, and go into the same viewing room as before.

"Ah, boys, welcome," the Mayor says, turning away from the mirror to greet us.

Behind him, in the Arena of the Ask, is Mr Hammar, wearing a rubber apron. Seated in front of him, a naked man is screaming.

The Mayor presses a button, cutting off the sound mid-cry.

"I understand the identification scheme is complete?" he asks, bright and clear.

"As far as we know," I say.

"Who's that?" Davy asks, pointing at the man.

"Son of the exploded terrorist," the Mayor says. "Didn't run when his mother did, foolish man. Now we're seeing what he knows."

Davy curls his lip. "But if he didn't run off when she did–"

"You both have done a tremendous job for me," the Mayor says, clasping his hands behind his back. "I'm very pleased."

Davy smiles and the pink rush fills his Noise.

"But the threat is finally upon us," the Mayor continues. "One of the original terrorists caught in the prison attack finally told us something useful." He looks back thru the mirror. Mr Hammar is blocking most of the view but the man's bare feet are curling tightly against whatever Mr Hammar's doing to him. "Before she unfortunately passed away, she was able to tell us that, based on the patterns of the recent bombings, we can almost certainly expect a major move by the Answer within days, perhaps as soon as tomorrow."

Davy glances over to me. I keep looking at a middle point beyond the Mayor on the blank wall behind.

"They'll be defeated, of course," says the Mayor. "Easily. Their force is so much smaller than ours that I can't see it lasting more than a day at most."

"Let us fight, Pa," Davy says eagerly. "You know we're ready."

The Mayor smiles, smiles at his own son. Davy's Noise goes so pink you can't hardly look at it.

"You're being promoted, David," the Mayor says. "Into an army position. You will be Sergeant Prentiss."

Davy's smile almost explodes off his face in a little boom of pleased Noise. "Hot damn," he says, as if we weren't there.

"You will be at Captain Hammar's side as he rides into battle at the front of the first wave," the Mayor says. "You will get your fight exactly as you want."

Davy's practically glowing. "Aw, man, *thanks*, Pa!"

The Mayor turns to me. "I'm making you Lieutenant Hewitt."

Davy's Noise gives a sharp change. "*Lieutenant?*"

"You will be my personal bodyguard from the moment the fighting starts," the Mayor goes on. "You will remain by my side, protecting me from any threats that may approach while I superintend the battle."

I don't say nothing, just keep my eyes on the blank wall.

I am the Circle and the Circle is me.

"And this is how the Circle turns, Todd," says the Mayor.

"Why does he get to be a lieutenant?" Davy asks, Noise crackling.

"Lieutenant isn't a battle rank," the Mayor says smoothly. "Sergeant is. If you weren't a sergeant, you wouldn't be able to fight."

"Oh," Davy says, looking back and forth to each of us to see if he's being made a fool of. I don't think nothing about that.

"There's no need to thank me, Lieutenant," the Mayor teases.

"Thank you," I say, my eyes still on the wall.

"It keeps you from doing what you don't want," he says. "It keeps you from having to kill."

"Unless someone comes after you," I say.

"Unless someone comes after me, yes. Will that be a problem for you, Todd?"

"No," I say. "No, sir."

"Good," says the Mayor.

I look back thru the mirror. The naked man's head has lolled lifelessly onto his chest, drool dripping from his slack jaw. Mr Hammar is angrily taking off his gloves and slapping them on a table.

"I am very blessed," the Mayor says warmly. "I have achieved my ambition to put this planet back on track. Within days, maybe even hours, I will crush the terrorists. And when the new settlers come, it will be me who puts out a proud and peaceful hand to welcome them."

He raises his hands, like he can't wait to start putting 'em out. "And who will be right beside me?" He holds his hands out to the two of us. "Both of you."

Davy, buzzing pink all over, reaches out and takes his pa's hand.

"I came into this town with one son," the Mayor says still holding out his hand to me, "but it has blessed me with another."

And his hand is out, waiting for me to take it.

Waiting for his second son to shake his hand.

"Congrats, *Lieutenant* Pigpiss," Davy says, hopping back into Deadfall's saddle.

"Todd?" Ivan says, stepping away from his post as I climb onto Angharrad. "Can I have a word?"

"He outranks you now," Davy says to him. "You'll address him as Lieutenant if you don't want to be digging bogs on the front lines."

Ivan takes in a deep breath, as if to calm himself. "Very well, *Lieutenant*, may I have a word with you?"

I look down on him from Angharrad's back. Ivan's Noise is busting with violence and the gunshot to his leg and conspiracies and resentments and ways to get back at the Mayor, openly thought, as if to impress me.

"You should keep that quiet," I say. "You never know who might hear."

I slap Angharrad's reins and off we go back down the road. Ivan's Noise follows me as I go. I ignore it.

Feeling nothing, taking nothing in.

* * *

"He called you *son*," Davy says, looking ahead as the sun disappears behind the falls. "Guess that makes us brothers."

I don't say nothing.

"We should do something to celebrate," Davy says.

"Where?" I say. "*How?*"

"Well, we're officers now, ain't we, brother? It's my understanding officers get *privileges*." He looks over at me sideways, his Noise bright as a flare, filled with things I used to see all the time in old Prentisstown.

Pictures of women with no clothes.

I frown and send him back a picture of a woman with no clothes and a band on her arm.

"So?" Davy says.

"Yer sick."

"No, brother, yer talking to *Sergeant* Prentiss. I may finally be *well*."

He laughs and laughs. He feels so good some of it actually touches my own Noise, brightening it whether I want it brightened or not.

"Oh, come *on*, Lieutenant Pigpiss, you ain't still pining for yer girl, are ya? She left you *months* ago. We need to get you someone new."

"Shut up, Davy."

"Shut up, *Sergeant* Davy." And he laughs again. "Fine, fine, you just stay at home, read yer book—"

He stops himself suddenly. "Oh, damn, sorry, no, I didn't mean that. I forgot."

And the weird thing is, he seems sincere.

There's a moment of quiet where his Noise pulses again with that strong feeling he's hiding—

That something he's trying to bury that makes him feel–

And then he says, "You know…" and I can see the offer coming and I don't think I can bear it, I don't think I could live another minute if he says it out loud. "If you ever wanted me to read it for–"

"No, Davy," I say quickly. "No, thanks, no."

"You sure?"

"*Yes*."

"Well, the offer's there." His Noise goes bright again, blooming as he thinks about his new title, about women, about me and him as brothers.

And he whistles happily all the way back to town.

I lay on my bed with my back turned to Mayor Ledger, who's chomping down his dinner as usual. I'm eating, too, but I've also got my ma's book out, just looking at it, lying on the blankets.

"People are wondering when the big attack's gonna happen," Mayor Ledger says.

I don't answer him. I run my hand over the cover of the book like I do every night, feeling the leather, touching the tear where the knife went in with the tips of my fingers.

"People are saying it'll be soon."

"Whatever you say." I open the cover. Ben's folded map is still inside, still where I stashed it. It don't even look like Davy bothered to open the book, not once in the whole time he had it. It smells a bit like stables, now that I know where it's been, but it's still the book, still *her* book.

My ma. My ma's words.

Look what's become of yer son.

Mayor Ledger sighs loudly. "They're going to attack here, you know," he says. "You'll have to let me out if that happens."

"Can't you keep quiet for five seconds?" I turn to the first page, the first entry my ma wrote on the day I was born. A page full of words I once heard read out.

(read out by–)

"No gun, no weapon." Mayor Ledger's standing now, looking out the windows again. "I'm defenceless."

"I'll take care of you," I say, "now *shut the hell up*."

I'm still not turned to him. I'm looking at my ma's first words, the ones written in her hand. I know what they say but I try to sound them out across the page.

Muh-y. My. It's *My.* I take a deep breath. *Dee. Dee-arr. Dee-arr-ess. Dee-arr-ess-tuh.* Which is *Dearest*, which seems mostly right. *My Dearest.* And the last word is *Son*, which I know, having heard it so clearly today.

I think about his outstretched hand.

I think about when I took it.

My Dearest Son.

"I've offered to read that for you," Mayor Ledger says, not able to hide his groan at the sound of my reading Noise.

I turn round to him, looking fierce. "I said, *shut up!*"

He holds his hands up. "Fine, fine, whatever you say." He sits back down and adds a last sarcastic word under his breath. "*Lieutenant.*"

I sit up. Then I sit up higher. "What did you say?"

"Nothing." He won't meet my eye.

"I didn't tell you that," I say. "I didn't say a word."

"It was in your Noise."

"No, it wasn't." I'm getting to my feet now. Cuz I'm right. I ain't been thinking bout nothing since I came in for dinner except my ma's book. *"How did you know?"*

He looks up at me but there ain't no words coming outta his mouth and his Noise is scrambling for something to say.

And it's failing.

I take a step towards him.

There's a *ker-thunk* at the door and Mr Collins lets himself in. "There's someone here for you," he says to me, then he notices my Noise. "What's going on?"

"I ain't expecting no one," I say, still staring at Mayor Ledger.

"It's a girl," Mr Collins says. "She says Davy sent her."

"Dammit," I say. "I *told* him."

"Whatever," he says. "Says she won't talk to no one but you." He chuckles. "Pretty little piece, too."

I turn at the tone of his voice. "Leave her alone, whoever she is. That ain't right."

"Best not take too long up here then." He's laughing as he shuts the door.

I stare back at Mayor Ledger, my Noise still high. "I ain't thru with you."

"It was in your *Noise*," he says, but I'm already out the door and locking it behind me. *Ker-thunk.*

I stomp my way down the stairs, thinking of ways to get the girl away without Mr Collins bothering her, without her having to go thru any of that for any reason, and my Noise is boiling with suspishuns and wonderings about Mayor Ledger and things beginning to come clear when I get to the bottom of the steps.

Mr Collins is waiting, leaning against the wall of the lobby with his legs crossed, all relaxed and smiling. He points with his thumb.

I look over.

And there she is.

34

LAST CHANCE

{VIOLA}

"LEAVE US," Todd says to the man who let me in, not looking away from me when he says it.

"*Told* you she was a piece," the man says, smirking as he disappears into a side office.

Todd stands there staring. "It's you," he says.

But he isn't moving towards me.

"Todd," I say and I take a step forward.

And he takes a step back.

I stop.

"Who's this?" he says, looking at Lee, who's doing his best to act like a real soldier behind me.

"That's Lee," I say. "A friend. He's come with me to–"

"What are you doing here?"

"I've come to get you," I say. "I've come to rescue you."

I see him swallow. I see his throat working. "Viola," he finally says. My name is all over his Noise, too. Viola Viola Viola.

He puts his hands up to the sides of his head, grabbing his hair, which is longer and shaggier than when I saw it last.

He looks taller, too.

"Viola," he says again.

"It's me," I say and I take another step forward. He doesn't step back so I keep coming, crossing the lobby, not running, just getting closer and closer to him.

But when I get to him, he steps back again.

"Todd?" I ask.

"What are you *doing* here?"

"I've come for you." I feel my stomach sink a little. "I said I would."

"You said you wouldn't leave without me," he says and in his Noise I can hear loud irritation at how he sounds. He clears his throat. "You *left* me here."

"They took me," I say. "I had no choice."

His Noise is getting louder now and though I can feel happiness in it–

Oh, Jesus, Todd, there's *rage*, too.

"What have I done?" I say. "We need to go. The Answer are going–"

"So yer part of the Answer now?" he snaps, bitterness suddenly rising. "Part of those *murderers*."

"Are you a soldier now then?" I say back, surprised, heat growing in my voice, too, pointing to the A on his sleeve. "Don't talk to me about *murder*."

"The Answer killed the Spackle," he says, his voice low and angry.

And the bodies of the Spackle in his Noise.

Piled high, one upon the other, tossed there like garbage.

The *A* of the Answer written on the wall.

And Todd in the middle of it.

"They might as well have killed me along with them," he says.

He closes his eyes.

I am the Circle and the Circle is me, I hear.

"Viola?" Lee says from behind me. I turn. He's crossed half the lobby.

"Wait outside," I say.

"Viola–"

"*Outside.*"

He looks so concerned, so ready to fight for me, my heart skips a little. He broadcast as loud as he could that I was his prisoner on the way here, so loud other soldiers thought he was covering up for a rape he was going to commit and whistled him good luck as we passed. Then we hid by the cathedral, seeing Davy Prentiss riding away from here, thinking things I wouldn't want to see again, thinking about how a *celebration* was due to him and Todd.

And so we pretended to be the celebration.

And it worked.

Kind of upsetting how easily it worked, frankly.

Lee shifts from foot to foot. "You call me if you need me."

"I will," I say, and he waits a second, then steps out the front door, keeping it open to watch us.

Todd's eyes are still closed and he repeats I am the Circle and the Circle is me which I have to say sounds an awful lot like something from the Mayor.

"We didn't kill the Spackle," I say.

"*We?*" he says, opening his eyes.

"I don't know who did it, but it wasn't us."

"You sent a bomb to kill them the day *you* blew up the tower." He's almost spitting the words. "Then you came back on the day of the prison break and finished the job."

"Bomb?" I say. "What bomb–?"

But then I remember–

The first explosion that made the soldiers run away from the communications tower.

No.

She wouldn't.

No, not even her. *What kind of people do you think we are?* she said–

But she never did answer the asking.

No, *no*, it's not true and besides–

"Who told you that?" I say. "Davy Prentiss?"

He blinks. "What?"

"What do you mean *what*?" My voice is harder now. "Your new best friend. The man who *shot* me, Todd, and who you ride to work with laughing every morning."

He clenches his hands into fists.

"You been *spying* on me?" he says. "Three months I don't see you, three months I don't hear *nothing* from you and you been *spying*? Is that what yer doing in yer spare time when yer not blowing people up?"

"Yeah!" I yell, my voice getting louder to match his. "Three months of defending you to people who'd be only too happy to call you enemy, Todd. Three months of wondering why the hell you're working so hard for the Mayor and how he knew to go right for the ocean the day after we spoke." He winces, but I keep going, thrusting out my arm and pulling up the sleeve. "Three months wondering why you put *these* on women!"

His face changes in an instant. He actually calls out as if he felt the pain himself. He puts a hand over his mouth to stifle it but his Noise is suddenly washed with blackness. He moves the fingertips of his other hand within reach of the band, hovering over my skin, over the band that'll never be removed unless I lose my arm. The skin is still red, and band 1391 still throbs, despite the healing of three mistresses.

"Oh, no," he says. "Oh, no."

The side door opens and the man who let me in leans out. "Everything all right out here, Lieutenant?"

"Lieutenant?" I say.

"We're fine," Todd chokes a little. "We're fine."

The man waits for a second, then goes back inside.

"*Lieutenant?*" I say again, lowering my voice.

Todd's leant down, his hands on his knees, staring at the floor. "It wasn't me, was it?" he says, his voice quiet, too. "I didn't–" He gestures again at the band without looking up. "I didn't do it without knowing it was you, did I?"

"No," I say, reading things in his Noise, reading his numbness at them, reading all the horror that sits way down below that he's working so hard to ignore. "The Answer did it."

He looks up fast, filled with asking marks.

"It was the only way I could come and find you safely," I say. "The only way I could get past all the soldiers marching around town was if they thought I'd already been banded."

His face changes again as this sinks in. "Oh, Viola."

I breathe out heavily. "Todd," I say. "Please come with me."

392

His eyes are wet but I can see him now, I can see him finally, I can see him in his face and in his Noise and in his arms as they drop to his sides in defeat.

"It's too late," he says and his voice is so sad my own eyes start to wet. "I've been dead, Viola. I've been dead."

"You haven't," I say, moving a bit closer to him. "These are impossible times."

He's looking down now, his eyes not focused on anything.

Feeling nothing, his Noise says. **Taking nothing in.**

I am the Circle and the Circle is me.

"Todd?" I say and I'm close enough to reach his hand. "Todd, look at me."

He looks up and the loss in his Noise is so great it feels like I'm standing on the edge of an abyss, that I'm about to fall down *into* him, into blackness so empty and lonely there'd never be a way out.

"Todd," I say again, a catch in my voice. "On the ledge, under the waterfall, do you remember what you said to me? Do you remember what you said to save me?"

He's shaking his head slowly. "I've done terrible things, Viola. *Terrible* things–"

"*We all fall*, you said." I'm gripping him hard now. "We all fall but that's not what matters. What matters is picking yourself up again."

But he shakes me off.

"No," he says, turning away. "No, it was easier when you weren't here. It was easier when you couldn't see–"

"Todd, I've come to save you–"

"*No.* I didn't have to think about nothing–"

"It's not too late."

"It *is* too late," he says, shaking his head. "It is!"

And he's moving away.

Away from me.

I'm losing him–

And I get an idea.

A dangerous, dangerous idea.

"The attack's coming tomorrow at sundown," I say.

He blinks again in surprise. "What?"

"That's when it happens." I swallow and step forward, trying to keep my voice steady. "I'm only supposed to know the fake plan, but I found out the real one. The Answer are coming over the hill with the notch in it just to the south of here, just to the south of this *cathedral*, Todd. They're coming right here and I'm sure they're coming right for the Mayor."

He looks nervously at the side door but I'm keeping my voice down. "There are only two hundred of them, Todd, but they're fully armed with guns and bombs and a plan and a hell of a leader who isn't going to stop until she topples him."

"Viola–"

"They're *coming*," I say, moving closer again. "And now you know when and from where and if that information gets to the Mayor–"

"You shouldn't have told me," he says, not meeting my eye. "I hide things but he figures them out. *You shouldn't have told me!*"

I keep moving forward. "Then you have to come with me, don't you? You *have* to or he wins for ever and ever and he'll be the one to rule this planet and he'll be the one who greets the new settlers–"

"With his hand outstretched," Todd says, his voice suddenly soft.

"What?"

But he just extends his hand out into the empty air, staring at it. "Greeting it with his son."

"Well, we don't want that either." I look nervously round to the front door. Lee is sticking his head in, trying not to look too out of place, but there are soldiers marching by out front. "We don't have much time."

Todd's hand is still outstretched.

"I've done bad things, too," I say. "I wish everything was different but it isn't. There's only now and here and you *have* to come with me if we have any chance of making this come out any good at all."

He doesn't say anything but his hand is still out and he's looking at it and so I move forward another step and I take it in my own.

"We can save the world," I say, trying to smile. "You and me."

He looks into my eyes, searching, trying to read me, trying to see if I'm actually here, if It's actually true, if the things I say are real, he searches and he searches–

But he doesn't find me.

Oh, Todd–

"Going somewhere?" says a voice from across the room.

A voice from a man holding a gun.

* * *

It's a different man from the one who let us in, a man I've never seen before.

Except once, in Todd's Noise.

"How did you get out?" Todd says, surprise rippling through him.

"You wouldn't leave without *this*, would you?" he says. In his non-gun hand, he's got the journal of Todd's mother.

"You *give* that to me!" Todd says.

The man ignores him and waves his gun at Lee. "Come inside now," he says. "Or I will ever so happily shoot our dear friend Todd."

I look back. Lee's got flight all over his Noise but he sees the gun pointed at Todd, sees my face, and comes forward, his Noise saying so loud that he won't leave me here that it almost distracts me from the gun.

"Drop it," the man says, referring to Lee's rifle. Lee sends it clattering to the floor.

"You liar," Todd says to the man. "You coward."

"For the good of the town, Todd," the man says.

"All that moaning," Todd says, his voice and Noise fiery. "All that bitching and moaning about how he's ruining everything and yer just another spy."

"Not at first," the man says, walking towards us. "At first I was just how you saw me, the former Mayor disgraced and left alive in all his inconvenience." The man passes Todd and comes up to me, putting Todd's book under one arm. "Give me your pack."

"What?" I say.

"Give it to me." He swings his arm back and points the gun right at Todd's head. I slide the pack off my shoulders and give it to him. He doesn't even open it the regular way, just feels along the bottom, feeling right for the secret pouch, the secret pouch where if you press right, you can feel my gun.

The man smiles. "There it is," he says. "The Answer don't change, do they?"

"You touch a hair on her head," Todd says, "and I'll kill you."

"So will I," Lee says.

The man keeps smiling. "I think you have a competitor, Todd."

"Who *are* you?" I say, annoyance at all this protection making me brave.

"Con Ledger, Mayor of Haven, at your service, Viola." He gives a little bow. "Since that's who you must be, isn't it?" He walks around Todd. "Oh, the President was very interested in the Noise of your dreams, my boy. *Very* interested in what you thought about while you were sleeping. About how much you miss your Viola, how you would do anything to find her."

I see Todd's face starting to glow red.

"And suddenly he became far more agreeable to me, asking me to pass along certain information to you, see if we could get you to do what he wanted." Mayor Ledger looks ridiculous, all the things he's carrying, a gun in one hand, pack in the other, book under his arm, and still trying to appear threatening. "I must say, it worked a treat." He winks at me. "Now that I know when and where the Answer are going to attack."

Lee's Noise rises and he takes a furious step forward.

Mayor Ledger cocks the pistol. Lee stops.

"Like it?" asks the Mayor. "The President gave it to me when he gave me my own key."

He smiles again then sees how we're all looking at him. "Oh, stop it," he says. "If the President defeats the Answer then all this will be over. All the bombings, all the restrictions, all the curfews." His smile's a bit weaker now. "You have to learn how to work *within* the system for change. When *I'm* his deputy, I'll work very hard to make things better for every- one." He nods at me. "Women, too."

"You'd better shoot me," Todd says, Noise coming off him like flame. "Cuz there ain't no way yer life is safe if you ever put down that gun."

Mayor Ledger sighs. "I'm not going to shoot *anyone*, Todd, not unless–"

The side door suddenly opens and the man who let me in steps out, surprise lighting up his face and Noise. "What're you–"

Mayor Ledger points the gun at him and pulls the trigger three times. The man falls back into the doorway and all the way to the floor until only his feet are sticking out.

We all stand there, shocked, echoes of gunfire still ring- ing off the marble floors.

There's a clear picture in Mayor Ledger's Noise, of himself with a black eye and split lip, of the man on the floor giving him the beating.

He looks back at us, sees us staring at him. "*What?*"

"Mayor Prentiss ain't gonna like that," Todd says. "He knows Mr Collins from old Prentisstown."

"I'm sure the prize of Viola and the Answer's attack

will make up for any other misunderstandings." Mayor Ledger's looking around now, trying to find a place to free up his hands. He finally just tosses the book to Todd, as if he doesn't want it any more. Todd bobbles it in his hands but catches it.

"Your mother wasn't much of a writer, Todd," Mayor Ledger says, bending forward and zipping open the pack with his free hand. "Barely literate."

"You're going to pay for that." Todd looks back at me and I realize I'm the one who said it out loud.

Mayor Ledger digs around in my bag. "Food!" he says, his face lighting up. He takes out a crested pine from the top and immediately shoves it in his mouth. He digs some more, finding bread and more fruit, taking bites of almost everything. "How long were you planning on *staying*?" he asks, his mouth full.

I see Todd starting to edge forward.

"It's not like I can't hear you," Mayor Ledger says, waving the gun again, digging down to the bottom of the bag. He stops, his hand deep inside, and looks up. "What's this?" He feels around a little more and starts to drag something larger out of the pack. At first I assume it's the gun but then he shakes it free of the bag.

He stands up.

And looks curiously at the Thrace bomb in his hand.

There's a second where it can't be true. There's a second where my eyes can't be seeing what they're seeing, not believing that I know what a bomb looks like by now. There's a moment where it's in his hand but it doesn't mean anything, it doesn't mean anything at all.

But then Lee gasps beside me and it all makes sense, it all makes the worst goddam sense I can even think of.

"*No*," I say.

Todd spins around. "What? What is it?"

Time slows down to nothing. Mayor Ledger turns it over in his hand and a beeping starts, a fast beeping, a beeping obviously set to go whenever anyone searched through my bag and picked it up, the pulse in his hand setting it off, a bomb you know is going to kill you if you let go of it.

"This isn't–" says Mayor Ledger, looking up–
    But Lee is already reaching for my arm–
    Trying to grab it so we can bolt for the front door–
    "Run!" he's yelling–
    But I'm jumping forward, not back–
    And I'm pushing Todd sideways–
    Stumbling towards the room where the dead man fell–
    Mayor Ledger isn't trying to shoot us–
    Isn't doing anything–
    He's just standing there, realization dawning–
    And as we're falling through the doorway–

And rolling over the dead man–

And curling into each other for protection–

Mayor Ledger tries to throw the bomb away from himself–

Releasing it from his hand–

And–

BOOM

– it blasts him into a thousand pieces, tearing out the walls behind him and most of the room we're falling into and the heat from the explosion singes our clothes and our hair and rubble comes tumbling down and we force ourselves under a table but something hits Todd hard in the back of the head and a long beam falls across my ankles and I feel both of them break and all I can think as I yell out at the impossible pain is *she betrayed me she betrayed me she betrayed me* and it wasn't a mission to save Todd, it was a mission to *kill* him, and the Mayor, too, if she was lucky–

She betrayed me–

She betrayed me *again*–
And then there's darkness.

Some time later, there are voices, voices in the dust and rubble, voices drifting into my pain-addled head.

One voice.

His voice.

Standing over me.

"Well, well," says the Mayor. "Look who we have here."

PART VI

THE ASK AND
THE ANSWER

35

VIOLA IS ASKED

[TODD]

"LET HER GO!"

I pound my fists on the glass but no matter how hard I hit it, it ain't breaking.

"LET HER GO!"

My voice is cracking from the strain but I'll go and go till it gives out completely.

"YOU LAY A FINGER ON HER, I'LL KILL YOU!"

Viola is strapped to the frame in the Arena of the Ask, her arms back and up, the skin around the metal band burning red, her head twixt the little buzzing rods that keep her from hearing Noise.

The tub of water is below her, the table of sharp tools to her side.

Mr Hammar stands there waiting, arms crossed, and Davy, too, watching nervously from the far door, across the room.

And the Mayor is there, calmly walking round her in a circle.

* * *

All I remember is the *BOOM* and Mayor Ledger disappearing in a fury of fire and smoke.

I woke up here, my head aching, my body filthy from dirt and rubble and dried blood.

And I got to my feet.

And there she was

Beyond the glass.

Being Asked.

I press the button again for the speaker in the room. "LET HER GO!"

But no one acts like they can hear me at all.

"I do this with the greatest reluctance, Viola," says the Mayor, still walking in his slow circle. I can hear *him* perfectly clear. "I thought we might be friends, you and I. I thought we had an understanding." He stops in front of her. "But then you blew up my home."

"I didn't know there was a bomb," she says and I can see the pain across her face. There's dried blood all over her, too, cuts and scratches from the explozhun.

But it's her feet that look the worst. Her shoes are off and her ankles are swollen and twisted and black and I just know the Mayor ain't given her nothing for the pain.

I can see it on her face.

See how much she's hurting.

I try to pull up the bench behind me so I can smash it thru the window but it's bolted into the concrete.

"I believe you, Viola," says the Mayor, re-starting his walk. Mr Hammar stands there smirking, watching it all, once in a while looking up to the mirror where he knows I'm standing and smirking some more. "I believe your dismay at your betrayal by Mistress Coyle. Though you can hardly be surprised."

Viola don't say nothing, just hangs her head.

"Don't hurt her," I whisper. "Please, please, please."

"If it helps," says the Mayor. "I'm not entirely sure I would take it personally. Mistress Coyle saw a way to get a bomb right into the heart of my cathedral, destroying it, perhaps destroying me in the process."

He glances up to me at the mirror. I pound my fists on it again. There's no way they can't hear *that* but he ignores me.

Davy looks over, tho, his face as serious as I've seen it.

And even from here I can hear the worry in his Noise.

"You presented her with an opportunity she couldn't pass up," the Mayor continues. "Your extreme loyalty to Todd might actually get you inside where any other bomber might not. She probably didn't wish to kill you, but there it was, a chance to take me down, and weighed up against that, you were finally expendable."

And I'm looking at her face.

It's pulled down sad, pulled down so sad and defeated.

And I feel her silence again, feel the yearning and the loss that I first felt out in the swamp a lifetime ago. I feel it so much my eyes get wet and my stomach tightens and my throat clenches.

"Viola," I say. "Please, Viola."

But she don't even look up.

"And so if that's all you mean to her, Viola." The Mayor's leaning down in front of her now, looking into her face. "Then maybe you finally know who your real enemy is." He pauses. "And who your real friends are."

Viola says something real quiet.

"What was that?" the Mayor asks.

She clears her throat and says it again. "I only came for Todd."

"I know." The Mayor stands again and starts his walk. "I've grown fond of Todd, too. He's become like a second son to me." He looks over at Davy, whose face flushes. "Loyal and hardworking and truly making a contribution to the future of this town."

I start pounding my fists again. "YOU SHUT UP!" I scream. "YOU *SHUT UP!*"

"If *he's* with us, Viola," the Mayor says, "and your Mistress is against you, then surely your path is clear."

But she's already shaking her head. "I won't tell you," she says. "I won't tell you anything."

"But she betrayed you." The Mayor comes round to her front again. "She tried to kill you."

And at that, Viola lifts her head.

She looks him right in the eye.

And says, "No, she tried to kill *you*."

Oh, good girl.

My Noise swells with pride.

That's my girl.

The Mayor gives a signal to Mr Hammar.

Who takes hold of the frame and plunges her into the water.

* * *

"NO!" I scream and start pounding again. "NO, GODDAMMIT!" I go to the door of the little room and start kicking it as hard as I can. "VIOLA! *VIOLA!*"

I hear a gasp and run back to the mirror–

She's up outta the water, coughing up liquid and spitting hard.

"We are running short on time," says the Mayor, picking a speck of lint off his coat, "so perhaps we should come right to it."

I'm still pounding on the mirror and shouting while he talks. He turns and looks over to me. He can't see me from his side but his eyes lock right on mine.

"VIOLA!" I scream and pound the glass again.

He's frowning a little–

"*VIOLA!*"

And he strikes me with his Noise.

It's *way* stronger than before.

Like a shout of a million people right in the middle of my brain, so far inside I can't reach it to protect myself and they're screaming YER NOTHING YER NOTHING YER NOTHING and it feels like my blood is boiling and my eyes are popping outta my skull and I can't even stand and I stagger back from the mirror and sit down hard on the bench, the slap ringing and ringing and ringing, like it ain't never gonna stop–

When I can open my eyes again, I see the Mayor stopping Davy from leaving the Arena and then Davy looking back towards the mirror.

And in his Noise he's worried.

Worried about *me*.

"Tell me when the Answer is going to attack," the Mayor says to Viola, his voice colder now, harder. "And from where."

She shakes her head, sending water drops flying. "I won't."

"You will," says the Mayor. "I truly am afraid you will."

"No," she says. "Never."

And she's still shaking her head.

The Mayor glances up to the mirror, finding my eye again tho he can't see me. "Unfortunately," he says, "we don't have time for your refusals."

He nods at Mr Hammar.

Who plunges her into the water again.

"STOP!" I shout and pound. "STOP IT!"

He holds her there–

And holds her there–

I pound so hard my hands are bruising–

"LET HER UP! LET HER UP! LET HER UP!"

And she's thrashing in the water–

But he's still holding her there–

She's still under water–

"*VIOLA!*"

Her hands are pulling hard against the binds–

The water is splashing everywhere with her struggling against it–

Oh jesus oh jesus oh jesus oh jesus viola viola viola viola–

I can't–

I can't–

"NO!"

Forgive me–

Please forgive me–

"IT'S TONIGHT!" I shout. "AT SUNSET! OVER THE
NOTCH IN THE HILL SOUTH OF THE CATHEDRAL!
TONIGHT!"

And I'm pressing the button as I shout it again and
again–

"TONIGHT!"

As she struggles under the water–

But no one looks like they hear me.

He's turned the sound off–

He's turned the *effing sound off*–

I go back to the window and pound–

But no one's moving–

And still she's underwater–

No matter how hard I slam my fists against the glass–

Why ain't it breaking–

Why ain't it ruddy *breaking*–

The Mayor gives a signal and Mr Hammar lifts up the frame.
Viola swallows air in huge raking gulps, her hair (longer than
I remember) stuck against her face, twisting in her ears, the
water falling off her in great ropes

"You're in control here, Viola," the Mayor says. "Just tell
me when the Answer are attacking and this will all stop."

"TONIGHT!" I scream, so loud my voice is cracking like dried mud. "FROM THE SOUTH!"

But she's shaking her head.

And no one can hear me.

"But she betrayed you, Viola." The Mayor's making his voice do that fake surprised thing. "Why save her? Why–?"

He stops, as if realizing something. "You have people you care about in the Answer."

She stops shaking her head. She don't look up but she stops shaking her head.

The Mayor kneels down in front of her. "All the more reason to tell me. All the more reason to let me know where I can find your mistress." He reaches forward and pulls a few wet strands of hair away from Viola's face. "If you help me, I guarantee they won't be harmed. I only want Mistress Coyle. Any other mistresses can remain in prison and everyone else, innocent victims of inflamed rhetoric no doubt, can be released once we've had a chance to talk to them."

He gestures for Mr Hammar to hand him a towel which he uses to wipe Viola's face. She still don't look at him.

"If you tell me, you'd be saving lives," he says, gently sponging away the loose water. "You have my word on that."

She finally raises her head.

"Your word," she says, looking right past him at Mr Hammar.

And her face is so angry even *he* looks surprised.

"Ah, yes," the Mayor says, standing. He hands the towel back to Mr Hammar. "You should look upon Captain Hammar as an example of my mercy, Viola. I spared his life." He's walking again but when he passes behind her he looks over to me. "Just as I shall spare the lives of your friends and loved ones."

"It's tonight," I say, but my voice is a rasp.

How can he not hear me?

"Then again," he's saying, "if you don't know, perhaps your good friend Lee will tell us."

Her head goes right up, eyes wide, breath heavy.

I don't know how he coulda survived the explozhun–

"He doesn't know anything," she says quickly. "He doesn't know when or where."

"Even if I believed that," the Mayor says, "I'm sure we would have to Ask him long and hard before we could possibly be sure."

"Leave him alone!" Viola says, trying to turn her head to follow him.

The Mayor stops just in front of the mirror, his back to Viola, his face to me. "Or perhaps we should just ask Todd."

I pound the glass right at his face. He don't even flinch.

And then she says, "Todd would never tell you. Never."

And the Mayor just looks at me.

And he *smiles*.

My stomach sinks, my heart drops, my head feels so light I feel like I'm going to drop right to the ground.

Oh, Viola–

Viola, please–

Forgive me.

"Captain Hammar," the Mayor says and Viola's plunged

into the water again, unable to not scream out in fright as down she goes.

"NO!" I shout, pressing myself against the mirror.

But the Mayor ain't even looking at her.

He's looking right at me, as if he could see me even if I was behind a brick wall.

"STOP IT!" I shout as she's thrashing again—

And more—

And more—

"VIOLA!"

And I'm pounding even tho I think my hands are breaking—

And Mr Hammar is grinning and holding her there—

"*VIOLA!*"

And her wrists are starting to bleed from where she's pulling—

"I'LL KILL YOU!"

I'm shouting into the Mayor's face—

With all my Noise—

"I'LL *KILL* YOU!"—

And still holding her there—

"VIOLA! *VIOLA!*"—

But it's Davy—

Of all people—

It's Davy who stops it.

"Let her up!" he suddenly shouts, striding forward from his corner. "Jesus, yer gonna kill her!" And he's grabbing the frame and lifting it outta the water and the Mayor gives Mr

Hammar a sign to let him and Davy gets Viola back up and out, her throat roaring from taking in the air and coughing it right back out again with all the water.

No one says nothing for a minute, the Mayor just staring at his son like he was some new kinda fish.

"How can she help us if she's dead?" Davy says, his voice wobbly, his eyes not meeting no one's. "Is all I meant."

The Mayor stays quiet. Davy backs away from the frame and returns to his spot near the door.

Viola coughs and hangs from her bindings and I'm pressed so close against the window it's like I'm trying to crawl *thru* it to get to her.

"Well," the Mayor says, clasping his hands behind his back, looking at Davy. "I think perhaps we've learnt what we need to know anyway."

He walks over to a button on the wall and presses it. "Would you please repeat what you said earlier, Todd?"

Viola looks up at the sound of my name.

The Mayor walks back over to the frame, lifting up the little Noise-baffling rods from the sides of her face and she looks all around as she can suddenly hear my Noise.

"Todd?" she says. "Are you there?"

"I'm here!" I yell, my voice now booming thru the Arena so everyone can hear me.

"Please tell us again what you said a few moments ago, Todd." The Mayor's looking at me again. "Something about tonight at sunset?"

Viola looks up to where the Mayor's looking, surprise on her face, surprise and shock. "No," she whispers and it's as loud as any shouting.

"Viola deserves to hear you say it again, Todd," the Mayor says.

He knew. He could hear my Noise the whole time, *course* he could, he could hear my shouting, even if she couldn't.

"Viola?" I say and it sounds like I'm begging.

And she looks into the mirror, searching for where I might be. "Don't tell him!" she says. "Please, Todd, don't—"

"One more time, Todd," the Mayor says, putting his hand on the drowning frame, "or she goes back into the water."

"Todd, no!" Viola shouts.

"You bastard!" I yell. "I'll kill you. I swear it, I'll KILL YOU!"

"You won't," he says. "And we both know it."

"Todd, please, no—"

"Say it, Todd. Where and when?"

And he starts lowering the frame.

Viola's trying to look brave but her body is curling and twisting, trying to keep any part of it outta the water. "No!" she's yelling. "NO!"

Please please please—

"NO!"

Viola—

"Tonight at sunset," I say, my voice amplified over her shouts, over Davy's Noise, over my own Noise, just my voice filling everything. "Over the notch in the valley south of the cathedral."

"*NO!*" Viola screams—

And the look on her face—

The look on her face about *me*—

And my chest tears right in two.

The Mayor pulls back the frame, lifting her away from the water and setting her back down.

"No," she whispers.

And it's only then that she actually starts to cry.

"Thank you, Todd," the Mayor says. He turns to Mr Hammar. "You know where and when, Captain. Pass on the orders to Captains Morgan, Tate and O'Hare."

Mr Hammar stands to attenshun. "Yes, sir," he says, sounding like he just won a prize. "I'll take every single man, sir. They won't know what hit 'em."

"Take my son," the Mayor says, nodding at Davy. "Let him see all the battle he can stomach."

Davy's looking nervous but proud and excited, too, not noticing the odd twist Mr Hammar's smile has taken.

"Go," the Mayor says, "and leave none alive."

"Yes, *sir*," Mr Hammar says as Viola lets out a little sob.

Davy snaps a salute at his father, trying to make his Noise look brave. He sends the mirror a look meant for me, a look of sympathy, his Noise full of fear and excitement and more fear.

Then he's following Mr Hammar out the door.

And then there's just me, Viola and the Mayor.

I can only look at her, hanging from the frame, her head down, crying, still tied up and soaking wet and so much sorrow coming from her I can practically feel it on my skin.

"Tend to your friend," the Mayor says to me, just on the other side of the glass again, his face close to mine. "I return to my burnt-out home to prepare for the new dawn."

He don't even blink, don't even act like nothing's even happened.

He ain't human.

"All too human, Todd," he says. "The guards will escort both of you to the cathedral." He raises his eyebrows. "We have much to discuss about your futures."

36

DEFEAT

{ V I O L A }

I HEAR TODD come into the room, hear his Noise come first, but I can't look up.

"Viola?" he says.

I still don't look up.

It's over.

We've lost.

I feel his hands on the binds at my wrists, pulling at them, finally getting one free, but my arm is so stiff from being held back it hurts more when it's released than it did when it was bound.

Mayor Prentiss has won. Mistress Coyle tried to sacrifice me. Lee's a prisoner if that wasn't a lie and he's not already dead. Maddy died for nothing. Corinne died for *nothing*.

And Todd–

He comes around in front of me to take off the second bind and when it's loose and I fall from the frame, he catches me, kneeling us gently down to the floor.

"Viola?" he says, holding me against himself, my head against his chest, the water on me soaking into his dusty uniform, my arms out, not able to grab anything, the metal band throbbing.

And I glance up to see the shiny silver *A* on his shoulder.

"Let me go," I say.

But he still holds me there.

"Let me *go*," I say, louder.

"No," he says.

I try to push him away but my arms are so weak and I'm so tired and everything is over. Everything is over.

And still he holds me.

And I start to cry again and I feel him hold me tighter and I cry harder and when my arms can move a little I put them around him and cry even harder because of how he feels and how he smells and how his Noise sounds and how he's holding me and his worry and his fretting and his care and his softness–

And I didn't know until just now how much I missed him.

But he told the Mayor–

He *told* him–

And I have to try and push him away again, even though I can hardly bear to do it.

"You told him," I say, choking it out.

"I'm sorry," he says, his eyes wide and terrified. "He was drowning you and I couldn't, I just couldn't–"

And I look at him and there I am in his Noise, dropping down into the water with him pounding on the other side of the mirror and worse, I can see what he felt, see the hopeless *rage* of it, see him unable to save me–

And his face is so worried.

"Viola, please," he says, begging me. "*Please*."

"He'll kill them," I say. "Every one of them. Wilf is there, Todd. *Wilf*."

He looks horrified. "Wilf?"

"And Jane," I say. "And so many others, Todd, *all* of them. He'll slaughter them and that'll be the end. That'll be the end of *everything*."

His Noise goes black and barren and he sort of crumples down next to me, splashing in the little puddle that's formed around us. "No," he says. "Aw, no."

I don't want to say it but I hear my voice saying it anyway. "You did exactly what he wanted. He knew exactly how to get it out of you."

He looks at me. "What choice did I have?"

"You should have let him kill me!"

And he's looking at me and I can see his Noise trying to find me, trying to find the real Viola that's deep down in this mess and pain, I can see him looking–

And for a minute I don't want him to find me.

"You should have let him kill me," I say again quietly.

But he couldn't, could he?

He couldn't and still be himself.

He couldn't and still be Todd Hewitt.

The boy who can't kill.

The *man* who can't.

We are the choices we make.

*   *   *

"We have to warn them," I say, feeling ashamed and not looking into his eyes. "If we can." I grab the edge of the tub of water to pull myself up. Pain shoots up my legs from my ankles. I call out and fall forward again.

And once more, he catches me.

"My feet," I say. We look at them, bare and swollen badly, turning ugly shades of blue and black.

"We'll get you to a healer." He puts an arm around me to lift me.

"No," I say, stopping him. "We have to warn the Answer. That's the most important thing."

"Viola–"

"Their lives are more important than my–"

"She tried to *kill* you, Viola. She tried to blow you up."

I'm breathing hard, trying not to feel the pain from my legs.

"You don't owe her nothing," he says.

But I feel his arms on me and I'm realizing things don't seem so impossible any more. I feel Todd touching me and there's anger rising in my gut but it's not at him and I grunt and I pull myself up again, leaning on him to keep me there as I stand. "I *do* owe her," I say. "I owe her the look on her face when she sees me alive."

I try to take a small step but it's too much. I cry out again.

"I have a horse," he says. "I can put you on her."

"He's not just going to let us leave," I say. "He said guards would escort us back to him."

"Yeah," he says. "We'll see about *that*."

He puts his arm further around me and leans down to put his other arm under my knees.

And he lifts me in the air.

The pull on my ankles makes me cry out again but then he's holding me up, carrying me like he did down the hillside into Haven.

Holding me up.

He remembers it, too. I can see it in his Noise.

I put my arm around his neck. He tries to smile.

And it's crooked like it always is.

"We just keep on having to save each other," he says. "We ever gonna be even?"

"I hope not," I say.

He frowns again and I see the clouds roiling in his Noise. "I'm sorry," he says quietly.

I grab the cloth of his shirt front and squeeze it tight. "I'm sorry, too."

"So we forgive each other?" The crooked smile climbs up one more time. "Again?"

And I look right into his eyes, right into him as far as I can see, because I want him to hear me, I want him to hear me with everything I mean and feel and say.

"Always," I say to him. "Every time."

He carries me to a chair and then goes over to the door and starts pounding on it. "Let us out!" he shouts.

"This does mean something, Todd," I say, taking as little breath as possible because my feet are throbbing. "Something we have to remember."

"What's that?" He pounds on the door again and says "ow" quietly with how it's hurting his hands.

"The Mayor knows I'm your weakness," I say. "All he has to do is threaten me and you'll do what he wants."

"Yeah," Todd says, not looking back. "Yeah, I knew that already."

"He'll keep trying it."

He turns around to face me, fists clenched at his sides. "He won't be laying his eyes on you. Not never again."

"No." I shake my head and wince at the pain. "It can't be that way, Todd. He has to be stopped."

"Well, why's it have to be *us* that stops him?"

"It's got to be somebody." I arch my back a certain way to keep any weight off my feet. "He can't win."

Todd starts kicking at the door. "Then let yer Mistress do it. We'll get to her somehow, warn 'em if we can, and then we're outta here."

"Out of here where?"

"I don't know." He starts looking around for something that might knock down the door. "We'll go to one of the abandoned settlements. We'll hide out till yer ships get here."

"He'll beat Mistress Coyle and then he'll go right for the ships." I gasp a little as I turn my head to follow him. "There's only a small number of people awake when they land, Todd. He can overpower them and keep everyone else asleep as long as he wants. He doesn't ever have to wake them up if he doesn't want to."

He stops his search. "Is that true?"

I nod. "Once he destroys the Answer, who's left to stop him?"

He clenches and unclenches his fists again. "We have to do it."

"We find the Answer first," I say, trying to pull myself upright. "We warn them–"

"And tell 'em exactly what kinda leader they got."

I sigh. "We're going to have to stop both of them, aren't we?"

"Well, that's easy, ain't it?" Todd says. "We tell the Answer all about yer mistress and then someone new will lead 'em." He looks at me. "Maybe you."

"Maybe *you*." I take a minute to try and catch my breath. It's getting harder. "Either way, we have to get out of here."

And then the door suddenly opens.

A soldier stands there with a rifle.

"I have orders to take you both to the cathedral," he says.

And I think I recognize him.

"Ivan," Todd says.

"Lieutenant," Ivan nods. "I've got my orders."

"You're from Farbranch," I say, but he's staring at Todd, not blinking. I can hear something in his Noise, something–

"*Lieutenant*," he says again in a way that seems like some kind of signal.

I look at Todd. "What's he doing?"

"You have orders," Todd says, concentrating on Ivan. I can hear stuff flying between their Noises, fast and blurry. "*Private Farrow.*"

"Yes, sir," Ivan says, standing at attention. "Orders from my superior officer."

Todd looks at me. I can hear him thinking.

"What's going on?" I say.

I see Lee rise in Todd's Noise. He turns back to Ivan. "Is there another prisoner? A boy? Blond shaggy hair?"

"There is, sir," Ivan says.

"And if I ordered you to take me to him, you'd do it?"

"You *are* my superior officer, *Lieutenant*." Ivan's looking harder at Todd now. "I'd have to follow any orders you gave me."

"Todd?" I say, but I'm beginning to understand.

"I've been a-trying to tell you this for some time, Lieutenant," Ivan says, impatience in his voice.

"Are there any higher ranking officers on the premises than me?" Todd asks.

"No, sir. Just myself and the guards. Everyone else has gone off to fight the war."

"How many guards?"

"Sixteen of us, sir."

Todd licks his lips, thinking. "Would they regard me as their superior officer, too, Private?"

Ivan looks away for the first time, glancing quickly behind him before saying again in a lower voice, "There is some concern with our current leadership, sir. They might be persuaded."

Todd stands up straighter, pulling at the hem of his uniform jacket. I notice again how tall he is, how much taller than the last time I saw him, how his face is lined in a way that's not at all boyish, how his voice is deeper and fuller.

I look at him, and I begin to see a man.

He clears his throat and stands at attention before Ivan.

"Then I order you to take me to the prisoner called Lee, Private."

"Even though I have been instructed to take you straight to the President," Ivan says in an official voice, "I feel I cannot disobey your direct order, *sir*."

He steps back out of the door to wait. Todd comes to my chair and kneels down in front of me.

"What are you planning?" I ask, trying to read his Noise, but it's spinning so fast I can hardly keep up with it.

"You said it's us who has to stop him cuz no one else will," he says, the crooked smile inching higher. "Well, maybe there's a way we can."

37

THE LIEUTENANT

[TODD]

I FEEL VIOLA WATCHING ME as I leave and follow Ivan down the hallway. She's wondering whether we can trust him.

I wonder it, too.

Cuz the answer's no, ain't it? Ivan joined the army as a volunteer, saving his own skin in Farbranch, and I remember him slinking up to me all those months ago even before it happened and telling me he was on the side of Prentisstown. He probably couldn't wait to join the army when it marched into town and then he led troops here and was even a Corporal.

Till Mayor Prentiss shot him in the leg.

You go where the power is, he said to me once. *That's how you stay alive.*

So maybe he thinks he's found the new power.

"Exactly what I'm a-thinking, *sir*," Ivan says, stopping outside a door. "He's in here."

"Can he walk?" I say as Ivan unlocks the door–

But Lee's already jumping out with an *AAAAAAAAHHHHHHHH!!!* and knocking Ivan over and punching him again and again in the face and I have to grab his shoulders and pull him back and he turns to me fists ready till he sees who it is.

"Todd!" he says, surprised.

"We need–" I start.

"Where is she?" he shouts, already looking round, and I have to step forward to keep Ivan from smashing the back of his head with a rifle.

"She's hurt," I say. "She needs bandages and splints." I turn to Ivan. "You got those here?"

"We got a first aid kit," Ivan says.

"That'll do. Give it to Lee and he'll take care of Viola. Then tell the men I wanna talk to 'em out front."

Ivan's glaring at Lee, Noise blaring.

"That's an order, *Private*," I say.

"Yes, *sir*," Ivan says, all sour, before he disappears down the hallway.

Lee goggles at me. "*Yes, sir?*"

"Viola'll explain." I push him after Ivan. "You get those bandages on her! She's hurting!"

That gets him moving. I turn about face and go towards the lobby. Two guards watch me walk past. "What's going on?" one of 'em asks.

"What's going on, *sir*," I snap without turning round. I walk out the front door of the Office of the Ask, down the little path and out the front gate.

Where it's almost peaceful.

And there's Angharrad.

Davy musta brought her.

"Hey, girl," I say, coming up on her slow, rubbing her nose. **Boy colt?** says her Noise. **Todd?**

"It's all right, girl," I whisper. "It's all right."

Hurt, she says, sniffing at the dried blood still on my face. She takes her big wet tongue and gives me the sloppiest lick right across my mouth and cheek.

I laugh a little and rub her nose again. "I'm okay, girl, I'm okay."

Her Noise keeps saying my name, **Todd Todd**, as I move to where my bag is still tied to the saddle. My rifle's still there.

So's my ma's book.

I'll bet Davy brought that, too.

I untie Angharrad's reins from the post and lead her out onto the road a little bit till she's pointing right at the gate with the big silver **A**. "Gotta give a little speech," I say, tightening the saddle. "Better from up top of you."

Boy colt, she says. **Todd**.

"Angharrad," I say.

I put my foot in a stirrup, hop up and swing my leg round till I'm sitting in the saddle, looking up at the sky. It's not darkening yet but the sun's getting down towards the falls. Afternoon is ticking away.

There ain't much time.

"Wish me luck," I say.

"Forward," Angharrad whinnies. "Forward."

* * *

The guards look up at me and back to Ivan who's trying to get 'em to stop talking, which would only help if they shut up the clatter of their Noise, too, cuz it's wailing like sheep on fire.

"He's a *lieutenant*," Ivan's saying to 'em.

"He's a *boy*," another guard says, one with ginger hair.

"He's the *President's* boy," Ivan responds.

"Yeah, and you were sposed to take him into town, Private," says another with a big pot belly and Corporal stripes on his sleeve. "Don't tell me yer disobeying a direct order."

"The Lieutenant gave me a different direct order," Ivan says.

"And he overrules the President, does he?" says Ginger Hair.

"Come on!" Ivan shouts. "How many of you got this assignment as punishment for something?"

That quiets 'em.

"Yer an idiot if you think I'm following a boy to face the President," says Corporal Pot Belly.

"Prentiss *knows* stuff," says Ginger Hair. "Stuff he shouldn't."

"He'd have us shot," says another soldier, a tall one this time, with sallow skin.

"By who?" says Ivan. "The army's all off fighting the war while the President sits in his blown-up cathedral a-waiting for me to show up with Todd here."

"What's he doing there?" asks Ginger Hair. "Why ain't he with the army?"

"Ain't his style," I say. They all look up at me again. "The

431

Mayor don't fight. He rules, he leads, but he don't pull no triggers and he don't get his hands dirty." Angharrad feels my nervousness and steps a little to one side. "He gets other people to do it for him."

Plus, I try to hide in my Noise, *he wants to talk to me*.

Which in a way feels worse than war.

"And yer gonna overthrow him, are ya?" asks the Corporal, crossing his arms.

"He's just a man," I say. "A man can be defeated."

"He's more'n a man," Ginger Hair says. "People say he uses his Noise as a weapon."

"And if you get too close to him, he can control your mind," says Sallow Skin.

Ivan scoffs. "That's all just grandmothers' tales. He can't do nothing of the sort–"

"Yes, he can," I say, and once again, all eyes turn on me. "He can hit you with his Noise and it hurts like hell. He can look into yer mind and try to force you to do and say the stuff he wants. Yeah, he can do all that."

They're staring at me now, wondering when I'm gonna get to the part that's helpful.

"But I think he's gotta make eye contact to do it–"

"You *think*?" says Ginger Hair.

"And the Noise hit ain't fatal and he can only do it to one person at a time. He can't beat all of us, not if we all come at once."

But I'm also hiding in my Noise how much stronger it was when he hit me in the Arena just now, how much more potent.

He's been working on it, sharpening his weapons.

"Don't matter," says Sallow Skin. "He'll have his own guards. We'd be walking right into our deaths."

"He'll be expecting you to escort me," I say. "We can walk right past the guards to where he's waiting."

"And why should we follow you, *Lieutenant*?" asks the Corporal, getting sarcastic on my rank. "What's in it for us?"

"Freedom from tyranny!" Ivan says.

The Corporal rolls his eyes. He ain't the only one.

Ivan tries again. "Because as soon as he's gone, *we* take over."

Less eye-rolling this time, but Sallow Skin says, "Anyone wanna be ruled by President Ivan Farrow?"

He says it to get a laugh but it don't get any.

"What about President Hewitt?" Ivan says, looking up at me with a weird glint in his eye.

Corporal Pot Belly scoffs and says again, "He's a *boy*."

"I'm not," I say. "Not no more."

"He's the only one a-willing to go after the President," Ivan says. "That speaks for *something*."

The guards look from one to another. I can hear all the askings in their Noise, all the doubts rattling around, all the fears confirming one another, and in their Noise I hear the idea being defeated.

But in their Noise I also hear how it can be saved.

"If you help me," I say, "I'll get you the cure."

They all shut right up.

"You can do that?" Ginger Hair asks.

"Naw," says the Corporal. "He's bluffing."

"It's stockpiled in the cellars of the cathedral," I say. "I saw the Mayor put it there himself."

"Why do you keep calling him *the Mayor*?" Sallow Skin asks.

"You come with me," I say. "You help me take him prisoner and every man here gets all the cure he can carry." They're listening to me now. "It's about ruddy time Haven became Haven again."

"He's taken it from the entire army," Ivan says. "We bring down the President, give 'em the cure, and who do you think they'll start a-listening to?"

"It won't be you, Ivan."

"No," says Ivan, giving me that look again. "But it could be *him*."

The men look up at me, up on top of Angharrad, with my rifle and my dusty uniform and my idea and my promises and there's a rustle thru their Noise as each man asks himself, is he desperate enough to take the chance?

I think of Viola, sitting in the Arena, sitting there as everything I want to save, everything I'd do anything for.

I think of her and I know exactly how to convince 'em.

"All the women are banded," I say. "Who do you think's gonna be next?"

Lee's pulling the last bandages round Viola's feet when I come back in and her face is looking way less pained.

"Can you stand?" I ask.

"Only a little."

"Don't matter," I say. "Angharrad's outside. She'll take you and Lee to find the Answer."

"What about you?" Viola says, sitting up.

"I'm gonna face him," I say. "I'm gonna take him down."

She *really* sits up at that.

"I'm coming with you," Lee says instantly.

"No, yer not," I say. "Yer telling the Answer to call off their attack *and* yer telling them just how Mistress Coyle works."

Lee's mouth sets firm but I can see his Noise roiling in anger over the bomb. He woulda died, too. "Viola says you can't kill."

I send her a dirty look. She's got the good grace to look away.

"I'm gonna kill him," Lee says. "I'm gonna kill him for what he did to my sister and mother."

"If you don't warn the Answer," I say, "there'll be a lot more dead people to make him pay for."

"He can *have* Mistress Coyle," Lee says but I can already see other people churning in his Noise, Wilf and Jane and other men and other women and Viola and Viola and Viola and Viola.

"What are you going to do, Todd?" she asks. "You can't just face him one on one."

"It won't be one on one," I say. "I got some of the guards to come with me."

Her eyes open wide. "You *what*?"

I smile. "Got me a little mutiny going."

"How many?" Lee asks, his face still serious.

I hesitate. "Seven," I say. "I couldn't get 'em all to agree."

Viola's face drops. "You're going to fight the Mayor with seven men?"

"It's a chance," I say. "Most of the army's off marching to their final battle. The Mayor's *waiting* for me. It's the least guarded he's ever gonna be."

She watches me for a second, then she puts one hand on Lee's shoulder and one hand on mine and lifts herself to her feet. I can see her catch herself at the pain but Lee's wound the bandages tight and even if they ain't bone-fixers then at least they let her stand for a second or two.

"I'm coming with you," she says.

"No, yer not," I say at the same time as Lee yells, "Not a chance!"

She sets her jaw. "And what makes either of you think you have a say in the matter?"

"You can't walk," I say.

"You have a horse," she says.

"It's yer chance to get *safe*," I say.

"He's expecting *both* of us, Todd. You walk in there without me, your plan is over before you even speak."

I put my hands on my hips. "You said yerself the Mayor will use you against me if he gets the chance."

She kisses her teeth as she tests the weight on her ankle. "Then your plan had better work, hadn't it?"

"Viola–" Lee starts but she stops him with a look.

"Find the Answer, Lee. Warn them. You haven't got much time."

"But–"

"*Go*," she says again, more firmly.

And we both see her rise in his Noise, we both *feel* how much he don't wanna leave her. It's so strong, I have to look away from him.

But it sorta makes me wanna hit him, too.

"I'm not leaving Todd," she says. "Not now I've found him again. I'm sorry, Lee, but that's the way it is."

Lee takes a step back, unable to keep the hurt outta his Noise. Viola's voice softens. "I'm sorry," she says again.

"Viola–" Lee says.

But she's shaking her head. "The Mayor thinks he knows everything. He thinks he knows what's coming. He's just sitting there *waiting* for me and Todd to show up and try and stop him."

Lee tries to interrupt but she don't let him.

"But what he's forgetting," she says. "What he's forgetting is that me and Todd, we ran halfway across this planet together, by *ourselves*. We beat his craziest preacher. We outran an entire army and survived being shot and beaten and chased and we bloody well *stayed alive* this whole time without being blown up or tortured to death or dying in battle or anything."

She takes her hand off Lee so she's balancing just against me.

"Me and Todd? Together against the Mayor?" She smiles. "He doesn't stand a chance."

38

MARCH TO THE CATHEDRAL

{ VIOLA }

"DID YOU MEAN what you said in there?" Todd says, pulling the strap on the saddle. His voice is low and he's keeping his eyes on the horse work. "Bout him not standing a chance against us?"

I shrug. "It helped, didn't it?"

He smiles to himself. "I gotta go talk to the men." He nods over to Lee, standing away from us, hands in his pockets, watching us chat. "You try and make this easy on him, okay?"

He gives Lee a wave and goes to where our escort of seven soldiers stands huddled by the big stone gate. Lee comes over.

"Are you sure about this?" he says.

"No," I say, "but I'm sure of Todd."

He breathes out through his nose, looking at the ground, trying to keep his Noise flat. "You love him," he says. Not an asking, just a fact.

"I do," I say. Also a fact.

"In *that* way?"

We both look over at Todd. He's gesturing with his arms and telling the men what we're planning and what they should do.

He's looking like a leader.

"Viola?" Lee asks.

I turn back to him. "You need to find the Answer before the army does, Lee, if you can at all."

He frowns. "They may not believe me about Mistress Coyle. A lot of people need her to be right."

"Well," I say, gently taking up the reins of the horse. **Boy colt?** she thinks, watching Todd, too. "Think of it this way. If you can reach them and we can take care of the Mayor, this could all be over today."

Lee squints into the sun. "And if you don't take care of him?"

I try to smile. "Well, then, you're just going to have to come rescue us, aren't you?"

He tries to smile back.

"We're ready," Todd says, coming back over.

"This is it," I say.

Todd holds out his hand to Lee. "Good luck."

Lee takes his hand. "And to you," he says.

But he's looking at me.

After Lee's set off into the woods, running to scale the hills and intercept the Answer before the army does, the rest of us start our march down the road. Todd leads Angharrad, who keeps saying **Boy colt** over and over again in her Noise, nervous at someone new on her back. Todd murmurs things to keep her calm, rubbing her nose and petting her flank as we go.

"How do you feel?" he asks me as we approach the first set of dormitories.

"My feet hurt," I say. "My head, too." I rub my hand on my sleeve where the band is hiding. "And my arm."

"Other than that?" He smiles.

I look at the guards around us, marching in formation, as if they really are escorting me and Todd to the Mayor as ordered: Ivan and another in front, two behind, two to my right and the last to my left.

"Do you believe we can beat him?" I ask Todd.

"Well," he says and laughs, low, "we're going, ain't we?"

We're going.

Up the road and into New Prentisstown.

"Let's pick it up," Todd says, a bit louder.

The men pick up the pace.

"It's deserted," whispers the guard with flaming red hair as we pass through areas with more and more buildings.

Buildings but no people.

"Not deserted," another guard says, one with a big belly poking out in front of him. "In hiding."

"It's spooky without the army," the red-haired one says. "Without soldiers marching up and down the street."

"*We're* marching, Private," Ivan says. "We're soldiers, too."

We pass houses with shutters closed tight, store fronts with locked shutters, roads with no carts or fissionbikes or even people walking. You can hear the ROAR from behind closed doors but it's half the volume.

And it's *scared*.

"They know it's coming," Todd says. "They know this could be the war they've been waiting for."

I look around from atop Angharrad. No homes have any lights on, no faces peep out of windows, no one even curious as to what this band of guards is doing around a horse carrying a girl with bandaged feet.

And then the road bends and there's the cathedral.

"Holy moly," says the red-haired guard, as we come to a stop.

"You lived through *that*?" the pot belly says to Todd. He whistles in appreciation. "Maybe you *are* a bit blessed."

The bell tower still stands, though it's hard to see how, teetering on top of an unsteady ladder of bricks. Two walls of the main building stand, too, including the one with the coloured glass circle.

But the rest of it.

The rest of it's just a pile of stone and dust.

Even from behind, you can see that most of the roof has caved in and the largest parts of two walls have been blown out onto the road and the square in front of it. Arches lean dangerously out of balance, doors are twisted off their hinges, and most of the inside lies open to the world, receiving the last of the sun as it heads down to the horizon.

And there's not one soldier guarding it.

"He's unprotected?" says the red-haired one.

"That sounds like something he'd do," Todd says, staring at the cathedral as if he can see the Mayor somewhere through the walls.

"If he's even inside," Ivan says.

"He is," Todd says. "Trust me."

The red-haired soldier starts backing away down the road. "No way," he says. "We're walking to our deaths here, boys. No way."

And with a final frightened look, he takes off running back the way we came.

Todd sighs. "Anyone else?" The men look to each other, their Noises wondering why they came in the first place.

"He'll put the band on you," Ivan says. He nods up at me. I pull up my sleeve and show them. The skin is still red and hot to the touch. Infection, I think. The first aid creams aren't doing what they're supposed to.

"And then he'll enslave you," Ivan continues. "I don't know about you, but that's not why I joined the army."

"Why *did* you join?" asks another guard but it's clear he doesn't want an answer.

"We take him down," Ivan says. "And we're heroes."

"Heroes with the cure," says the pot belly, nodding. "And he who controls the cure–"

"Enough talking," Todd says and I hear the discomfort in his Noise about how this is going. "Are we gonna do this or not?"

The men look to one another.

And Todd raises his voice.

Raises it so it commands.

Raises it so even *I* look at him.

"I said, are we *ready*?"

"Yes, sir," the men say, seeming almost surprised to hear it coming out of their mouths.

"Then let's go," Todd says.

And the men start marching again, *step step step*, crunching through the loose gravel scattered across the road, down a small slope, through the town and towards the cathedral, getting bigger and bigger the closer we get.

We file past some trees and I look to our left, to the hills on the southern horizon.

"Sweet Jesus," Pot Belly says.

Even from here you can see the army marching in the distance, a single black arm twisting up a path too narrow for them, up to the summit of the hill with the notch on top, up to where they'll meet The Answer.

I look at the setting sun.

"Maybe an hour," Todd says, seeing me check. "Probably less."

"Lee won't get to them in time," I say.

"He might. There must be short cuts."

The snake of the army slithers up the hillside. So many there's no way the Answer will be able to fight them if it comes to open battle.

"We can't fail," I say.

"We won't," Todd says.

And we reach the cathedral.

We march up the side. This is where most of the damage is, the whole north wall having collapsed straight onto the road.

"Remember," Todd murmurs to the men, as we climb over rubble. "Yer taking two prisoners to see the President like you were ordered to do. Nobody needs to be thinking nothing but that."

We pick our way down the road. The pile of stones is so high you can't see into the cathedral. The Mayor could be in there anywhere.

We come around the corner to where the front used to be, now just a gaping hole into the vast lobby and sanctuary, still watched over by the bell tower and by that circle of coloured glass. The sun, behind us, shines right into it. Open rooms hang from upper walls, their floors crumbling. Half a dozen redbirds pick through the remains of food and worse in amongst the stones. The rest of the structure leans in on itself, like it's grown suddenly tired and might fall down to rest at any time.

And inside its shell–

"No one," Ivan says.

"That's why there aren't any guards," says Pot Belly. "He's with the army."

"He's not," Todd says, looking around, frowning.

"Todd?" I ask, sensing something–

"He told us *himself* to bring Todd here," Ivan says.

"Then where is he?" asks Pot Belly.

"Oh, I'm here," says the Mayor, stepping out of a shadow that shouldn't have been able to hide him, almost seeming to step straight out of the brick, out of a shimmer where he couldn't be seen.

"What the devil–?" says Pot Belly, stepping back.

"Not the Devil," the Mayor says, taking his first steps down the rubble towards us, his hands open at his sides. The guards all raise their rifles at him. He doesn't even look like he's armed.

But here he comes.

"No, not the Devil," he says, smiling. "Much worse than that."

"Stop where you are," Todd says. "There are men here who would happily shoot you."

"I know it," the Mayor says, stopping on the bottom step of the cathedral entrance, resting one foot on a large stone toppled there. "Private Farrow, for example." He nods at Ivan. "Still seething for being punished for his own incompetence."

"You shut your mouth," Ivan says, looking down the barrel of his rifle.

"Don't look into his eyes," Todd says quickly. "Nobody look into his eyes."

The Mayor slowly puts his hands in the air. "Am I to be your prisoner then?" He takes a look around at the soldiers, at all the guns pointed at him. "Ah, yes, I see," he says. "You have a plan. Returning the cure to the people, capitalizing on their resentment to install yourselves in power. Yes, *very* clever."

"That ain't how it's gonna be," Todd says. "Yer gonna call off the army. Yer gonna let everyone be free again."

The Mayor puts a hand to his chin like he's thinking about it. "The thing is, Todd," he says, "people don't really *want* freedom, no matter how much they might bleat on about it. No, I should think what will happen is that the army will crush the Answer, that the soldiers accompanying you will be put to death for treason, and that you and I and Viola will have that little chat about your future I promised."

There's a loud snap as Ivan cocks his rifle. "You think so, do you?"

"Yer our prisoner and that's the end of it," Todd says, taking out a length of rope from Angharrad's saddle bag. "We'll just have to see how the army reacts to that."

"Very well," the Mayor says, sounding almost cheerful. "But I should send one of your men to the cellar so you can start taking the cure immediately. I can read all your plans perfectly clearly, and you wouldn't want that."

Pot Belly looks back. Todd nods at him and Pot Belly jogs on up the steps past the Mayor. "Just back and down," the Mayor points. "The way's quite clear."

Todd takes the rope and walks towards the Mayor, moving past the guns pointed at him. My hands are sweating into the reins.

It can't be this easy.

It can't–

The Mayor holds out his wrists and Todd hesitates, not wanting to actually get near him. "He tries anything funny," Todd says, without looking back. "Shoot him."

"Gladly," Ivan says.

Todd reaches forward and starts winding the rope around the Mayor's wrists.

We hear footsteps in the cathedral. Pot Belly comes jogging back, out of breath, his Noise a storm.

"You said it was in the cellar, *Lieutenant*."

"It is," Todd says. "I saw it there."

Pot Belly shakes his head. "Empty. Completely empty."

Todd looks back at the Mayor. "Then you moved it. Where is it?"

"Or what?" the Mayor says. "You'll shoot me?"

"I'd actually *prefer* that option," Ivan says.

"*Where did you move it?*" Todd says again, his voice strong, angry.

The Mayor looks at him, then looks around at all the men, and finally looks up to me on horseback.

"It was you I was worried about," he says. "But you can hardly walk, can you?"

"Don't you look at her," Todd spits, stepping closer to him. "You keep yer filthy eyes *off* her."

The Mayor smiles again, his hands still out, loosely bound by rope. "Very well," he says. "I'll tell you."

He looks around at everyone again, still smiling.

"I burnt it," says the Mayor. "After the Spackle sadly left us, there was no more need and so I burnt every last pill, every last plant that the pills were made from, and then I blew up the processing lab and blamed it on the Answer."

There's a shocked silence. We can hear the ROAR of the army in the distance, marching up that hill, keeping on towards their goal.

"You're a *liar*," Ivan finally says, stepping forward, gun still raised. "And a stupid one, at that."

"We can't hear yer Noise," Todd says. "You can't have burnt it all."

"Ah, but Todd, my son," the Mayor says, shaking his head. "I have never taken the cure."

Another silence. I hear suspicions rising in the Noise of the men. I even see a few of them step back, thoughts of the

Mayor's power, thoughts of what he can do. Maybe he *can* control his Noise. And if he can do *that*–

"He's lying," I say, remembering Mistress Coyle's words. "He's the President of Lies."

"Well, at least you finally called me *President*," the Mayor says.

Todd gives the Mayor a shove. "Tell us where it is."

The Mayor stumbles back a step, then regains his balance. He looks around at us all again. I can hear everyone's Noise rising, Todd's most of all, red and loud.

"I tell no lies, gentlemen," says the Mayor. "If you only have the right discipline, Noise can be controlled. It can be silenced." He looks around at each of us again, his smile reappearing. "It can be used."

I AM THE CIRCLE AND THE CIRCLE IS ME, I hear.

But I can't tell if it's from his Noise–

Or Todd's.

"I've had just about enough of this!" Ivan shouts.

"You know, Private Farrow," says the Mayor, "so have I."

And that's when he attacks.

39

YER OWN WORST ENEMY

[TODD]

I FEEL THE FIRST STRIKE of Noise fly by me, a *whooshing* of concentrated words and sound and pictures rushing over my shoulder, straight for the men with rifles. I flinch away and dive for the ground–

Cuz the men start firing their guns–

And I'm right in the way–

"Todd!" I hear Viola shout but the rifles are firing and the men are screaming and I roll on the rubble, jarring my elbow, and whip round to see Corporal Pot Belly on his knees in front of Angharrad, his back turned, both hands on the sides of his head, screaming wordlessly down into the ground, Viola watching him, wondering what the hell is going on. Another guard has fallen on his back, fingers in his eyes, as if he's trying to dig them out, and a third lies unconshus on his stomach. Two others are already running back into the city.

The Noise flies from the Mayor, louder and stronger than anything I've seen before.

Way louder than at the Office of the Ask.

Loud enough to take out five men at once.

Only Ivan still stands, one hand up to his ear and the other trying to aim his rifle at the Mayor but weaving it dangerously around–

BANG

A bullet smacks the ground in front of my eyes, sending dust and dirt up into them–

BANG

Another bounces off stones deep in the cathedral–

"IVAN!" I shout.

BANG

"Stop firing! Yer gonna get us killed!"

BANG

His rifle goes off right by Angharrad's head. She rears up and I see Viola grab the reins, surprised, holding on for dear life–

And then I see the Mayor is walking forward and forward and forward–

His eyes on the men he's attacking–

Coming past me–

And I don't even think–

I leap from the ground to stop him–

And he turns and sends his Noise straight at me–

The world goes all bright, terribly, painfully bright, like everyone can see how much you hurt, everyone watching and laughing and nowhere to hide and YER NOTHING YER NOTH-ING YER NOTHING all bound up tight like a bullet right thru you, telling you everything that's wrong with you, everything you ever done bad in yer life, telling you yer worthless, yer dirt, YER NOTHING, yer life ain't got no point nor reason nor purpose and you should just tear down the walls of yerself, ripping apart who you are and either die or give it up as a gift, as a gift to the one who can save you, as a gift to the man who can control you, who can take it all away, who can make everything fine fine fine–

But not even Noise can stop a body when it's moving.

I feel all these things and I'm still flying at him and I still hit him and I still knock him over on the steps of the cathedral.

He grunts as the air is crushed out of him and the Noise attack stops for a second. Corporal Pot Belly calls out and falls over and Ivan's gasping for breath and Viola's calling out "Todd!" and then a hand is around my neck and it's pushing my head up and the Mayor is looking right into my eyes–

And this time it hits me full blast.

"Give me the rifle!" the Mayor is shouting, standing over Ivan, who's crouched on the ground below him, hand over his ear again but the rifle still pointed up at the Mayor. "Give it to me!"

I blink, grit and dust in my eyes, wondering for a second where I am–

YER NOTHING YER NOTHING YER NOTHING YER NOTHING

"Give me the rifle, *Private!*"

451

The Mayor's screaming at Ivan, hitting him over and over again with Noise blasts and Ivan is sinking to the ground–

But his rifle's still aimed–

"Todd!"

I see horse legs beside my head. Viola's still up on Angharrad. "Todd, wake up!" she's yelling. I look up at her. "Thank God!" she yells and her face is a picture of frustrayshun. "My stupid feet! I can't get off the goddam horse!"

"I'm okay," I say, tho I don't know if I am, and I lean myself up, my head spinning.

YER NOTHING YER NOTHING YER NOTHING YER NOTHING

"Todd, what's going on?" Viola says as I grab a rein to help me stand. "I hear Noise but–"

"The rifle!" shouts the Mayor, stepping closer to Ivan. "Now!"

"We have to help him," I say–

But I flinch back at the strongest attack yet–

A flare of Noise so white you can almost see the air bending twixt the Mayor and Ivan–

And Ivan grunts sharply and bites his tongue–

Blood spilling from his mouth–

Before he screams like a child and falls back–

Dropping the rifle–

Dropping it right into the Mayor's hands.

He lifts it, cocks it and aims it at us in one fluid move. Ivan lies twitching on the ground.

"What just happened?" Viola says, too angry it seems to care much about the rifle.

I put my hands in the air, still holding the reins.

"He can use Noise," I say, keeping my eyes on him. "He can use it like a weapon."

"Just so," says the Mayor, smiling again.

"All I heard was shouting," she says, looking at the men lying on the ground, still breathing but out cold. "What do you mean, a weapon?"

"The truth, Viola," the Mayor answers. "The best weapon of all. You tell a man the truth about himself and, well," he nudges Ivan with his boot, "they find they have trouble accepting it." He frowns. "You can't kill him with it, though." He looks back up at us. "Not yet, anyway."

"But…" She's not believing this. "How? How can you–?"

"I have two maxims that I believe, dear girl," the Mayor says, coming slowly towards us. "One, if you can control yourself, you can control others. Two, if you can control *information*, you can control others." He grins, his eyes flashing. "It's been a philosophy that's worked out rather well for me."

I think about Mr Hammar. About Mr Collins. About the chanting I used to hear coming from the Mayor's house back in my old town.

"You taught the others," I say. "The men from Prentisstown, you taught them how to control their Noise."

"With varying degrees of success," he says, "but yes, none of my officers has ever taken the cure. Why should they? It's a weakness to have to rely on a drug."

He's nearly on us now. "I am the Circle and the Circle is me," I say.

"Yes, you were certainly making an impressive beginning,

weren't you, Todd? Controlling yourself while you did the most unspeakable things to those women."

My Noise turns red. "You *shut up* about that," I say. "I was only doing what you told me—"

"*I was only following orders*," the Mayor mocks. "The refuge of scoundrels since the dawn of time." He stops two metres away from us, rifle pointed firmly at my chest. "Help her off the horse, please, Todd."

"What?" I say.

"Her ankles, I believe the problem was. She'll need your help walking."

I still have the reins in my hand. I have a thought I try to bury.

Boy colt? Angharrad asks.

"I assure you, Viola," the Mayor says to her. "If you think about running on that beautiful animal, I will put more than one bullet through Todd." He looks back at me. "However much pain it might cause me."

"You let her go," I say. "I'll do anything you want."

"Now where have I heard that before?" he says. "Help her down."

I hesitate, wondering if I should slap Angharrad's flanks anyway, wondering if I should send Viola riding off into the distance, wondering if I could get her safe—

"No," Viola says and she's already working her leg round the saddle. "Not a chance. I'm not leaving you."

I take her arms and help her down. She has to lean on me to stand but I keep her up.

"Splendid," says the Mayor. "Now let's go inside and have that chat."

* * *

"Let us start with what I know."

He's brought us into what used to be the room with the round coloured glass window in it but it's now open to the air on two sides and above, the window still there, looking down, but looking down on rubble.

Looking down on a little cleared area with a broken table and two chairs.

Where me and Viola sit.

"I know, for example," the Mayor says, "that you did not kill Aaron, Todd, that you never took your final step towards becoming a man, that it was Viola here who put the blade in all along."

Viola takes my arm and squeezes it tight, letting me know it's okay that he knows.

"I know that Viola told you the Answer were hiding at the ocean when I let you escape to go speak with her."

My Noise rises in anger and embarrassment. Viola squeezes my arm harder.

"I know that you've sent the boy called Lee to warn the Answer." He leans against the broken table. "And of course I also know the exact time and place of their attack."

"Yer a monster," I say.

"No," the Mayor says. "Just a leader. Just a leader who can read every thought you have, about yourself, about Viola, about me, about this town, about the secrets you think you're keeping, I can read *everything*, Todd. You're not listening to what I'm saying." He's still holding the rifle, watching us sit before him. "I knew everything about the

Answer's attack this morning before you even opened your mouth."

I sit up in my chair. "You what?"

"I had the army gathering before we even started Asking Viola."

I start to rise. "You tortured her for *nothing*?"

"Sit down," the Mayor says and a little flash from him weakens my knees enough that I sit right back down. "Not for nothing, Todd. You should know me well enough by now to know that I do not do *anything* for nothing."

He sits up from the broken table, showing again that he likes to walk and talk.

"You are completely transparent to me, Todd. From our first proper meeting here in this very room until how you sit before me today. I've known everything. *Always*."

He looks at Viola. "Unlike your good friend here, who's a little tougher than I imagined."

Viola frowns. If she had Noise I'm sure she'd be slapping him around a bit.

I get a thought—

"Don't try it," the Mayor says. "You're not nearly that advanced yet. Even Captain Hammar has yet to master it. You'd merely end up hurting yourself very badly." He looks at me again. "But you *could* learn, Todd. You could advance far, farther than any of those poor imbeciles who followed me from Prentisstown. Poor Mr Collins barely worth more than a butler and Captain Hammar just another garden-variety sadist, but you, Todd, *you*." His eyes flash. "You could lead armies."

"I don't wanna lead armies," I say.

He smiles. "You may have no choice."

"There's always a choice," Viola says by my side.

"Oh, people like to say that," the Mayor says. "It makes them feel better." He approaches me, looking into my eyes. "But I've been watching you, Todd. The boy who can't kill another man. The boy who'd risk his own life to save his beloved Viola. The boy who felt so guilty at the horrible things he was doing that he tried to shut off all feeling. The boy who still felt every pain, every twitch of hurt he saw on the face of the women he banded."

He leans down closer to my face. "The boy who refused to lose his soul."

I feel him. He's in my Noise now, rummaging around, turning things over, upending the room inside my head. "I've done bad things," I say and I don't even mean to say it.

"But you *suffer* for them, Todd." His voice is softer now, almost tender. "You're your own worst enemy, punishing yourself far more than I could ever hope to. Men have Noise and the way they handle it is to make themselves just a little bit dead, but *you*, even when you *want* to, you can't. More than any man I've ever met, Todd, you *feel*."

"Shut up," I say, trying to look away, not being able to.

"But that makes you *powerful*, Todd Hewitt. In this world of numbness and information overload, the ability to feel, my boy, is a rare gift indeed."

I put my hands to my ears but I can still hear him in my head.

"You're the one I couldn't break, Todd. The one who wouldn't fall. The one who stays innocent no matter the blood on his hands. The one who *still* calls me Mayor in his Noise."

"I'm not innocent!" I shout, my ears still plugged.

"You could rule by my side. You could be my second in command. And when you learn to control your Noise, you may have power to overtake even *mine*."

And then the words thunder thru my whole body.

I AM THE CIRCLE AND THE CIRCLE IS ME.

"Stop it!" I hear Viola shout but it's from miles away.

The Mayor puts a hand on my shoulder. "You could be my son, Todd Hewitt," he says. "My real and true heir. I've always wanted one that wasn't–"

"Pa?" we all hear, cutting thru everything like a bullet thru fog.

The Noise in my head stops, the Mayor steps abruptly back, I feel like I'm able to breathe again.

Davy stands behind us, rifle in one hand. He's led Deadfall up to the steps and is looking over the rubble to the three of us here. "What's going on? Who are the men out there on the ground?"

"What are you doing here?" the Mayor snaps, frowning. "Is the battle already won?"

"No, Pa," Davy says, climbing over the rubble towards us. "It was a trick." He plants his feet next to my chair. "Hey, Todd," he says, nodding in greeting. He glances at Viola but he can't hold her eye.

"*What* was a trick?" the Mayor demands but he's already looking angry.

"The Answer ain't coming over the hill," Davy says. "We marched way back deep into the forest but there ain't no sign, not nowhere."

I hear Viola take a little gasp, a bit of pleased surprise

escaping from her even as she tries to hold it back.

The Mayor looks her way, his eyes fierce, his face thinking and thinking.

And he raises his rifle at her.

"Something you'd like to tell us, Viola?"

40

NOTHING CHANGES, EVERYTHING CHANGES

{VIOLA}

TODD'S ALREADY UP and out of his chair, standing between me and the Mayor, his Noise raging so loud and furious the Mayor takes a step back.

"You see the power in you, my boy?" he says. "This is why you watched her being Asked. Your suffering makes you *strong*. I'll teach you how to harness it and together we'll–"

"You hurt her," Todd says, clearly and slowly, "and I'll tear every limb from yer body."

The Mayor smiles. "I believe you." He hoists the rifle. "Nevertheless."

"Todd," I say.

He turns to me. "This is how he wins. Playing us off each other. Just like you said. Well, it stops here–"

"Todd–" I'm trying to stand up but my stupid ankles won't hold me and I stumble. Todd reaches for me–

But it's Davy–

Davy catches me by the arm, stopping the fall and then lowering me back into the chair. He won't meet my eye. Or Todd's. Or his father's. His Noise flushes yellow with embarrassment as he lets me go and steps back.

"Why, thank you, David," the Mayor says, unable to mask his surprise. "Now," he says, turning back to me, "if you would please be so kind as to inform me of the Answer's *real* plan of attack."

"Don't tell him nothing," Todd says.

"I don't *know* anything," I say. "Lee must have reached–"

"There wasn't sufficient time and you know it," the Mayor says. "It's obvious what's happened, isn't it, Viola? Your Mistress misled you once more. If the bomb went off as it should have, it wouldn't have mattered if you had the wrong information because you and, she hoped, *I* would be dead. But if you were caught, well, then. The best liar is the one who believes her lie is true."

I don't say anything because how could she have misled me if it was only something Lee overheard–

But then I think–

She *wanted* him to overhear it.

She *knew* he wouldn't be able to not tell me.

"Her plan worked perfectly, didn't it, Viola?" The shadow from the setting sun reaches the Mayor's face, covering him in black. "One twist after another, lies building on lies. She played you exactly how she wanted, didn't she?"

I glare at him. "She'll beat you," I say. "She's as ruthless as you are."

He grins. "Oh, *more*, I should say."

"Pa?" Davy asks.

The Mayor blinks, like he forgot his son was there. "Yes, David?"

"Um, the *army*?" Davy's Noise is full of bewilderment and exasperation, trying to make sense of what his father's doing but not finding much relief. "What're we sposed to do *now*? Where're we sposed to go? Captain Hammar's waiting for yer orders."

All around us the low, frightened ROAR of New Prentisstown seeps out of the houses, but still no faces at the windows, and from over the hill with the notch, the blacker, twistier buzz of the army. You can still see them up the hillside, shiny like a trail of black beetles sliding off one another's shells.

And here we sit, alone with the Mayor and his son, in the open ruins of the cathedral, like we're the only people on the planet.

The Mayor looks back at me. "Yes, Viola, tell us. What are we supposed to do now?"

"You're supposed to fall," I say, staring back at him, not blinking. "You're supposed to lose."

He smiles at me. "Where are they coming from, Viola? You're a clever girl. You must have heard *something*, seen some clue as to her real plans."

"She ain't telling you," Todd says.

"I *can't*," I say, "because I don't *know*."

And I'm thinking, I really *don't* know–

Unless the thing she told me about the east road–

"I'm waiting, Viola." The Mayor raises the rifle at Todd's head. "On pain of his life."

"Pa?" Davy says, shock coming out of his Noise. "What're you *doing*?"

462

"Never you mind, David. Get back on your horse. I'll have a message for you to take to Captain Hammar presently."

"Yer pointing the gun at *Todd*, Pa."

Todd turns around to look at him. So do I. So does the Mayor.

"You ain't gonna shoot him," Davy says. "You can't." Davy's cheeks are red now, so dark you can even see them in the sunset. "You said he's yer second son."

There's an uncomfortable silence as Davy tries to hide his Noise.

"You see what I mean by power, Todd?" the Mayor says. "Look at how you've influenced my son. You've already got yourself a follower."

Davy looks at me, right in the eyes. "Tell him where they are." There's worry all over his Noise, anxiety at how things are playing out. "C'mon, just tell him."

I look back at Todd.

He's looking at Davy's rifle.

"Yes, Viola, tell me, why don't you?" the Mayor says. "Your best speculation. Are they coming from the west?" He looks up towards the falls, the highest point on the horizon, where the sun's disappearing behind the zigzag road carved down the hill, the hill I've only been down once and never gone back up. The Mayor turns. "The north, perhaps, though they'd have to cross the river somehow? Or a hill to the east? Yes, maybe even over the hill where your Mistress blew up the tower and any chance you had of communicating with your people."

I clench my teeth again.

"Still loyal, after all that?"

I don't say anything.

"We could send out troops, Pa," Davy says. "To different parts. They gotta come from *somewhere*."

The Mayor waits for a minute, staring us down. He finally turns to Davy and says, "Go tell Captain Hammar–"

He's interrupted by a distant *BOOM*.

"That's due east," Davy says, as we all look up even though there's a wall of the cathedral in the way.

It *is* east.

It's exactly the road she told me it was going to be.

She made me think the truth was a lie and a lie was the truth.

If I get out of this, we're going to have words, her and me.

"The Office of the Ask," the Mayor says. "Of course. Where else would they–"

He stops again, cocking his head, listening out. We hear it several seconds after he does. The Noise of someone running full out towards the cathedral from the back, up the road we took to get here, around the side of the cathedral and up to the front, coming upon us, gasping.

It's the red-haired guard, the one who fled. He's obviously barely registering who he's seeing as he stumbles into the wreckage of the building. "They're coming!" he shouts. "The Answer is coming!"

There's a burst of Noise from the Mayor and the red-haired soldier falls back, catching himself. "Calm down, Private," the Mayor says, his voice slinky, snake-like. "Tell us clearly."

The guard pants, seemingly unable to catch his breath. "They've taken the Office of the Ask." He looks up at the

Mayor, caught by his eyes. "They killed all the guards."

"Of course they did," the Mayor says, still holding the red-haired soldier's gaze. "How many are there?"

"Two hundred." The red-haired soldier isn't blinking now. "But they're releasing the prisoners."

"Weapons?" asks the Mayor.

"Rifles. Tracers. Launchers. Siege guns on the backs of carts." Still the stare.

"How goes the battle?"

"They're fighting fierce."

The Mayor cocks an eyebrow, still staring at him.

"They're fighting fierce, *sir*," the guard says, still not blinking, like he couldn't look away from the Mayor if he tried. There's another *BOOM* in the distance and everyone except the Mayor and the soldier flinches. "They're coming for war, sir," says the soldier.

The Mayor keeps the stare. "Then you should be trying to stop them, shouldn't you?"

"Sir?"

"You should be taking your rifle and preventing the Answer from destroying your town."

The soldier looks confused but he's still not blinking. "I should..."

"You should be on the front line, soldier. This is our hour of need."

"This is our hour of need," the soldier mumbles, like he's not hearing himself.

"Pa?" Davy says but the Mayor ignores him.

"What are you waiting for, soldier?" the Mayor says. "It's time to fight."

"It's time to fight," says the guard.

"Go!" the Mayor suddenly barks and the red-haired guard springs away, back down the road towards the Answer, his rifle up, yelling incoherently, running back to the Answer as fast as he ran away from them.

We watch him go in stunned silence.

The Mayor sees Todd staring at him, mouth agape. "Yes, dear boy, better at *that*, too."

"You as good as killed him," I say. "Whatever you did–"

"What I did was make him see his duty," the Mayor says. "No more, no less. Now, as *fascinating* as this discussion is, we're going to have to settle it later. I'm afraid I'm going to have to have Davy tie you both up."

"*Pa?*" Davy says again, startled.

The Mayor looks at him. "Then you'll ride to Captain Hammar, tell him to bring the army down the road with all speed and fury." The Mayor casts his eyes to the far hillside where the army waits. "It's time we brought this to an end."

"I can't tie him up, Pa, it's *Todd*."

The Mayor doesn't look at him. "I've had just about enough of this, David. When I give you a direct order–"

Boom!

He stops and we all look up.

Because it's different this time, a different kind of sound. We hear a low *whoosh* and a rumble starts to fill the air, getting louder as the seconds pass.

Todd looks at me, confused.

I just shrug. "Nothing I ever heard before."

The roar starts to get louder, filling the darkening sky.

"That don't sound like no bomb," Davy says.

The Mayor looks at me. "Viola, is there–"

He stops and then turns his head.

And we all realize–

It's not coming from the east.

"Over there," Davy points, raising his hand towards the falls, towards where the sky is bright pink with sunset.

The Mayor looks at me again. "That's too loud for a simple tracer." His face tightens. "Have they got missiles?" He takes a step so big he's almost on top of me. "*Have they built missiles?*"

"You *back off*!" Todd yells, trying to get between us again.

"I will *know* what this is, Viola!" the Mayor says. "You will tell me!"

"I don't *know* what it is!" I say.

Todd's shouting and threatening, "You lay a *finger* on her–"

"It's getting louder!" Davy shouts, putting his hands to his ears. We all turn and watch the western horizon, watch as a dot rises, getting lost in the last of the sun before reappearing, growing larger as it comes.

As it comes straight for the city.

"*Viola!*" the Mayor shouts, through clenched teeth, sending some Noise at me but I don't feel whatever it is that men feel.

"I DON'T KNOW!" I yell.

And then Davy, who hasn't stopped watching it, says, "It's a ship."

41

THE MOMENT OF DAVY PRENTISS

[TODD]

IT'S A SHIP.

It's a ruddy *ship*.

"Yer people," I say to Viola.

But she's shaking her head, tho not to say no, just staring at it as it rises over the falls.

"Too small for a settler ship," Davy says.

"And too early," the Mayor says, aiming his rifle at it as if he could shoot it from this distance. "They're not due for another two months at least."

But Viola still ain't looking like she can hear any of this, hope rising on her face so painful it hurts my heart just to see it. "A scout," she whispers, so quiet I'm the only one who hears it. "Another scout. Sent to look for me."

I turn back to the ship.

It clears the crest of the falls, soaring out over the river.

A scout ship, just like the one she crashed in back in the

468

swamp, killing her parents and stranding her here all those months and lifetimes ago. It still looks as big as a house, stubby wings looking too short to keep it in the air, flames coming outta the tail end as it flies flies flies down the river, using it as a road hundreds of metres below.

We watch it come.

"David," the Mayor says, his eyes still on it. "Get my horse."

But Davy's got his face up to the sky, his Noise opening up in wonder and amazement.

And I know exactly how he feels.

Nothing flies on New World except the birds. We got machines that go down the roads, fissionbikes, a few fissioncars, but mainly we just got horses and oxes and carts and our feet.

We don't got *wings*.

The ship comes down the river, nearing the cathedral and flying almost right over us, not stopping, so close you can see lights on the underside and the sky above the exhaust shimmering with the heat. It flies right on past, down the river.

Down east towards the Answer.

"*David!*" the Mayor says sharply.

"Help me up," Viola whispers. "I have to get to them. I have to *go*."

And her eyes are wild and her breath is heavy and she's staring at me so hard it's like a solid thing I can feel.

"Oh, he'll help you up," the Mayor says, pointing the gun. "Because you're coming with me."

"*What?*" Viola says.

"They're *your* people, Viola," the Mayor says. "They're going to be wondering where you are. I can either bring you to them right away." He looks at me. "Or I can sadly inform them that you died in the crash. Which would you prefer?"

"I'm not going with *you*," she says. "You're a liar and a murderer–"

He cuts her off. "David, you'll remain guard over Todd while I take Viola to her ship." He looks back at her. "I think you know first-hand my son's eagerness with a gun if you don't cooperate."

Viola looks furiously at Davy. I look at Davy, too, standing there, rifle in hand, looking back and forth twixt me and his pa.

His Noise roiling.

His Noise saying clearly there ain't no way he's *ever* gonna shoot me.

"Pa?" he says.

"Enough of this, David," the Mayor frowns, trying to catch Davy's eye–

And catching it.

"You will do what I say," he says to his son. "You will tie Todd up with the rope he so helpfully brought and you will stand guard over him and when I return with our newly arrived guests, everything will be peaceful and happy. The new world will begin."

"New world," Davy mumbles, his eyes glazing over, just like the ginger-haired soldier, askings and doubt being pushed outta his Noise.

As he bends to the will of another.

I get an idea.

Forgive me, Davy.

"You gonna let him talk to you like that, Davy?"

He blinks. "What?"

He looks away from his pa.

"You gonna let him point a gun at me and Viola?"

"Todd," the Mayor warns.

"All that Noise you say you hear," I say to the Mayor but I still look at Davy, still hold his eye. "All the way you say you know *everything*, but you don't know yer own son very well, now, do ya?"

"David," the Mayor says.

But *I* got Davy's eye now.

"You gonna let him get his way again?" I say to him. "You gonna let him boss you round with no reward?"

Davy watches me nervously, trying to blink away the mess his pa's put in his head.

"That ship changes everything, Davy," I say. "A whole new batch of people. A whole city's worth to try and make this place something better than the stinking boghole it is."

"*David*," the Mayor says. There's a flash of Noise and Davy flinches.

"Stop it, Pa," he says.

"Who do you want to get to that ship first, Davy?" I say. "Me and Viola to get some help? Or yer pa so he can rule them, too?"

"Be *quiet*!" says the Mayor. "Are you forgetting who has the gun?"

"Davy has one, too," I say.

* * *

There's a bit of a pause as we all see Davy remember he's holding a rifle.

There's another flash of Noise from the Mayor and another flinch from Davy. "Jesus, *Pa*, effing quit it already!"

But he looks at his pa to say it.

And his pa catches his eyes again.

"Tie Todd up and get my horse, David," the Mayor says, holding his stare.

"Pa?" Davy says, his voice gone quiet.

"My horse," says the Mayor. "He's out back."

"Get between them," Viola hisses at me. "Break the eye contact!"

I move but the Mayor turns the gun on her without taking his eyes off Davy. "One move, Todd."

I stop.

"Bring me my horse, son," says the Mayor, "and we'll greet the new settlers side by side." He smiles at his son. "You'll be my prince."

"He said that before," I say to Davy. "But not to you."

"He's controlling you," Viola shouts. "He's using his Noise to—"

"Please tell Viola to be quiet," the Mayor says.

"Be quiet, Viola," Davy says, his voice soft, his eyes not blinking.

"*Davy!*" I shout.

"He's just trying to control you, David," the Mayor says, his voice rising. "Like he's done from the start."

"*What?*" I say.

472

"From the start," Davy mumbles.

"Who do you think's held you back from promotion, son?" the Mayor's saying it and he's saying it right into the middle of Davy's brain. "Who do you think tells me all the things you do wrong?"

"Todd?" Davy says weakly.

"He's *lying*," I say. "Look at me!"

But Davy's overloading. He's just staring frozen at his pa, not moving at all.

The Mayor gives a heavy sigh. "I see I have to do this myself."

He comes forward, gesturing us back with his rifle. He grabs Viola and lifts her to her feet. She cries out from the pain in her ankles. I move automatically to help but he pushes her forward so she's right in front of him, his rifle at her back.

I open my mouth to shout, to threaten, to damn him–

But it's Davy who speaks first.

"It's landing," he says quietly.

We all turn eastward. The ship is taking a slow circle, flying around a hilltop east of town–

Maybe even the one where the tower once stood–

It comes round again and hovers above the treetops–

Before slowly starting to lower itself out of sight–

I turn to Davy, too, see his eyes fogged and confused–

But he ain't looking at his pa no more–

He's looking at the ship–

And then he's turning his head and looking at me–

"Todd?" he says, like he's just waking up—

And his rifle is just there, just hanging from his hand—

And one more time—

Forgive me.

I lunge forward and snatch it from him. He don't even put up any resistance, just lets it go, lets it go right into my fingers and I'm already raising it and cocking it and pointing it at the Mayor.

Who's already smiling, his gun still in Viola's back.

"So it's a stand-off, is it?" he says, grinning from ear to ear.

"Let her go," I say.

"Please take your gun back from Todd, David," the Mayor says, but he has to keep looking at me, watching me with the gun.

"Don't you do no such thing, Davy."

"Stop it!" Davy says, his voice thick, his Noise rising. I sense him putting his hands to the sides of his head. "Can't you both just effing *stop it*?"

But the Mayor's still looking at me and I'm still looking at the Mayor.

The sound of the ship landing screams over the city, over the Noise of the army marching its way back down the hill, over the distant *booms* of the Answer making its way up the road, and over the terrified, hidden **ROAR** of New Prentisstown all around us, not knowing that their whole future depends on this, right now, right this second, me and the Mayor with our rifles.

"Let her go," I say.

"I don't think so, Todd." I hear a rumble of Noise coming from him.

"My finger's on this trigger," I say. "You try to hit me with yer Noise and yer a dead man."

The Mayor smiles. "Fair enough," he says. "But what you need to ask yourself, my dear friend Todd, is if, when you decide to finally pull that trigger, can you pull it fast enough so that I don't also pull my own? Will killing me kill your beloved Viola, too?" He lowers his chin. "Could you live with that?"

"You'd be dead," I say.

"So would she."

"Do it, Todd," Viola says. "Don't let him win."

"That ain't happening neither," I say.

"Are you going to let him point a gun at your own father, David?" the Mayor asks.

But he's still looking at me.

"Times are changing, Davy," I say, eyes still on the Mayor. "This is where we all decide how it's gonna be. Including you."

"Why's it have to be like this?" Davy asks. "We could all go together. We could all ride up on horseback and—"

"No, David," says the Mayor. "No, that won't do at all."

"Put the gun down," I say. "Put it down and end this."

The Mayor's eyes flash and I know what's coming—

"You stop that," I say, blinking furiously and looking over his shoulder.

"You cannot win this," the Mayor says and I hear his voice twice over, three times, a legion of him inside my head. "You cannot shoot me and guarantee her life, Todd. We all know you'd never risk that."

He takes a step forward, pushing Viola along. She calls out at the pain in her ankles.

But I find myself taking a step back.

"Don't look in his eyes," she says.

"I'm trying," I say, but even the *sound* of his voice is getting inside me.

"This isn't a loss, Todd," the Mayor is saying, so loud in my head it feels like my brain's vibrating. "I wish for your death no more than I wish for my own. Everything I said earlier was true. I want you by my side. I want you as part of the future we're going to create here with whoever steps out of that ship."

"Shut *up*," I say.

But he's still stepping forward.

I'm still stepping back.

Till I'm behind even Davy.

"I want no harm to come to Viola, either," the Mayor says. "All along I promised both of you a future. That promise still stands."

Even without looking right at him, his voice is buzzing in my head, weighing it down, making it seem like it's easier just to–

"Don't listen to him!" Viola shouts. "He's a liar."

"Todd," says the Mayor. "I think of you as my son. I really do."

And Davy turns to me, his Noise rising all hopeful, and he says, "C'mon, Todd, you hear that?"

And his Noise is reaching for me, too, eagerness and worry coming forward like fingers and hands, asking me, *begging* me to put the gun down, put it down and make everything all right, make it so all this stops–

And he says, "We could be brothers–"

And I cast my eyes to Davy's–

And I see myself in them, see myself in his Noise, see the Mayor as my father and Davy as my brother and Viola as our sister–

See the hopeful smile rising to Davy's lips–

And for the third time, I have to ask–

Forgive me.

I point the rifle at Davy.

"Let her go," I say to the Mayor, not quite able to look Davy in the face.

"Todd?" Davy asks, his forehead furrowing.

"Just do it!" I snap.

"Or you'll what, Todd?" the Mayor teases. "You'll shoot him?"

Davy's Noise is spilling over with more asking marks, with surprise and shock–

With a betrayal that's rising–

"Answer me, Todd," the Mayor says. "Or you'll *what*?"

"Todd?" Davy says again, his voice lower this time.

I look him briefly in the eyes and look away again.

"Or I'll shoot Davy," I say. "I'll shoot yer son."

Davy's Noise is pouring with disappointment, disappointment so thick it falls off him like mud. I don't even read no anger in his Noise, which makes it worse. He ain't even thinking of jumping me or punching me or wrestling the gun away.

The only thing in his Noise is me holding a gun on him.

His only friend holding a gun on him.

"I'm sorry," I whisper.

But he don't look like he hears.

"I gave you yer book," he says. "I gave you back yer book."

"You let Viola go!" I shout, looking away from Davy, anger at myself snapping my voice loud. "Or I swear to God–"

"Go ahead then," the Mayor says. "Shoot him."

Davy looks at the Mayor. "Pa?"

"Never much use as a son anyway," the Mayor says, still pushing Viola forward with the rifle. "Why do you think I sent him to the front line? I was at least hoping he'd die a *hero*'s death."

There's pain on Viola's face still but it ain't all her ankles.

"Never mastered his Noise," the Mayor continues, looking at Davy, whose Noise–

I can't say what his Noise is like.

"Never followed an order he couldn't get out of. Couldn't capture you. Couldn't take care of Viola. Only ever showed improvement because of *your* influence, Todd."

"Pa–" Davy starts.

But his pa ignores him.

"*You* are the son I want, Todd. Always you. *Never* this waste of space."

And Davy's Noise–

Oh, Jesus, Davy's Noise–

"LET HER GO!" I shout so I don't have to hear it. "I'll shoot him, I'll do it!"

"You won't," says the Mayor, smiling again. "Everyone knows you aren't a killer, Todd."

He pushes Viola forward again–

She calls out from the pain of it–

Viola, I think–

Viola–

I grit my teeth and raise the rifle–

I cock it–

And I say what's true–

"I would kill to save her," I say.

The Mayor stops edging forward. He looks twixt me and Davy and back again.

"Pa?" says Davy. His face is twisted and crumpled.

The Mayor looks back at me, reading my Noise.

"You would, wouldn't you?" he says, almost under his breath. "You'd kill him. For her."

Davy looks back at me, his eyes wet but anger rising there, too. "Don't, Todd. Don't do it."

"Let her go," I say again. "*Now*."

The Mayor's still looking twixt me and Davy, seeing that I'm serious, seeing that I'd really do it.

"Just put the gun down," I growl, not looking at Davy's eyes, not looking at his Noise. "*This is over*."

The Mayor takes in a long breath and lets it out.

"Very well, Todd," he says. "As you wish."

He steps away from Viola.

My shoulders relax.

And he fires his gun.

42

ENDGAME

{VIOLA}

"TODD!" I shout, the sound of the rifle shot blasting past my ear, erasing everything but him, the whole world reduced to not knowing if he's all right or not, if he's been hit, if–

But it's not him–

He's still holding up his gun–

Unfired–

Standing next to Davy–

Who falls to his knees–

Sending up two small clouds of dust as he hits the rubble–

"Pa?" he asks, his voice pleading, like a little kitten–

And then he coughs, spilling blood down his lips–

"Davy?" Todd says, his Noise rising like he's the one that's been shot–

And I see it–

A hole high in Davy's chest, in the fabric of his uniform, just below the base of his throat–

And Todd runs to him, kneeling down beside him–

"*Davy!*" he shouts–

But Davy's Noise is staring at his father–

Asking marks sent everywhere–

His expression shocked–

His hand reaching up to the wound–

He coughs again–

And gags–

Todd's looking at the Mayor, too–

His Noise railing–

"*What did you do?*" he shouts–

[TODD]

"*WHAT DID YOU DO?!*" I shout.

"I removed him from the equation," the Mayor says calmly.

"Pa?" Davy asks again, holding out a bloodied hand towards him–

But his pa is only looking at me.

"You were always the truer son, Todd," the Mayor says. "The one with the potential, the one with the power, the one I'd be proud to have serve by my side."

Pa? Davy's Noise says–

And he's hearing *all* of this–

"You effing *monster*," I say. "I'll *kill* you–"

"You'll *join* me," the Mayor says. "You know you will. It's only a matter of time. David was weak, an embarrassment–"

"*SHUT UP!*" I shout.

Todd? I hear–

I look down–

Davy's looking up at me–

His Noise swirling–

Swirling with askings and confuzhun and fear–

And **Todd?**–

Todd?–

I'm sorry–

I'm sorry–

"Davy, don't–" I start to say–

But his Noise is still swirling–

And I see–

I see–

I see the truth–

Here at the last–

He's showing me the truth–

The thing he's been hiding from me–

About Ben–

All in a messy rush–

Pictures of Ben racing up the road towards Davy–

Pictures of Davy's horse rearing–

Pictures of Davy firing his gun as he falls–

Pictures of the bullet hitting Ben in the chest–

Pictures of Ben staggering out into the bushes–

Davy too scared to go after him–

Davy too scared to tell me the truth after–

After I became his only friend–

I didn't mean it, his Noise is saying–

"Davy–" I say–

I'm sorry, he thinks–

And that's the truth all over–

He *is* sorry–

For everything–

For Prentisstown–

For Viola–

For Ben–

For every failure and every wrong–

For letting his pa down–

And he's looking up at me–

And he's begging me–

He's begging me–

Like I'm the only one who can forgive him–

Like it's only me who's got the power–

Todd?–

Please–

And all I can say is "Davy–"

And the fright and the terror in his Noise is too much–

It's too much–

And then it stops.

Davy slumps, eyes still open, eyes still staring back at me, eyes still asking (I swear) for me to forgive him.

And he lies there, still.

Davy Prentiss is dead.

{VIOLA}

"You're insane," I say to the Mayor behind me.

"No," he says. "You've been right all along, both of you. Never love something so much it can be used to control you."

The sun is down now but the sky is still pink, the Noise of the town still ROARs, there's another *Boom!* in the distance as the Answer approaches, and the ship must have landed by now. Its doors must be opening. Someone, probably Simone Watkin or Bradley Tench, people I know, people who know *me*, must be looking out, wondering what sort of place they've landed in.

And Todd kneels over the body of Davy Prentiss.

And then Todd looks up–

His Noise is boiling and burning and I can hear the grief in it and the shame and the *rage*–

And he gets to his feet–

And he raises his rifle–

I see myself in his Noise, I see the Mayor there, too, behind me, rifle pointed, eyes glinting with triumph.

And I know exactly what Todd is going to do.

"Do it," I say, my stomach dropping but it's right right right–

And Todd raises the rifle to his eye–

"*Do it!*"

And the Mayor shoves me hard, sending lightnings of pain up my legs, and I can't help it and I scream out and fall forward, forward towards Todd, forward towards the ground–

And the Mayor does it again–

Uses me to control Todd–

Because Todd can't help it either–

He jumps to catch me–

To catch me when I'm falling–

And the Mayor attacks.

[TODD]

My brain explodes, burning and raging with everything he fires at it and it ain't nothing like a slap at all, it's like fiery metal poked right into the centre of who I am, and as I jump forward to catch Viola, it hits me so hard my head snaps back and here it comes again, the Mayor's voice but somehow *my* voice, too, somehow *hers* as well and all of 'em saying YER NOTHING YER NOTHING YER NOTHING YER NOTHING—

Our bodies are still moving together and I feel us tumble into one another, feel the top of her skull crack into my mouth, and YER NOTHING YER NOTHING YER NOTHING she falls into my chest and my fumbling arms and we twist down onto the rubble together, a siren ripping off the roof of my head YER NOTHING YER NOTHING YER NOTHING and I feel the rifle fall and bounce away and I feel the weight of her against me and I hear her as if from the other side of the moons and she's calling my name and YER NOTHING she's saying "Todd" YER NOTHING YER NOTHING she's saying "Todd!" and it's as if I'm watching her from under water and I see her try to rise up on her hands to protect me but the Mayor's above her and swinging his rifle by the barrel and smacking her across the back of her head and she's falling to one side—

And my brain is boiling—

My brain is boiling—

My brain is boiling—

YER NOTHING YER NOTHING YER NOTHING YER NOTHING YER NOTHING—

And I see her eyes as they're closing—

And I feel her against me–

And I think *Viola*–

I think *VIOLA!*

I think ***VIOLA!!!!***

And the Mayor steps away from me like he's been stung.

"Whoo," he says, shaking his head as I blink away the buzz still rocketing from my brain, as my eyes refocus and my thoughts are mine again. "Told you you had some power in you, boy."

And his eyes are wide and bright and eager.

And he hits me again with his Noise.

I fling my hands up to my ears (not holding the gun, not holding the gun) as if that'll stop it but it ain't thru yer ears that you hear Noise and he's in there, inside my head, inside my self, invading it like I don't have any self at all YER NOTHING YER NOTHING YER NOTHING my own Noise swept up and hit against me, like I'm punching myself with my own fists YER NOTHING YER NOTHING YER NOTHING–

Viola, I think but I'm disappearing, I'm falling deeper into it, I'm weaker and my brain is rattling–

Viola–

{VIOLA}

Viola, I hear, as if from the bottom of a canyon. My head is aching and bleeding from the Mayor's blow and my face is in the dust and my eyes are half-open but they aren't seeing anything–

Viola, I hear again.

I open my eyes wide.

Todd's scooting back into the rocks, his hands over his ears, eyes squeezed shut–

And the Mayor is standing over him and I can hear the same shouting as before, the same kind of clanging, laser-bright Noise firing right at him and–

Viola, I hear in amongst all the clatter–

And I open my mouth–

And I shout–

[TODD]

"TODD!" I hear screamed from somewhere out there–

And it's her–

It's her–

It's her–

And she's alive–

And her voice is coming for me–

Viola–

Viola–

VIOLA–

I hear a grunt and the Noise in my head stops again and I open my eyes and the Mayor is staggering back, one hand up to his ear, the same reflex that everyone does–

That everyone does when they hear an attack of Noise.

VIOLA, I think again, right at him, but he ducks his head and raises the rifle at me. I think it again–

VIOLA

And again–

VIOLA

And he steps back and stumbles over Davy's body, falling

backwards along it and down into the rubble–

I push myself up–

And I run to her–

{VIOLA}

He runs to me, his hands open and reaching for me, taking my shoulders and rolling me up to a sitting position and saying, "Are you hurt, are you hurt, are you hurt–"

And I'm saying, "He's still got the gun–"

And Todd turns–

[TODD]

And I turn and the Mayor's getting to his feet and he's looking at me and here comes his Noise again and I roll outta the way and I hear it following me as I scramble over rocks, scramble back to where I dropped my rifle and–

And there's a gunshot–

And dust flies up in the air in front of my hands–

Hands that were reaching for the rifle–

And I stop–

And I look up–

And he's staring right back at me–

And I hear her call my name again

And I know she's understanding–

Understanding that I need to hear her say my name–

And that way I can use hers as a weapon–

"Don't try it, Todd," the Mayor says, looking down the barrel at me–

And I hear his voice in my head–

Not an attack–

The slinky, snaky, twisty verzhun of his voice–

The one that's him taking hold of my choices–

The one that's him turning them into his–

"You won't fight any more," he says–

He takes a step closer–

"You won't fight any more and that'll be the end of it–"

I turn away from him–

But I have to turn back–

Have to look into his eyes–

"Listen to me, Todd–"

And his voice is hissing twixt my ears–

And it would be so easy just to–

Just to–

Just to fall back–

Fall back and do what he says–

"No!" I shout–

But my teeth are locked together–

And he's still in there–

Still trying to get me to–

And I will–

I will–

YER NOTHING–

I'm nothing–

"That's right, Todd," the Mayor says, stepping forward, rifle bearing down on me. "You are nothing."

I'm nothing–

"But," he says–

And his voice is a whisper scratching across the deepest

part of me—

"But," he says—

"I will make you *something*."

And I look right up into his eyes—

Eyes that are an abyss I feel myself falling into—

Up and into the blackness—

And outta the corner of my eye—

{VIOLA}

I throw the stone as hard as I can, praying as it leaves my hand that my aim's as good as Lee said—

Praying, Please, God—

If you're there—

Please—

And *wham!*

It hits the Mayor right in the temple—

[TODD]

There's a terrible *ripping* feeling, like a strip is being torn right outta my Noise—

And the abyss is gone—

It's turned away—

And the Mayor lurches to the side, holding his temple, blood already dripping from it—

"*TODD!*" Viola shouts—

And I look at her—

Look at her arm outstretched where she threw the rock—

And I see her—

My Viola.

And I get to my feet.

He gets to his feet.

He stands up tall–

And I shout his name again–

"TODD!"

Because it does something–

It does something to him–

It does something *for* him–

The Mayor's wrong–

He's wrong for ever and ever–

It's not that you should never love something so much it can control you.

It's that you *need* to love something that much so you can *never be controlled*.

It's not a weakness–

It's your best strength–

"TODD!" I shout again–

And he looks at me–

And I hear my name in his Noise–

And I know it–

I know it in my heart–

Right now–

Todd Hewltt–

There's nothing we can't do together–

And we're gonna *win*–

The Mayor is looking up now, half crouched, blood seeping from twixt his fingers held against the side of his head–

He turns to look at me, a scowl on his face–

And here comes his Noise–

And–

VIOLA

I beat it back–

He flinches away–

But he tries again–

VIOLA

"You can't beat us," I say–

"I can," he says, clenching his teeth. "I will."

VIOLA

He flinches again–

He tries to raise the rifle–

I hit him extra hard–

VIOLA

He drops the rifle and staggers back–

I can hear his Noise buzzing at me, trying to twist its way in–

But his head is hurting–

From my own attacks–

From one well-thrown rock–

"What exactly do you think this proves?" he spits. "You've got power, but you don't know what to do with it."

VIOLA

"Looks like I'm doing fine," I say.

And he smiles, teeth still clenched. "Are you?"

And I notice my hands are shaking–

I notice my Noise is flying, sizzling like a bright thing–
I can't feel my feet below me–

"It takes practice," the Mayor says. "Or you'll blow your mind apart." He stands up a little straighter, trying to lock my eyes again. "I could show you."

And right on cue, Viola yells *"TODD!"*

And I hit him with everything I got–
Every bit of her behind me–
Every piece of anger and frustrayshun and nothingness–
Every moment I didn't see her–
Every moment I worried–
Everything–
Every little tiny thing I know about her–
I send it right into the centre of him–

VIOLA

And he falls–
Back and back and back–
His eyes rolling up–
His head twisting round–
His legs buckling–
Falling falling falling–
Right to the ground–

And lying there still.

{ VIOLA }

"Todd?" I say.

494

He's shaking all over, almost to the point of not being able to stand, and I can hear an unhealthy-sounding whine cutting through his Noise. He wobbles a little as he takes a step.

"Todd?" I try to get to my feet but my ankles–

"Jeez," he says, crumpling down beside me. "That takes it outta you."

He's breathing heavy, his eyes unfocused.

"Are you all right?" I ask, putting a hand on his arm.

He nods. "I think so."

We look back at the Mayor.

"You did it," I say.

"*We* did it," he says and his Noise is getting a little clearer and he sits up a little straighter.

His hands are still shaking, though.

"Poor bloody Davy," he says.

I grip his arm. "The ship," I say quietly. "She's going to get there first."

"Not if I can help it," he says. He stands up and he swoons for a second but I hear him call Acorn with his Noise.

Boy colt, I hear clearly and Davy's horse tugs free of where he's tied and walks up over the rubble, boy colt, boy colt, boy colt.

Todd, I hear from farther out and there's more clopping of hooves as Angharrad follows Acorn in and stands beside him. "Forward," she nickers. "Forward," Acorn nickers.

"Absolutely forward," Todd says to them.

He puts an arm under my shoulders to lift me up. Acorn sees in his Noise and kneels down so it's easier for me to get up top. When I'm sat in the saddle, Todd slaps his flank gently and up he stands.

Angharrad comes close to Todd and starts to kneel, too, but, "No, girl," he says, petting her nose.

"*What?*" I say, alarmed. "What about you?"

He nods at the Mayor. "I have to take care of him," he says and doesn't meet my eye.

"What do you mean, take care of him?"

He looks past me. I turn. The beetle march of the army has reversed its course and stretches to the bottom of the hill now.

It'll be marching here next.

"Go," he says. "Get to the ship."

"Todd," I say. "You can't kill him."

He looks at me and his Noise is a muddle and he's still struggling to stay upright. "He deserves it."

"He does but–"

But Todd's already nodding. "We are the choices we make."

I nod back. We understand each other. "You'd stop being Todd Hewitt," I say. "And I ain't losing you again."

[TODD]

I give a little snort when she says *ain't*.

"I'm gonna have to stay with him, you know," I say. "Yer gonna have to go to the ship as fast as you can and I'm gonna have to wait for the army to come."

She nods, even tho there's sadness there. "And what'll you do then?"

I look over at the Mayor, still sprawled on the rocks, unconshus and moaning slightly.

I feel so *heavy*.

But I say, "I reckon they might not be too unhappy to see him beaten. I reckon they just might be on the lookout for a new leader."

She smiles. "And that'll be you?"

"And if you meet the Answer?" I say, smiling back. "What'll you do then?"

She brushes her hair outta her eyes. "I reckon they may need a new leader, too."

I step forward and I put my hand near hers on Acorn's side. She don't look at my face, just slides her hand till the tips of our fingers are touching.

"Just cuz yer going there and I'm staying here," I say. "It don't mean we're parting."

"No," she says and I know she understands. "No, it certainly doesn't."

"I ain't parting from you again," I say, still looking at our fingers. "Not even in my head."

She pushes her hand forward and laces her fingers in mine and we both look at 'em wrapped together.

"I have to go, Todd," she says.

"I know."

I look deep into Acorn's Noise and I show him where the road is, where the ship landed, and how fast fast fast he's gotta run.

"Forward," he whinnies, loud and clear.

"Forward," I say.

I look back up at Viola.

"I'm ready," she says.

"Me, too," I say.

"We'll win," she says.

"I reckon we just might."

One last look.

One last look where we know each other.

Right down to our souls.

And I slap Acorn hard on the flanks.

And off they go, over the rubble, right down the road, tearing hard towards the people who (I hope I hope I hope) can help us.

I look down at the Mayor, still lying on the ground.

I hear the army marching down the hill, three kilometres away, if that.

I look for the rope.

I see it but before I pick it up, I take a second to close Davy's eyes.

{VIOLA}

We fly down the road, and it's all I can do not to fall off and break my neck.

"Watch for soldiers!" I shout in the space between Acorn's flattened-back ears.

I have no idea how far into town the Answer's managed to march, no idea if they'll wait to see who I am before they blow me off the road.

No idea what her reaction will be if she sees me–

When she sees me–

When I tell her and everyone else the things I've got to tell them–

"Faster if you can!" I shout and there's a jolt like an engine firing and Acorn goes even faster.

She'll head for the ship. No doubt about that. She'll have seen it land and gone straight for it. And if she gets there first, she'll tell them how sorry she is that I died so tragically, how I fell so cruelly at the hands of the tyrant the Answer are trying to overthrow, how if the scout ship has any weapons that can be used from the air–

Which it does.

I lean down farther in the saddle, biting hard against the pain in my ankles, trying to make us go even faster.

We get well past the cathedral, down through the rows of shuttered-up shops and bolted-in houses. The sun is completely down, everything turning to silhouette against the darkening of the sky.

And I think about how the Answer will respond when they find out the Mayor's fallen–

And what they'll think when they find out *Todd* did it–

And I think of him–

I think of him–

I think of him–

Todd, Acorn thinks.

And we race down the road–

And I nearly tumble off as a *BOOM* rises in the distance.

Acorn judders to a halt, twisting round to keep me on his back. We turn and I look–

And I see the fires burning down the road.

I see houses on fire.

And stores.

And grain sheds.

And I see people running this way through the smoke, not

soldiers, just people, running past us in the dark.

Passing us so fast they don't even stop to look at us.

They're fleeing from the Answer.

"What is she *doing*?" I say out loud.

Fire, Acorn thinks, nervously clattering his hooves.

"She's burning everything," I say. "She's burning it all."

Why?

Why?

"Acorn–" I start to say.

And a horn blows a deep, long call across the entire valley.

Acorn whinnies sharply, no words in his Noise, just a flash of fear, of terror so sharp I feel my heart leap, echoed by the disbelieving gasps of some of the people running past me, many of them shouting out and stopping, looking behind me, back towards the city and beyond.

I turn, even though the sky's too dark to see much.

There are lights in the distance, lights coming down the zigzag road by the falls–

Not the road the army is on.

"What is it?" I say to no one, to anyone. "What are those lights? What was that *sound*?"

And then a man, stopped next to me, his Noise bright and circling with amazement, with disbelief, with fright as clear as a knife, whispers, "No."

He whispers, "No, it can't be."

"*What*?" I shout. "What's happening?"

And the long, deep horn sounds again across the valley.

And it's a sound like the end of the world.

THE BEGINNING

THE MAYOR WAKES before I even finish tying his hands.

He moans, pure, real Noise ratcheting from him, the first I've ever heard outta his head, now that he's off guard.

Now that he's been beaten.

"Not beaten," he murmurs. "Temporarily waylaid."

"Shut up," I say, pulling the ropes tight.

I come round the front of him. His eyes are still misty from my attack but he manages a smile.

I smack him cross the face with the butt of the rifle.

"I hear one stitch of Noise coming from you," I warn, pointing the barrels at him.

"I know," says the Mayor, a grin still coming from his bloody mouth. "And you would, wouldn't you?"

I don't say nothing.

And that's my answer.

The Mayor sighs, leaning his head back as if to stretch

his neck. He looks up into the coloured glass window, still standing, impossibly, in a wall all its own. The moons are rising behind it, lighting up their glass verzhuns just a little.

"Here we are again, Todd," he says. "The room where we first properly met." He looks around himself, at how he's the one tied to the chair now and I'm the one out here. "Things change," he says, "but they stay the same."

"I don't need to hear you talking while we wait."

"Wait for what?" He's growing more alert.

His Noise is disappearing.

"And you'd like to be able to do that, too, wouldn't you?" he says. "You'd like just for once to have no one know what you're thinking."

"I said, shut up."

"Right now, you're thinking about the army."

"Shut *up*."

"You're wondering if they really *will* listen to you. You're wondering if Viola's people can really help you–"

"I'll hit you again with the damn rifle."

"You're wondering if you've really won."

"I have really won," I say. "And you know it."

We hear a *BOOM* in the distance, another one.

"She's destroying everything," the Mayor says, looking towards the sound. "Interesting."

"Who is?" I ask.

"You never met Mistress Coyle, did you?" He stretches one shoulder and then the other against his binds. "Remarkable woman, remarkable opponent. She might have beaten me, you know. She might really have done it." He smiles wide again. "But you've done it first, haven't you?"

"What do you mean *She's destroying everything?*"

"As always," he says, "I mean what I say."

"Why would she do that? Why would she just blow things up?"

"Twofold," he says. "One, she creates chaos so it's harder to fight her as an orderly enemy. And two, she obliterates the safety of those who won't fight, creating the impression that she cannot be beaten, so that everyone's that much easier to rule when she's done." He shrugs. "Everything's a war to people like her."

"People like you," I say.

"You'll be swapping one tyrant for another, Todd. I'm sorry to be the one to tell you."

"I won't be swapping nothing. And I told you to be quiet."

I keep the rifle pointed at him and go to Angharrad, watching us both from a cramped space in the rubble. **Todd**, she thinks. **Thirsty**.

"Is there a trough still out front?" I ask the Mayor. "Or did it get blown up?"

"It did," the Mayor says. "But there's one round the back where my own horse is tied. She can go there."

Morpeth, I think to Angharrad, the name of the Mayor's horse, and a feeling rises in her.

Morpeth, she thinks. **Submit**.

"Attagirl," I say, rubbing her nose. "Damn right he'll submit."

She pushes me playfully once or twice then clops off outta the rubble, making her way round the back.

There's another *BOOM*. I have a little flash of worry for

505

Viola. I wonder how far down the road she's got by now. She must be getting near where the Answer is, she must be—

I hear a little stirring of Noise from the Mayor.

I cock the gun.

"I *said*, don't try it."

"Do you know, Todd?" he says, like we were having a nice lunch. "The attacking Noise was easy. You just wind yourself up and slam someone with it as hard as you can. I mean, yes, you have to be focused, tremendously focused, but once you've got it, you can pretty much do it at your will." He spits away a little blood pooling on his lip. "As we saw with you and your *Viola*."

"Don't you say her name."

"But the other thing," he continues. "The *control* over another's Noise, well, I must say, that's a *lot* trickier, a *lot* harder. It's like trying to raise and lower a thousand different levers at once and sure on some people, some *simple* people, it's easier than others and it's surprisingly easy on crowds, but I've tried for years to get it to work as a useful tool and it's only recently I've had any level of success at all."

I think for a minute. "Mayor Ledger."

"No, no," he says brightly. "Mayor Ledger was *eager* to help. Never trust a politician, Todd. They have no fixed centre, so you can never believe them. *He* came to *me*, you see, with your dreams and things you said. No, no control there, just ordinary weakness."

I sigh. "Would you just be *quiet* already?"

"My point is, Todd," he presses on, "that it's only today that I've been able to even come close to forcing *you* to do what I want you to do." He looks at me, to see if I'm getting it. "Only today."

Another *BOOM* in the distance, another thing destroyed by the Answer for no good reason at all. It's too dark to see the army but they must be marching into town by now, down the road straight to here.

And night is falling.

"I know what yer saying," I say. "I know what I've done."

"It was all you, Todd." He keeps his eyes on me. "The Spackle. The women. All your own action. No control needed."

"I know what I've done," I say again, my voice low, my Noise getting a warning sizzle to it.

"The offer's still open," the Mayor says, his voice low, too. "I'm quite serious. You have power. I could teach you how to use it. You could rule this land by my side."

I AM THE CIRCLE AND THE CIRCLE IS ME, I hear.

"That's the source," he says. "Control your Noise and you control yourself. Control yourself," he lowers his chin, "and you can control the world."

"You killed *Davy*," I say, stepping up to him, gun still pointed. "Yer the one with no fixed centre. And now yer *really* gonna shut the hell up."

And then a low and powerful sound rumbles thru the sky, like some giant, deep horn.

A sound God would make when he wanted yer attenshun.

I hear whinnies from the horses out back. I hear a filament of shock race thru the still-hiding Noise from the people of

New Prentisstown. I hear the steady marching of the army's feet collapse into a racket of sudden confuzhun.

I hear the Mayor's Noise spike and pull back.

"What the hell was that?" I say, looking up and around.

"No," the Mayor breathes.

And there's *delight* in it.

"What?" I say, poking the rifle at him. "What's going on?"

But he's just smiling and turning his head.

Turning it towards the hill by the falls, by the zigzag road coming down into town.

I look there, too.

Lights are at the top.

Lights are starting to come down the zigzag.

"Oh, Todd," the Mayor says, amazement and, yeah, it's *joy* coming thru his voice. "Oh, Todd, my boy, what *have* you done?"

"What is it?" I say, squinting into the dark, as if that'll help me see it clearer. "What's making that—"

A second horn blast comes, so loud it's like the sound of the sky folding in half.

I can hear the ROAR of the town rising, so many asking marks you could drown in 'em.

"Tell me, Todd," the Mayor says, his voice still bright. "What exactly were you planning on doing when the army arrived?"

"What?" I say, my forehead furrowing, my eyes still trying to see what's coming down the zigzag road, but it's too far and too dark to tell. Just lights, individual points of 'em, moving down the hill.

"Were you going to offer me up for ransom?" he goes on,

still sounding cheerful. "Were you going to give me to them for execution?"

"What were those blasts?" I say, grabbing him by the shirt front. "Is that the settlers landing? Are they invading or something?"

He just looks in my eyes, his own sparkling. "Did you think they'd elect you leader and you'd single-handedly usher in a new era of peace?"

"I'll lead them," I hiss into his face. "You watch me."

I let him go and climb up one of the higher piles of rubble. I see people poking their heads outta their houses now, hear voices calling to one another, see people start running to and fro.

Whatever it is, it's enough to get the people of New Prentisstown out of hiding.

I feel a buzz of Noise at the back of my head.

I whip round, pointing the gun at him again, climbing back down the rubble and saying, "I *told* you, none of that!"

"I was just trying to keep our conversation going, Todd," he says, false innocence everywhere. "I'm very curious to know your plan for leadership now that you'll be head of the army and President of the planet."

I want to punch the smile off his face.

"What's going on?" I shout at him. "*What's coming down that hill?*"

There's a third blast of the horn sound, even louder this time, so loud you can feel it humming thru yer body.

And now people in town are really starting to scream.

"Reach in my front shirt pocket, Todd," the Mayor says. "I think you'll find something that once belonged to you."

I stare at him, searching him out for a trick, but all that's there is that stupid grin.

Like he's winning again.

I push the rifle at him and use my free hand to dig in his pocket, my fingers hitting something metal and compact. I pull it out.

Viola's binos.

"Really remarkable little things," the Mayor says. "I do so look forward to the rest of the settlers landing, seeing what new treats they bring us."

I don't say nothing to him, just climb back up the rubble and hold the binos to my eyes with my free hand, clumsily trying to get the night vision to work. It's been a long time since I–

I get the right button.

Up pops the valley, in shades of green and white, cutting thru the dark to show me the town.

I raise them up the road, up the river, to the zigzag on the hill, to the points of lights coming down it–

And–

And–

And oh my God.

I hear the Mayor laugh behind me, still tied to his chair. "Oh, yes, Todd. You're not imagining it."

I can't say nothing for a second.

There ain't no words.

How?

How can this be *possible*?

An army of Spackle is marching for the town.

Some of 'em, the ones near the front, are riding on the backs of these huge, wide creachers covered in what looks like armour and a single curving horn coming out the end of their noses. Behind 'em are troops, cuz this ain't a friendly march, nosiree, it ain't nothing like that at all, there are troops marching down the zigzag road, troops marching over the lip of the hill at the top of the falls.

Troops that are coming for battle.

And there are thousands of 'em.

"But," I say, gasping, hardly able to get the words out. "But they were all *killed*. They were all killed during the Spackle War!"

"All of them, Todd?" the Mayor asks. "Every single one of them on this whole planet when all we live on is one little strip? Does that make sense to you?"

The lights I've been seeing are torches carried by the Spackle riding on the creachers' backs, burning torches to lead the army, burning torches that light up the spears that the troops carry, the bows and arrows, the clubs.

All of 'em carrying weapons.

"Oh, we beat them," says the Mayor. "Killed them in their thousands, certainly, every one within miles of here. Though they out-numbered us by a considerable margin, we had better weapons, stronger motivation. We drove them out of this land on the understanding that they would never return, never get in our way ever again. We kept some of them as slaves, of course, to rebuild our city after that war.

511

It was only fair."

The town is really **ROAR**ing now. The marching of the army has stopped and I can hear people running about and screaming to each other, stuff that don't make no sense, stuff of disbelief, stuff of fear.

I run back down the rubble to him, pushing the gun hard into his ribs. "Why did they come back? Why *now*?"

And still he grins. "I expect they've had time to work on how they might get rid of us once and for all, don't you? All these years? I expect they were only looking for a reason."

"What reason?!" I shout at him. "Why—"

And I stop.

The genocide.

The death of every slave.

Their bodies piled up like so much rubbish.

"Quite right, Todd," he says, nodding like we're talking about the weather. "I suspect that must certainly be it, don't you?"

I look down at him, understanding coming too late like always. "You did it," I say. "Of *course* you did it. You killed every Spackle, every single one, made it look like it was the Answer." I push the rifle into his chest. "You were *hoping* they'd come back."

He shrugs. "I was hoping I'd have the chance to beat them once and for all, yes." He purses his lips. "But it's you I have to thank for speeding the plan along."

"Me?" I say.

"Oh, yes, definitely you, Todd. I set the stage. But you sent them the messenger."

"The messen—?"

512

No.

No.

I turn and run up the rubble again, binos back on, looking and looking and looking.

There's too many, they're too far away.

But he's there, ain't he?

Somewhere in that crowd.

1017.

Oh, no.

"I should say, *Oh, no* is right, Todd," the Mayor calls up to me. "I left him alive for you to find, but even with your *special relationship*, he wasn't very fond of you, was he? No matter how much you tried to help him. You're the face of his torturers, the face he took back to his brothers and sisters." I hear a low laugh. "I really wouldn't want to be you right now, Todd Hewitt."

I spin round, looking at the horizon on all sides. I spin round again. There's an army to the south, one to the east, and now one marching down from the west.

"And here we sit," says the Mayor, still sounding calm. "Right in the middle of it all." He scratches his nose on his shoulder. "I wonder what those poor people on the scout ship must be thinking."

No.

No.

I spin round once more, as if I could see them all coming. Coming for me.

My mind is racing.

What do I do?

What do I *do*?

The Mayor starts whistling, as if he had all the time in the world.

And Viola's out there–

Oh, Jesus, she's out there in it–

"The army," I say. "The army's gonna have to fight them."

"In their spare time?" the Mayor says, raising his eyebrows. "When they've got a few free minutes from fighting the Answer?"

"The Answer will have to join us."

"Us?" says the Mayor.

"They'll have to fight alongside the army. They'll *have* to."

"You really think that's how Mistress Coyle is going to play it?" He's smiling but I can see his legs starting to bounce up and down now, energy coursing thru him. "She'll see herself and them as having a common enemy, now won't she? You mark my words. She'll try to negotiate." He catches my eye again. "And where will that leave you, Todd?"

I'm breathing heavy. I don't got no answer.

"And Viola's out there," he reminds me, "all on her own."

She is.

She is out there.

And she can't even *walk*.

Oh, Viola, what have I done?

"And under these circumstances, my dear boy, do you really think the army is going to want you as leader?" He laughs as if it was always the dumbest idea anywhere. "Do you think they'll trust *you* to lead them into battle?"

I spin round again with the binos. New Prentisstown is

in chaos. Buildings burn to the east. People run thru the streets, running away from the Answer, running away from the Mayor's army, and now running away from the Spackle, running all direkshuns with nowhere to go.

The horn blasts again, shaking glass outta some of the windows.

I spy it in the binos.

A great long trumpet, longer than four Spackle put together, carried on the backs of two of the horned creachers, being blown by the biggest Spackle I've ever seen.

And they've reached the bottom of the hill.

"I think it's time you untied me, Todd," the Mayor says, his voice a low buzz in the air.

I spin around to him, aiming the gun one more time. "You won't control me," I say. "Not no more."

"I'm not trying to," he says. "But I think we both know it's a good idea, don't you?"

I hesitate, breathing heavy.

"I've beaten the Spackle before, you see," he says. "The town knows it. The army knows it. I don't think they'll be quite so eager to discard me and unite behind you now that they know what we're up against."

I still don't say nothing.

"And after all this betrayal from you, Todd," he says, looking right up at me. "I *still* want you by my side. I *still* want you fighting next to me." He pauses. "We can win this together."

"I don't want to win this with you," I say, looking down the barrel. "I *beut* you."

He nods as if in agreement, but then he says one more

time. "Things change, but they stay the same."

I hear marching feet getting closer to the church. A troop from the army's finally pulled itself together enough to come into town. I can hear them heading down a side road, towards the square.

There ain't much time.

"I don't even mind that you tied me up, Todd," the Mayor says, "but you have to let me go. I'm the only one who can beat them."

Viola–

Viola, what do I do?

"Yes, Viola, again," he says, his voice slinky and warm. "Viola out there among them, all by herself." He waits till I'm looking him in the eye. "They'll kill her, Todd. They will. And you know I'm the only one who can save her."

The horn blasts again.

There's another *BOOM* to the east.

The feet of the Mayor's soldiers getting closer.

I look at him.

"I beat you," I say. "You remember that. I beat you and I'll do it again."

"I have no doubt you will," he says.

But he's smiling.

VIOLA I think right at him, and he flinches.

"You save her," I say, "and you live. She dies, you die."

He nods. "Agreed."

"You try to control me, I shoot you. You try to attack me, I shoot you. Got it?"

"I've got it," he says.

I wait a second more but there ain't no more seconds.

There ain't no more time to decide nothing.

Only that the world's marching to meet up right here, right now.

And she's out there.

And I ain't never parting from her again, not even when we're not together.

Forgive me, I think.

And I go behind the Mayor and untie the rope.

He stands up slowly, rubbing his wrists.

He looks up at another blast of the horn.

"At last," he says. "No more of this slinking, secret fight, no more running after shadows and all this undercover cloak and dagger nonsense." He turns to me, catches my eye, and I see behind his smile the real glint of madness. "Finally, we come to the real thing, the thing that makes men men, the thing we were *born* for, Todd." He rubs his hands together and his eyes flash as he says the word.

"*War.*"

END OF BOOK TWO